Holiday Hoax

A FAKE MARRIAGE BILLIONAIRE ROMANCE

MAGGIE COLE

PULSE PRESS INC

One

GEORGIA PEACH

"Excuse me," a deep voice states in annoyance. A hard frame pushes past me.

"Whoa!" I cry out. My right heel skids on the slick floor, and the four boxes of cupcakes I'm carrying wobble. I grab his arm to catch my balance, barely saving the treats I baked for my new co-workers from falling to the ground.

He spins, tilts his head down, and pins his blue eyes on me. He clenches his chiseled jaw, further exhibiting his irritation.

Praline and a hint of citrus mixes with sandalwood, stirring something deep in my core. His broad shoulders fill out the designer, probably custom-made suit jacket. Biceps you'd only get with hours in the gym, but not over the top, sculpt the sleeves. Thick, wavy chestnut hair, that's still slightly damp, perfectly frames the features of his face, and matches his short-trimmed goatee and mustache.

"You good now?" he asks.

I gape at him.

What a jerk!

Why does he look like he's having a dying duck fit so early in the morning?

Kill them with kindness, my grammy says in my head.

I force a smile, doing my best to make it not look fake. In my most cheerful voice, I reply, "Got my balance back."

"Great." He narrows his eyes.

Confused why he looks angrier, I ask, "Do you want a cupcake?"

His head jerks back a bit before he catches himself. He squares his shoulders and cocks an eyebrow. "Cupcake?"

I nod toward the boxes. "Yes. I baked them. It's my grammy's secret recipe. It's my first day at my internship. I wanted to do something nice for my new co-workers and boss."

He scoffs. "Well, it can't be a secret if you have it, now can it?"

I open my mouth, but nothing comes out.

His eyes drift to my yellow sundress and matching button-down sweater. Heat fills me as he slowly moves his leering gaze up, as if he's imagining what I look like naked. He lingers on my breasts, then gives me a challenging stare, uttering, "Well, aren't you, Little Miss Sunshine?"

I don't think I've ever encountered anyone so boldly nasty upon first meeting yet so sinfully seductive at the same time. My insides quiver, and I lift my chin, willing the fire to leave my cheeks. I reply as cheerfully as possible, "Bless your heart for noticing."

He grunts, then glances at my hand still digging into his forearm. "If you can stand on your own two feet, I've got important things to do."

Horrified, I release him. I smirk, "Balance is good now. Have a great day."

He gives me a final disproving look, shoves his security card through the scanner, and pushes through the metal bar. I ogle his toned ass even after he steps into the elevator, then reprimand myself. He spins, catches me, and his smug expression reignites the zings flying through my core. Neither of us breaks our gaze until the doors are completely shut.

What an arrogant, miserable man.

I can't let him ruin my first day.

I take several deep breaths, continue through the gate, and go up to the top floor. The doors open and I step out of the elevator. A woman with curly red hair, emerald eyes, a form-fitting navy dress, and a matching jacket smiles at me. "Can I help you?"

"I'm Georgia, the new intern," I answer.

Her face brightens. "Ah, yes! I'm Victoria, Mr. Cartwright's director of operations. You'll be working with me."

"You're so young to be a director," I blurt out in awe. Then I cringe for my outburst. "Sorry."

She laughs. "No apologies necessary. You're right. I'm thirty, but Mr. Cartwright prefers to promote employees within the corporation. I started as an intern like you. So work hard, and the sky's the limit." She winks.

I won't be here that long. Only a few years of saving and I can open my bakery.

Best to keep my thoughts to myself on the first day.

I hold the boxes out to her and say, "That's great to hear. I baked some cupcakes for everyone. Is there somewhere I can put these?"

"Oh, that was sweet of you. What kind?" She eyes the boxes.

"A variety," I take four steps, set the boxes on the receptionist's counter, and open one lid. Motioning to each row, I continue, "These are chocolate raspberry, caramel coffee swirl, vanilla madagascar, and strawberries and cream. Do you want to pick one before the others choose?"

She snatches a chocolate-raspberry one. "They all look delicious, but this one is calling my name."

Joy fills me. It's what my grammy always claimed she felt whenever anyone ate hers. I beam. "Guess it's yours, then. Where should I put them?"

"Let me show you where the break room is, and you can leave them there," she replies and leads me through the office.

I set the cupcakes on the table, then follow her on the tour. My interview was with human resources personnel and on a different floor. And it's night and day different.

Everything about this area screams an exclusive vibe. Almost as if you're lucky just to be permitted to step foot in it. Plus, it's quieter. There are several private offices and way more men in suits, whereas the human resources floor had mostly cubicles and women.

Victoria introduces me to everyone as we make our way around the different work suites. Even though the spaces are enclosed, each is visible through the glass except for one. She stops in front of the closed door and asks, "Ready to meet the big boss?"

Tinted glass covers the entire room, so you can't see inside. A gold-plated sign reads "Mr. Sebastian Cartwright, Vice President."

My stomach flips. I don't know why I'm suddenly intimidated. Everyone I met on the tour has been friendly. Maybe it's because of the stark contrast between his office and the others. Perhaps it's just first-day jitters reappearing. Regardless, I hesitate.

Victoria must sense my nerves. She offers, "He's always really busy, so if he doesn't have a lot of time, don't take any offense, okay?"

I square my shoulders and nod. "Sure."

"And he's really a big teddy bear underneath his persona," she adds.

Her statement only makes my butterflies flutter harder.

Why would she need to say that?

She knocks.

A muffled, "Come in," hits my ears.

She opens the door and announces, "I wanted to introduce you to our new intern who'll be working closely with us." She steps inside.

I follow and freeze. My heart pounds harder. Goose bumps pop out on my skin while I squeeze my thighs closer together.

No, no, no!

Not him!

The Dallas skyline makes a breathtaking backdrop, competing with the exquisite eye candy sitting in front of it. Unfortunately, it's the rude man from the lobby.

He looks up from his desk. Shock fills his expression, mirroring my own. He quickly catches himself, hardening his features and grinding his molars. A beam of sunlight streams through the window. It hits his chestnut hair and outlines his chiseled body as if he's somehow an angel.

Disguised as the devil.

"Sebastian Cartwright, meet Georgia Peach," Victoria declares.

He rises, furrows his eyebrows, and questions, "Georgia Peach? Is that a joke?"

Embarrassment mixes with pride. I've heard every joke under the sun growing up about my name. But it's mine, and I've come to accept it. Now that I'm an adult, I thought others would be more mature about it, but apparently, Mr. Grumpy Pants only looks like he has class and maturity. I pull it together and proudly state, "No, it's not."

"Georgia Peach, the cupcake lady," he mutters.

"Do you want one? I can go to the break room and get it before they're all gone," I retort in a chipper voice.

He stares at me as if I'm crazy, replying, "No." He turns quiet, assessing me, and tension grows thicker with every breath we take.

Victoria clears her throat. Unable to hide her uncomfortable tone, she asks, "So you two have met?"

He snaps his sneer at her. "Yes. In the lobby. Ms. Peach didn't introduce herself."

I blurt out, "I was supposed to know it was you?"

"Yeah. Everyone knows me. You're no different, so don't pretend to be."

"I had no idea who you were. Why would I know you anyway? I doubt we hang out in the same circles," I argue.

He scoffs. "Of course we don't. But I'm sure you did your homework researching our company?"

My pulse races. I retort, "Yes, I did. But only the CEO's photo is on the website. It only mentions your name, along with other heads of the corporation."

"I'm all over the internet. Let's not act like you didn't do a search on me," he accuses.

Appalled at his audacity, I insist, "I did no such thing."

He grunts. "Sure you didn't."

"I didn't," I claim again, glaring at him.

Tense silence fills the air.

Victoria glances between us, then clears her throat. She interjects, "Not everyone cares to know you, Sebastian."

He acts like he doesn't hear her, keeping his scowl pinned on me.

She continues, "While we have your attention, are there any additional documents you'll need this morning for your meetings?"

He crosses his arms, and his biceps strain against the expensive fabric of his suit jacket. I curse myself when my eyes drift to them. He catches me and fixates his sexy yet lewd gaze on me. If anyone else looked at me like that, I'd slap them. But something about the way he studies me is irresistible. It creates an uncomfortable ache in my body. He finally shakes his head. "Not that I'm aware of. As of now, everything is adequate, Victoria." He glances at her, then pins his intimidating stare on me once again.

Why does he have to be so hot?

He's not.

I'm a liar.

I do everything in my power not to appear scared of him and announce, "I look forward to working with you, Mr. Cartwright."

His lips purse in an expression I'm unsure how to take. My pulse quickens as he replies in a dry voice, "Welcome to Cartwright Enterprises."

"Thank you," I cheerfully state, then spin and leave, exhaling deeply the moment I step out of the room. I go to the desk Victoria assigned to me and turn.

"Like I said, he's a teddy bear once you get to know him," she states.

"Sure he is," I reply.

She offers a smile, then points to a pile on my desk. "If you can start with those files, I'd appreciate it."

I nod. "Of course."

She starts to leave, then stops and adds, "He really is great once he drops his guard. He's just a bit aloof when he first meets people."

"Aloof?" I challenge. It's not exactly the word I would have chosen, but I guess it's more politically correct.

She nods, claiming, "Underneath the hard exterior is a brilliant, very generous man."

"Sure," I reply, then sit in my chair. "Should I tell you when I'm finished with each file or the entire pile?"

"If you can send me the individual files, that would be great."

I give her a little salute. "On it!"

She grins and leaves.

I turn on the computer and punch in the passcode written on a sticky note. It prompts me to create a new one, and I stare at Sebastian's closed door, thinking for a minute, then type in, *Kill-HimWithKindness4Ever.*

There. That will remind me to stay calm.

A message in the portal pops up.

Mr. Cartwright: *I need the spreadsheet for Gulf Oil updated for the ten o'clock meeting.*

Victoria: *Georgia, it's in your pile. Can you focus on that first?*

Me: *Absolutely.*

I pull the correct folder and study the notes on the spreadsheet. I find the corresponding file on the computer and update the formulas. When I finish, I email it to Victoria and Sebastian, then click on the message box.

Me: *I finished the spreadsheet for Gulf Oil. Would you like paper copies?*

Mr. Cartwright: *Yes, that is how we do things around here.*

My stomach clenches. I shake my head, press print, then type another message.

Me: *How many copies would you like?*

Mr. Cartwright: *Victoria, please inform Georgia where she can find pertinent information.*

Victoria: *Will do.*

I breathe through my anger, and my grammy's words fill my head. *"No one is responsible for your feelings except you."*

Hard to say when Mr. Grumpy Pants is your boss.

Her voice claims, *"He can only affect you if you let him."*

I shake it off as Victoria approaches my desk.

"Sorry," I quickly state.

"No worries. It won't take long before you know these things," she claims, then takes control of my mouse. She clicks a dropdown box on the schedule. "This is where you'll find Mr. Cartwright's upcoming appointment notes. If you select the description, it'll state who is attending the meeting. You'll always make copies for each person in attendance, plus two extras in case there are any surprises."

"Great. Thanks for showing me," I say.

"No problem. You'll need to add them to the presentation fold-ers," she adds, then returns to her office.

The meeting with Gulf Oil has five people listed. I make eight to include Sebastian and the two extras. I take them off the printer, then knock on his door.

"Yeah?" he calls out.

I open the door and approach him at the desk. He doesn't look up, and I wonder if it's just to be a bigger jerk and add to his intimidation factor.

In a condescending tone, he finally states, "Is there something you need, *Ms. Peach*?"

I try to ignore his obvious jab at my name and reply, "I'm here to add the spreadsheets to the presentation folders."

"Do you want a reward for doing your job?" he questions.

I gape, then catch myself. "No, of course not."

"Then why are you bothering me with this?"

Unsure how to respond, I don't answer him.

He sits back in his chair and arches his eyebrows. "Well?"

"Don't you have the folders?" I quiz.

He sighs. "No, Ms. Peach. I do not have the folders. Those are in the conference room, which is where I meet people."

I point to the huge table in his office. "You don't meet with people there?"

He snorts. "Of course not. How would I ever exit the room when I'm ready if they're in my office?"

Stupidity washes over me, but then I catch myself again. I force another smile and chirp, "It's my first day, Mr. Cartwright. Excuse my ignorance. I'll make sure these are updated. I won't concern you over this issue ever again."

He refocuses on his computer screen, muttering, "Good."

I hightail it out of his office, go to the conference room, and find the folders in a stack. I position the spreadsheets in the same spot as the sample folder and glance around the room.

A buffet cabinet has a pitcher of water, glasses, coffee, mugs, cream, and sugar on it. It seems cold to me. Surely if this is the room where clients meet, there should be a bit more life to it, right?

I go to Victoria's office and knock.

She looks up from her desk. "Hey, Georgia. What can I help you with?"

"I added the spreadsheets to the folders."

"Great."

I hesitate.

"Is something wrong?" she asks.

"Gulf Oil is an important client, correct?" I quiz.

"Yes. They're one of our largest," she admits.

I step closer, confessing, "I don't want to be disrespectful, but the meeting room looks a bit...um...cold."

Surprise fills her expression.

I quickly add, "I was wondering if I could take one of the vases of fresh flowers from the break room and put it in there? Also, maybe add a plate of my cupcakes?"

She shrugs. "Sure. That would be nice."

"Great. Thanks. I won't take a long time to do it," I state. Then I go into the break room. I look for a platter and find it and several empty vases.

It gives me another idea.

I take one set of flowers and cut the stems. I position them in a glass globe so they're the perfect size for the conference room table. Then I pick up the other vase and take both to the conference room. The big one I put on the buffet cabinet.

I return to the break room and place a dozen cupcakes on the platter. Then I take them to my desk. I find a package of colored sharpies in my desk drawer and make four signs with the flavors of the cupcakes on each. I go back into the conference room and place the platter and signs on the buffet cabinet.

Satisfaction fills me when I assess the room. The Dallas skyline is just as impressive here as Sebastian's office. But now, the flowers and cupcakes add a touch of warmness that wasn't present before.

I return to my desk and get lost in the pile of folders. Sebastian steps out of his office and states, "Follow me."

I glance up. "Where are we going?"

He huffs. "To the meeting with Gulf Oil."

"Oh. You want me in the meeting?" I ask, surprised.

His eyes turn to slits. "Are you not Victoria's intern?"

"Yes, of course."

"Tell me, *Ms. Peach*. Why did you choose to apply at Cartwright Enterprises?" he interrogates.

The hairs on my neck rise. I open my mouth, but nothing comes out.

His arrogance grows. "Let me guess. You heard how we have more young professionals in the C-suite than any other company in Dallas, and you want to climb up the career ladder as fast as you can?"

No, I wanted to earn money for my cupcake bakery.

"I-I..." I swallow the lump in my throat, suddenly needing a glass of water to quench my dry mouth.

"I didn't promote more young professionals than any other corporation by letting them sit at their desks. Hands-on experience— that's what Cartwright Enterprises is about and why people excel here. You have an MBA, but that isn't going to get you where you want to be without learning," he lectures.

He knows I have my MBA?

He undresses me with his eyes again and lowers his voice, adding, "Isn't that what you want? Hands-on experience?"

Every inch of my skin flushes. My gape only grows.

A level of arrogance so powerful it radiates around him appears. He keeps me in his heated stare another moment, then orders, "Let's go." He motions for me to go ahead of him.

I rise and stroll down the hall, knowing he's checking out my booty the entire time. No matter how much I tell myself not to strut, I can't help it. I sway my hips to torment him, not for more attention, I tell myself.

I'm lying once again.

I glance behind me and catch his gaze right where I felt it. I stop walking, shift on my feet, and arch my eyebrows.

His eyes dart to mine. "Is there a problem, *Ms. Peach*?" he challenges.

"You can call me Georgia," I blurt out, tired of hearing him say my last name like it's a joke.

He takes my words the wrong way, and I curse myself. His smug expression tells me he's clueless about why I don't want him to call me *Ms. Peach.*

There's no doubt. Sebastian Cartwright, my new boss, thinks I'm into his attention on my backside and any other part of my body.

I am.

No, I'm not.

Liar!

He steps closer, eliminating the gap between us. His intoxicating scent annihilates me for the second time this morning. His lips twitch as he says, "Well, then, Georgia, is there a reason you're making our clients wait?"

My words jumble in my head. I stutter, "N-no." I spin and walk into the conference room.

There are four men and Victoria in the room. They all have coffee and a cupcake in front of them, except Victoria, who states, "I already had one for breakfast."

"Where did you buy them? My daughter would love these for her birthday party," one man asks.

Victoria rises, motioning toward me. "Georgia made them."

The men stand too, and the one who stated he wanted them for his daughter's party steps in front of me. He gives me a once-over, lingering a bit longer than I'd prefer, then holds out his hand. "Ben Eiler. Nice to meet you. Any chance I can get a few dozen of these by Saturday? My ex-wife thinks I can't plan my daughter's party without her help, and I'm on a mission to show her she doesn't know who she's messing with."

"Umm...I...ummm..."

"Georgia's our new intern," Sebastian interjects, stepping so close to me his body heat mingles with mine.

Ben glances at Sebastian, then back at me. "Tell me you aren't too busy to help me out, Georgia? It'll go a long way during our contract negotiations today." He winks in a flirtatious way.

"Are we dealing with cupcakes instead of oil prices?" Sebastian asks in a disapproving tone.

Ben's eyes light up further as he continues to study me. "Well, yes. We sure are. What do you charge for these?"

"I haven't sold them yet," I confess.

"Why not?" he asks.

"I'm saving up for my own bakery someday," I declare.

"Is that so?" Sebastian mumbles.

I cringe inside. *Why did I announce that?*

"You want a partner? I'll back you," Ben claims.

I gape, then compose myself. "Thank you for your offer, but this is something I need to do on my own."

He chuckles. "Can't argue with that kind of entrepreneurial spirit. But what do you say, Georgia? Can you help me out?"

Something tells me that I'm in a no-win situation. Sebastian moves even closer to me, and I assess his forced smile.

"Well?" Ben asks.

I try to contain my excitement about my first client, confirming, "Sure. I can make that happen."

"Perfect. I'll give you my number so you can get all the details," Ben declares.

"I'm sure your assistant can handle this," Sebastian suggests.

Ben's challenging stare says otherwise. He proclaims, "I think I'll handle this one."

Sebastian's face hardens.

Ben takes another bite of his cupcake and mumbles, "Remind me to take one of these for the road."

"Georgia, have a seat," Sebastian orders, pulling out a chair, his commanding eyes full of irritation.

I obey, trying to contain my giddiness. Sebastian Cartwright is not going to rain on my parade. I have my first client.

Two

SEBASTIAN CARTWRIGHT

Georgia Peach.

What kind of parents name their child Georgia Peach?

Were they on drugs?

Did they hate her upon birth?

A small part of me feels sorry for Georgia. I can imagine how badly the kids teased her while growing up.

She's not a moron. She could have legally changed it.

I would have if I were her.

Her name is as annoying as her perky tits, sunshine attitude, and royal-blue doe eyes.

She looks so innocent.

I bet she's only dated super-nice guys who don't know what they're doing in the bedroom.

I could corrupt her twenty four -year-old virginal body.

Okay, she can't be a virgin.

Maybe she is.

Nah. She probably lost her virginity to her longtime high school boyfriend, who came the minute he shoved his small little cock inside her tight pussy.

I should teach her what it's like to be with a real man.

HR would love that.

I glance through the tinted glass at her long legs crossed under her desk. She twists a lock of her blonde hair around her finger, studying a piece of paper. She furrows her eyebrows, releases her hair, then marks the paper. Her pink tongue shoots out, slowly licking her bottom lip.

I groan, slide my hand inside my pants, and stroke the raging hard-on I've had since I ran into her in the lobby. The moment she opened those pouty lips and her southern accent came out, I was a goner.

But I knew if she worked in this building, I needed to stay away from her.

Then she showed up in my office with her little cupcake dreams, compounding my annoyance.

What is the point of an MBA if you aren't going to use it?

She's obviously using Cartwright enterprises as a stepping stone until her fantasy operation can come to fruition. Watching our clients eat her cupcakes all day and rave about them only irritated me more.

If Ben Eiler thinks he's going to have his way with her, he's got another thing coming.

She's an employee. I need to stay away from her.

She's not long-term.

Maybe I should have her sign a contract, tell her I'll pay her double her salary to service my needs and keep her at my beck and call.

I chuckle, trying to imagine her face if I proposed that arrangement, stroking myself faster.

She rises and walks toward my door. There's a knock.

I remove my hand from my pants, scoot closer to my desk, and bark, "Come in."

"Is there anything else you need before I leave tonight, Mr. Cartwright?" She turns her dazzling smile on me, making my cock hurt more.

Yeah, come over here. I'll bend you over the desk and fuck that chirpy little attitude of yours right out of you.

The lights are dim, signaling it's past seven. It's to save electricity, but I also prefer it after a long day. I glance at the window, realize it's already dark out, and then refocus on her. "No. I'm good."

"Okay. I'll see you tomorrow," she says and spins.

"Wait!" I order.

She freezes, then turns back. "Yes?"

"Why are you here so late?" I question. The others left at least an hour ago.

She shrugs. "I wanted to get a head start on the files Victoria gave me for tomorrow."

I study her, staring at her tits, covered in her yellow dress and sweater, for so long she nervously shifts. When I pin my gaze back on hers, I state, "You're on salary."

"Yes, I'm aware."

"There's no overtime for staying later," I point out.

"I wasn't staying to earn overtime," she claims.

Hook, line, and sinker.

"No? Then what were you staying late for when everyone else but me has left?" I ask, just to watch her squirm.

A moment passes, and it's like watching a lightbulb go off in her brain. Crimson colors her cheeks, and she stutters, "I-I told you I wanted to get a head start."

"Is that all?" I ask, enjoying every minute of making her uncomfortable. And there's no more debating. I'll have my way with her sooner rather than later. It'll be a new challenge to see what she'll allow me to do to her.

Remember HR.

I'll cover my butt.

"Well?" I ask when she continues to gape at me.

She squares her shoulders and lifts her chin. I have to give her credit. A lot of interns have tried to seduce me. I'm one of Dallas's top bachelors to snag, and they all want a piece of my fortune. Yet I don't fancy those offers. What's the fun if it's too easy? I can get laid anywhere. Plus, doing it with someone on my payroll is a headache.

I'll make an exception for her naive ass though.

She reiterates, "I wanted to get a head start on tomorrow. Since it's Thanksgiving this Thursday, I didn't want to get behind due to the day off."

I almost roll my eyes. Thanksgiving is just another excuse for people not to work. I snicker. "Granny coming to town to cook you a turkey?"

Her eyes glisten and her voice shakes. "No. She died six months ago."

Now I feel like a total jackass. I add, "Sorry. I didn't mean to—"

"If there's nothing else, I'll see you tomorrow," she states, not waiting for me to reply before shuffling out of the office.

I rush toward the door and call out, "Hey!"

She spins, puts her hand on her hip, and asks, "What?"

"I didn't mean to be a dick about your grandma," I claim.

"Yes, you did. Goodnight," she replies, then practically runs to the elevator.

Her response shocks me. Most people don't call me out on my bullshit. I stare at her pert ass, fisting my hand at my side, feeling a tad guilty. It's what happens every now and then—the guy who used to care about hurting people's feelings shows up.

I watch her disappear in the elevator, reprimand myself for apologizing to her, and try to shake him away. My days of caring about women are over. Every time I put my heart on the line, it got squashed. After my fourth fiancée, and last failed attempt to find love, I vowed to use women for my physical needs and stay single forever. All of them were just using me for the Cartwright name and money. It didn't matter if they were from the small town I grew up in or Dallas. Every time I got used, it cut me deeper.

Ms. Peach is lying about not knowing who I was before this morning.

She seemed genuinely shocked.

It's an act.

The last five years, I've stuck to my rules, and I no longer get emotionally attached. It's easier, there aren't any surprises, and I don't become a lovestruck fool.

I pace my office, wishing I hadn't thought of my past romantic failures and trying to no avail to get Little Miss Sunshine out of my head. So I decide I need to work out again. I go home, change, and step into my gym, sweating for several hours. But nothing gets her voice, with her southern phrases and accent, out of my mind.

Plus, her round ass and long legs were made to torture men.

I finally get into the shower, jack off, and toss my pre-packaged, macro-balanced meal into the microwave.

A vision of her gourmet, sugar-scented cupcakes pops into my head.

I mumble, "Who eats cupcakes in today's age anyway?"

More annoyance fills me thinking about all the clients who ate and raved about them while my mouth watered as I resisted trying one.

A few times, I had to check myself. Georgia would say something in the meeting, and I couldn't help but scowl to cover up my attraction toward her. From time to time, Victoria gave me her "What the hell is wrong with you?" expression.

Nothing I did seemed to faze Little Miss Sunshine, which only irritated me further. And every time she ran her pink tongue over her lips, my cock ached.

The microwave dings. I eat my food without tasting it, then slide into bed.

All night, I toss and turn, thinking about the mergers and acquisitions I have on my plate and the contracts that need to get renewed. Eventually, the never-ending question rears its ugly head.

When will my father finally retire?

He keeps saying he's going to, but he puts it off another twelve months every year. So I'm not going to hold my breath that come January, I'll be the new CEO of Cartwright Enterprises.

To distract my thoughts, Georgia pops back into my mind. I get another hard-on and jack off to visions of her sucking me dry with her plump, pink lips.

By four thirty, I give up trying to sleep. I go back into the gym, run several miles on the treadmill, pump a few weights, take a shower, and start to feel a little bit better.

I glance at myself in the mirror. Trying to convince myself it's true, I state, "It's coming soon. I know it's coming soon." The anxiety I'm constantly battling while trying to show my father I'm ready to take over grows bigger the closer I get to January. I've tried to tap into the "the universe will give you what you ask for" mentality, but so far, it's not working for me.

After my pep talk, I go into the kitchen, prepare the same protein shake I drink every morning, then guzzle it down. I brush my teeth and step outside to the parking garage.

I get in my truck, and I'm halfway to the office when my father's name pops up on my dashboard screen.

Something inside me makes me hesitate. He only calls when something isn't to his liking or there's a problem. It rings again, and I answer, "Dad, what's going on?"

"Well, good morning to you too," he says.

I grunt. "Didn't know you called to exchange niceties. What's going on?"

"Jesus, it's barely dawn, and you already have an attitude for the day, huh?" he comments.

"Dad, can you get to the point of whatever this conversation is?" I demand.

"Why aren't you coming home tomorrow?" he questions.

I grip my fingers on the steering wheel tighter. "I told Mom I have a lot of work to do. I don't have time to come home for one day."

"It's Thanksgiving. You should be coming home for the weekend, not just one day," he says.

I tug at my hair, claiming, "I don't have time for that, and you know it. I've got a lot on my plate. Remember what it was like when you were running things?"

Years ago, he moved back to the ranch. He used to commute between Dallas and home, but he put me in charge of running the operations so he could back off a little. It's where I wanted to be anyway. I can't stand the small town I grew up in. There's not a lot going on, too much gossip, and memories I'd rather forget. And I'd rather work for a week with no break than put up with all the country-girl-turned wannabe Dallas socialites who'd love to sink their claws into me.

"It's a holiday. You're meant to be with family," my father restates.

I remind him, "Dad, you know what's at stake. I've got to renew these contracts. We also have the new acquisition to close."

"I thought you wanted to be the new CEO," he challenges.

The hairs on the back of my neck rise. I angrily accuse, "Let me guess. You're not retiring again."

"Didn't say that," he declares.

"I'm tired of you waving the carrot in front of me, then holding it out another twelve months," I admit.

He chuckles. It's loud and riles me up more. He replies, "Well, I guess your patience is about to pay off."

"Bullshit," I utter.

"Watch your language."

"Dad, I don't have time for this. What are you going to hold over my head now?" I inquire, not convinced he'll actually retire.

"I'm not holding anything over your head, son. But you've got two choices."

"Here we go," I say and turn onto the main road where my office is located.

"Son, your mother's upset. It's the holidays. You should be here with your brothers and sisters and us. Plus, you haven't seen your nieces or nephews in a while. You need to come home every now and then," he states.

"I don't like it there. There's nothing in your small town I need," I tell him for the millionth time.

He sighs. "The oil wells are here. So are the cattle and all the employees who run the ranch. Seems to me like you need that to run the corporation."

I point out, "They do their job, and I do mine, so they still have one."

"Sebastian, you have to come home for the Christmas holidays. You're going to be here December 1st, and you aren't leaving until January 1st," he informs me.

My gut dives. "No way!"

"Did I stutter?"

"I'm not coming home for a month. That's ridiculous."

25

He drops another bomb. "Then I guess I'll name Alexander as the new CEO on January 2nd when I announce my retirement."

I can feel the blood draining from my cheeks. I seethe, "So this is what you had up your sleeve? You know Alexander isn't anywhere near capable of doing what I do here in Dallas."

"Maybe not, but your brother understands family values. And Cartwright Enterprises was built on family values," my father says matter-of-factly.

I sarcastically laugh. "So I don't have values because I don't like to come home?"

"Part of family values is spending time with your family. And especially on the holidays."

"Dad, a lot is going on here. I can't do my job if I'm there instead of in Dallas."

"That's not true. There are video meetings and all sorts of technology nowadays, as you always point out," he throws in my face.

My gut dives further. "These meetings are better handled one-on-one."

"You can go back to Dallas for a meeting or two if I approve it. But my guess is you won't have to," he claims.

"You can't be serious," I mutter, cringing at the thought of having to spend a few days, much less a month, in the small town.

"I'm not making your decision for you. It's your choice. But, Sebastian, come home for a month and spend time with your mother and the rest of the family, or I'm naming your brother as CEO."

"That's ridiculous," I protest again.

"Don't test me on this, Sebastian," he threatens.

"Dad—"

"Call your mother today and let her know what your decision is," he orders, then hangs up.

I slap the steering wheel several times, miss a red light, and run right through it. A siren wails, and I glance in the rearview mirror. I groan and pull over.

A cop parks behind me, gets out of his vehicle, then gives me a ticket and a stern lecture.

I barely hear a word. When he releases me, I drive another block, enter my office building, and step off the elevator on the top floor. I turn the corner toward my office and groan inside.

I forgot about her.

Georgia's at her desk. She crosses, then uncrosses her legs. The pencil skirt she's wearing hits mid-thigh when she's seated. Her blouse is buttoned up, but a peek of her cleavage shows through.

My raging hard-on returns, and that's before she looks up at me, beaming.

She drawls, "Good morning, Mr. Cartwright. How was your night?"

"Fine," I grumble, then go into my office and close the door. I step toward my desk and freeze.

Goddamn her.

I reach for the gold-frosted cupcake that has a plastic turkey stuck in it. The scent of sugar flares in my nostrils, and I almost cave before I toss it in the trash.

Don't need empty calories, I tell myself.

Doesn't she know sugar and carbs only turn to fat?

I don't need to add time to my workout to work off her baked goods.

I glance through the glass.

How does she keep those curves, baking all the time?

I spend hours burying myself in work, trying to forget about the conversation earlier with my father, until he texts me.

Dad: *Why haven't you called your mother yet?*

Me: *I'm working.*

Dad: *You have ten minutes to call her, or I'm going to tell your brother he's the new CEO.*

What the fuck is his problem? My brother doesn't even want to be CEO.

Maybe he does.

What if things have changed?

And all of a sudden, now he wants extra responsibility?

My inner demons fight me. New anxiety explodes within me like fireworks.

My father texts me again.

Dad: *Two minutes.*

I cave and pick up the phone, calling my mother.

She answers, "Sebastian! How are you, dear?"

I lie, "I'm good, Mom."

"Are you calling to tell me you're coming home for Thanksgiving?" she asks wishfully.

I grimace, unable to believe what's about to come out of my mouth. "No. I still can't come. I've got a lot of work to do here."

Disappointment fills her voice. She lays on the guilt. "Oh, honey, I really wish that you'd make time for us. Please tell me you're coming home for Christmas."

I take a deep breath and stare out at the Dallas skyline, forcing myself to reply, "That's what I'm calling to talk to you about."

Hope fills her tone. "Oh?"

My irritation peaks. I swallow it down, informing her, "I'm coming home for the month."

"A month!" she shrieks.

I squeeze my eyes shut. "Yeah. I'll be there on December 1st. I'm leaving on New Year's Day."

As soon as that clock strikes midnight, I'm out of there.

"Oh, Sebastian. I'm so happy to hear this. Everyone will be so excited," she declares.

Sure they will.

One thing I can always count on is being the black sheep of the family. I prefer the excitement of the city to the dull quiet of the country. The family gatherings I wouldn't mind, if everyone in town wouldn't try to pry into my business or point out my failures when they indulge in their gossip.

So I prefer to be by myself. It's easier that way. I reply, "Alright, Mom, I gotta go. I'll talk to you later. Let Dad know what's happening."

"I sure will. I'm so excited. Are you bringing anybody this year?" she inquires.

Here we go...

I answer, "I haven't thought that far."

"So you aren't dating anyone?" she asks.

"I didn't say that," I claim, then regret the words.

"You are?" she pries.

"Mom, I have to go. We can discuss this later," I say, to buy myself some more time.

She blurts out, "There are a couple of women I'd really like to introduce you to if you come alone. I know you're super picky, but I think—"

"Mom, do not try to set me up," I warn.

"Honey, you're getting older. I need some more grandbabies," she tells me for the millionth time.

"Mom, please."

This is going to be such a disaster. Why did I agree to do this?

Because I've worked my ass off to become CEO.

I quickly state, "I've got a meeting and need to go. Love you. Bye." I hang up and put my forehead on the desk, groaning.

What am I going to do for a month?

Go nuts.

She's probably already inviting all the single women in town to hang out at our house and attend the parties.

How many parties will they have?

I count the family birthdays in December plus holidays in my head and groan.

Too many.

I rack my brain about what to do. I debate about bringing home a fake fiancée, but then I cringe.

All the gossips will be placing bets on if I make it to the altar or not. I should have learned after the first, at the very most, the second time. Four times was asking to give them extra ammo.

I kept thinking each one would never hurt me.

I thought they were different.

I'm an idiot.

Why do I care what the gossips say?

I don't care.

Yes, I do.

God, I hate my life sometimes.

There's a knock on my door, pulling me out of my thoughts. I sit up straight at my desk, answering, "Come in."

Georgia bounces into my office with her little perky tits waving in the air like two flags telling me to come hither.

Jesus, she's got a killer body.

She smiles, and her eyes widen, bustling with that innocence that I want to corrupt.

To hell with human resources. I should shut the door and show her what Sebastian Cartwright's really about.

She strolls to the side of my desk, and her rose-scented perfume flares in my nostrils. And I swear she bathes in sugar, which only adds to my torment. She puts a file on my desk, then opens it. She says, "I found a—" Her eyes lock on my trash can.

My chest tightens.

Hurt fills her expression. She blinks hard, then pins her blues on me. "There's a big error in your spreadsheet. I think you can negotiate a twelve percent increase at your two o'clock meeting." She taps the highlighted column, then spins and walks out.

Three

GEORGIA

The Next Day

Everything feels strange this year. It's the first time I've not gone back to Savannah or been with my grammy for the holidays. Since she died six months ago, there's no reason to return to my hometown. No one is left.

When I was little, my parents were always on the road. They had musical ambitions, so they traveled the country, singing. One night, their tour bus crashed, and the little time I did get to spend with them was gone. I became an orphan.

I'd already been living with my grandfather and grandmother in Georgia. In some ways, it didn't seem any different even though there was grief. And I noticed how sad my grandparents became.

My grandfather had a harder time hiding it than my grandmother. I'd catch him staring at my mother's picture and crying some nights.

But my grammy's saying was, "when life gives you lemons, you turn them into lemonade." So even though my parents were gone, I didn't feel the loss like a child might have. Sure, it hurt, but if they hadn't been so absent, I imagine I would have had a harder time adjusting.

Ever since I can remember, I'd spent every holiday with my grammy. This will be the first year I stay in Dallas for Thanksgiving and Christmas.

Most of the friends I met in college when I was getting my MBA have left. They've gotten jobs around the country or returned to their hometowns to be closer to their families. The only friend I have in town is Melanie. She's married with a four-year-old son and a two-year-old daughter.

One night, we were talking. I was having a hard time contemplating spending the holidays without my grammy. Then I heard her voice telling me to turn lemons into lemonade. That led to me volunteering to host Thanksgiving for Melanie and her family since her and her husband's parents are all in Ohio.

Now that I have plans, I'm feeling excited about Thanksgiving. I plan on making a big, traditional meal. So even though I'm waking up a little bit sad today, I need to do what my grammy would do.

I glance at my clock. It's five a.m., but I can't sleep. My guests are arriving around ten this morning, and we're going to eat around eleven o'clock. So, I roll out of bed to start the turkey. I already brined it and prepped some of the sides last night.

I go into the kitchen, pull the turkey out, and prepare it in the roaster. I start the water for the sweet and white potatoes. Then I mix a can of mushroom soup with fresh green beans.

After I'm finished, I leave the kitchen and return to my bedroom. I jump in the shower, dry my hair, and am in the middle of putting my foundation on when my phone buzzes.

I swipe at the screen and chirp, "Happy Thanksgiving, Melanie!"

Her voice sounds raspy as she replies, "Happy Thanksgiving."

My red flags wave. "Melanie, what's wrong?"

"I'm so sorry, Georgia. The kids were throwing up all night. Their temperatures are slightly over one hundred. Even Darren's got a fever."

"Oh no," I say, as disappointment shoots through me.

She continues, "I'm so sorry. There's no way we can come over."

My gut drops, but I assure her, "It's okay. Is there anything I can get or do for you?"

She sneezes several times.

I pull the phone away from my ear. When she stops, I bring it back.

"Sorry. No, I'm just really sorry. I feel horrible leaving you on your own today. Plus, it was going to be so much fun."

I take a deep breath, trying to sound happier than I feel. "It's okay, don't worry about me. Just get better. If I can do anything, just let me know."

"I will. Thanks. Bye." She hangs up.

I stare at myself in the mirror. *What am I going to do now? I have a ton of food with no one to eat it.*

I blink back tears, but grief overwhelms me and wins. My cheeks turn wet.

A memory of my grandparents on Thanksgiving comes to my mind. Loneliness rears its ugly head. It's something I've felt way too much of lately.

"Stop moping," my grammy says in my head.

I pull myself together and go out to the kitchen. The aroma of turkey fills the air. I stare at all the food, trying to figure out what to do.

I have to finish making everything. Otherwise, it'll go to waste.

I can take it over to Melanie's.

Doing my best not to sink into a pity party, I turn on some music and finish making everything. I save two servings for myself and text Melanie.

Me: *I'm going to drop food off. I know y'all are sick, but you can have some when you feel better.*

Melanie: *That's sweet of you, but don't feel obligated.*

Me: *I'm not going to be able to eat all this, and I don't want it to go bad.*

Melanie: *Okay, thanks. Just leave it outside our door so you don't get sick.*

Me: *No problem.*

I package everything in containers I saved when I cleaned out my grammy's house. They keep the food warm, and I stare at the worn-out fabric. It's off-white with little turkeys on it. It's another bittersweet feeling.

I stop myself from getting on another pity-party train and text Melanie.

Me: *Hey, I'm leaving in five minutes. Can you make sure I get my containers back? These were my grammy's.*

Melanie: *Of course. I'll take good care of them.*

Me: *Thanks.*

I find a box and put everything in it. Then I take everything to my car. I drive to Melanie's, ring her bell, put everything on the front porch, then text her.

Me: *Food's here.*

Melanie: *Thanks, girl. I'm so sorry, again.*

Me: *It's okay. Just get better.*

I return to my apartment and stare at the wall.

What am I going to do now?

I should just crawl into bed and forget about this entire day.

"That's not the answer," my grammy's voice states in my head.

The empty, lonely, depressed feeling that I hate continues to grow. I almost get trapped in it and go into my bedroom, but I stop myself.

Maybe I should go to work.

"It's a holiday," my grammy reprimands.

I say out loud, "At least if I go to the office, I can get more caught up on the backlog of work."

My grammy tsks me, and it's so vivid I shudder.

"At least Mr. Grumpy Pants won't be there," I add.

No matter what I do to convince myself to go, I can't get my grammy's horrified expression out of my head. Then I hear her say, *"Bake. It's what you love best. You'll feel better if you bake."*

Deciding it's better to use my free time on something I love, I pull out ingredients and debate about what to make.

Tomorrow's Black Friday. Make something fun for the day.

It's funny how I've never gone shopping on Black Friday. My grammy taught me how to watch my pennies, but she and I always spent the day preparing the house for Christmas and baking cookies, fudge, and other holiday treats.

Tomorrow I have to work. We have several important meetings with bigwigs who are in town for the holiday. So I try to remember how many people will be at each meeting. Then I add in the staff who always eat them. By the end of the afternoon, I have six dozen double chocolate fudge cupcakes with dark chocolate frosting. And just like my grandma stated in my head, I do feel better.

I heat up the Thanksgiving meal I cooked, pour a glass of White Zinfandel, and put it on a TV tray. There are several Christmas movies on, so I eat my dinner and drink two glasses of wine while watching them, but my thoughts begin to wander.

For the life of me, I can't figure out why I'm thinking what I am, but thoughts of Sebastian won't leave my head.

What's he doing today?

Is he with his girlfriend?

Ugh! I'm sure she's a runway model or something fabulous like that.

Maybe he's single.

Fat chance.

Doesn't matter. I don't care about him! He's rude and obnoxious.

Maybe he just needs someone good in his life to morph into the nice person that must be deep inside him.

Like way deep.

Way, way, WAY deep.

"You can't change a man," grammy's voice stated.

The second movie ends, tearing me out of my thoughts. I decide to go to bed early, but I regret it.

All night, I have dreams about Sebastian. His praline, citrus, and sandalwood scent flares so powerfully that I swear I'm not dreaming. I can smell it.

In one dream, snow's falling and he's kissing me. Not in a way anyone's ever kissed me before either. He uses his tongue as a weapon, assaulting my mouth until I'm unable to stand without his arm holding me tight to his waist.

In another, we're in a barn. He pushes me onto the hay bales and pins his body over mine, murmuring the dirtiest things I've ever heard. What's crazier is I'm not offended, not one little bit. Every word that comes from his mouth makes my core stir faster.

Then there's the last one. He's dragging his tongue on my cleavage, then past my belly button and on to my most private region. I grip his chestnut hair and push him closer to my body. An earthquake of adrenaline annihilates my entire being. I wake up in a sweat, shaking and horrified that I'm dreaming of my rude boss who hasn't said a nice thing to me since I started working for him.

Plus, he tossed my cupcake in the garbage. If he didn't want it, he could have waited until after hours to do that, given it to someone else, or put it in the break room.

My alarm rings shortly after that dream. Relief fills me that I not only got through Thanksgiving but that I'm scheduled to go to work. I don't want to sit at home and think about how I'm alone on the holidays. But then I'm disturbed, thinking about the dreams I had of Sebastian.

I convince myself I'll just ignore him. Besides, it's not like he knows my thoughts. So I get ready for work and then text Melanie.

Me: *Hey, girl, how are you feeling?*

Melanie: *Oh, this flu is so bad. I'm so glad we didn't see you the day before we got this.*

Me: *Do you need anything?*

Melanie: *No, but thanks for the food. It'll come in handy once we can eat again.*

I cringe.

Me: *Yikes. Well, my offer still stands if you need anything.*

Melanie: *Thanks, girl. I'll let you know if something pops up.*

I load the cupcake boxes into my car and head to work. It doesn't take long to get to Cartwright Enterprises. I make my way through the building, saying my good mornings to the security guards and other people I've started to get to know within the last few days. When I get up to our floor, I take the boxes back to the break room and start separating them on the platters for the different meetings.

Victoria comes in, peeks over my shoulder, and asks, "Oh, what do we have today?"

"Black Friday cupcakes. They're double chocolate fudge with dark chocolate frosting," I inform her.

She snatches one out of the box. "I shouldn't, but I couldn't get through the pumpkin pie yesterday. So I deserve this."

"Oh? Why not?" I question.

She huffs. "I couldn't stop comparing it to your pumpkin pie cupcakes you brought in on Wednesday."

"Really?"

She nods. "Yep."

"Well, sorry I ruined your pie," I offer.

She shrugs. "No biggie. How was your Thanksgiving?"

"It was great," I lie before I ask, "How was yours?"

"Oh, lots of family drama. You know how it is," she says.

I just smile. Actually, I don't know. My family didn't really have drama. It was only the three of us. I was a good kid, so I didn't cause my grandparents any problems. I always wondered what it would be like to have a big family. But I guess I'll never know. I pick up a platter and reply, "I'm going to get the room ready for the first meeting."

"Later," she says and gives a small wave.

When I get to the conference room, I run smack into Sebastian. Several cupcakes smash into his suit jacket. I exclaim, "Oh no! I'm so sorry!"

He glances down at the frosting stain, then back at me, scowling.

I set the platter down and try to wipe the dark concoction off with my finger, but it only makes it worse.

"Stop," he demands.

A shiver runs down my spine. It's the same way he spoke to me in one of my dreams. I slowly glance up. His intoxicating scent teases me, sending tingles to my core and heat rushing to my cheeks.

He locks his blues on mine, then clasps his fist around my hand. He moves my frosting-covered fingers near his mouth and asks, "What is this?"

"Dar—" I clear my throat. "Dark chocolate frosting."

He repositions them in front of my mouth. "Do you smell that?"

My insides quiver, but it's not from fear. Zings ping-pong around my body like a professional game. I swallow hard, trying to find my breath, and manage, "The frosting?"

"The sugar," he states.

Confusion fills me. I answer, "Yes."

"Do you eat your cupcakes?"

"Sometimes," I admit.

"Go on then," he goads, pushing my fingers closer to my lips.

"What?" I ask.

Something plays in his expression, but I don't know what it means. "Show me you eat what you bake. Go on." He pushes my fingers past my lips, and I have no choice but to suck the frosting off.

His breathing turns into short pants. Time seems to stand still as neither of us breaks our gaze, and he continues to keep my fingers positioned in my mouth.

For a moment, I forget I'm at work. The chocolatey sweetness dances on my tongue as Sebastian clenches his jaw.

He finally releases my hand and steps back. "Good to know you aren't trying to poison me." His eyes dart down my body, in his lewd way, then back to my eyes.

"Why would I do that?" I inquire, my heart pounding so fast, I wonder if it's possible for it to explode.

He leans into my ear, and in the same voice as in my dream, he murmurs, "Georgia, Georgia, Georgia."

Every time he says my name, I overheat. In my current predicament, it's not helping matters. I squeeze my thighs together, then whisper, "Yes, Sebastian?"

His hot breath hits my ears, and goose bumps break out on my skin. He inhales as if he's smelling me, then adds, "I think you owe me a clean suit."

Dizziness hits me. I grip the part of the jacket with the frosting to steady myself. I reply, "I can take this to the dry cleaners."

He softly chuckles, but it only confuses me.

"You don't want me to?" I blurt out.

He retreats. His lips twitch, and he steps back, slowly unbuttoning his jacket.

Oh my gosh! Oh my gosh! Oh my freaking gosh!

I'd never seen Sebastian without a suit jacket on. He lowers the coat, his muscles flexing just like in my dream before he pushed me onto the hay. I try to tear my eyes off his torso, but it's like they're glued to his pecs.

He tilts my chin, which only adds to my embarrassment. His eyes shine with arrogance, and he slings his coat over his shoulder. "I think we have more important things to discuss, Georgia."

"What?"

He shuts the conference room door, pulls a chair away from the table, and motions for me to sit.

I obey and wait for him.

He takes the chair next to me and states, "I have a proposal for you."

The hairs on my neck rise. I tilt my head and furrow my eyebrows. "A proposal?"

He grins, which is the first time I've ever seen him smile. My heart skips a beat as he asks, "How would you like to get your cupcake bakery started in the New Year?"

Shocked, I gape at him, unsure how to answer.

Amusement fills his expression. He stays quiet.

I blurt out, "Is this a trick?"

He shakes his head. "No. Are you serious about your dream or not?"

"Of course I am," I assert.

He leans closer. "Okay, then I'm only going to ask you one more time. How would you like to start your cupcake bakery in the New Year?"

"This upcoming year? As in a few months?" I ask.

"Yes."

"That's not possible," I reply, adding up the little money I have in my bank account.

"Where's Little Miss Sunshine's optimism gone?" he challenges.

I glare at him. "Stop calling me that."

"Why? You are, aren't you?" he retorts.

"Just because I choose to—"

"Look, we're getting off topic here. Do you want your bakery or not? If there were no obstacles in the way, is that what you'd do?" he interrogates.

I don't hesitate. "Of course I would."

He studies me for several moments.

I confess, "You're making me nervous."

"Don't be," he orders.

I stay silent, my pulse racing faster with every passing second.

He finally drops the bomb. "Marry me until January 2nd, and I'll give you enough money to open your bakery."

Four

SEBASTIAN

A Few Hours Earlier

So far, my Thanksgiving week has been super productive. I got a ton of work done yesterday since no one was in the office. The only thing I can complain about is that I had a moment of weakness.

Since it was Thanksgiving, nothing was open. I didn't think about food before I left. I figured I had some meals in the fridge at work.

I was wrong and paid for my mistake.

When lunchtime rolled around, I hadn't eaten since breakfast and was starving. Georgia left her cupcakes in the breakroom. Those damn turkey cupcakes were inside a glass-covered cake plate, tormenting me.

I didn't eat only one. I binged four of them before I left for the night, cursing myself every time I polished one off.

I had underestimated Georgia's cupcakes. They weren't good. They were amazing.

And addictive.

It only made me more annoyed. The last thing I needed was a cupcake obsession.

When I got home, I spent two hours in the gym. I still felt guilty. It took me years to create my strict regime so I could eliminate the excess weight of my childhood. And I'm going to be CEO of Cartwright Enterprises. Come January 2nd, I'll be the face of the corporation. I can't have cupcake rolls. I can imagine all the fun the gossips would have with that.

Pissed at myself, I went to bed and got up at three a.m. to burn off some more calories, still feeling guilty about my binge. At five, I went into the office.

For hours, I've been working. I hit send on an important email regarding a contract I need to close immediately and my phone dings. I glance at the screen and groan.

Mom: *Here's somebody I think you should meet. Her name's Carolina. She's a lovely girl.*

A picture of a blonde pops up. She's got fake everything... hair, lips, eyelashes. Her cleavage is pushed so high, there's no doubt her boobs are fake too. I'm not against implants if a woman wants them, but at least be a bit discreet about them.

She should take some pointers on being natural from Georgia.

I need to stop thinking about Georgia, I reprimand myself.

Mom: *Or Jessica's available. She told me she loves Dallas and would consider moving there for the right person.*

"I bet she would," I mutter.

A brunette pops up on my screen next. Everything about her resembles my last fiancée.

Not reliving that nightmare.

Mom: *Of course, Carmine's really, really nice. She can't wait to have babies.*

A nerdy-looking redhead fills the screen. I suppose she's good-looking, but I'm pretty sure she should marry a boring accountant or something.

I'm about to text my mom to stop when another text pops up.

Mom: *What about Sarah? She's beautiful, isn't she? She's competing in the Miss Texas pageant.*

A photo of a Latino woman in a glittery gown followed by one of her in her bikini with a sash over it comes through.

That's all I need. A pageant queen.

She should take lessons from Georgia on how to not overdo the makeup.

Stop thinking about Georgia!

Good God, my mother really doesn't know me at all.

I text my mom back.

Me: *I told you I'm in a relationship. Stop texting me these pictures. I'm not interested in any of these women. Nor will I ever be.*

Mom: *Who is it? Tell me. You said that, but you didn't give me any details. I thought you were making it up, Sebastian.*

Great. Even my mother can see through my lie.

I scrub my face.

What am I doing? I have to leave on Monday. There's no way I can go home alone now.

Why did I say that?

Instead of fessing up, I only go deeper.

Me: *You'll meet her when I bring her home.*

Mom: *You're bringing her home? You must be serious, then?*

The pit in my stomach grows. This is bad. I'm not dating anyone right now. I have my women who I utilize when I want to fuck, but I wouldn't bring any of them home, especially for a month.

Mom: *Sebastian? Give me details!*

Me: *I've got important meetings. I don't have time to talk about this. I'll talk to you later. STOP YOUR MATCHMAKING.*

I toss my phone on the desk upside down and press my hands to my forehead. *What am I going to do?*

I can't go home. It's going to drive me nuts.

If I don't, I'm not going to be CEO. I've worked too damn hard to have my father name my brother head of this corporation over me.

I need a fake fiancée. That'll appease everyone for a month.

Fiancée number five?

The shame I feel around my failed relationships cyclones in my stomach. I pound my head against the back of my chair.

No more fiancées, whether real or fake.

Think! What would be better?

I pace my office, then it hits me—I need a fake wife. I will gladly pay a woman a fortune if it means my family leaves me alone while I'm home.

Georgia's chipper voice tears me out of my thoughts. She's practically singing good morning to everybody she comes across.

I stare at her through my tinted window, watching her carrying six boxes.

Six.

Does the woman do anything besides bake?

Is she on drugs and that's what makes her so happy?

If so, they should market it to the rest of the world so they can walk around in a blissful haze of happiness.

No. That would be annoying.

I stare at her round ass, wondering why she can't be ugly. At least then I wouldn't have to jack off to her every time I take a shower.

She turns the corner, and the urge to follow her fills me. Instead, I head to the conference room, needing to get out of my office. I pace the room, staring at the beautiful morning glow of the Dallas skyline, trying to figure out my problem. If I don't, my mother will have every single woman in town over at the house at all hours of the day and night.

I need the perfect woman. Someone sweet and kind but not a door-mat. One who my family and the entire town will fall in love with; who fools them into thinking she genuinely loves me.

Not like the others.

My chest tightens, thinking of all the other Christmases I brought a fiancée home thinking she was the one, only to learn her true intentions.

Focus, I reprimand myself. I shake it off, racking my mind over who I can turn into my fake wife.

The woman has to be someone I'd be attracted to, so gorgeous is a must. She needs to get along easily with people and eagerly dive into all the annoying activities my family will force upon her.

Where am I going to find someone with these qualities in less than four days?

Panic sets in as I mentally flip through the Rolodex of women I know. No one has the traits I need or is anyone I can put up with for more than a day.

I curse myself again for my past relationships. If I hadn't been naive enough to think any woman would want me for me and not for my money, I wouldn't be in this predicament.

Love doesn't exist. At least, not for me. It's a cruel reality, but at least I know and understand the truth. And I used to believe in marriage. I wanted nothing more than what my parents have. But eventually, all my fiancées' true colors shone through. They only wanted me for my wealth, status, and power.

Then there was the issue of my sexual tastes. The women all tried to act like they were into it, but I knew they didn't like it when I talked dirty or wanted them at my mercy. Deep down, they were prudes. I saw it in their faces, and people can only pretend for so long until their real selves surface.

I have money, so it shouldn't be this hard.

My parents instilled good financial sense into my siblings and me. I'm not cheap, but I don't like to be reckless with my fortune. However, this is one time where I'm willing to overpay to get what I need.

It's the price for my promotion.

Frustrated beyond belief, I'm about to leave the room when Georgia bounces through the door. She runs right into me, and her platter of cupcakes hits my chest. My expensive, tailor-made suit coat gets frosting on it.

She gets flustered and tries to wipe it off me, but it only makes it worse.

The aromas of roses and chocolate mix in the air, and my skin electrifies. My cock hardens again. All the days I've spent in the office with a painful erection take their toll. I cross all HR boundaries and make her suck the frosting off her finger just to see how far I can push her.

And damn if she doesn't like it. I see it. Her innocent eyes widen as she submits to my whim. And there's no way for her to hide her attraction toward me. It only fuels me to want to tap into the dirty desires I've imagined since I ran into her in the lobby. Then everything becomes clear.

I don't need to look anywhere except in front of me.

Georgia Peach.

She can be my fake wife.

It's time to get what I want.

I take a quick moment to assess the situation like any other business deal.

What does she want?

She wants a bakery for her cupcakes.

I resist lecturing her on how ridiculous that is. The woman has an MBA, for God's sake. She should use it to make as much money as possible. Besides, who would waste all that time and energy to get the education she has for a silly cupcake bakery?

It doesn't matter. That's what she wants.

I lead her to the table and order her to sit. Then I state, "I have a proposal for you."

She tilts her head and furrows her eyebrows, questioning, "A proposal?"

I continue, "How would you like to get your cupcake bakery started after the New Year?"

She gapes at me. I stay quiet, and she finally blurts out, "Is this a trick?"

"No. Are you serious about your dream or not?"

"Of course I am," she asserts.

I lean closer. "Okay, then I'm only going to ask you one more time. How would you like to start your cupcake bakery after the New Year?"

"This upcoming year? As in a few months?" she questions.

"Yes."

"That's not possible."

"Where's Little Miss Sunshine's optimism gone?" I challenge.

She glares at me. "Stop calling me that."

"Why? You are, aren't you?" I push.

"Just because I choose to—"

"Look, we're getting off topic here. Do you want your bakery or not? If there were no obstacles in the way, is that what you'd do?" I question, reminding myself I need to win her over, not push her away.

She doesn't hesitate. "Of course I would."

I study her, trying to push out of my mind all the sordid ways I plan on having her at my beck and call for a month.

Stay focused.

"You're making me nervous."

"Don't be," I reply.

She turns quiet again.

I decide straightforward is the best option. I demand, "Marry me until January 2nd, and I'll give you enough money to open your bakery."

Her jaw drops to the floor. "Marry you until January 2. Are you crazy?"

Here we go. Time to close this deal.

I chuckle. "Not at all."

"Why? What would make you want to marry me? I don't understand," she admits. Her face turns redder, and she backs her chair away from me.

I close the space between us, sling my arm around her, lean an inch from her face, and murmur, "Georgia, Georgia, Georgia."

Her body stiffens. She meets my gaze. "Sebastian, is this a joke?" She holds her breath.

I turn serious and back away, deciding she needs to breathe. I confess, "No. I need a fake wife. And I'm willing to pay."

Appalled, she questions, "Excuse me? I'm not a prostitute!"

I groan. "No one said you're a prostitute, Georgia, nor would anyone think that."

"But you're asking me to marry you for payment," she points out.

"So? Marriages are just contracts of convenience," I state.

More horror fills her expression. "Is that what you believe?"

"Prove to me it's not," I challenge.

"It's-it's not!"

I shrug. "Whatever. You stay in a fairyland believing what you want, and I'll believe what I know to be true. Either way, I need a wife, and you want a cupcake bakery."

A disgusted look replaces her horror.

I cross more HR lines. "Oh, don't get your panties in a twist."

Insulted, her head jerks backward.

But I gotta keep going because I've already come this far. I continue with the belief that the truth is the best option. "My father has given me an ultimatum. I have to go home from December 1st to January 2nd in order to become CEO. If I don't, he's naming my brother, Alexander, as the head of the company. So I need a fake wife. You in or out?"

Her eyes turn to slits. "But why?""

"Because my mother isn't going to stop pushing women on me the whole time I'm there," I admit.

"So just deal with it," Georgia asserts. She doesn't understand that that's not possible.

I sigh. "Here's the thing, Georgia. It's not that easy. You don't know my mother. She'll literally have every single woman in town at our house at all times of the night and day. Plus, I don't want to deal with it. I need to work. You know, all the projects we have to get finished before the end of the year. I don't have time for my mother's matchmaking games. It'll be a complete nightmare for me if I don't bring home a fake wife."

She stares at me as if processing everything. I wait until she accuses, "So you're going to trick your family?"

I sit back and cross my arms. "Georgia. Did you hear what I just said?"

"But it's your family. You'd be lying to them."

And this is why she's so perfect.

I nod. "Yep."

She tilts her head. "So you think it's okay to lie?"

"Oh please, Georgia. Let's not go into your Girl Scout routine."

"Excuse me?" she says, offended once again.

I reprimand myself. I need to get the ball through the hoop, not send her running. I lean closer. "Sorry. Here's the deal. I'll pay you $100,000 if you become my wife and then divorce me on January 2nd."

Shock fills her face.

I add, "I'll put it in writing in a prenup. Think of it as a business contract."

She looks at me like I'm crazy.

"Think about it. You'll have all the money you need to open your cupcake bakery. Isn't that what you said you wanted instead of working for me?" I wait a beat, then add, "Which I know you really don't want to be doing."

She blurts out, "I like my job here."

"I didn't say you didn't. I said that it's not what you really want to be doing," I clarify.

In a worried voice, she repeats, "I like my job here, and I'm grateful for it."

I hold my hands in the air. "No one said you didn't, Georgia. Look, all I'm trying to do is create a win-win for both of us. I get my mother off my back, and you get paid for your cooperation in exchange. You'll have plenty to open your cupcake bakery."

She bites her lip. Too much time passes without her saying anything.

"What's the problem? You can have everything you've ever wanted. And all you have to do is marry me."

"Marriage is forever, not a contract, Sebastian," she scolds.

I wave my hand in front of my face. "Not in my world. And we won't even be married for thirty days. We can annul it, and it'll be like it never even happened—except you'll be $100,000 richer with resources to chase your dream. Win for me. Win for you."

It's like I can see the wheels in her mind spinning.

She's too wholesome.

I can't wait to make her spread her legs for me.

I lean closer. "Think about it. People can be paying for all those cupcakes instead of you slaving away for free."

"Not everything is about money, Sebastian."

I scoff. "Everything's about money, Georgia. If it wasn't, then why do you want to open a bakery? Hmm?"

"None of your business," she reprimands, then turns her head and stares out the window, biting her lip.

"Georgia," I say, my tone demanding.

She turns back, locking her innocent blues on mine.

"This is your shot at having exactly what you want. All you have to do is work for it in a little different way."

"What, by sleeping with you?" she blurts out.

I can't hold my cockiness back. I smirk. "You don't like sex?"

Her face turns as red as a cherry. She opens her mouth, but nothing comes out.

All it makes me think of is fisting her hair and shoving my dick between those plump, pink lips. I drag my fingers over the back of her hand.

She squirms in her seat and scoots it away from the table.

I firmly question, "$100,000, Georgia. What's it going to be?"

She rises, scolding, "This isn't right, Sebastian. This is warped."

I chuckle. "As long as I get what I want, I don't care what you call it. It's a deal on paper to me. Nothing more."

"We'd be lying to everybody—your family...the people who love you!" she exclaims.

I rise, voicing, "I told you what I don't want to deal with when I go home. Stop judging me. Go think about it for a few hours. Smell your cupcakes and think about your dreams instead of putting obstacles in front of them. No one gets ahead in life by not seizing the opportunities they're given. You've got until noon. I don't have time to deal with your wishy-washy ideals."

She huffs. "They aren't wishy-washy ideals. You just dropped a bomb on me."

"Yeah, that's life. Deal with it."

Hurt fills her expression.

A part of me hates when she looks at me like that, but not enough to back down. I dangle her dream in front of her again. "$100,000, Georgia. Decide if your dreams are worth a month of your life or ten years, because you and I both know that's what it'll take for you to save what I'm offering." I leave the room and don't look back, going straight to my office. I shut the door and pace, taking deep breaths.

She better say yes.

Just the way she acted means she's perfect.

But all women pretend they don't care about money.

She has to say yes.

My nervousness continues to grow throughout the morning. I have to force myself to stay focused in my meetings. Between them, I stare at Georgia, getting increasingly obsessed with the idea of her as my fake wife.

Consummating our marriage is going to be a challenge. I doubt she won't make me work for it. But I'll win her over. By the time January 2nd rolls around, I'll have had my fun with my blushing bride. Any naive innocence she now has will be destroyed.

I sit back in my chair, staring out at the Dallas skyline, coming up with rebuttals about how I'll convince her to do this if she comes into my office at noon and turns my offer down.

She will be mine. There's no doubt about it. And I'm going to enjoy every minute of biting into Georgia Peach.

Five

GEORGIA

I return to my desk, but the shock doesn't seem to wear off.

He's serious. He wants me to marry him.

$100,000 to marry him for less than thirty days.

Is he crazy?

I glance toward Sebastian's office, but I can't see anything because of the tinted glass. I refocus on my computer screen, wondering what I should do.

I should say no, but he's right. It'll take me years to open only one bakery. By next spring, I could have my first one.

No, this is wrong.

The message system pops up.

Sebastian: *Victoria, I have Georgia working on a project all day. She won't be in any of our meetings. Please make sure that you don't give her any other projects.*

My stomach flips.

I look toward his office again and then curse myself. He's probably staring at me right now.

What am I going to do?

Victoria: *No problem. I'll assign her project to somebody else this morning.*

Sebastian: *Thank you. Georgia, I expect a full report by noon. Please keep in mind the goals of both parties.*

My stomach dives again. I need to say no to this. This is just bad, bad, bad.

It's $100,000.

That's not going to get me what I need.

There's more to my cupcake business than what I've revealed to Sebastian. I've spent hours creating spreadsheets and a solid business plan. I know everything right down to the penny of what it'll cost me.

My dream is so much bigger than one bakery. I plan to franchise it. I want my grammy's recipes, and the joy I know it'll spread, to be everywhere. Plus, I want everyone to know about her. That's why I got my MBA. I wanted to understand the ins and outs of building a corporation.

I could have told Sebastian, but something tells me the less he knows, the better. It's clear he thinks I'm silly wanting to start a bakery, so I'd rather keep my plans to myself.

Let him eat crow someday when he sees how successful my business becomes.

But I can't marry him. It's wrong.

I continue to freak out and then decide I need to write a list of pros and cons. I make two columns and start with the cons.

This is totally crazy.

We'd be lying. Maybe it's not a big deal to Sebastian, but it is to me. Deception is never good.

I'd have to spend the month with Sebastian.

I freeze. *Or is that a pro?*

No, no, no! It's a definite con.

I move to the pro side.

My first bakery would be open.

I flip back to the cons. *It's not going to get me my entire franchise.*

I stare at the list, going over all the items until I feel crazy. Then it hits me.

I need to negotiate.

I put my pen down, feeling guilty for even contemplating this. Yet I can't get Sebastian's warning out of my head about not letting an opportunity pass me by.

I need a million dollars to do what I want and have a little cushion for emergencies.

I can't go in there asking for a million dollars though.

Why not?

Am I really considering this?

This is my chance. Sebastian's right. I need to seize the opportunity.

But marry him and then get divorced...or annulled? That goes against all my beliefs. My grammy would turn in her grave.

I continue to stare at my screensaver, wondering how much I should start with.

Two million? No, that gives him too much room to negotiate. Sebastian Cartwright is known to be ruthless in his negotiations.

Three million? Yes! I need to start with three million. That way, he'll feel like he won by getting me down to a third, and I'll get the million dollars I need.

I glance at my pros and cons sheet. I add to the pros. *I'll have money to start the charity with the cupcake profits.*

I've always wanted to start a charity for children. I could do that and other good with the profits from the bakeries.

This is starting to look better and better, but I review the cons again.

It's morally wrong.

But is it?

What if I don't have sex with him?

Golly gee, I'm not having sex with him!

He expects me to.

No, I'll make it very clear I'm not having sex with him.

I write on the paper under pros: *No sex.*

Is that really a pro?

Ugh!

More time passes. I continue to fret over my decision. At a quarter to noon, I get a text. It's from an unknown number, but there's no doubt who it's from.

Unknown Caller: *You're putting too much thought into this. This is a business transaction. I doubt your MBA professors would tell you not to snatch this opportunity up.*

His text comes a little too late. I've already been thinking of it that way for the last few hours. But it doesn't make me any less nervous. This is beyond my comfort zone and not anything I ever considered doing. Not that I even thought entering a fake marriage would ever be something someone would present to me for money.

Another text comes through.

Unknown Caller: *Your dreams coming true after 30 days... Or your dreams after years of grinding it out. Or maybe somebody does what you're planning on doing and beats you to the punch. How many cupcake bakeries can there be in Dallas?*

Oh, I really dislike him for putting that thought in my head. But it's not Dallas I'm worried about...it's how many cupcake franchises can there be in the world?

Okay, I need to do this and stop contemplating it.

I get up. It's 11:55, but I chicken out before I knock on his door. Instead, I hightail it to the break room to get a bottle of water.

A bunch of my co-workers are sitting around the table eating my Black Friday cupcakes.

"These are great, Georgia, just like every day," Sam calls out.

"Thanks," I say. Then I decide if Sebastian Cartwright wants me to marry him, he's going to prove it to me because I'm worth it.

And so are my cupcakes.

I grab a cupcake, say goodbye to everybody, and find my courage. I lift my chin and square my shoulders, walking through the office. Taking a deep breath, I knock on Sebastian's door.

"Come in," he calls out.

I open the door, and my pulse skyrockets. I freeze.

Lord have mercy.

Sebastian's on his treadmill, wearing nothing but a pair of shorts and running shoes. Sweat coats his skin, making him look like a glistening rock of muscles.

I groan inside. *Could a man be any more perfect?*

His lips twitch. "See anything you like? Maybe it'll make your decision a little easier," he suggests, punching the treadmill so it stops. He jumps off it and tosses a towel around his neck.

"Don't flatter yourself," I retort, then go to his desk and sit down. I put the cupcake on it.

"Little hungry?" he sneers.

I ignore his comment, informing him, "I'm considering your proposal."

He gives me his challenging stare, questioning, "Considering it? What's there to consider, Little Miss Sunshine?"

I refrain from scolding him, lock eyes, and try to appear confident. My insides shake like a wet dog. I demand, "It'll cost you $3 million."

He jerks his head backward, then scoffs. "Money doesn't matter, huh?"

I put on my biggest smile and sweetly reply, "I have things I want to do with my life."

"What could possibly require $3 million?" he inquires.

I tilt my head, bat my eyelashes, and say, "Sorry, none of your business."

He clenches his jaw, then replies, "I'll give you $200,000."

"Nope."

"Georgia, it's less than thirty days. It's not like it's your whole life. $200,000 for less than thirty days is more than adequate."

"Technically, it's thirty-three days," I assert.

"But less than thirty for marriage," he argues.

"Doesn't matter. It's my time," I respond.

He scowls. "Fine. $300,000."

"That won't do. I need $3 million," I claim again.

"Georgia, this isn't how negotiations work. I go up, and you've got to come down."

"Why should I come down? I'm not the one with the problem that needs to be solved. You are," I remind him.

He chuckles. "Sure, Georgia. And money for your cupcake bakery is just going to fall out of the sky and into your bank account, isn't it?"

I hate that he has a point. But I respond, "Flattery will work a lot better than insults."

He grunts, then repeats, "$300,000."

"$2.5 million," I state and cross my arms over my chest.

He glances at my arms, and I swear he's imagining what my breasts look like naked. I should be angry, but something about his dirty stare stirs everything in my core, heating it until it's like lava bubbling and needing to flow down a volcano.

"But this offer comes with perks, darling," he drawls.

My cheeks burn, and I glare at him, not wanting to encourage him to describe his perks. I demand, "What's it going to be, Sebastian? Are you taking my offer?"

He replies, "$400,000."

"No."

Several minutes pass, with him giving me his intimidating stare. He finally offers, "$500,000."

I rise. "No. And I'm not into playing your games, Sebastian."

His voice rises. In all the meetings I've sat in, I've never heard him lose his cool. It makes me think he's even more desperate to make this deal than I initially anticipated. He asserts, "Georgia, you have to come down. It's for thirty-three days. Nobody in their right mind would do that."

I chirp, "Nobody in their right mind would ask their employee— sorry, their *intern*—to marry them, then lie to their family over the holidays. And for what? So you don't have to deal with your mother pushing women on you," I say in a disapproving tone.

He snorts. "You don't know my mother. Lower your offer, Georgia, or you're getting squat."

I shake my head.

"Fine, I'll find someone else," he threatens.

"Really? Will you?"

He scrubs his hands over his face. "You have to give me something."

I cave a bit. "Fine. $2 million. That's fair," I claim, knowing there's no way he'll go for it.

He shakes his head. "No. I'll give you $600,000."

"Sorry." I walk toward the door.

"Georgia. Sit down," he orders so strongly I jump.

I take a breath and spin. "Why? You're not being reasonable."

"I just offered you $600,000 for thirty-three days of pretending to be my wife. There are much worse jobs in the world that would pay you way less money," he claims.

I go over to the corner of his desk and sit on it. Then I cross my legs.

Surprise fills his expression, as if he didn't think I had it in me to do something so naughty. He stares at my thighs and swallows hard.

"Up here," I coo.

His blues dart to mine. He declares, "$700,000. Final offer."

I pretend to pout. "Oh, I'm sorry. I guess I'll just have to walk." I slowly uncross my legs and scoot my booty off the desk. I lean down. "Although, your offer did sound kind of fun."

His eyes widen a bit, but he catches himself. "$800,000."

"No, sorry." I bat my eyes again.

"Georgia, I'm not paying you $2 million. Give me another number. What's your final offer? And don't test me on this. If you do, I'm pulling out my Rolodex of women, and I'll find some-body else."

I huff. "Your Rolodex of women? Do you know how ridiculous that sounds?"

He gives me an "I don't give a shit" look. Then he declares, "Think what you want, Georgia. You have an opportunity right now in front of you. Either take it or don't, but I guarantee you, if you wake up tomorrow and you could have had all the money you needed to start your bakery and don't, you'll regret it."

My butterflies flutter, and not in a good way. I question, "Why? Are you going to fire me?"

He shakes his head. "Of course not. I'm not that kind of an asshole."

"But you are an asshole, right?"

He sincerely appears shocked. "Did you just cuss, Little Miss Sunshine?"

His comment irritates me. "Whatever, Sebastian. How bad do you want me to be your fake wife?"

He grabs me and pulls me onto his lap.

"What are you doing?" I shriek.

He puts his hand on the back of my head and holds it firmly in front of his face. The sweat from his thighs penetrates the fabric of my dress. I push my palm against his wet pecs.

He demands, "Give me your final offer. Let's make this happen."

My stomach somersaults. Is it too early to put my cards on the table or not? I decide it's a tad too early. "$1.5 million."

He shakes his head. "A million dollars. That's it. That's my final offer. There's no more. And if you don't take it, you won't have this offer in front of you anymore. It'll be over, Georgia. Don't test me on this," he warns.

I've seen Sebastian in dozens of meetings over the last week. And I know that this is his point of no return. Several clients walked out and ended up calling him back after they left. Sebastian didn't give them the final deal. He made it worse, and they still ended up taking it.

But it's also exactly what I wanted. I pretend to think for a minute.

He arches his eyebrows. "Really? You're thinking about a million dollars?"

I finally sigh as if I'm not happy, "Fine. A million dollars."

"Don't look so upset," he orders, then glances at my lips. "I'll have the attorney draw up the paperwork."

My heart pounds so hard I think it'll tear through my chest cavity. I jump back to my feet. "Well, there are some other things we have to discuss."

"What's that?" he questions.

I put my hand on my hip. "One, I'm not sleeping with you."

He smirks. "Is that so?"

"I'm not going to be a prostitute, Sebastian," I declare.

"Like I previously stated, I didn't say you were," he claims.

"I mean it. I'm not going to be your prostitute."

"Fine, you're not my prostitute. And by the way, I don't have to pay to get sex," he says.

"Whatever," I mutter.

"Georgia, do you really want me to tell my attorney to put that in the contract?" he challenges.

I think about it for a moment. He has a good point. This is embarrassing enough. So I answer, "No, you don't have to put it in the contract, but let's just make sure you're clear about it."

"Fine. I'm clear. Are we good?" he questions.

"Not yet." I sit back on the desk, cross my legs, then lean over him, informing him, "There's one more thing you have to do."

He hesitates, glances at my legs, then lowers his voice. "What's that?"

I grab the dessert and hold it under his nose. "You have to eat my Black Friday cupcake."

Annoyance fills his expression and voice. "Why would I eat your cupcake, Georgia?"

"Because that's what people do for their wives or their fiancées... Am I your fiancée now?" I inquire.

He grunts. "Yeah, I suppose you are. Although I haven't put a ring on your finger yet, have I?"

I shrug. "I don't really care about that."

"Sure, you don't," he utters.

"I don't," I declare.

"What kind of woman doesn't care about a big fat diamond?" he challenges.

"Me."

"Why?"

I don't answer his question. I state, "I only care about you eating my cupcake."

"What does me eating your cupcake matter?" he inquires.

I tilt my head. "I'm going to be your wife, and you're going to be my husband. You have to know what my cupcakes taste like. And since you throw them in the trash, which, by the way, will no longer be acceptable, you have to eat one and tell me your honest thoughts. But you can't lie to me, Sebastian."

His eyes dart between my face and the cupcake.

I huff. "Seriously, why do you have an issue with my cupcakes?"

"I didn't say I did," he lies.

"You didn't have to," I accuse.

He stays silent, looking at my cupcake like it's a death sentence.

"You really have an issue this big with eating a cupcake? You're going to blow the whole deal when it's a nonnegotiable request?"

He finally snatches the cupcake out of my hand. "Fine, I'll eat it." His annoyed expression deepens as he unwraps it.

I stay still, watching him eat every bite and taking several sips of water in between. When he's done, he asks, "Are you happy?"

I shake my head. "No, I want to know what you thought about it."

"It's fine," he says.

"You told me you wouldn't lie, Sebastian. One thing I don't want is lies between us. I mean, we're going to be lying to everybody else, but you and I cannot have lies. If I catch you lying to me, I'll blow your little plan up, money or not," I warn.

"Don't threaten me," he scolds.

"I'm not. No lies between us is another nonnegotiable."

He scowls. "What's your point about the cupcake, Georgia?"

"I want to know your honest opinion," I push, not even sure myself why I care so much what Sebastian Cartwright thinks about something so dear to my heart.

He finally admits, "It's delicious. Are you happy?"

I jump off his desk and pat the top of his sweaty head. "Yeah, I'm happy. Have your attorney draw up the paperwork. Make sure you give me time to review it before I have to sign. And don't try anything sleazy, or I'll walk."

"Why would I do that?" he asks.

I give him my "I don't believe you" look.

He grumbles, "Fine. I'll text you when the prenup is done. Go home and pack. We're leaving Monday morning."

SEBASTIAN

"Mr. Cartwright, Huck Peterson's on line two," my receptionist says over the intercom.

Huck Peterson's been my family attorney forever. He's older and known for doing things that aren't always on the up-and-up, yet no one can ever prove it. It's exactly why my family keeps him around.

I hit the button for the second line, then spin my chair so I'm staring at the Dallas skyline. "Huck," I answer.

He drawls, "Sebastian, what gives me the pleasure of talking to you today?"

For the last two hours, I've debated what to say. I decided straightforward is the best. "I have something I need you to do, but it's between you and me."

He chuckles, stating, "Meaning that I shouldn't tell your old man?"

My insides churn. If my father finds out what I'm doing, I'm toast. I don't care if he knows once I'm already named CEO, but if he gets any whiff of what I'm up to, there will be consequences.

Huck's my father's friend, but he's also known for his discretion. Plus, it's not the first time I've had him do things for me under the radar. Still, I'm a bit nervous about this one. I've never intentionally deceived my family. I take a deep breath and reply, "Yeah, it means exactly that. Can I count on you?"

Huck lowers his voice. "Have I ever talked to your father about anything you've told me not to?"

My lingering worries dissolve. "No, you haven't. And that's why I'm trusting you with this delicate matter."

"Which is?" he inquires.

I tap my fingers on the arm of my chair, informing him, "I need a prenup in the next few hours."

Silence fills the line.

My gut flips. The quiet lasts so long that I wonder if he hung up. I ask, "Huck? Are you still there?"

"First of all, do you think I'm at your beck and call, Sebastian? I do have other clients and a busy law firm to run," he lectures.

I chuckle. "Yeah, yeah, yeah. Whatever. I know you're just going to paste a bunch of clauses together and fill in a few sentences, then charge me an arm and a leg, along with a rush fee," I declare.

"Insulting me is not going to get you anywhere, Sebastian," he warns.

I continue, "Listen, I need a prenup. I don't have time to wait, so can we cut to the meat and potatoes of this ordeal?"

"Which one's this for? And why do you need it so fast?"

I cringe inside. After I overheard my first fiancée discussing how she'd be rich once she married me, I had Huck draw up prenups for the following three. Not that I ever got to see how good his prenups hold up, since I never made it down the aisle. But all of those were long negotiations, which should have been my first clue. The memories of going through that process aren't ones I ever wanted to revisit, but here I am, doing it again.

Negotiations are over, I remind myself.

A million dollars.

Georgia is crazy to believe I'll ever let that get into her bank account.

I ignore my tightening chest and announce, "I need a prenup, and I need it to say that I'm going to annul it by January 2nd."

He barks, "What are you talking about, Sebastian?"

"I'm not going into details with you, Huck. I need what I need," I state.

"Well, you're going to have to give me a little bit more detail than that if you want me to do this, kid," he says.

I hate every time he calls me "kid." It's a reminder that I'm not fully respected the way my father is, but there's no one besides Huck who can do this for me. I don't trust anyone else. So I admit, "My father gave me an ultimatum. I have to go home for the holidays between December 1st and January 2nd. If I don't, he'll name Alexander CEO and not me."

Huck whistles. "Well, that's a pretty big ultimatum."

I nod. "Yeah, and you know how my mother is."

Huck chuckles. "Yep, I sure do."

"Then you understand why a fake wife is the only way to stop her from trying to hook me up with every blood-sucking, available woman in town," I claim.

"Just pretend this new woman is your fiancée," he offers.

I grunt. "And have everyone tossing that she's number five in my face? No thanks."

"Seems like a little embarrassment is an easier road to travel down," he suggests.

I rise, pace my office, and scrub my face. "No. I've made up my mind. Now, listen, I need to ensure this prenup is ironclad, Huck."

He caves. "All right. It's your bed to lie in. Give me the details."

Relieved, I reveal, "It needs to say that on January 2nd when we annul the marriage, she gets a million dollars."

"Are you insane?" Huck accuses.

"That's what she insisted upon. She negotiated better than you do," I confess.

Huck's tone gets rougher. "She better have some good benefits for that amount of money."

The hairs on my neck rise as I claim, "I said the paperwork needs to state she gets it. I didn't say I wanted you to not put in loopholes."

He mutters, "Poor girl. She has to put up with you and then you're going to cut her paycheck."

"Since when are you a stand-up type of guy?"

He ignores my comment, asking, "What kind of loopholes are you looking for?"

"I don't know. You're the attorney, so figure it out. Make sure I can pay her less than a million but not less than $100,000 when this is over. But she needs to think she's getting a million dollars,"

I add, feeling a tad guilty. But I'm not a reckless billionaire. What Georgia asked for is greedy, as far as I'm concerned.

Huck's sinister little laugh fills the phone. "All right. I can do that. So let's talk about some things. What else do you want in there besides the fact she gets a million dollars? What would be some things she could do that would break the contract?"

I ponder his question for a moment, then say, "No cheating." Georgia may think we're not sleeping together, but she'll be at my mercy before she knows it. And I'll be damned if another man touches her.

"Is she like fiancée number three?" he inquires.

A sting pierces me, revisiting how I found the woman I planned on marrying making out at dinner with a business colleague. I reply, "No. She's nothing like her. But put it in there."

He continues, "Fine. Besides the nondisclosure clause, what else?"

I pace some more, then answer, "She has to engage with my family at all times. She can't talk bad about me. Oh, and she has to show me PDA everywhere we go," I assert, unable not to smile.

Yep, I'll have her naked in no time once she knows what it's like to have my lips on hers.

Huck mutters, "So your new wife's not too fond of you, I take it?"

I don't answer him.

He adds, "Don't most women love to be fawned over by Sebastian Cartwright?"

I blurt out, "Georgia isn't like most women." My pulse quickens just thinking about her sucking the frosting off her fingers.

"So her name's Georgia. What's her last name?"

"Peach," I state.

"Sorry, did you say Peach?" he questions.

"Yes. Her name's Georgia Peach."

"You've got to be kidding me," he notes.

"No, I'm not. And she's just as annoyingly chipper as the name," I relay.

The sound of Huck lighting up his cigar hits my ears. He takes a deep puff and slowly lets it out. He asks, "Anything else besides the standard clauses?"

"Remind me of the standard clauses?"

"Waiving her right to sue you for any damages that might occur, that type of stuff," he answers.

I reply, "Not that I can think of."

"Okay. I'll get right on it. I'll have it over to you within a few hours."

"Thanks, Huck," I say, relieved this will get done quickly.

He adds, "Yeah, but it'll cost you for the rush job."

I groan. "Of course it will. Send me the bill. Just cover my ass and add in the loopholes."

"No problem." He hangs up.

A few hours pass. I try to do my work and keep looking at Georgia's empty desk. An uncomfortable feeling fills me. I've gotten used to seeing her behind the desk, crossing those long legs of hers.

I text her.

Me: *Are you packing?*

Georgia: *Yes, but how do I know I'm taking the right type of clothes?*

Me: *It's the country.*

Georgia: *So? Should I not bring anything nicer?*

Me: *Pack whatever you want. I'll give you my credit card to go shopping with my sisters and mom when you get there.*

Georgia: *I don't need your credit card to buy clothes.*

Me: *You're going to be my wife. It'll look a little sketchy if you pull yours out.*

Georgia: *Why don't you tell me what type of clothes I'll need and I won't need to go shopping?*

Surprised, I stare at her text. *What woman doesn't want to take my credit card and shop?*

Don't be fooled again. It has to be an act to trick me into thinking she doesn't want my money. After all, she did negotiate a million dollars.

Me: *Pack what you want. If you need something else, then you'll go shopping.*

I wait for another text but nothing arrives. I try to get lost in my work, but I keep staring at her empty desk.

I text her again.

Me: *Leave your granny panties at home.*

Georgia: *Excuse me?*

Me: *My wife wouldn't have them.*

Georgia: *What would your wife have?*

Me: *Thongs. Those cheeky ones that have the round part of your ass showing. See-through bikinis. Crotchless for fun and games.*

Minutes pass.

Me: *Are you going to church to pray for my sins?*

Georgia: *What if I was?*

Me: *I'd tell you to stop praying. It won't absolve me from my deviant actions.*

Georgia: *No one is looking at my underwear.*

Me: *The staff who does the laundry will.*

Georgia: *I'll do my own laundry.*

Me: *That's now how it works in the Cartwright household, Sunshine.*

Georgia: *Stop calling me that.*

I grin. Something about getting under Georgia's skin fuels me.

Me: *So leave your granny panties at home. You can come get my card and go buy some this weekend if needed.*

Georgia: *I don't need your card. I can pay for my own underwear. Besides, who says I even own granny panties?*

Me: *Sure, Miss Million Dollar Negotiator.*

Georgia: *Don't be a sore loser, Sebastian. And I'll earn every penny of the million having to be stuck with you for a month.*

Oh, you're going to earn it by making all my indecent thoughts become a reality.

There's a ding, and I turn to my computer. An email pops up from Huck. I open it.

Sebastian,

. . .

Here's the prenup. Let me know if you have any questions or any issues. I can meet you tomorrow at noon so you can both sign. Hopefully, your bride-to-be doesn't have any issues with anything.

Huck

I read through the document, satisfied with all the details he put in it. As I thought, it's the same template as my other three prenups, only this one is much simpler. There are no amounts for children we may have or extra amounts earned for so many years of marriage.

I'm sure Georgia won't break any of the things I had him add, so I'm unsure what Huck has up his sleeve to make sure I don't pay her the million.

I reread it a few times, then send it to her. I shoot her another text.

Me: *The prenup's in your inbox. I need to know immediately if there are any changes. Let me know.*

When she doesn't answer me back, I start to get antsy. I pace the office, shooting one message off after another and staring at her empty desk. I try calling but it goes into her voicemail, which only makes my dick hurt again. Then I text some more messages. I'm sure it's a bit overboard, but her lack of response makes me think she's getting cold feet. And the longer it goes on, the more my worries take hold.

I remind myself that I always get what I want.

Georgia Peach isn't going to be the exception. I'll get her to sign this and become my wife. And it's only a matter of time before I have her in all ways.

Seven

GEORGIA

My half-packed suitcase lies open on my bed. I keep adding things and taking them out.

What do you take for a month at someone's house when you don't even know the people whose place it is?

I barely know Sebastian.

I'm marrying a guy I barely know.

What is wrong with me? I shouldn't be doing this.

More guilt fills me, and my feet grow colder.

I'll always have to tell any future guys I date that I've been married before.

What will I tell them? The truth?

That's going to showcase the good parts about me.

I'm sure Sebastian will have a confidentiality clause in the prenup. Does that mean I'll have to lie for the rest of my life?

It'll be annulled.

It'll still be on record that I was married.

I need to get out of this.

My phone rings, and I glance at the screen, then answer, "Hey, Melanie. How are you feeling?"

"Much better today. No one's puked in the last twelve hours!" she chirps.

I wince and hold my stomach. The mere thought of vomit makes me want to gag. I reply, "That's good."

She continues, "I thought we could reschedule Thanksgiving for next Saturday. It gives us a week to completely heal, and we can still celebrate the holiday?"

"That sounds—" My mouth turns dry. *What am I going to tell her?*

"What's wrong?" she questions.

"I won't be in town until after New Year's," I blurt out.

"Why? Where are you going?" she asks.

I take a minute, then state, "Sebastian has work he has to do at his family's ranch, so I'll be staying there."

Silence fills the line. She finally clears her throat and inquires, "Sebastian?"

"My boss."

"Yes. It's the first time I haven't heard you call him Mr. Cartwright," she points out.

My face heats. I quickly lie, "He told me not to."

She digs further, pushing, "Why the sudden change?"

My heart races faster. Melanie is my only friend in Dallas. I've never lied to her. Yet, I'm unprepared. I didn't think about what I would tell her regarding this situation.

"Georgia?"

I go further into my untruth, answering, "He said that since we're going to be working closely together, I need to call him Sebastian. That's all."

"Who else is going to his ranch?"

"Why all the questions?" I ask.

"Why are you defensive?" she retorts.

"I'm not," I claim.

"Then why do you sound it?"

I stay silent.

She repeats, "Who else from work is going?"

I take a few breaths, hoping she can't hear me. I fess up. "It's just me."

Tension grows over the line until she lowers her voice and asks, "Are you having an affair with your boss?"

"No! He's an arrogant, rude man!" I declare.

"Then why is he taking you when you're only the intern?"

Sebastian's words from the first day I started ring in my ears. I remark, "He said hands-on experience is what Cartwright Enterprises is about and why people excel there."

She dramatically whispers, "Georgia, does Sebastian Cartwright have the hots for you?"

"No!" I proclaim, but my cheeks burst with heat. The thought of sitting on his lap while sweat dripped down his pecs earlier today makes me shudder.

It's going to be a long month not giving in to the temptation of doing naughty things with him. I can try to deny my attraction toward him all I want, but at the end of the day, I can't lie to myself. Nothing about Sebastian, including his infuriatingly arrogant ways, is a turn-off. I wish I could say it was, but it's not.

"Are you sure? It seems odd to me," Melanie comments.

"Yep, I'm sure. Anyway, I need to pack. Can I call you in a few days?" I ask, needing to change the subject. I don't want to risk violating the prenup before I even sign it. I've never been closer to making my dreams happen. I'm not going to ruin my chances by not controlling my mouth.

"All right. But I want all the details," she states.

"Melanie, it's not like that," I claim.

She snorts. "Sure it's not. Have a good trip."

"It's not. Bye," I say and hang up. I glance back at my suitcase, and my worries haunt me again.

I take out my jeans, sweaters, and the dresses I packed and place them on my bed. Then I stare at them, questioning everything all over again. I consider calling Sebastian and begging him to tell me what kind of clothes people wear for the events we'll be at, but my pride won't allow me to.

He can deal with whatever I wear while I'm there.

He'll make me go shopping.

I'm not using his credit card.

I repack the items on my bed into the suitcase, then look at my list.

Underwear and bras.

My stomach flips. I go to my drawer and open it, debating about what to bring.

How did he know I have granny panties?

Is it because he doesn't see me as sophisticated as the women he dates?

Or sexy?

Of course I'm not. I'm simple, and they're probably spectacular.

The thought hurts, but I know it's true. After being called out by him about not knowing who he was, I researched him online. I've seen the women Sebastian takes to charity events. I'm nothing like them. They all look like they stepped out of the Dallas Country Club, ready for a magazine shoot. I wouldn't know how to compete if I tried.

I'm not competing. This is strictly business, I remind myself.

I refocus on my panty drawer. More butterflies wake up in my belly. I pick up a pair of comfortable panties and a thong.

Why am I stressing over this? Sebastian isn't going to see my panties.

We'll be sharing a room. He'll probably take it upon himself to go through my drawers.

New stress fills me. Sharing a room with Sebastian for a month isn't something I thought about, but there's no way we'd be able to stay in a different room if we're married.

I'll make him sleep on the floor.

I grab a mix of matching comfortable bra-and-underwear sets and sexy ones. I toss them in my suitcase, along with socks. Then I go into my closet and pull out an overnight bag. I set it next to my nightstand to fill with my toiletries the morning of departure.

Glad to have that out of the way, I go to the family room, grab my phone out of my pocket, and sit on the couch. I glance at the screen and gape.

Is he crazy?

There's a slew of missed calls and text messages from Sebastian. I begin to read them.

Sebastian: *The prenup's in your inbox. I need to know immediately if there are any changes. Let me know.*

Thirteen minutes later.

Sebastian: *Why aren't you responding?*

Seven minutes later.

Sebastian: *Hello?*

Two minutes after.

Sebastian: *This isn't a good start to our marriage.*

Four minutes after.

Sebastian: *You do realize it's Friday on a holiday weekend. If we need any changes—although we shouldn't—time is running out.*

One minute later.

Sebastian: *I'm going to spank you for not responding to me.*

My insides quiver, and butterflies take off. Spank me? Is he into that? Something about it sounds horrifying, yet not. I clench my thighs, trying to imagine it.

Is that what he does to his women?

Do they like it?

Ten minutes later.

Sebastian: *I meant it. Your peachy ass is going to be stained red with my hand mark.*

Tingles race down my spine, and I swallow hard. I continue reading another message sent six minutes later.

Sebastian: *Is something wrong with the prenup?*

Sebastian: *Are you intentionally ghosting me?*

I laugh, toss my phone on the couch, and grab my laptop. I decide it's best to let him sweat it out some more. I open the email and prenup.

Most of it is standard legal jargon. There are confidentiality and nondisclosure clauses. I read through them. It all seems normal.

I continue reading the terms. Everything is about what I have to or am not permitted to do, or I'll default on the prenup and not get paid. Very conveniently for Sebastian, there's nothing that says how he could default. I make a note of it and study the terms.

No cheating.

No talking bad about Sebastian.

Must engage in public displays of affection (PDA) and make it look real.

Must interact with family and friends at all times.

Since we're not having sex, does he really think I'm going to go have sex with someone else with a ring on my finger?

Yeah, he probably does.

Well, he's not having sex with anyone either. I wouldn't put it past him to try. I'm not going to be made a fool.

What does interacting with his family mean? I need to have him clarify that. Is it every minute of every second I have to be with his family? Just at events? What? How is that even measurable?

The bullet point stating I can't talk badly about Sebastian makes me roll my eyes.

That's going to be difficult.

No, I can handle that one. Just have to remind myself every day to kill him with kindness.

I make a note to add that he defaults if he talks bad about me. This marriage is a two-way road, not a one-way lane.

PDA and make it look real. My flutters take off again, my heart races, and my pulse creeps up. We agreed to no sex, so what is this about?

This needs to be scratched from the list.

The last part states that $1,000,000 will be paid to Georgia Peach on January 2nd. The money will be deposited into my bank account as soon as the annulment papers are signed. The one I have my wages deposited into is listed.

My nerves creep up again, and my internal debate continues.

Am I really going to do this?

It's a million dollars.

I can have my franchise. I can make everything happen now instead of waiting years.

Yes, I'm going to do this.

It's not like I'm prostituting myself. Sebastian Cartwright is not touching me.

PDA clause.

I'll get it removed.

I need to talk to him.

My cell phone rings, showing his name. Does he have ESP? I answer, "You need to have some patience."

His deep drawl comes through the line. "Listen, Sunshine. We've only got a little time to get any issues resolved. You're pushing it. Did you review the prenup?"

"I'm reviewing it now."

"And?"

I point out, "You need to work on your patience since you texted and called me so many times."

He grunts. "Whatever. What are your issues with it?"

My pulse creeps up. "For a start, this is a one-way prenup."

"No, it's not. Both our names are on it," he claims.

"Don't patronize me. Everything is about what I can or can't do. If there are ways that I can break the terms, then there need to be ways that you can be in breach too," I point out.

Silence fills the line.

"I'm not signing if it's not a two-way street," I declare.

"Fine. What do you want to add to it?" he asks.

"I'm not allowed to cheat, but you're not allowed to cheat either. You aren't making a fool out of me," I proclaim.

"I don't have any plans of doing anything of the sort. I'm just going to be working all month," he replies.

"Sure you will."

His tone sounds like I offended him. He questions, "What's that mean?"

I tell another white lie, "Nothing."

He deeply exhales. "What's your next issue, Georgia?"

"Please clarify the not engaging with your family terms. What exactly does that mean?"

He answers, "It means what is stated."

I huff. "Does it mean I don't get a minute to myself all day long? Is it only for events? That's subjective, so you need to clarify it."

"Of course I don't mean that you can't have a minute to yourself," he states.

I order, "Well, clarify it in writing or take it out. I'm not letting something subjective stop you from paying me."

A few moments pass, then he caves. "I'll have the attorney add that you need to be present at family events."

"Good."

"Next issue?" he questions.

My butterflies spark to life again. I inquire, "What does engage in PDA mean, Sebastian?"

"Are you really this technical?" he quizzes.

"Yeah, I am because I don't trust you."

He dramatically gasps, then asserts, "You don't trust me, but you're marrying me."

"Ha ha," I scoff.

"Georgia, I'm not out to screw you," he claims.

It doesn't appease my worries. This is Sebastian Cartwright. He's known for his shrewd money skills. And he agreed to pay me way more than he wanted.

He adds, "The whole point of taking you is so you can act like a good little wife while I get my business done."

"We agreed to no sex," I reminded him.

"PDA isn't sex."

"Then tell me what it is so I'm not surprised," I demand.

"Really? Has no man ever shown their desire for you in public before? Or are you one of those women who has to keep everything on lockdown unless you're in the bedroom?" he arrogantly questions.

I shift in my seat. It's not a secret Sebastian has way more experience than I do. I've never dated anyone who wasn't a perfect gentleman. Something tells me there's nothing gentlemanly about my future husband.

Scared, I blurt out, "Deal's off."

"What? No," he says.

"I said no sex."

"We're getting married, Georgia. We'll be newlyweds. We have to act like it in front of others. That's not sex though," he states.

"What does PDA mean to you, Sebastian? I want to be very clear and have it in writing," I restate.

"You want me to put in writing what PDA means?" he questions.

"Yes, I do."

He groans. "Okay, fine. What's PDA to you, innocent woman?"

"Insulting me isn't going to get you anywhere," I warn.

He snaps, "Well, what is it?"

Embarrassment fills me. I confess, "I don't know. Holding hands, kissing in public, hugging."

"Okay. Well, that's what it means," he says.

"Sebastian, I don't want any of your games on this."

"Georgia, keep your panties on. Wait, maybe you shouldn't keep your panties on," he teases.

"See, this is exactly what I'm talking about," I tell him.

"Calm down. I'm a man of my word," he claims.

Something about his statement doesn't make me feel like he's a man of his word. I'm not letting my guard down yet. "Spell it out in the prenup, Sebastian, or I'm not signing this."

"Fine. I'll have the attorney spell it out. Anything else?"

"When will I be able to review the annulment papers?"

"You want to review the annulment papers?"

"Yes."

"The annulment papers that annul that our marriage took place, which gives you a million dollars in your bank account?" he questions.

"Correct."

In a frustrated tone, he inquires, "Georgia, why are you worried about the annulment papers?"

I admit, "I'm trying to do my due diligence."

"Listen, Sunshine. It's Friday on a holiday weekend. I already had to jump through hoops to get my attorney to do this prenup. Now I need to go back to him and have him work on these amendments. You can review the annulment paperwork before you sign it, okay? I'll give you plenty of time, but you can't expect me to get him to draw up those papers this weekend," Sebastian remarks.

I consider his statement and decide he's right. I concede but stipulate, "Then add in that if you don't give me at least a week to review the annulment papers, then you're in breach."

"Are you serious?"

"Yes, I am serious, Sebastian."

"Fine, I'll have it added. Anything else?"

I ponder it for a moment, then reply, "No. That's it."

"Good. Now it's my turn."

Goose bumps pop out on my skin. "Your turn for what?"

"My attorney and I will meet you at your place tomorrow. Then we're leaving," he reveals.

My stomach dives. "I thought we were going Monday?"

"Change of plans per my father. We're expected for breakfast on Sunday morning, so that means we need to be there Saturday night," he informs me.

I stay quiet.

"We can sign the prenup before we leave," he offers.

It'll be real. There will be no turning back.

I blurt out, "Don't we have to get married before we leave?" I hadn't thought about that detail yet.

"No. The wedding will be the following Saturday," he announces.

The hairs on my neck rise. "With your family?"

His voice stays neutral. "Yes. You'll plan it with my mother. It'll make her happy. I'm sure all my sisters will stick their noses in as well."

I fret, "You didn't tell me your family would be present."

His tone turns to annoyance. "You didn't think I was going to marry you without my family there, did you? By the way, which of your family members do you want me to fly in?"

My heart squeezes so tight it becomes hard to breathe. I take a minute to answer. "I don't have any family members I want there."

He sternly claims, "Georgia, my parents will think it's odd if your family's not there. They need to be there."

I squeeze my eyes shut and try to keep emotion out of my voice, but I can't. It shakes as I admit, "Sebastian, I don't have any living relatives."

Silence fills the line. He finally clears his throat and asks, "What are you talking about?"

"Don't make me repeat it," I beg.

To my surprise, Sebastian doesn't push it. He finally states, "Okay. It'll just be my family, then. Well, that and probably the whole freaking town."

"The town?" I blurt out.

"Chill. They don't matter," he orders, but it doesn't calm my nerves. He adds, "I'll send over the new revisions as soon as I get them. Make sure you reply to my messages."

"Okay."

"I'll see you at noon tomorrow. Be ready to leave after we sign," he directs and hangs up.

I stare at my phone with my stomach diving.

What am I getting myself into?

Eight

SEBASTIAN

I pull up to Georgia's apartment complex and cringe. It's in a run-down part of town, and the paint on the building peels away from the concrete wall.

I lock my vehicle, remove a suitcase and matching overnight bag from the bed of my truck, and carry them up the steps. Annoyance fills me when I reach for the doorknob. It's not locked. Anyone can walk right in.

She'd be a prime target for all sorts of crimes just by walking to her car.

After she gets my money, she can move.

She's not getting that million dollars. She's only getting a hundred thousand. She'll use it for her bakery and stay here.

I make a mental note to gift her a five-year free lease at one of my condos near the office as a parting gift once the annulment is signed.

That'll soften the blow when she doesn't get the million dollars.

The old elevator creaks as it makes its way to the ground level. I step inside and wonder when it got serviced last. The entire lift shakes on its way to the fifth floor, then comes to a jolting stop.

I shake off my irritation and step off the death trap, strolling down the hallway that's just as outdated as the front of the building. When I get to Georgia's unit, I knock.

The smell of sugar faintly swirls in the air. It makes my stomach growl as I wait. And wait. And wait some more.

My stomach churns, and I knock again.

Did she change her mind?

I should have closed this deal last night.

The sound of her releasing a security chain fills my ears. It only adds to my frustration. She should have a dead bolt, not just a chain that someone can easily cut through. The door opens, and my heart skips a beat.

Georgia's long blonde hair falls in loose curls over her shoulders. She's wearing brown knee-high boots and a long-sleeved, blue floral dress. A worn denim jacket caps off the outfit. Her skin glows, competing with her doe-eyes and lush mouth that I'm more than willing to have on mine.

She chirps, "Good afternoon, Mr. Cartwright."

My lips twitch. I love it when she calls me Mr. Cartwright. Or Sebastian. Hearing her say my name in her sugary-sweet voice stirs so many deviant thoughts. One way or another, I'm making her mine during this fake marriage. She'll be begging me for it, and I can't decide if I'll make her call me Mr. Cartwright or Sebastian when she does.

I'll switch it up depending on how I have her.

"I think it's best if you stick with Sebastian from now on. My family will think it's odd if you don't." I drag my gaze over her body, lingering on her tits and between her legs, then slowly lock it on hers. Flames ignite on her cheeks, and I lower my voice and add, "Until it's more appropriate, that is."

"More appropriate?" she questions, nerves filling her expression.

"Yep." I step inside, and she retreats. I push the luggage in front of her.

"What's that for?" she inquires.

"This is for you. Go fill it," I order.

"I have my own luggage."

I snort. "Of course you do. What's the brand?"

She wrinkles her forehead. "What does that matter?"

I cross my arms. "It matters because my wife wouldn't be rolling around non-designer luggage."

"What's wrong with an off-brand?" she challenges.

I fake a yawn. "You're smart. Figure it out."

She tilts her head and gives me a disapproving look.

I shake my head, relaying, "There's no way my wife wouldn't have the best of the best. Did you forget I'm rich?"

She rolls her eyes, stating, "So I have to be a snob?"

"Why does having the best make you a snob?" I ask.

She huffs. "It shouldn't matter what brand your luggage is."

I point to the suitcase and overnight bag. It's a new luxury brand called Southern Gal. It's a white cream with brown and gold leather trim. When I saw it, I thought it looked perfect for her, especially going to the country. It's nothing my previous fiancées would have chosen, but they were more into Dallas high society. But part of the reason I chose Georgia is that she's not like them. I'm confident she can do Dallas high society or country. I question, "You don't like what I chose for you?"

She studies it, then refocuses on me. "It's a beautiful set."

A spark of satisfaction ignites in me. I'm glad I got it right and she approves. Then I reprimand myself for caring what she thinks.

I'm not going to get close to this girl.

I'm going to use her for what I want. Then we're both moving on.

The last thing I need is someone messing with me again.

"Good. Glad you like it. Go switch your stuff out," I assert.

She puts her hand on her hip and tilts her head up at me. "Don't be bossy, Sebastian. If I'm going to be your wife, you don't get to boss me around like in the office. You need to treat me with respect."

I lean into her ear. "If you want me to treat you like you're my wife, then we're going to have to eliminate this no-sex thing."

Her face turns as red as a cherry tomato. Her blue eyes spark against her flushed cheeks, turning my cock harder.

There's a knock on the door. I tear my gaze off her and open the door, instructing, "Huck, come on in."

Huck steps inside, removes his cowboy hat, and nods to Georgia. "Ma'am. I assume you're Ms. Georgia Peach?"

Georgia beams. "Yes, I am. And you are?"

He holds his hand out. "Huck Peterson, the attorney."

"Nice to meet you. Even if it's for this weird arrangement that Sebastian and I have," she says, giving me an uncomfortable look.

Huck chuckles. "Ms. Peach, there's no need for any embarrassment here. I've had a lot of strange contracts in my life, and I can assure you, this isn't the craziest."

"No?" she questions.

"No, ma'am. Is there a place we can sign?" he inquires.

"Sure. Why don't we go to the table?" she suggests.

I step between them. "Hold up. Georgia, go pack."

Her eyes turn to slits. "Why do I need to pack now? Don't you want me to sign?"

"I have another issue I need to talk with Huck about real quick."

"About our prenup?" she quizzes.

"No. Something that doesn't concern you," I lie. "Can you please go pack and give us a minute?"

Distrust fills her expression, but she finally leaves the room, wheeling the suitcase and overnight bag behind her.

When she's out of earshot, I keep my voice low and ask Huck, "The revisions are all done?"

He nods. "Of course."

I glance behind me to ensure she's still unable to hear, then inquire, "And I'm protected?"

"Stop asking dumb questions," he demands.

I pat him on the back and go to the table. I sit down and take in Georgia's apartment.

Unlike the rest of the building, everything looks fresh and spruced up. The appliances, counter, and fixtures are outdated, but the paint looks new. A rustic vibe makes it feel homey, and bright fake flowers add a bit of cheer.

It's so her.

It's the opposite of my sleek, modern penthouse, but I like how she's made the drab place feel warm and cozy.

Huck puts his briefcase on the table, then pulls out a set of paperwork and several pens. He asks, "Do you want to look through it?"

I snort. "That's what I pay you for. Remember the big bucks?"

"Yeah, yeah, yeah," he grumbles.

Georgia comes bouncing out of her bedroom, dragging the suitcase and overnight bag. I get up and pull the chair next to mine out. She sits, and Huck pushes the paperwork toward her.

He asks, "Would you like me to review this with you, Ms. Peach?"

She straightens her shoulders and picks up the paperwork. "Let me read it first."

The prenup isn't as long as the other's Huck wrote for me, but it feels that way. Georgia reads every single detail.

Halfway through it, I question, "Didn't you review it last night?"

"Yes, but I'm making sure it's the same one," she admits.

"Do you think I'm going to screw you over?" My chest tightens, which surprises me. I never feel guilty about getting what I want. And it would be negligent to give her a million dollars for doing barely anything. The hundred thousand she'll end up with is more than fair.

She scoffs. "I don't put it past you, Sebastian. And didn't you learn in school that you're supposed to read contracts before you sign anything?"

"That's what I have my attorney for," I reply.

She smirks. "Yeah, *your* attorney. Not mine. No offense, Mr. Peterson."

He chuckles. "No offense taken, but I assure you it's the last revised version I sent you via email."

She gives him a big smile, lacing her voice with honey, asserting, "Then you won't mind if I continue to read it over so I'm comfortable signing?"

He shakes his head. "No, ma'am. I'm here to answer any questions you have as well."

"Great. Thank you." She returns to reading the paperwork.

I sit back in my seat, tapping my hands on my thighs, getting more nervous the longer she takes to read.

She finishes and reaches for the pen. She signs her name, and relief fills me.

"You'll need to initial each page as well," Huck instructs.

She doesn't hesitate and obeys. Then she shoves the papers at me. "It's your turn."

I scribble my initials and signature and hand the pen to Huck.

He notarizes the document, then states, "I'll email both of you copies later today."

"Thank you," Georgia chirps.

"Great. We need to get going," I announce, rising.

Huck puts the papers in his briefcase and places his cowboy hat back on his head. He nods to Georgia. "Ma'am. It was nice meeting you."

"You too. Hey, I have something for you."

"Oh?" he asks.

She goes to the counter and picks up a small box. There are four larger ones next to it. She states, "This morning, I baked cupcakes for a birthday party and also to take to Sebastian's family. I set these aside for you."

Of course she did.

That's why it smells like sugar in here.

Huck's face lights up like a Christmas tree. He drawls, "Well, aren't you a sweetheart. Thank you."

She hands him the box and adds, "There's a variety in there. Hope you love them."

"I'm sure I will. The grandkids are coming over today, so it'll be a nice treat for them," he declares.

I wouldn't have thought her expression could get any happier, but it does. Something stirs in me, but it's not the normal annoyance I feel. I try to place what it is, but I can't. All I know is it makes me feel good.

I shake off whatever it is, then watch Huck kiss her on the cheek and thank her again. "Sebastian," he states, then leaves.

Huck kissed her before I did.

That's just wrong.

"Okay, soon-to-be Mrs. Sebastian Cartwright. Let's get moving," I order.

Georgia freezes. A scared look fills her expression. Or maybe it's disgust?

Does she despise marrying me that much?

She opens her mouth, shuts it, then paces her small apartment. "I feel like I'm forgetting something."

"You're not."

"But I feel like I am."

I assure her, "If you forget anything, I'll buy it for you when we get to town."

"I don't know what it is," she frets. Her breath shortens, and I wonder if she's a few steps away from an anxiety attack.

Time to show her the perks of having my last name.

I close the distance between us, and she retreats until she's up against the wall. I slide my hands on her cheeks, tilt her head up, and lower my mouth an inch from hers. I murmur, "I know what you forgot."

"What?" she breathes.

I press my lips against hers, parting them with my tongue. She gasps, then pushes her palms on my chest.

I slide my tongue deeper into her mouth, moving closer until my heart is pounding against her frame. She whimpers, begins flicking her tongue against mine, and her hands relax.

Jesus Christ. Ms. Georgia Peach is the best kisser I've ever had the pleasure of putting my mouth on.

It's not what I expected.

I thought she'd be decent but that I'd have to train her on everything.

I couldn't have coached her to kiss like this. And I'd never have guessed she'd create the heat racing through my blood only from a kiss.

Her tongue teases me, and my cock twitches against her stomach. Her knees buckle, and she moves her hands up my chest. She glides her fingers up my neck and into my hair, slightly tugging on it.

I groan inside. This woman is a surprise in so many ways, but this...well, this is only going to make me more impatient to have her.

Where did she learn to kiss like this?

I retreat a bit but can't resist and go back for some more. Sugar swirls with her rose perfume, and I lose myself in her. The room disappears. It's her and me and all the thoughts of what I want to do to her.

I slide my hands under her dress, grabbing her round ass I've been dreaming of groping. I mumble, "We can be late."

"Late?" she whispers, then her tongue darts back against mine.

I kiss her some more, then test out the waters. I slip my hand to the front of her body and drag a finger over her slit, groaning inside when I learn she's already wet. I demand, "Show me your bedroom."

She freezes, then removes her tongue from mine and shuts her mouth. A mix of emotions appears in her eyes.

Does she want to fuck me?

Yes. Those are fuck-me eyes.

Will she let me?

I drill my gaze into hers, challenging, "Let's move this to the other room." I inch my finger over her panties again.

She squares her shoulders and pushes me away from her. She steps out of my grasp and asks, "What are you doing?"

"I thought we should get our first kiss out of the way. You don't want to look out of sorts when it comes time for our PDA. It didn't seem like you weren't enjoying it," I taunt, then sniff my fingers.

She gapes at me, watching as I lick my digit.

Her eyes widen. She continues looking at me like she's not sure what just happened or what she should be doing.

But one thing is clear. She's not disgusted by my little display. I've seen enough women to know what category they're in, and it shocks me to realize she's not offended. That only gives more fuel to my overactive fantasies.

How filthy will she let me get with her?

We need to be naked right now.

I know what will get her to shed that dress...

I reach into my pocket and pull out a ring box. I hold it in front of her. My gut flips, surprising me again.

It's strange. I've bought four different engagement rings. But I was never nervous when I asked any of those other women. There was never a question in my mind about whether they would say yes or not. But everything about giving Georgia a ring creates a nervous circus in my belly.

"What is that?" she asks.

"Open it," I encourage.

She takes a deep breath, then opens the box. Her head jerks backward, and she opens her mouth, closes it, then bites on her lip. It's not the expression I expected.

"You don't like it?" I blurt out.

She swallows hard, then takes the ring out of the box. "Ummm...it's a beautiful piece."

"A beautiful piece? That's a four-carat flawless diamond from Tiffany's," I state.

"Yes, I can see that," she utters.

"But you don't like it?" I ask, confused. All the women I've dated would have been more than pleased to flash that ring around town.

"I um... I think I'm not used to wearing such an over-the-top ring," she admits.

She doesn't like it. How is this possible?

She quickly adds, "But I guess it's what your wife would wear, right? Something really big?"

The disappointment I try to shake off doesn't go away. I shouldn't care if she likes it or not, but it bugs me.

Maybe she's trying to trick me into thinking she doesn't like it.

She only wants me to think she doesn't care about money or material things.

I remind myself that she tried to get a million dollars out of me, so I shouldn't buy this little act of hers. But if Georgia is lying, she's doing a hell of a job. She's still uncomfortably assessing the ring. I suggest, "Why don't you try it on?" I take the ring and then shove it on her finger.

She holds her hand out, staring at it and continuing to furrow her eyebrows.

It does look huge on her.

Every woman wants a ring that big.

She smiles, but I think it's forced. She clears her throat and says, "Thank you. It's beautiful."

My erection loses all steam. I realize there's no way I'm getting in her pants right now. I ask, "Are you ready to go?"

"Yeah, I suppose so." She grabs the handle of her suitcase.

"I've got that," I state. I take it away from her and lead her toward the door, rolling the luggage with me.

She stays quiet, and we leave her apartment. She takes a key out of her pocket, locks the door, and we go to the elevator.

"Oh shoot! I need to go back!" she exclaims when the elevator arrives.

"What for?" I ask.

"The cupcakes!" She rushes down the hall.

I groan and hold my hand against the doors for so long, a loud beep fills the air.

Georgia reappears, puts the four boxes on the ground, and relocks her apartment. She picks them back up and joins me. We get in the elevator, and it screeches.

"This is a death trap," I grumble.

She winces, confessing, "The building needs a bit of TLC."

I grunt. "A bit? This place is falling apart. You really should live somewhere that at least has a front door that locks. Oh, and that chain needs to go. You should have a dead bolt."

"No one's ever bugged me. My neighbors are all nice," she claims.

I shake my head, declaring, "It's not safe."

The elevator slams to a stop, and I clench my jaw. The doors open, and I motion for her to go first. She steps out and we continue outside.

I put the luggage in my covered truck bed, the boxes of cupcakes in the back seat, then I open the passenger door for Georgia.

She scoots in, and her dress hikes up her legs. My erection springs forth again. She catches me ogling them and tugs at the fabric.

I tear my gaze off her and get in the truck.

There's a two-hour drive ahead of us, and all I can think is how delicious my new little peach will be when I finally bite into her.

Nine

GEORGIA

Sebastian and I don't say much at the beginning of our journey. I stare at the way-too-big ring that's now on my finger, wondering why any woman would want such a large rock.

It's not that I can't appreciate a beautiful ring, but this is so huge it feels borderline gaudy.

At least on me.

I feel bad I offended Sebastian. He tried to hide it, but I clearly did.

I continue staring at the ring, flustered over it and our kiss.

Well, kisses.

And his large hands all over me.

What am I going to do all month?

I always knew keeping Sebastian in line would be challenging, but now I know what it's like to kiss him and have his flesh pressed against mine. I could easily have caved and let him have his way with me. I'm sure I would have enjoyed it, but I would have hated myself after.

I don't judge people for casual sex. What they do is their decision. I've never had anything casual, but I know in my gut that having sex with anyone I'm not in a serious relationship with won't be good for me.

I tear my eyes off the monstrosity on my finger and my heart beats harder. Sebastian makes it race every day when I see him in his suit. When he showed up in his jeans and T-shirt, I could have fainted. And just like his suits that hug his body in all the right places, so do these clothes.

Plus, seeing him in non-work clothes reminds me that this arrangement we have is happening. Now that I've signed the prenup, there's no going back.

I squeeze my thighs together, continuing to take in his chiseled features.

Why haven't I ever been kissed like that before?

Oh gosh, this is so bad.

I cannot be falling for him.

He veers onto the expressway and catches me ogling him. He smirks as he says, "I think we need to get to know each other, Georgia. If we're going to fool my parents and everyone else, we need to know stuff."

"Okay," I reply, agreeing. It makes sense if I'm going to be his fake wife.

He turns his dimpled smile on me, asking, "How old were you when you lost your virginity?"

I gasp. "That's not your business."

"I think it's something every husband knows about their wife. Wouldn't you think? No secrets?" he challenges.

My pulse creeps up. *Is this guy for real?*

"Come on, Georgia, spill it," he orders.

I turn it on him. "How old were you?"

He doesn't hesitate. "Fourteen."

I blurt out, "You were fourteen years old?"

He shrugs. "Yeah. What's the big deal?"

"It just seems very young to me," I claim.

He grunts. "I'm a dude. That's what we do."

"A dude?"

"What? You've never heard that word before?"

I try to hold my smile back but can't. "No, I just never imagined Mr. Cartwright calling himself a dude."

He leans closer, claiming, "I'm not the stick-in-the-mud you probably think I am."

"I never said that."

He grunts. "Spill it, Ms. Peach. How old were you?"

I put my hands over my face and moan. "Why are we talking about this?"

"I told you. Now you have to tell me," he asserts.

I cave. "Fine. I was nineteen."

He gives me a look like he already knew that.

I ignore his reaction and change the subject. "What's your favorite color?"

He wiggles his eyebrows. "Blue. Like your eyes."

My flutters take off, but I reprimand, "Are you going to be sweet-talking me this whole month? Because it's annoying."

He chuckles. "I'm the annoying one? Isn't that more like your personality? To sweet-talk people so you can manipulate them?"

"Manipulate them?" I question, insulted.

"Okay, wrong word. But you know what I mean, Little Miss Sunshine."

I give him a dirty look.

"You can't even be pissed at me without looking cute," he states.

My butterflies multiply.

He inquires, "What's your favorite color?"

"Yellow."

He grins. "I knew it."

"How?"

Arrogance washes over him, and I curse myself for the zings I get flying through my core. He answers, "Yellow like sunshine."

I slap my hand on his chest. "Stop with the sunshine talk."

"Why? You're like the happiest person I know. Unless it's an act?" He cocks an eyebrow.

Hurt, I declare, "No. It's not an act. Is that what you think I am? Fake?"

"Not at all."

"I feel like you're degrading me when you say it."

He locks eyes with me. "Georgia, I'm not degrading you."

111

"You aren't?"

"No. Your little sunshiny attitude is starting to wear on me," he says and winks, then turns his focus back to the road.

His statement does nothing for my overactive senses. I ask, "What's your favorite type of music? Let me guess. It's country."

He groans. "Hell no."

Surprised, I reply, "No? But didn't you grow up in a small town?"

"So? It doesn't mean I like country," he claims.

"You don't like any of the songs?" I question.

"Some of the newer stuff is okay, but that old-school twangy stuff, no. It drives me nuts."

"So, what do you like?"

"Rock, mostly. How about you?"

I ponder the question for a moment. "Well, I like everything except elevator music, techno, or that really Gothic stuff."

He smiles as if I'm amusing him. "What's your favorite food?"

"Pecan pie," I state.

His eyes widen. "Pecan pie is your favorite food?"

"Yeah. Why do you act like that's bad?"

"What is it with you and sweets?"

"Do you have a problem with sweets?"

"Yeah, it's called sugar. Do you not know how bad it is for you? It kills people," he claims.

"Everything in moderation is fine," I assure him.

He shakes his head as if I'm crazy.

For some reason, I feel insulted. I accuse, "Is this some warped idea you have that women should be stick poles?"

His eyes widen. "When did I say I wanted women to be stick poles?"

"Well, if it looks like a frog and jumps like a frog..."

He scowls. "Don't accuse me of things you know nothing about."

Tense silence fills the cab. I finally break it, asking, "So what's your favorite food?"

"Tex-Mex or barbecue."

"Ah, very Texan of you, Mr. Cartwright," I tease.

"Don't even try to tell me you don't like Tex-Mex or barbecue," he asserts.

"You can't go wrong with either. I'd happily eat those dishes any day of the week."

"Whew! No one in my family would let me marry you if you didn't like that kind of food," he teases.

"Good to know," I claim. "So, tell me about your family and how you grew up. I probably should know some stuff about them. Right?"

He turns on his blinker, looks over his shoulder, then veers into another lane, passing a semi. He answers, "We grew up on the ranch. As you know, we've got thousands of cattle, but we also have horses, chickens, goats, and lambs."

"That sounds like a good way to grow up," I state.

He continues, "My mom and dad have been together forever. My dad's name is Jacob. My mom's name's Ruby. But you probably already knew that."

"Yes," I admit. The Cartwright family is known all over Dallas, and his parents have even been featured in articles.

"So, let's see, my brother, Alexander, is thirty-four. He's got two kids, but..." Sebastian clutches his jaw for a minute, and I notice his fingers grip the steering wheel tighter. "His wife died of cancer shortly after his second son was born."

"Oh no! I'm so sorry!" I offer.

Sebastian mutters, "Is what it is. There's also my brother, Mason. He's twenty-nine. Jagger's twenty-seven. They're both single, which doesn't make my mother happy, of course. And then I have my sister, Evelyn. She's thirty-five and the perfect one."

I laugh. "The perfect one?"

"Yep. She and her husband have three kids, along with the white picket fence. It's what my mother wants for all of us."

"You don't want that? It sounds nice to me."

He grunts. "No way. That's boring."

"Why is it boring?"

"It just is."

I sigh. "Okay. So do you have any other sisters?"

"Yep. Three."

"Wow! So there's..." I count it in my head. "Eight of you?"

He chuckles. "Yep. That's what happens on ranches. There's nothing else to do. You fuck, then fuck some more," he says.

The thought of Sebastian's finger on my panties sends a shudder down my spine.

"Sorry. I didn't mean to use obscenities in front of you, my dear wife," he jokes.

I roll my eyes again. "So what about your other sisters?"

"They're all single too, which doesn't make my mother happy. Ava's thirty-one. Willow's twenty-five, and Paisley is twenty-one. She's going to graduate from college in the spring."

"I bet it was fun growing up with all of them," I comment.

A nostalgic look passes over Sebastian's face. "Yeah, I guess it was. There were always tons of things to do. My siblings and I were always getting into trouble. Well, Evelyn didn't get in trouble, but Ava did. Willow and Paisley are a lot younger than me. So I was pretty much grown and out of the house by the time they started doing their shenanigans."

The ache I always feel when thinking about how I don't have any family left rears its ugly head. I mumble, "You're lucky to have them."

Silence fills the vehicle. He finally says, "All right, enough about me. Tell me about your childhood."

My chest tightens. Having to tell Sebastian anything about me makes me feel vulnerable for some reason. It's like the less he knows of me, the better, but I also know that I can't keep everything from him. We do have to fool his family, and they're sure to ask. Especially when we start planning the wedding.

I still can't believe I'm about to get married, not even for thirty days, and for money. I push the guilt out of my mind and start off, "Well, my mom and dad were musicians."

He cuts across a lane. "Really? What kind?"

I hesitate, then answer, "Country. The old twangy kind."

"You're lying to make me feel bad," he accuses.

"Nope!"

"Sorry. Hope I didn't insult you," he offers.

"You didn't."

"So, do you really like that type of music?" he asks.

"I don't know. It's okay. I don't have anything against it, but it's not my favorite," I answer honestly.

"You said your parents *were* musicians. What happened?"

My stomach dives. I take a minute to gather my thoughts and inform him, "I grew up with my grammy and my grandpa because my parents were always on the road. I was only five when their tour bus smashed into the side of a concrete bridge. There weren't any survivors." I look out the window, blinking hard. I rarely get emotional over my parents. Typically, it's over my grammy. Maybe it's because I'm about to get married and not one person I know will be there, even if it is a fake union.

Sebastian's voice fills with sympathy. He grabs my hand and squeezes it. "I'm sorry to hear that. That must have been hard for you."

Something about Sebastian being sympathetic makes me nervous. I pull my hand away and clasp it with my other hand in my lap, claiming, "It's fine. There's nothing I can do to change it."

Silence fills the air, and tension grows between us. He questions, "And what happened to your grandparents?"

"My grandfather died of a heart attack about five years ago. My grandmother died over the summer from a stroke."

"That's tough, Sunshine," Sebastian states.

I turn back toward the window, glancing at the cars we're racing past.

"You don't have any siblings?" Sebastian questions.

That ache grows bigger. I shake my head. "No, it's just me."

"Hmm," is his only reply to that.

I don't want to ask him what his hmm is about, so I change the subject. "What will your family think of me?"

He grins, and my heart skips another beat. He states, "They're going to love you."

"Why do you think that?" I inquire.

He gives me a look like I'm crazy. "Because you're perfect."

Heat rushes to my cheeks again.

He continues, "You're polite and charming. You've got the southern girl act down perfectly."

"I don't put on an act," I insist.

He waves me off. "You know what I mean. Plus, you're hot. Sexy. You check all the boxes."

More embarrassment fills me.

He thinks I'm hot and sexy?

This is not good.

I don't think anyone's ever thought I was sexy before.

I stay quiet, growing flustered and thinking about our kiss again.

Sebastian gets off at an exit. "Well, get ready for the country. It's going to be nothing but farmland from here on out."

My stomach churns with nerves. This is something I never thought I would do, yet here I am.

We don't speak the rest of the ride. My anxiety kicks into full gear when he pulls through the large gate.

What if they don't like me?

It doesn't matter. It's only for a month.

Sebastian pulls in front of a large ranch home, and five young children come running over. A little girl yells, "Uncle Sebastian!"

He gets out of the truck, and she jumps into his arms. He hugs and tickles her. She squeals.

The other kids jump on him, and it takes a few moments for him to hug all of them. His face lights up, and it warms my heart to see him with them.

He'd make a good father.

Don't go there.

He turns to me and says, "This is Georgia. Georgia, meet my brother Alexander's boys, Wilder and Ace. These are my sister Evelyn's kids, Isabella, Emma, and Jacob, Jr."

"Nice to meet you," I say.

"Welcome to our home," Isabella says, then jumps on me as she did to Sebastian.

I laugh and hug her back. "Thank you!"

"I'm six, Emma's five, Jacob's three, Wilder is ten, and Ace is eight," she informs me.

"Wow! Those are all great ages," I declare.

"My birthday is in a few weeks, so I'll be seven soon!" She aims a bright smile at me.

"Sebastian!" a woman's voice calls out.

I turn and recognize his parents from the articles in the paper. I assume the other two people are one of his brothers and sisters.

His mom hugs him and his dad leans down and kisses my cheek. "I'm Jacob, and this is my wife, Ruby."

Ruby steps forward and embraces me. "It's so nice to meet you, Georgia. Sebastian told me all about you last night."

I glance at Sebastian.

He slides his arm around my waist and tugs me into him, then kisses the top of my head. "That's Alexander and Evelyn. Everyone, meet Georgia."

"Is that a ring?" Evelyn asks, then exchanges a glance with Alexander.

Sebastian's grip tightens on me. "Yes. And you're all going to be busy this next week."

"Why is that?" Evelyn asks.

He drops the bomb. "We're getting married next Saturday."

"What?" his brother blurts out.

"You heard me."

"In a week?" his mom shrieks. "Why didn't you say anything on the phone?"

Sebastian's body tenses.

"We wanted to surprise you," I offer.

"That's right. And with our busy schedules, we thought the timing was perfect since everyone is here," he adds.

"Well, this is...oh, this is perfect!" his mom declares, her eyes filling with tears.

"Mom, don't," he orders.

"Oh shush!" She throws her arms around both of us again.

"Can I be in the wedding?" Isabella asks, tugging on my dress.

"Isabella! That's rude to ask!" Evelyn reprimands. She says to me, "Sorry!"

I laugh. "It's okay." I crouch down so I'm at eye level with Isabella. "What do you think about you and Emma being flower girls?"

"Yes!" She claps.

"Perfect." I rise, and Sebastian winks at me. My butterflies go crazy again.

His father declares, "Sebastian, I need to tear you away from your bride for a bit. You too, Alexander."

"Dad, we just got here," Sebastian claims, glancing at me.

"It's okay. I'll be fine," I assure him.

"You sure?" he asks, voice full of concern, which surprises me.

I didn't expect Sebastian to consider if I was comfortable enough with his family to be left alone with them. It makes me wonder if I judged him too early out of the gate. "Yes. I'm sure," I insist. Then I take a step toward the house.

Sebastian grabs my hand and pulls me back into him.

"Whoa!" I utter.

His lips twitch. "Aren't you forgetting something?"

"What?" I ask.

He tugs me closer and gives me a semi-chaste kiss, making me want more. But he pulls back. "That."

I can't help but smile. I murmur, "Oh. Thanks."

"Georgia gets upset if I don't kiss her before we part. Don't you?" he states.

Embarrassment surges through me. This is his family and a bunch of strangers, and he's basically insinuating I have to kiss him every time we part?

He smirks. "It's okay. My family won't judge you for wanting my lips on yours all the time."

Oh, I see what he has up his sleeve.

I laugh and tilt my head, accusing, "Don't you mean *you* don't like parting ways without kissing *me*?"

"Oh, such lovebirds," his mom coos, tearing us out of our locked gazes.

He pats my ass, releases me, and declares, "I won't be gone long."

And as bad as it is, everything about his statement makes me happy.

Ten

SEBASTIAN

"We have a lot to plan," Mom chirps. She puts her arm around Georgia's shoulder. "Let's go inside, and we can discuss everything you've ever dreamed about for your wedding."

Panic washes over Georgia's face, but she quickly reels it in. She nods. "Sounds good." She smiles bigger at me. "I'll make sure I run all the options by you."

Oh, hell no.

I smile back. "Remember we talked about this? Whatever you want, I'll make happen, Sunshine."

She steps closer, batting her lashes. She lowers her voice, asking, "Don't you remember our conversation last night?"

"Last night?" I question.

She widens her eyes into that innocent expression I'm dying to see under my naked body. She answers, "Yes. When I told you how important it was to me that *you engage* in the process of planning for our big day."

"Engage in the—" I clench my jaw.

So she's going to throw the "engage with my family" clause of our contract in my face?

She trails her hand down my arm, and it's kind of hard to stay mad at her. A rush of adrenaline shoots down my spine as she coos, "You promised me you'd take part. Remember?"

"Jeez, don't be such an idiot, Sebastian. No bride wants to plan their wedding without their soon-to-be husband's input," my always-perfect-at-everything sister states.

I glance at her. "Stay out of my business, Evelyn."

Georgia gasps, then slides her hand on my cheek, forcing me to lock eyes with her. "Don't be mean to your sister. She's just stating the facts."

And I'm officially upset with her again...except for my dick that's straining against my zipper. Georgia's hand on my body is a straight-up tease.

She steps closer and pulls my head down so her lips are near my ear. Her hot breath taunts my skin. In her sticky-sweet southern voice, she murmurs, "I know you'd never promise me something and not come through, Sebastian." She moves her face an inch from mine and pins her blues on me.

I've underestimated my wife-to-be. She's something I never thought she'd be—cunning.

Game on, Ms. Peach.

I grab her ass again and tug her closer to me. "You're right, Sunshine. I'll tell you what, you get all the options together, and we'll discuss it in bed tonight, okay?"

A flush crawls up her neck

I add, "I promise I'll go through every detail with you with a fine-toothed comb."

More red burns her cheeks. I stare her down until she smiles and replies, "Perfect."

I hold my hand on her ass for another moment, just because I want to. She's got a round bottom that I'm starting to think God made exclusively for my palm. I'm craving to see my imprint on her juicy little cheek. I finally release her. She spins and walks away with my mom and sister. I watch her booty until I can't see her anymore, growing harder by the second.

Alexander whistles once she's inside. "Bro, you got a looker there."

"Sure do," I state, still shocked at her ability to turn the tables on me. But I'm not upset. I love nothing more than a challenge, and since I've met Georgia, she's offered me plenty of them. This turn of events is refreshing. It'll only make the month more interesting.

"Sebastian, how long have you been dating her?" my father asks.

I grind my molars. I knew it would only be a matter of time before he grilled me. I answer, "Not long, but when you know, you know. And don't worry, Huck came over, and we signed the prenup today."

It's a sore topic. I argued with my father about a prenup with my first fiancée, Molly. He could see right through her and knew she only wanted a claim to the Cartwright fortune. She was the only fiancée I had who was from our town, yet she had all the aspirations to become a Dallas socialite.

I had no clue. We never got as far as negotiating a prenup. I overheard her talking to her mother about ways they were both planning to spend my family's money once we got hitched.

After that, I never again had another girlfriend from this town and wanted to get as far away from it as possible. When I asked Kara, Cindy, then Nicky to marry me, a prenup wasn't even a question. Negotiations were long and hellacious with all three of them.

My father nods. "Good. Although, she's got spunk in her. I hope you never have to use it."

"I won't," I claim, but my gut churns. I've never lied to my family on this level. And I already know they will be disappointed when they hear I'm divorced.

Annulled.

Like that little difference will make my parents any happier.

But I'll be CEO, and my father won't be able to hold it over my head any longer.

"Let's go see your brothers. They're training a new Thoroughbred," my father informs me.

The racing side of our business is newer. My brothers all love horses. I used to, but I haven't ridden in a long time. Being in the city, there aren't a lot of opportunities, and I avoid coming home at all costs. It's not because I don't love my family, but I'm busy with work and can't stand half the people in this town.

My father leads us to the stables.

Alexander states, "You're in time for the race on Tuesday night. We've got two new ones entered."

"That was faster than expected, wasn't it?" I question. I don't know much about this business since I spend my time developing the big money makers for our family, which are oil and cattle.

My brother Mason sees me and jumps off a horse. "Sebastian!"

Jagger leans against the fence and spins, then wraps his arms around me. "Bro, about time you got here."

"Where's your woman? Mom wouldn't stop obsessing over who you were bringing," Mason asks, then gives me a guy hug over the fence.

My father answers, "She's inside planning their wedding for next Saturday."

My brothers gape at me.

"Don't everyone speak at once," I tease.

"This Saturday? As in a week?" Jagger asks.

"Yep. No time like the present," I declare.

"Well, shit. Congratulations," he states.

"You're a crazy bastard. Mom's going to be a basket case this week," Mason claims.

"Sorry," I say, knowing he's telling the truth.

"Don't speak about your mother that way," my father warns.

My brothers and I exchange a look. My father always sticks up for my mother, even though he knows we speak the truth.

I turn toward him. "So why did you bring me down here? What did you want to talk about?"

He points to the horse Mason was on. "See that horse?"

"Yeah. He's beautiful," I declare, assessing his reddish-brown coat. It's a lot brighter than most chestnut-colored horses.

"Your mom picked him, so I named him Red Ruby. He's running faster than any current contenders, including Penny Lane," my father claims.

Penny Lane's a Kentucky Derby favorite. I whistle. "For real?"

"Yes. And I want you to sell some contracts for breeding him while his time is hot," Dad declares.

I groan inside and ask, "Why me? No offense, but that's peanuts compared to our other businesses."

"Because this is another avenue you need to get your feet wet in if you're planning on being CEO," he asserts.

And there's the maybe I'll be CEO, maybe I won't that he's always waving in front of me.

I cross my arms and lean against the fence. "And why is this important?"

Dad states, "A CEO needs to know all areas of his corporation."

"Fine. I'll add it to the 50,000 other things taking priority before the end of the year," I grumble.

"Good. I'll see you all back at the house," Dad says, then pats my back and walks away.

When he's out of earshot, Alexander offers, "I'll help you line it all up. It shouldn't take me long. I can go over it with you so he thinks you did it."

"Thanks," I reply, grateful my brother's always had my back.

"Just don't fuck this next month up. Dad's threatening to make me CEO, and you know damn well I don't want that job," Alexander admits.

My brother might be smarter than me. He's more than capable of running our corporation, but he doesn't have the desire like I do. He wants to stay on the ranch, raise his kids, and tend to the labor side of our business.

"I won't," I promise. Then I ask all my brothers, "So, what's new?"

"Same old shit, different day," Mason claims.

I scoff, "So I take it Mom's all over your asses about getting hitched?"

"You got it," Jagger interjects.

"You don't want to know who she tried to hook me up with, claiming I'd have an awesome mother for the boys," Alexander adds.

I groan. "That woman's impossible. Who was it?"

"Teeny Tina," he states.

"The vertically challenged girl?" I ask in horror. She's the shortest woman in town. My brothers and I are all over six feet and she barely hits four and a half feet. And it's not Tina's height but everything else about her. She has a super-high-pitched voice and never stops talking.

"She's not a midget. She's vertically challenged," Mason says, trying to imitate my mother's voice.

I chuckle. "Shut up. She didn't."

"Oh, she did," Alexander says.

"Has Mom lost her mind?" I inquire.

Alexander shakes his head. "Apparently, she thinks I'm desperate. Be happy you brought home your bride-to-be. She had a slew of them ready to attend a welcome home party. The only reason she was going to throw it was to get you hitched and pumping out grandbabies."

His statement only makes me more grateful that Georgia agreed to our arrangement. I would have gone insane if I had to deal with my mother's matchmaking skills and constant nagging about finding a good woman.

"Speaking of Georgia, I better go check on her. Who knows what thoughts Mom and Evelyn are putting in her head."

"Don't forget about Ava, Willow, and Paisley. They're home too. It'll be a full-on shit-show of a trip down memory lane, starring you," Mason warns.

My stomach flips. Mason's right. My sisters and mother will have Georgia filled in on my entire life, including things I'm not proud of and I'd rather not remember.

Mason and Jagger go back to training the horse while Alexander and I return to the house. Wilder runs up to me, slaps my arm, and says, "Tag, you're it!"

"Oh no you don't!" I declare, then run after him. I spend the next half hour playing with the kids. Then I go inside, feeling happier than I have in a while. I do miss my family.

If only they'd come to Dallas more often, I think. Then I freeze outside the kitchen door.

Ava states, "His second fiancée, that Kara chick, she was the most annoying. She had that whiny voice that she'd use on Sebastian when she wanted something. It drove me nuts."

"I beg to differ. I would rather have listened to her than the third one, Cindy. She was horrible. Remember how she made him hire a team of people to do her hair and makeup every day she was here? As if anyone around the ranch cared about her appearance," Paisley interjects.

Willow groans but adds, "She was horrible. At least Sebastian got smarter on the fourth one."

"How is that?" Georgia asks.

I cringe inside. I should interrupt this conversation, but it's like I can't move. Maybe I'm a sucker for punishment, eavesdropping and not stopping it. Yet no matter how much I will myself to step into the room, I can't.

"She wanted a prenup gift," Willow informs her.

"Sorry?" Georgia asks, confused.

Ava interjects, "Nicky tried to get Sebastian to buy her a limited-edition Porsche for signing the prenup."

"Wow," Georgia replies.

My mother voices, "I think Molly's the one who really broke his heart though. Jacob knew she was only after his money. He begged Sebastian to get a prenup, but he refused. Thank God he learned what she was after before he walked down the aisle. You would have thought he'd pick better women after that heartbreak."

"They all sound awful," Georgia declares in a soft voice.

"Didn't he tell you this stuff?" Ava inquires.

A moment of silence passes. The hairs on my neck rise as I wait to see how Georgia will respond.

She finally answers in her chipper tone, "Sebastian and I still have a lot to learn about each other. He told me about his fiancées but not the details. And I can understand if he doesn't want to rehash his past relationships. After all, they're in the past, right?"

"Yes, dear. They are, thank goodness. I was scared he was never going to open his heart again. He changed after each failed engagement. That's why I'm so happy you're here, and he finally found the one. I can tell you're different from the others," Mom says.

Each failed engagement. I squeeze my eyes shut.

"Yeah, especially since you don't have a mile-long list of ridiculously expensive wedding must-haves that no one will ever care about," Evelyn comments.

I finally force myself to move, but it's not into the kitchen. I need air. I should have guessed my sisters and mother would gossip with Georgia the first minute they had her alone.

What do I care?

It's embarrassing that more than one woman used me.

It's not my issue. My ex-fiancées are the ones who are in the wrong.

But I chose to love them when they didn't deserve me. That's on me.

I make my way through the house and step out onto the back patio. The pool has a cover over it for the winter. The lounge chairs as well. I pace the concrete, making a circular pattern, with my thoughts going down a black hole I try to avoid whenever possible.

This is why I don't come home.

Gossips are everywhere. My sisters and mom are just products of this stupid little town.

Once January 2nd hits, I'll have more for them to add to their arsenal.

Darkness sets in, but it does nothing to disperse my demons. I keep walking, feeling like I might crawl out of my skin, when Georgia interrupts me.

"There you are," she practically sings.

I turn and stare at my beaming fake fiancée. I seethe, "What do you want?"

Her eyes widen. She jerks her head back, then swallows hard.

"Well?" I demand.

She crosses the patio and steps in front of me, tilting her head up to drill her doe-eyed glare into me. "We're going to eat dinner soon."

"Did you have fun?" I snarl.

Confusion fills her expression. She stares at me momentarily, then questions, "You're going to be nasty to me because I made you agree to look at the wedding details?"

I had forgotten about her little trick. While I thought it made her more interesting when it happened, it now makes me see through her innocent attitude.

She's no different than the others.

She negotiated a million dollars.

She wants money just like all the others did.

I don't answer her question. Crossing my arms, I ask, "Did you play your role? Or are you in breach of the contract?"

Hurt flits across her features. "Why are you being so mean right now?"

I circle my arm around her waist, pin her against me, then fist her hair. I tug it, and she gasps.

Her lips part and her breath hitches. Blue flames ignite in her eyes, searing hotter and hotter until she glances at my lips.

There's my innocent peach. Ready to be defiled.

"Were you under the impression I was a nice guy?" I murmur.

She stays quiet, her chest pushing into mine, making me wonder what her tits look like naked.

I'll find out tonight.

She finally asks again, "Why are you upset with me?"

"You did a good job fooling my family," I comment, then stare at her plump mouth, remembering how good her tongue felt massaging mine.

"Isn't that what you wanted?" she questions, then teases me further by licking her lips.

My body hardens. I slide my hand under her dress and panties. Her bare ass is smooth, and I once again note how my palm fits perfectly around it.

"What are you doing, Sebastian?" she asks, pushing her hands against my pecs.

I hold her tighter, claiming, "I'm establishing my PDA rights."

"No one is here," she comments.

"So? I paid a million dollars for you. I can do what I want," I declare.

She slaps me so hard, it stings. I step back and put my hand over my cheek, crying out, "What the fuck, Georgia!"

Her expression explodes with anger. Her lips tremble, and she jabs my chest. "Don't you treat me like I'm your whore. I'm not, Sebastian!" She spins and moves toward the house.

"Georgia, wait," I call out, following her. I grab her arm and spin her around.

"No! Don't touch me right now!" she warns, her eyes glistening.

Something tells me that I better back off. I hold my hands in the air. "Okay."

She shakes her head at me, then opens the door.

"There you are! We're ready to—Georgia, what's wrong?" Evelyn asks. Her eyes dart between us.

"Oh, your brother is just being your brother. I need to freshen up. Where's the closest bathroom?" Georgia asks.

"I'll take you," I offer.

"No," she replies, giving me a look that makes me want to crawl into a hole.

What did I just do?

God, I really am an asshole.

"First door on the left," Evelyn instructs.

"Thanks," Georgia says, flying past her.

Evelyn puts her hand on her hip and stands in the doorway. "Sebastian, why is Georgia upset?"

"None of your business. Move," I order.

"What did you do to her?" she demands.

"Nothing."

"It didn't look like nothing."

"Evelyn, mind your own business," I assert.

"Whatever you did, you better make it right, Sebastian. She looks really upset," Evelyn claims.

My chest tightens, and disappointment and shame fill me. Evelyn is my pain-in-the-ass sister, always sticking her nose where it doesn't belong. She's only a year younger than me, but she acts like the matriarch of our family. We've always butted heads. I typically ignore what she says, but right now, her words sting more than Georgia's slap.

My family spilled the beans about my past. Why am I taking it out on Georgia?

She wants my money.

I approached her to marry me.

One hundred grand wasn't enough, though, was it?

I can't blame the woman for negotiating higher. I would have.

So did all my past fiancées...

"I said to mind your own business. Now move," I repeat.

My sister finally steps aside, but she never stops giving me a look of death.

I move toward the bathroom where Georgia should be and wait.

She finally opens the door, sees me, and freezes.

I start with, "Look, I'm—"

"Don't you dare, Sebastian Allen Cartwright! I don't want to hear your fake apology or any other warped thing in your head. And don't you dare touch me, just don't!" she threatens, then brushes past me.

She knows my middle name?

It's public record.

Still...

My gut dives so deep I feel nauseous. I've officially screwed things up. And something tells me that it's not going to be easy to get it back on track.

Eleven

GEORGIA

Sebastian's family is already seated when I enter the dining room. There are so many of them that his father had an oversized rectangular table made so everyone can eat together.

"Sit here!" Isabella orders, then tells Emma, "Move over so we can both sit by Georgia!"

Emma hops over as instructed.

Evelyn scolds, "Maybe Georgia wants to sit by Sebastian."

"Nope, that's okay," I chirp, quickly sitting in the seat between the girls so I can stay away from Sebastian a little bit longer.

I'm still angry with him. I can't believe he did that to me, and I still don't understand why he's so upset.

Sebastian grabs a chair across from me and gives me another guilty expression. I try to ignore him, but it's hard with him directly facing me, giving me puppy dog eyes.

He even mouths, *"Sorry."*

Since when does Sebastian Cartwright apologize?

Ruby, Ava, and Paisley carry dinner to the table. There's prime rib, roasted root vegetables, couscous, and huge dinner rolls. Everything smells and looks delicious, and I realize how hungry I am.

Everyone gets situated with food on their plates, then we start eating. I engage in conversations, trying to avoid getting into any discussion with Sebastian. He keeps trying to pull me into them, but I answer curtly and then refocus on someone else.

He's crossed the line this time. I've never felt so disrespected. I almost told him to rip up the prenup, but then I swallowed my pride, focusing on my end goal.

But if he thinks he can overstep and treat me horribly the entire month, he's wrong.

When dinner is over, Alexander asks, "What's for dessert?"

Ruby replies, "Leftover pies from Thanksgiving."

Alexander groans, "Again?"

"Hey, there's a lot left. I can't be baking every single day, you know," she claims.

Sebastian jumps up out of his chair. "Hold on. Georgia brought something you'll all love." He winks at me, and my panties melt. He's too gorgeous for me not to react to his flirtatious gesture.

This isn't real. He's only acting.

He's a jerk. Don't forget it!

My gut flips. I had forgotten to bring in the cupcakes. What will his family think of them? Will they react how he did when I first brought them into the office?

"What did you bring us?" Emma asks.

"You have to wait and see," I answer.

"No fair!" she whines.

"Tell us!" Isabella demands, tugging on my arm.

I laugh, saying one of my grammy's phrases. "Patience gets rewarded."

Sebastian returns, carrying the boxes. Instead of his normal scowl, his face radiates something I've not seen on him before. I want to say it's pride, but that would be foolish. Sebastian Cartwright has nothing but mediocre thoughts about my cupcakes.

Isabella claps. "Ooh, Uncle Sebastian. What's inside?"

He sets the boxes on the table, announcing, "These are the world's best cupcakes."

I should be happy he said something nice about my cupcakes, but I don't trust him after what he did to me.

"Forgiveness, forgiveness, forgiveness," my grammy says in my head, which is what she used to always tell me whenever I'd get upset with someone.

Yet I'm having a hard time figuring out how to let this one go. I can't stay mad at him all month, but I also refuse to be his doormat.

Sebastian opens the box and takes a caramel apple one out. He holds it close to Isabella's mouth.

She shrieks, "I get the first one!"

Sebastian unpeels the wrapper. But instead of giving it to her, he takes a big bite. With his mouth full of cupcake, he says, "Sorry, I get the first one."

"Uncle Sebastian!" She laughs, then adds, "I want the pink one!"

He chuckles and hands her a strawberry-lemon one.

"What kind are they?" Ruby asks.

I point to each cupcake. "Caramel apple, pumpkin with cream cheese frosting, peanut butter chocolate, and strawberry-lemon."

"They look amazing," Alexander states and snatches a peanut butter cupcake.

Everybody chooses what they want and begins raving about how wonderful they taste.

Joy fills me just like it does whenever anyone claims they love my desserts, but relief also fills me. It hits me how much I want the Cartwrights' approval.

Sebastian announces, "Georgia's going to open a cupcake bakery."

"Really? That's amazing," Willow states.

I nod. "It's always been my dream."

"These are amazing. What's the secret?" Ruby asks.

"They're my grammy's recipes. I've never told anyone. Although, soon I'll have to, I guess. I mean, if I'm going to go commercial with it."

"But you'll tell me, right?" she says with a hopeful look on her face.

I laugh, and offer, "Yeah, I can do better than that. I'll show you how to make them while I'm here."

"Ooh. Can I help?" Isabella asks.

"Sure," I answer, putting my arm around her and kissing her on the head. The girls are just gorgeous, as are the little boys, and everyone in Sebastian's family are different than I expected. They're all so nice, and it makes me wonder why he doesn't want to come home more often. If this were my family, I'd want to be around them. Plus, they all seem sincere.

Unlike him.

Forgiveness, forgiveness, forgiveness.

Ugh!

His mom states, "It's nice to see you eat a dessert, Sebastian."

He freezes and gives her a hardened look.

"What? I'm just saying," she claims.

I interject, "He doesn't eat them very often."

"Well, you know why, right?" Willow asks.

"He has a fat complex?" I blurt out.

"He used to be fat," Jagger mentions, stuffing more of his cupcake in his mouth.

Sebastian Cartwright was fat? No way.

I glance at Sebastian. He clenches his jaw.

"Well, he had diabetes, if you want to know all the details," Ruby adds.

Shock hits me, along with a bit of worry. I ask him, "You had diabetes?"

"I was a kid. I liked sweets. I ate a lot of them. That's what happens when you eat too much sugar. I keep telling you this. So, yeah, I was diabetic, but I reversed it, and I'm trying not to ever have it again," he defensively admits.

"With that strict diet you keep and all the workouts, you don't need to worry about it anymore, Sebastian. I've told you several times you can relax a little bit," his mom says.

Sebastian's face grows red. "Excuse me for not wanting to be diabetic, have to shoot myself up with insulin, put my limbs at risk of amputation, and die early."

I make a note to figure out how to make some sugar-free cupcakes for him that don't taste horrible. But then I scold myself. I'm not going to be married to him long enough to worry about that. Besides, why should I do anything for him when he's been so mean and disrespectful to me?

Still, it can't be easy turning down cupcakes all the time when I'm throwing them in his face.

I thought Sebastian was just overly worried about his fit body. This new information makes me feel bad for tempting him every day in the office.

Evelyn rises, breaking the tension, and proclaiming, "Time for ornaments."

The kids get excited again and race into the other room.

Evelyn demands, "Georgia, you have to make one too."

"Is this a Cartwright thing?" I ask.

"Yeah, we do it every year. Then tomorrow, when the tree gets cut down and brought in, everyone has their new ornaments and old ones to put on the tree," she informs me.

"Oh. That's a great tradition. I'd love to make one," I admit and go into the other room.

Card tables are set up around the living room and are covered with tablecloths. Every imaginable art supply is available including stickers, glitter, glue, markers, and paints. Fake snow, tiny bunches of holly, construction paper, cotton, and other things are scattered all over the tables. Everyone gets a huge clear bulb to fill and decorate.

I decide to create a Christmas cupcake. I use construction paper to form a fake wrapper. I fill the bulb with dark-red glitter, then use cotton as the frosting. I sprinkle green glitter over it and paint the year on the lower corner of the wrapper.

I'm almost done with one when Sebastian sits down next to me. He grabs one of the bulbs, quizzing, "So you're an artist too, huh?"

I shrug, then question, "You're going to make an ornament?"

"Yeah. Is that okay?" he asks, giving me a look that makes me think he's still walking on eggshells around me.

"Of course," I reply, reprimanding myself for holding a grudge.

"You sure?"

"Yes. I just didn't think you'd be into this," I admit.

He picks up a bulb. "I'm a professional. And you're going to love mine."

"Why is that?"

"You'll see." He fills the bulb with green glitter, paints a red heart on the outside, then holds it in front of the tiny craft fan until it's dry. He adds S + G in the middle of the heart, then adds the year at the bottom. He holds it out and winks, stating, "First ornament for us."

I stare at it with mixed emotions. Part of me wishes his statement were true, but after this holiday is over, I'll no longer be part of the Cartwright family.

I'll be a memory like his other fiancées.

Something about that thought pains me.

I shake off the odd feeling, force a smile, then get up and focus on helping the kids make their ornaments.

We spend the rest of the evening playing with the kids. Isabella and Emma want me to tuck them in and tell them a story, so I read them *Green Eggs and Ham* by Dr. Suess. Emma falls asleep, and Isabella can barely keep her eyes open. I kiss them both on the head and leave the room.

Sebastian's in the hallway, leaning against the wall. "It looks like you have a fan club," he comments.

"They're adorable," I confess.

He nods, then stares at me a moment before asking, "Ready for bed?"

Nerves fill me. My stomach flips. The comment from the backyard flashes in my head.

It must register on my face because he lowers his voice and adds, "I was an ass. And I *am* sorry. Are you going to hate me forever, Sunshine?"

I want to fully trust him, but it's hard, especially when I have to share a room with him. But I need to get over this, or the next month will be miserable. I square my shoulders, warning, "Don't do it again."

"I won't. Promise," he vows.

"Okay. You're forgiven."

"Just like that?" he asks.

"Yep."

He grins. "Good. Thanks."

A moment of silence passes between us, then he slings his arm around my waist, stating, "Let me show you our room."

More butterflies fill my gut. How is it that a week ago I was starting a new job, and now I'm pretending to be my boss's fiancée?

My utterly arrogant, way-too-sexy, and probably overly experienced boss who would use me and leave me with a broken heart without having an ounce of guilt.

That's not fair.

It's true.

I push my fears to the back of my mind and step into the bedroom suite. Our suitcases are already there. I point at the dresser. "Am I allowed to use that?"

"Use as many drawers and as much closet space as you want. There's plenty of room," he announces.

It shouldn't surprise me. The dresser and the closet are huge. Still, I glance at them in awe. I start to unpack and offer, "Thanks."

When I get to my underwear, Sebastian teases, "Ah, you did bring the granny panties?"

I spin on him, snapping, "Can you leave me alone? And stop judging me for everything. I'm just tired of it."

He puts his hands in the air and sighs. "Georgia, I thought we made peace? I'm sorry I was a dickhead."

Okay, so maybe I need to work on the forgiveness part.

"You weren't just a dickhead. You were offensive, rude, and disrespectful!" I scold.

He nods. "I know. I'm sorry. What do I have to do to make this right?"

"How about you stop being mean to me?"

"Okay. I will."

"Why were you so nasty to me anyway?" I ask, putting my hand on my hip.

He opens his mouth, then snaps it shut.

His silence makes me angrier. I snap, "I'm waiting for an answer. I at least deserve that, don't you think? And be honest, Sebastian. Don't feed me your lies."

He furrows his eyebrows. "Do you really think that badly about me?"

Guilt fills me. But I'm not ready to back down. I feed him some of his own silence.

"Guess I have a lot to work on," he mutters.

"I'm still waiting for an honest answer," I declare.

He grinds his molars, glances at the ceiling, then refocuses on me. He admits, "I hate everyone talking about me behind my back, especially, about my past failed relationships. It makes me angry. A part of me is still upset that I fell for all their deceit. And I should have known they were all users, but I didn't. So, I'm sorry I get a little unhinged when anyone talks about it behind my back."

His answer makes me let down my guard a little bit. It was devastating to hear from his sisters and mom what his ex-fiancées did to him. Who acts like that anyway? I soften my tone. "I can understand why that would hurt you."

"Can we not talk about it anymore?" he asks.

"Okay. But I will say that I think they're horrible people."

"Yeah, they are. And I wish it didn't make me angry anymore, but it does."

I blurt out, "Maybe you need to work on some forgiveness, then."

He scrunches his face. "Forgiveness? I didn't do anything to them. Regardless of what you think about me, I was good to them. I can assure you that I was nothing but good, beyond generous, and kind."

"I didn't say you weren't, Sebastian. But if you're this angry about it and it makes you do stupid things like what you did to me in the backyard, then you need to work on forgiving them."

"I don't understand."

"You have to forgive them for what they've done. It doesn't mean you have to forget it, but if you forgive them, at least it won't hurt as badly."

He stares at me for a while, then states, "I'm going to shower. Do you need anything?"

My butterflies kick up again. The thought of his sweaty chest when he pulled me onto his lap in the office flashes in my mind. I reply, "No, I'm okay. I'll keep unpacking."

"All right, Sunshine." He winks and goes into the bathroom, and my pulse creeps up.

I stare at the bed, thinking thoughts that I shouldn't have anywhere in my mind. I tear my eyes off it, then finish unpacking.

He steps out of the bathroom in nothing but a towel. His skin glistens, taut over his ripped flesh, as if he's some kind of god.

My cheeks heat, and I gape at him.

"Is that drool?" he teases.

Flustered, I grab my pajama bottoms and tank top. I rush past him, closing the bathroom door and locking it.

I toss my hair into a knot, take a quick shower, then brush, floss, and rinse with mouthwash. I get dressed, then stare at myself in the mirror.

There's nothing to worry about.

It's Sebastian Cartwright—Mr. Smooth Moves.

I take a deep breath, lift my chin, then open the door. I point to the couch. "You can sleep there."

He looks at me in horror. "What?"

I point to the floor. "Or you can sleep there."

He chuckles. "This is a king-size bed, Sunshine. There's plenty of room for both of us."

"Too bad for you that I still don't trust you." I smirk.

He groans. "Seriously, Georgia? I'm not sleeping on the couch. I'm tall. There's no way I'll fit on that thing. Look at it. It is a love seat."

I shrug. "The floor will work, then."

"I'm a thirty-six-year-old man. I don't sleep on the floor, especially a wood one," he claims.

A tad of guilt appears, but I push it away. I cross my arms and give him my most challenging stare.

He grumbles, "Fine. I'll sleep on the floor."

"Okay. Thanks." I slip under the covers.

Sebastian shakes his head at me, goes into the closet, and returns with a blanket and a pillow. He mutters, "This is ridiculous."

"Shh. I'm tired," I claim and turn off the light.

He pleads, "Can we please act like adults? I can sleep on the other side of the bed, far away from you?"

"Nope," I reply, then snuggle down under the covers.

Silence fills the air. It feels like a long time, but it's probably only a few minutes. All of a sudden, I hear a stirring.

Sebastian's warm body slides next to mine under the covers.

I jump up and turn the light on, accusing, "What are you doing?"

He asserts, "I'm not sleeping on the floor, Georgia. I'm sorry, but no. You could have put that in the prenup, but you didn't. So you're just going to have to deal with me sleeping next to you. Got it?"

"I'm not okay with this," I state, but it sounds weak. The heat from his body makes me want to move closer.

"Well, you should have put it in writing," he murmurs, his hot breath tingling my ear.

"And you're back to being rude and disrespectful," I tell him.

He huffs. "Me? You want me to sleep on a wood floor. Who's the real rude one in this situation?"

I bury my face in the pillow, uttering, "You're impossible."

"Are you going to keep the light on all night or turn it off?" he asks.

What Sebastian Cartwright wants, he always gets.

He wants me.

He doesn't really want me. He wants to use me for the next month and then discard me.

Not letting that happen.

I turn off the light, then slide back under the covers. "Make sure you stay on your side of the bed."

His intoxicating scent of praline and a hint of citrus mixed with sandalwood seems to grow more intense. My pulse skyrockets and my heart rapidly beats. Sebastian slides his arm under my back and tugs me into his body, rolling me so I'm facing him.

"What are you doing? I told you to stay on your side of the bed."

He chuckles. "I am on my side of the bed. But you're on my side of the bed too."

"Sebastian," I reprimand, but I also don't move. I can't. His warm frame feels too good against mine. I curse myself for not moving.

He grabs my thigh and slings my leg over his body.

"What are you doing?" I shriek again.

"Shh. This is better, admit it," he challenges.

"Says who?" I manage to get out. But he's right. Every part of our bodies entwined feels like heaven.

"Do you have something against cuddling?" he murmurs, his lips against my hair.

"I didn't know it was in my contract to cuddle," I retort.

"Calm down. I won't do anything."

I relax a little. "You promise you're not going to try anything funny?"

"Funny? Nope," he replies, but something feels fishy about it.

I stay quiet, trying to lower my racing pulse.

He adds, "Not unless you want me to."

I nudge him in the ribs. He laughs. "Ouch! Between that and your slap, you're pretty vicious, Sunshine."

Against the advice from the voice in my head, I snuggle closer to his chest and close my eyes. I warn, "Well, now you know what I'm capable of, so no funny business."

He grunts.

No matter how hard I try to sleep, I can't. All I can smell is him. All I hear is his breathing mixing with my pulse pounding between my ears. And tingles attack every part of my body.

What's worse is I don't think I've ever craved anyone before. Right now, at this moment, I'm not sure how I'm going to make it through the night with Sebastian Cartwright.

Then, he makes it even harder.

Twelve

SEBASTIAN

Georgia's sugary-rose scent flares in my nostrils, taunting me to break my promise to her.

I'm trying to be good. I don't want her pissed at me again, and her body is finally relaxed against mine.

Still, my cock is hard as steel. My palm hasn't left her upper thigh, and I'm surprised she's let me keep it there. I glance at the digital clock.

Ten minutes.

Six hundred seconds of holding myself back from disturbing her.

I cave, questioning, "What did you decide for the wedding?"

Her body stiffens, then she slowly rolls farther into me, lifting her head off my chest. Her blues are barely visible against the darkness, and her hot breath hits my chest. She answers, "We got off track."

The conversation about my ex-fiancées hits me again. I grunt. "Doesn't surprise me."

She asks, "What do you want for the wedding?"

I admit the only thing I truly care about. "That you show up and say 'I do.'"

She tilts her head, a smile playing on her lips. "Done deal. I signed the prenup, remember?"

The sting of too many failed attempts down the aisle reappears. I try to ignore it and inquire, "So what do you want for it?"

"Something simple," she states.

"Simple?" I ask, unable to comprehend it or hide my shock. All the women I asked to marry me wanted lavish, over-the-top events.

Her voice turns offended. "What's wrong with simple?"

I can't help myself and slide my hand along her cheek, dragging my thumb over her lips. I murmur, "Nothing is wrong with it, Sunshine."

She pins her eyebrows together, asking, "No?"

"No, not at all."

"Then why did you sound like it was?" she inquires.

My heart beats faster. I've already told Georgia way more than I ever thought I would. All I want to do is bury my past in the graveyard and never visit it again. Yet I should have known it would be impossible here. I have too many ghosts that everyone in town will be talking about, never mind my family, as they've already proven. I confess, "Everyone I've dated has wanted something extravagant enough for the front page of *Dallas High Society*."

Even in the dark, I see her roll her eyes. She says, "Well, that sounds like a very impersonal wedding to me."

I nod. "Yeah, I agree."

A moment passes, and she asks, "So... Is it okay if we keep it simple? Or does Sebastian Cartwright need a super-fancy wedding?"

I ponder her question. If I have an extravagant wedding of the century, it'll shut everyone up more. But if we keep it simple, at least it'll stop them from gossiping about how we went over the top. It'll shock the town for it to not be what they expect.

Yet something about Georgia wanting a simple wedding makes me want to give it to her, even if it's fake.

I answer, "If you show me how you're going to kiss me in front of everyone, I'll agree to simple."

Her cheek heats under my palm. A tiny laugh escapes her, and she states, "The groom kisses the bride, not the other way around."

"You have to fool everyone into thinking you're in love with me," I point out.

"Isn't that why we're getting married?"

Nerves flare in my belly. I've not felt anything of the sort since high school. "Yes, but you're going to have to kiss me like you can't get enough of me."

She takes several small breaths.

I flip her onto her back, then cage my body over hers.

She gasps but doesn't object.

I demand, "We need to practice."

"Do we?" she whispers.

I lean lower so my mouth is an inch from hers. My cock twitches against her, and I swear she pushes just a touch closer to me. She swallows hard, and I insist, "Practice makes perfect."

Her hands glide into my hair, and in a barely audible tone, she orders, "Then show me what you got, Sebastian Allen Cartwright."

Every time she says my name, my blood heats. Something about her saying my full name makes it boil. I don't hesitate, but instead of going right for her lips, I take my time. I dip to her neck, kissing her collarbone, then make my way up to her lobe.

Her breath hitches in my ear, her legs widen beneath me, and she arches her back, pushing her hard nipples into my pecs.

I kiss her forehead, then nose and cheeks. When I finally get to her lips, her fingers grip my skull, and a tremor runs through her body.

Her lips part as if welcoming me home, and everything I thought about our first kiss was wrong.

It's nothing compared to the fire she stokes inside me. She uses her tongue like a rolling pin, gently gliding it against mine, then pressing harder with every stroke until I'm dizzy with my little peach's ability to make me forget about anything but her.

My hand moves to her leg, and I tug on it. She bends it, slings it around my waist, then does the same with the other, and I think I've died and gone to heaven. Her grip intensifies, holding me closer. Her tongue massages mine with more fervor.

My fingers slide between us, grazing her nipple.

She whimpers, a sound so sweet I wish I had my phone recording it.

I trace the hard ridge, then move into a pinching motion, gliding my tongue around hers faster. My erection's so stiff, it pops out of my boxers.

I need to get these flannel pants off her.

I break our kiss, leaning into her ear, murmuring, "I want my mouth on your pussy."

She freezes, except for her hard breathing.

I move my hand to her pants and tug at the drawstring, ordering, "Lift your hips."

She takes a deep breath, then releases my hair, pressing her palms against my chest. She says, "Get off me, Sebastian."

"Why, Sunshine?" I question, not sure why she's stopping me.

"This isn't right," she claims.

My past haunts me again. I object, "Why? Because I said pussy?"

"No."

Surprised, I inquire, "Then what is it?"

She turns her face toward the wall.

I move it so she's facing me again. "Tell me why, Georgia. What makes it wrong? We're two consenting adults, are we not?"

Her bottom lip quivers.

A new thought hits me. I ask, "You don't like sex?"

"Of course I like sex," she replies.

Relief fills me. I continue, "Then if it's not because I said pussy, and it's not because you don't like sex, what's it about?"

She shuts her eyes for a minute.

I take it that she doesn't really want me to stop and arrogantly declare, "I promise you if you let me lick your pussy, you'll want me to do it again. In fact, I bet you that you'll beg for me to do it again."

Her eyes pop open. She blurts out, "This isn't real, Sebastian."

"Last time I looked, you and I were both real people," I retort.

She stresses, "*We* aren't real. Remember the prenup?"

I huff. "So? What about it?"

She sternly says, "This isn't love."

"So?" I ask again.

Her face hardens.

I retreat a tad, taunting, "Don't tell me you only have sex with someone when you think you're in love."

Offended, she argues, "Think?"

"Yeah. Love isn't real," I claim.

Appalled, she huffs. "Is that what you believe?"

"One hundred percent," I answer.

Tense silence fills the air. She finally pushes my chest again and says, "Practice is over. Get off me."

Groaning, I obey, stating, "Sex is sex, Sunshine. It's two people getting each other off. You shouldn't complicate a basic human need. Maybe you're just too young and naive to realize this."

She scoffs. "Gosh, you're sad."

Irritated, I question, "Sad?"

She tugs the covers over her and turns away from me. She mumbles, "You do you, Sebastian, and I'll do me."

"Don't get offended," I offer.

"Goodnight, Sebastian. Stay on your side of the bed," she firmly directs.

I sigh, pissed.

We were doing so well.

Am I the only one who felt the fireworks in our kisses?

No way. She did too.

Then why is she acting like a prude?

It's going to be harder than I thought to get into her pants.

Why did I choose to spend a month with a woman who believes in fairy tales?

My raging hard-on doesn't go away. I've never had a woman turn me down before. Usually, they'll let me get in their pants as soon as I try. It's all part of keeping me happy to get their claws in me.

Why doesn't Georgia play the usual game and dig hers into me?

She doesn't have to. She already gets a million dollars.

A hundred thousand. She's definitely not getting a million.

Is she lying or telling the truth that she's only had sex with someone she thought she loved?

The questions spinning in my mind are endless. Her sugary-rose scent never stops taunting me. I debate about spooning her round ass but decide against it. My cock is tormented enough.

I finally fall asleep around three in the morning, only to wake up at four. I finally give up and sneak into the closet. I grab shorts and a T-shirt, socks, and sneakers. I quietly slip out of the room and go into the gym.

I'm surprised to see Alexander there, although I shouldn't be. Ever since his wife died, he hasn't slept well either. Anytime I come home, he's usually covered in sweat by the time I step foot into the room.

He pushes the stop button on the treadmill and jumps off it. He takes a towel, wipes his face, then downs some water. He asks, "Can't sleep?"

I shrug. "Story of my life."

"Is Georgia still mad at you?"

I grunt. "Don't get me started."

He warns, "Better fix that before she changes her mind."

"What does that mean?" I snap.

He holds his hands in the air. "Bro, chill. I just meant I like her. She seems good for you."

I relax a bit. "How's that?"

"Lots of reasons. The first being that she doesn't kiss your ass. She challenges you," he asserts.

"Her challenges are getting under my skin," I mumble, then step on the treadmill and punch the settings.

He chuckles.

"Why are you laughing?" I ask.

"That's how I know she's good for you. Right there," he claims.

I ignore him.

He continues, "Did you ever wonder why none of those other women were right for you?"

The speed on the track moves faster. Hating my past, I accuse, "Do you honestly think I haven't asked myself a thousand times how my personal life became a joke?"

"Not a joke, bro," he declares.

"Easy for you to say."

"Okay, get past your ego for a minute."

"Not in the mood for your insults," I hurl.

He steps in front of my machine and crosses his arms. He watches me for a few moments and then adds, "Those women were all blood-sucking snobs."

"Tell me something I don't know, Alexander," I bark, then the incline adjusts, and I move into a slow jog.

He shakes his head. "If you knew it, then why did you continue falling for them?"

"Can we change the subject?" I ask.

He ignores my request. "Georgia isn't like them."

"No shit, Sherlock."

"So you finally got it right."

My little brother's self-proclaimed relationship expertise gets on my last nerve. I blurt out, "You don't even know her to be able to state that."

He arches his eyebrows. "So she's not the one for you but you're marrying her?"

Flustered, I claim, "I never said that."

"Oh, right. You said I don't know her enough to say you finally got it right," he replies.

"Congratulations, you can hear," I sneer and pick up my pace.

Alexander snorts, adding, "I saw enough. You've met your match, bro. It's about time."

Still unsure how he's claiming this when he just met Georgia, I say nothing.

"She's not a woman who'll just sit back and let you walk all over her," he states.

"You're making me rethink marrying her. It sounds like my life will be full of headaches and blue balls," I mutter.

He chuckles. "A bit. But it'll also be interesting. She'll keep you on your toes. That's the type of woman you want to grow old with."

"How would you know?" I accuse, then regret it the minute his face falls. I quickly apologize. "Sorry."

His face hardens. He grinds his molars, then announces, "I'm going to shower. See you at breakfast."

"Alexander," I call after him, knowing I crossed the line, but the door slams.

"Shit!" I shout, then hit the button to run faster, trying to work out my frustration and guilty feelings.

It doesn't work. My thoughts return to Georgia, and no matter what I do, I can't get the way her body felt under mine or how her tongue flicked in my mouth, out of my mind.

Mason and Jagger eventually enter the gym, but I'm not in the mood for conversation. I leave, creep into the bedroom, and stare at Georgia sleeping.

She's too beautiful for her own good.

Love. Ugh. How can she be so naive?

I tear my gaze off her, go into the bathroom, and shower. I spend extra time under the water, thinking about her and eliminating my hard-on. When I'm spent and feeling better, I dry off.

And I must be a sucker for punishment because instead of getting dressed and leaving the room, I toss on my boxers. I stand over Georgia for a moment, studying her in the darkness.

Her plump lips part slightly. The sound of her soft breath fills my ears. Her long eyelashes flutter briefly, and I think she's going to wake up, but they relax closed again.

Not wanting her to catch me being a creeper, I slide back into bed, then move over to her side. I sling my arm around her waist and take deep breaths of her sugary-rose scent.

Unlike with my normal insomnia, I fall back asleep. For the first time in years, I dream. But it's not good. It's a nightmare. And it freaks me out.

Georgia's shrieking at me with tears falling down her cheeks, but I can't comprehend what she's saying. I try to pull her into my arms, yet she won't let me. She pushes me away and runs.

I chase her, running faster and faster, but no matter how quickly I move, she outpaces me. Then, she disappears. I'm standing in the cold snow, wet and freezing.

The scene changes to my penthouse. I'm holding papers, but I feel empty. I glance at them again and read, *Annulment*. The bottom of the page has Georgia's signature scribbled on it.

I wake up in a sweat. Like my dream, Little Miss Sunshine isn't anywhere in sight. Panic fills me. I get out of bed, toss on a T-shirt and a pair of joggers, and leave the bedroom.

The smell of breakfast hits my nose. I call out, "Georgia," rushing through the house.

I go down several hallways and then yell louder, "Georgia!"

She steps out of the kitchen wearing a Christmas apron, with her hair in a high ponytail. Relief fills me. Confused, she pushes a rogue lock of hair behind her ear, and a white mark stains her cheek. She questions, "Why are you shouting? Where's the fire?"

I release a stress-filled breath, then swipe my thumb over the floury substance. I should have known she'd be baking, yet something feels comforting about it instead of the irritation I used to feel. I answer, "I didn't know where you were."

"Should I leave you a note on my whereabouts from now on?" she teases.

I chuckle, replying, "Maybe you should."

"I'm making breakfast with the girls."

I glance into the kitchen. Emma and Isabella have matching aprons. My sisters and mom are drinking coffee at the table, giving me funny looks.

I ignore them, trying to pull my thoughts together.

"Did you need something?" Georgia asks.

I slowly shake my head.

"Are you hungry? We're making pancakes," she states.

"I don't eat pancakes," I state.

"Your mom said your favorite breakfast food is pancakes."

"Was. I don't eat them anymore. They're bad for me," I admit.

"You can eat these. They're special," she declares.

"Special?" I ask, still feeling odd and trying to shake it off.

She nods. "It took a few hours to figure it out, but I think we nailed it."

"Why would it take hours? Pancakes are easy to make," I assert.

She informs me, "They're sugar-free protein pancakes."

I stare at her. My chest tightens and my stomach flips.

She quietly adds, "You can eat them and not worry."

More time passes.

Evelyn reprimands, "Jeez, Sebastian. You could say thanks. She's been slaving in here so you can stay on your stupid diet."

I shoot her a dirty look, then turn back to Georgia. I lock eyes with her, humbly saying, "Thanks, Sunshine."

She doesn't move for a moment. She finally offers a tiny smile and nods. She returns to the girls, and I fill a mug of coffee. I watch them finish making breakfast, confused over how off I feel.

For the first time in my life, I think a woman has made me speechless.

And I can't decide if I like or hate it.

Thirteen

GEORGIA

Nerves skyrocket in my gut. I add a stack of pancakes to a plate and set it in front of Sebastian, along with the homemade sugar-free syrup I figured out how to make.

He glances at it, then back at me with a worried look on his face.

"It's safe. Nothing's going to happen, Sebastian. I promise there's no sugar in it," I repeat.

"But they're fluffy," he comments, his face scrunched as he stares at the food.

"Yeah, I know," I say with pride.

"How's that possible? I've tried to make these things before. They never look like this. They're always dense. And they always taste like crap. These look like real pancakes."

I pretend to zip my lips and toss the key. "My secret. Well, Isabella, Emma, and my secret, right, girls?"

They giggle, then Isabella excitedly orders, "Try it, Uncle Sebastian! Try it! They're really good."

"I already ate one too," Emma chirps.

He smiles at his nieces. His dimple pops out, and my heart swoons a bit. Sebastian Cartwright is always eye candy, but watching him interact with his family shows me another side of him. And I like who he is around them.

Well, when he's not getting angry or hurt by what they tell me.

I refocus on the pancakes, and the nervous rumbling in my gut continues to grow. I want him to like them as much as I wanted him to like my cupcakes. But now, knowing Sebastian's health history and why he is how he is, something makes me really want him to like these. It doesn't seem fair that he has to worry so much and not enjoy food like the rest of his family does. And maybe he's a bit overboard, but I can't blame him for not wanting to risk his health.

Perhaps I shouldn't be doing anything nice for him after what happened last night. Especially since I woke up with his body wrapped around mine. Against my better judgment, I almost stayed there.

Almost.

But my resolve to not let Sebastian use me won. I quietly snuck out, knowing if I stayed, there was a good chance of something happening when he woke up. It wasn't easy to turn him down last night, but he made it clear sex doesn't mean anything to him. The last thing I need is to get caught up in an affair with Sebastian Cartwright, just to get tossed aside. I already know that come January 2nd, he'll be done with me.

Still, I couldn't resist attempting to figure out how to make him his favorite breakfast when I heard he loves pancakes but never eats them anymore. It seemed cruel, so I set out on a mission.

Now, it's the moment of truth.

Sebastian takes his fork and knife in his hands, cuts the stack of pancakes, and pours the syrup over it. Then he takes a bite.

Time stands still as he chews. My chest tightens, and I don't even realize I'm holding my breath.

He finally looks at me, announcing, "These are incredible."

"Yay." I clap.

The girls jump up and down, shrieking.

I laugh, telling them, "We did it."

"Seriously, how did you make these?" Sebastian inquires and shoves more into his mouth.

"As I said, it's my secret," I chirp, then go back to the counter and start to clean up the mess. The counter's a disaster zone, and not like when I bake. I usually clean up as I do each step, but Isabella and Emma had a blast helping me. I didn't want to interrupt their fun.

"I know the secret," Isabella taunts and sits down next to Sebastian.

He leans into her, demanding, "Tell me what it is."

She shakes her head. "Nope. Georgia told us we had to take it to our graves."

"Are we dying soon?" Emma asks.

"No, of course not," I say, horrified at the thought.

She giggles. "Okay. That's good. Isabella, let's go play dolls."

"All right." Isabella jumps up, and she and Emma run out of the room.

"Are you going to eat?" Sebastian asks.

"I already did," I inform him.

"Did you eat these?" he asks.

I shake my head. "No, I just had some eggs and bacon."

"You didn't try these?"

"Well, I sampled them while cooking them. So I guess I have had pancakes this morning."

"They really are great. Thanks," he restates. Zings fill me until they get replaced with nerves. He asks, "Where's your ring?"

I pick the flashy diamond up off the counter. "Right here. It's hard to wear while baking. The diamond's so big it gets dirty, so I took it off," I state, then slide it on my finger.

His face falls at that.

I try to concentrate on cleaning, but I can't get how wrong the ring is for me off my mind. I need to work better at pretending to love it.

"Have a seat," Sebastian orders when I finish cleaning. He pulls a chair out next to him. Something about his gesture makes my heart pitter-patter. I wish it didn't, but it does.

I sit down, and he continues to eat while Ruby announces, "We need to talk about this wedding. Where are we going to have it?"

"Yeah, time's ticking," Evelyn adds.

"What about the country club?" Ruby asks.

Sebastian groans. "That's so cliche, Mom. Plus, you know I avoid that place like the plague."

Ava scoffs. "I never understood why you don't like it. I love the country club."

He snaps, "It's a gossip haven. Even the men's locker room is, but of course, you would like it."

"Hey, be nice," Ruby chastises.

My gut dives. I feel bad for Sebastian. He seems to get upset about gossip, and I assume it's because he's been the center of it. So I assert, "Let's cross the country club off. It doesn't feel right."

He places his palm on my thigh, and tingles race down my spine, right to my core. I challenge myself not to shift on my seat and squeeze my thighs tighter.

His mom suggests, "What about the cattle museum?"

I blurt out, "You have a cattle museum?"

Sebastian grunts. "Yep."

"Like a shrine to cattle?" I tease.

"Exactly. How ridiculous is that?" Sebastian answers.

"Tsk. It's more for the children to study parts of cattle. You know this, Sebastian," Evelyn reprimands.

"Still stupid," he mutters, shrugs, then shoves more pancakes in his mouth.

"Not really. I think the kids love it," Ruby claims.

"I used to love it," Paisley admits.

Willow complains, "I hated going there. It's all bones and cattle parts and ... Ugh." She makes a face and then adds, "There are enough cattle on this ranch."

"Agreed," Sebastian says, turning toward me.

I exchange an amused glance with him.

He scoots closer and slides his arm around my shoulder.

Everything in me goes hot, making me feel flustered. Flashbacks of last night when he had his body over mine haunt me. I stiffen, scolding myself for wanting to feel that again. I almost pull away from him, but he leans closer.

He whispers, "PDA clause. Relax, Sunshine. I'm not going to try to come in you with my family around."

I gape at him.

Did he just say that in front of his whole family?

No, he whispered it.

Nobody heard.

He's so dirty.

Why do I like the fact that he talks so filthy?

Arrogance washes over him, and he gives me a challenging look as if he knows I like his perverted remarks.

Am I a pervert?

He kisses me below the ear, then tugs me even closer.

I try to relax and smile at his family. They're all giving us approving smiles, as if they're happy I'm in love with Sebastian.

No, no, no! I'm not in love with him.

He's definitely not in love with me.

He doesn't even believe in love. My heart dives at the truth.

How can we pretend to do this so well that we're actually fooling them?

This is so wrong. They're such nice people.

Paisley snaps her fingers, tearing me out of my guilt trip. "The college courtyard. That would be a great place. Georgia, you would love it. It's beautiful."

"You'll have to make an extra donation to get them to agree, Sebastian," Evelyn says.

Willow adds, "The Baxters had to pay half a million dollars, and they still had some things wrong with their day."

"Well, we don't want things going wrong," Ruby claims.

"Half a million dollars!" I exclaim.

Willow shrugs. "Yeah, it's not a big deal, Georgia. Don't worry about it. That's cheaper than what Sebastian was going to pay for a lot of his previous weddings."

Sebastian snarls, "Seriously? You're going to bring those up while I'm planning my wedding with my future wife?"

She cringes, offering, "Sorry."

I put my hand over Sebastian's, squeeze it, and interject, "That doesn't sound like a very good place. Let's skip that one."

Ava exclaims, "Oh my gosh! The Spiegel mansion! It's so amazing, especially at Christmas. You'll love it, Georgia."

"Plus, it has that huge ballroom," Ruby points out.

Sebastian shakes his head and closes his eyes. His body stiffens.

"What's wrong?" I quietly ask.

He locks his blues on mine, questioning, "I thought you wanted simple."

"I do."

"Does simple include a thousand guests?"

My mouth hangs open. I finally mutter, "A thousand? Are you serious?"

His face hardens. "Yeah. That's what it'll be like. Is that what you want?"

"No!" I declare, the thought of that many people making my stomach flip.

Relief washes over him. "Then the Spiegel mansion's not right. Just trust me on this."

"I trust you," I say, without even thinking about it.

Do I trust him?

No, I definitely don't trust him.

But a part of me does.

He turns toward his family and asserts, "We aren't inviting a ton of guests. It's going to be family and some close friends only."

"That'll be hard to whittle down. People will get offended," Ruby frets.

"Too bad. Blame it on me. Other options," Sebastian orders.

My heart swoons. Something about Sebastian's don't-argue-with-me tone always makes me weak-kneed.

Tension fills the air.

"When will your family be arriving?" Ruby questions.

"Ummm..." I swallow hard and blink back the unexpected grief I wish I didn't feel.

Sebastian tugs me closer to him. "Georgia's family has all passed. It's just us."

Just us, as if I'm one of them.

I'm not. Don't forget it.

Sympathetic smiles flash at me.

I shift in my seat, and Sebastian orders, "What are the other options?"

Silence fills the kitchen.

Willow slaps the table. "I've got it. The Hideaway Resort & Spa. Plus, we can spend all day getting ready with massages and detox baths."

Paisley informs us, "That's a no-go. They are booked solid until after the New Year. I couldn't even get a fifteen-minute hot towel service."

"Hot towel service?" Sebastian inquires.

"They put a hot towel over your face. It's infused with really nice-smelling oils," she answers.

"Sounds like a waste of money to me," he states.

She rolls her eyes. "You would think that. Anyway, I even offered to pay extra, but they said there isn't any possibility."

"Maybe you didn't offer enough. Sebastian, you'll just have to offer a huge sum of money that they can't say no to," Willow asserts.

All their talk about overpaying for things makes me uncomfortable.

I ask, "Is there anywhere we can go where Sebastian doesn't have to whip out his checkbook and break the bank?"

All their eyes widen, and amusement fills their faces.

Evelyn chastises Sebastian, "Have you not told your wife that you aren't just rich, you're wealthy?"

What's the difference?

I must be super naive.

Sebastian scrubs his face, groaning. "Evelyn, can you shut up?"

I state, "I don't want Sebastian wasting his money just because he has it."

His sisters all exchange another humorous glance.

Did I say something wrong?

This is so out of my comfort zone.

I'm not used to these sums of money they're talking about, nor am I used to wasting it. I'm not a cheapskate, but I don't see the point in tossing money out for nothing.

Ruby suggests, "What about the Lakeside Plaza?"

"You'll have the gorgeous sunset," Paisley claims.

Evelyn shakes her head, revealing, "There's an issue with the chemicals."

"Chemicals? What chemicals?" I question.

She answers, "They add chemicals so the water looks turquoise. It's really, really pretty, but something's not right. I was there a few weeks ago for the Smith wedding. Green algae was growing on the surface of the water and it had this horrible stench. Trust me. It's not what you want on your big day."

"We're running out of options," Ruby agonizes.

Several minutes pass until Ava suggests, "The Rustic Reserve. Georgia, it's beautiful."

"I've never heard of it," I admit.

"It's acres and acres of farmland and hay. The oil wells are no longer working, so it's more for events."

Evelyn interjects, "The Reserve doesn't do weddings during the holidays. They make too much from the lights."

"If Georgia wants it there, Sebastian needs to go negotiate. It should be what she wants," Ava stresses.

"No. I don't want him overpaying for something," I insist again.

"But it's perfect," Paisley whines.

"You'd love it," Willow adds.

"You seriously don't need to worry about the money," Evelyn claims.

"I don't want Sebastian..." Suddenly, the idea comes to me. I inquire, "Why can't we just have it here on the ranch?"

Everyone exchanges glances.

Sebastian states, "I think that's a great idea."

"You do?"

He nods. "Yeah, actually, it's perfect."

Ruby excitedly claims, "I've always wanted a wedding here."

Paisley notes, "Sebastian, do you remember when you were engaged to Molly, and you wanted your wedding here? She was appalled by the idea."

"She's such a snob, especially when she grew up here," Evelyn remarks.

Sebastian shoots them dirty looks, asking, "Can you two shut up, please?"

"Whatever." Paisley smirks.

Evelyn rolls her eyes, muttering, "Always so sensitive."

Sebastian rises and then leans over me. My heart beats faster, and my pulse creeps up. His intoxicating signature scent flares around me, making me slightly dizzy. He pins his blues to mine and questions, "Is that what you want? To get married here?"

My insides quiver as tingles move faster through my cells. I nod. "Yes. That sounds perfect."

Satisfaction washes over his expression. He gives me a chaste kiss, smiles, and offers, "Well, whatever you want, you can have, Sunshine. I'll show you the spot I think you'll like, later this afternoon." He winks, lingering a bit and keeping his intense gaze on mine.

Paisley clears her throat really loudly, pulling us out of our heated stare.

Sebastian stands straight, announcing, "I'll leave the rest of it to you ladies. I better go help my brothers."

He refocuses on me, drags his eyes over my body, then licks his lips.

My insides turn to lava, ready to boil over.

Right when I think I can't take his gaze anymore, he squeezes my shoulder and leaves.

Oh my gosh.

How does he do that?

Does he know what he's doing to me?

Of course he does. He does it on purpose.

His sisters and mom go into more details about the wedding and pull up pictures of decorations and other wedding ideas on the internet.

I barely hear them, having a hard time thinking about anything but Sebastian. I agree to things I don't even care about but that seem important to them. And the longer it goes on, the more nervous I become.

This is happening.

Six days and I'll be Mrs. Sebastian Cartwright.

Not even for a month, I remind myself, and I'm surprised by the disappointment filling me. It mixes with excitement, which I also reprimand myself for.

No matter how much I tell myself this isn't real, I can't help but feel like it is. I'm doing everything I can to not get swept up in it, but I don't think anything's ever been harder for me. Plus, I have to appear excited. After all, I am the bride, fake or real.

It's not real.

Ava slings her arm around me and confesses, "You're the type of girl I always saw Sebastian with."

I furrow my eyebrows. "What do you mean?" I quietly ask, unsure if it's a compliment or if I should be insulted.

She smiles. "Don't worry, I meant it in a good way."

I exhale in relief.

She continues, "You're real. Plus, I can tell you love my brother. And he loves you differently than those horrible women he was with before."

I open my mouth, but nothing comes out.

Evelyn interjects, "What Ava is trying to tell you is that Sebastian always brought home the wrong women. He finally picked the right one. And we're thrilled you're joining our family."

I blink hard, fighting so many feelings I wish I could make disappear, including the guilt and shame of what Sebastian and I are doing.

This is wrong. The Cartwrights are everything I could ever hope for in a family. They've welcomed me with open arms. I always assumed whoever I married would have a family that would be as kind as they are, so I already know it'll be hard to leave them behind. But we're also lying to them.

Ruby pulls me out of my thoughts, declaring, "There's one more thing that we have to take care of, and we're going to have to do it first thing tomorrow."

"What's that?" I ask.

She smiles brightly. "We've got to go wedding dress shopping."

Fourteen

SEBASTIAN

Mason jumps off the Thoroughbred he named Dynamite. He opens the gate and joins my other brothers and me, declaring, "I think he's ready."

"Looks like it," I agree. I've spent the morning with my brothers, watching Jagger and Mason train their new horses. I've tried to get Georgia off my mind, but I can't.

I keep thinking about how she made me pancakes so delicious, I'd happily eat them every morning. After last night, it surprised me she'd do anything nice for me, especially something that's above and beyond.

Mason secures the gate. "Dynamite's going to win. I can feel it."

I stare at the horse, wondering for the millionth time this morning if Georgia has ever ridden.

I bet she knows how. She seems to know how to do everything.

If she doesn't, I could show her.

I'll bring her down here. Make it into a date.

A date?

What am I thinking?

My father arrives with Wilder and Ace. He booms, "Boys, time to cut the tree down."

Jagger mutters, "Oh, what fun."

Mason adds, "Yippee."

Cutting the tree down is always a project. It depends on what my mother's chosen for the year. Some years, we have it easy. Other years, not so much.

I ask, "Where's Jacob, Jr.?" It seems like if the men are going, he should also get to experience it.

My dad looks at me in disapproval, claiming, "Three-year-olds don't belong in the tree field. It's too dangerous."

"God help your children when you and Georgia have them," Alexander claims.

Images of a slew of blond-haired, blue-eyed, happy kids next to a very pregnant, beaming Georgia fill my mind.

Maybe that's what I should do. Keep her barefoot and pregnant.

Jesus. I need to get a grip.

It's a colder day, so I grab one of the flannel Carhartts from the barn, knowing that the wind will be even harsher out where we're going. We get in the truck, and my brothers and I jump in the back cab with the kids. It takes about five minutes to get to the large field where my father planted Scottish Pines.

It's my mother's favorite type of Christmas tree. For their tenth wedding anniversary, he decided to create a whole field for her. They have a date night every year before Thanksgiving and come out here. She picks which tree she wants him to cut down, then it's our job to do it. We never know how big or small it will be. My mom keeps us on our toes.

The scent of pine whips through the air, and my father points to the biggest tree in the field. "That's the one, boys."

My brothers and I grumble obscenities. The tree's at least fifteen feet tall. It'll look amazing in our family room, which has a twenty-five-foot vaulted ceiling. The tree also has a full body, and it's hard to see any space through the limbs and needles.

Mason mutters, "That's going to take forever to decorate."

Jagger groans. "Guess we're clearing our schedules the rest of the day."

My father gives them dirty looks. "This is our Christmas tradition. Stop complaining. What are you teaching the boys?"

My brothers glance at our nephews. One thing my parents are serious about is their Christmas traditions. That and the family being together.

I used to believe it was more my mom, but the older they get, the more I think my father loves it just as much as she does.

I order, "Day's not getting any younger. Let's get this down."

My brothers and I start to unload the chainsaw and an ax. We pull the tarp out and put it where we plan on dropping the tree.

Alexander takes the chainsaw, and we all step back.

My father asks, "What are you getting your bride for Christmas?"

My stomach flips. Anxiety fills me. I didn't think about it.

What would Georgia want for Christmas?

I shrug, confessing, "I don't know. I haven't thought that far."

My father's eyes turn to slits. He disapprovingly states, "This is your wife's first Christmas with you, and you don't know what you're getting her?"

"I'll figure it out," I claim.

He shakes his head and says, "Son, you've got a lot to learn."

I ignore him and pretend I don't care.

But I do. As much as I don't want to, I now care about what I'm getting the woman I plan on marrying in less than a week and divorcing shortly after Christmas.

How did I get this so fucked-up?

Christmas gifts were never hard before this year. Anyone I dated always made it clear what they expected. All I had to do was tell my assistant to get it, and it would appear on my desk already wrapped.

Why didn't I think about this before I left Dallas?

I sort through all the expensive gifts I've gotten my girlfriends in the past. Brand-name perfume, hard-to-get jewelry, luxurious trips, designer purses, clothes, and shoes all fill my mind.

Nothing is good enough for Georgia. I continue to rack my brain, growing antsier and antsier, wondering what she'd appreciate.

Why do I even care?

It's just for show for my family.

This really isn't a big deal.

Yet the nagging voice in my head tells me that it is and I shouldn't mess this up. Plus, I've never done anything half-assed, so the last thing I want to do is disappoint her on Christmas, especially after her reaction to the ring.

I wince inside, still having a difficult time believing I got it so wrong. She tried to hide it, but I could see she despised the ring I chose.

It burns me that she hates it. Not because I love the ring, but because I didn't put the effort in to pick the right one. I went into the jeweler and pointed to the biggest one in the case, figuring she was just like my other fiancées.

She's not them.

It's only until January 2nd. She can do whatever she wants with the ring afterward.

Hell, it's worth a lot of money. She'll be happy I gave it to her when she goes and sells it.

Even that statement feels off. The more I get to know Georgia, especially after our conversation with my sisters and mom this morning, the more I get the impression she isn't all about money.

Then why did she negotiate a million dollars?

She wanted three!

The longer the debate about Georgia goes on in my head, the more confused I become.

"Timber!" the boys yell, tearing me out of my thoughts.

The pine drops to the ground on the tarp, which isn't surprising since Alexander is a pro at cutting down trees. Still, we all cheer.

We secure it on the tarp and tie it to the back of the truck. All of us hop back in the vehicle, and when we get back to the house, we drag it to the front steps.

Then the real work starts. It takes about an hour to move it inside the house and secure it on the tree stand. And even though it's a pain in the butt, I have to admit it makes it feel like Christmas.

Plus, all my nieces and nephews are running around and shrieking with excitement.

But the thing I notice the most is Georgia beaming. And that funny feeling in my gut sparks again.

I go over to her and kiss her since I know I can get as many as I want when my family's around. I ask, "Did you miss me?"

She looks flustered but recovers, stating, "Nope!"

"Ouch," I declare, pounding my heart.

She laughs and points to the stuff I tossed onto the chair, inquiring, "Since when do you wear cowboy hats?"

"When I'm here. Why? Does it get you riled up?" I tease.

She doesn't answer, just bats her eyes and smiles.

Is she flirting with me?

No.

She picks up the Carhartt flannel. "This makes you look kind of rugged."

Yes! She's flirting with me.

Why am I even wondering this?

My stomach flips some more, and my chest tightens. I try to think what to say to flirt back, but I'm suddenly speechless.

What is it about this woman that keeps making me forget how to speak?

I regain my cockiness and tug her closer to me, trying to ignore my growing erection. I lower my voice and suggest, "Is this what you're into? Do I need to dress down for you?"

Her eyes light up, and her face flushes. She claims, "I didn't say that."

"You didn't have to, Sunshine," I arrogantly state, then stare at her lips again until her cheeks turn the color of a tomato.

She pushes her hand against my pecs, and I secure my arm around her.

Then I invoke my PDA rights, palming her ass cheeks and leaning into her ear, murmuring, "Why don't you admit you think I'm cute?"

She laughs and whispers, "Do you ever get sick of being so full of yourself?"

Jesus. I don't think I've ever wanted to have sex with anyone so badly before.

I lower my voice even more and claim, "I'm pretty sure if you had let me lick your sweet pussy last night, you would have had no problems afterward seeing what it's like to be full of me." I retreat and pin my gaze on hers.

Her bottom lip trembles slightly. She takes a short breath, then clears her throat, announcing, "Why yes, Sebastian! I'd love to see you let the girls put makeup on you tonight!"

"What? Yes!" Isabella screams, grabs Sebastian's hand, and jumps up and down.

Once again, I'm speechless. Maybe I should be mad, since there's no way Isabella will let me out of this without me being the bad uncle, but I start to chuckle. I warn Georgia, "I think you messed with the wrong Cartwright."

She smirks.

"Sebastian, help with the lights," Dad orders.

I tear my gaze off my little peach and grab a string of lights.

Everyone stands around the tree, and my mom chirps, "I knew it'd be perfect when I saw it."

I glance at her. "You pick the biggest one."

"I know. I've been waiting for years for this tree," she claims.

"It's really pretty," Georgia says, staring at it like she's never seen a Christmas tree before.

Why does everything seem so special to her?

Is it real excitement?

I continue to stare at her until she catches me. I hand her the plastic reel, stating, "Let's start stringing, Sunshine."

We work for a few hours decorating the tree. Georgia and I continue to go back and forth, and we're both constantly laughing.

There are five ladders. Most of the time, my brothers and I are up there. Sometimes we let the kids go up. When it comes time to put the star on the tree, I hold it out to Georgia. I announce, "You get to put it on."

She glances up at the tree, her eyes wide and expression filled with fear. She replies, "That's okay. Someone else can do it."

"No, you have to do it. You're new to the family," I declare.

She assesses the tree again, and the color drains from her cheeks.

I ask, "What's wrong?"

She swallows hard. "I can't do it, Sebastian. I'm scared of heights."

I jerk my head back, shocked. How is she afraid of anything? She always seems so fearless. I taunt, "Well, that's kind of negative."

She scrunches her face. Her eyes dart between me and the top of the tree.

I continue, "This is something you need to overcome."

"Sebastian, I'm not getting on that ladder."

I put my arm around her waist and lead her toward the ladder, holding the star. "Come on. I'll do it with you."

"I can't," she claims.

"I'll make sure you don't fall. Just don't look down."

"Sebastian, no. I can't."

"Come on," I goad, tugging her into me. "It's not that tall."

She glances behind her, looking up at me, her mouth in an O.

"Since when do you chicken out?" I challenge.

She furrows her eyebrows.

"I'll be right behind you. Promise."

She takes a deep breath, then gives in. "Fine. I'll do it." She grabs the star and moves toward the ladder.

I step behind her. "Guys, make sure it doesn't wobble."

Mason holds one side of the ladder and Jagger the other.

I pat Georgia's ass. "Time's ticking."

She gazes up with determination, then climbs a few rungs. She freezes, fretting, "I don't think I can do this."

I step behind her on the first rung. "Sure you can. Don't look down. Just look at the goal. Top of the tree," I tell her, then pat her ass again.

She jumps slightly. "Sebastian."

I chuckle, teasing, "If you're going to stand there, you can't just expect me to look at it and not touch it."

"Sebastian," my mom scolds.

My brothers chuckle.

Georgia shakes her head and continues climbing, slowly making her way to the top.

When she gets there, I make sure my frame is tight behind hers. I instruct, "All you have to do is reach up and put it on there."

"But then I'd have to let go of the ladder," she worries.

"Yep. That's how it's done."

She winces, making a mistake by glancing down. She freaks. "Oh gosh. Oh gosh. Oh gosh. I'm going to fall!"

I tilt her chin back up. "No, you're not." I put my hand over hers with the star and move it toward the top of the tree, adding, "Almost done."

She takes another deep breath and then moves her other hand to the star, securing it tightly.

"There. You did it," I praise.

My family claps.

She laughs, but nervousness still coats her expression. "Okay. Can I get down now?"

"Sure. But the same rules apply. Don't look down," I order.

We slowly make it to the floor, one rung at a time.

She beams when we step away from the ladder, gazing up and declaring, "I did it!"

"Yes, you did," I say and then point up at the perfectly straight star.

"Point for me," she declares, and everyone laughs.

I lean closer to her, studying her face until she shifts on her feet. I inquire, "Are you ready to get out of here?"

She arches her eyebrows. "Where are we going?"

My chest tightens. "I need to show you where I think we should get married."

There's the perfect spot on the ranch. When I first proposed to Molly, I wanted to marry her there, but it wasn't ritzy enough for her. She wasn't going to do anything that didn't require lots of money. I never even brought it up to the other three.

Georgia is nothing like them.

She'll love it.

What if she doesn't?

Why do I even care? I ask myself for the millionth time today.

"Sure," she replies.

I guide her to the front hall, pull out her coat, and help her in it. Then I grab her hand and steer her through the yard.

"Where are we going?" she asks.

"It's about a ten-minute walk. Figured you'd be up for it."

"That's fine," she answers.

We stroll across my parents' land, and I point out the horses, questioning, "Do you know how to ride?"

"I've only done it a few times. I wouldn't say I know how to ride well."

"You want to learn while we're here? I'll teach you," I offer.

She glances at the horses and back at me. "Okay. Can you make sure I don't fall?"

I chuckle. "Don't tell me you're scared of horses too?"

"No, not really. But I want to make sure I know what I'm doing."

"Don't worry, Sunshine. I'll make sure you're safe," I tell her, then squeeze her hand.

We stay quiet the rest of the way and approach the brick building Dad uses as his office.

"Is that it?" she asks.

"Kind of," I state.

She arches her eyebrows.

I lead her around the border of thick hedges that are taller than me and up to a pink, arched door. I instruct, "Go ahead and open it."

She tilts her head. "What's inside?"

I wiggle my eyebrows. "It's a secret. You have to open the door."

She bites on her lip, then turns the knob. She steps inside and freezes.

Bright fall flowers in full bloom burst with color. Ivy climbs up the back of the brick office. Green grass fills the lawn. Cedar beams in a crisscross pattern support a glass ceiling that covers most of the secret garden.

I study her as she glances around, taking everything in. Her jaw drops toward the ground as she processes the area.

My nerves flutter again. "What do you think?"

She tears her eyes off the thick hedges and says, "Sebastian, this is incredible."

Relief fills me. I smile, nostalgically remembering all the years I played here with my siblings. I point to the ivy, suggesting, "That could be the backdrop for when we have our ceremony."

Georgia nods. "It's perfect."

I point toward the sky. "My mom didn't want it completely enclosed. She said fresh air was good, but she also wanted to be able to be here when it rained. Plus, she wanted us to have a spot to play outside during those times."

"It's gorgeous. Those beams are beautiful," she declares.

"Don't worry though. Dad had pieces created for the winter when it's colder. We can have those inserted so it closes the space and isn't freezing. Plus, we'll add heaters. And I'll have the glass cleaned so it's spotless."

"I'm not worried," she claims and continues to look at everything in awe. Then she asks, "Why did your family even suggest other places when you have this?"

My stomach churns. I admit, "Because my other fiancées wouldn't have ever agreed to get married here."

Georgia's eyes widen. "Why wouldn't they?"

I blurt out, "Because they're nothing like you, Sunshine."

She stares at me, and my heart feels funny again.

I'm falling for this girl.

No, I am not falling for her.

This is over on January 2nd. That's the deal. None of this is real.

She cautiously asks, "How am I not like the others?"

I opened Pandora's box, so now I've got to deal with it. Somehow telling her not to worry about it doesn't seem like it'll fly. So I step closer, place both hands on her cheeks, run my thumb over her chin, and confess, "They only cared about material things...about my money."

She takes short breaths, making my cock ache more. But her expression makes me think I made her uncomfortable, so I claim, "Sorry, we shouldn't talk about this."

"They didn't deserve you," she blurts out, then her cheeks heat under my palms.

Her statement affects me. I wish it didn't. I don't know what's happening to me. I don't normally let women get under my skin after everything I've been through. My pulse buzzes through my veins.

We say nothing for a while, just stand here staring at each other.

I finally step back and question, "So this is okay? You'd be happy to marry me here?"

She smiles. "Yeah, I would. It's perfect. Way better than anything I could ever imagine."

"What have you imagined?"

She shrugs. "I never really had a vision about a place when I thought about marriage. I just imagined the guy."

My pulse quickens. I dare to question, "And what about that guy? What's he like?" I step closer to her again, inhaling her sugary-rose scent.

She ponders my question but doesn't flinch. She finally answers, "He loves and adores me. And I love and adore him."

Flutters fill my stomach. "And?"

"And what more is there?" she questions.

"You never thought about anything else? What your ring looks like? What kind of food you'll serve your guests? The dress you'll wear? What he does for a living?" I interrogate.

She shakes her head and lifts her chin. "No, none of that matters."

"How does it not matter?" I quiz, wondering how she could mean that.

Doesn't every girl think about those things?

Is she telling the truth?

Is this a game to somehow trick me as the others did? Or does she really feel this way?

Something tells me that this is her. That there's nothing false about Georgia and that she doesn't lie.

She's lying to my family.

But I made her lie to my family.

"If you have that, nothing else matters, Sebastian," she claims.

I try to process what she's saying and deal with unfamiliar emotions growing more intense by the minute.

She looks around again and nods. "This will be perfect."

"So it can be your dream wedding, then," I joke.

Her face falls. She asserts, "No, Sebastian, it won't."

"What do you need, then?" I question, confused. Everything in my head screams that I need to make it into everything she's ever wanted.

"This is fine for us," she claims.

I can't help it any longer or stop myself. I close the distance between us and kiss her. Then continue kissing her until she's digging her fingers into my skull. Her body molds to mine, and all I can think is that she has to want me.

I murmur, "Don't worry, Sunshine. I'll give you your dream wedding."

She pulls back and then says, "No, you won't."

"Sure I will," I arrogantly claim.

She shakes her head. "You don't listen. My dream wedding will be with someone who adores me. Someone who loves me. And when I'm not under any false pretenses. I know you're not capable of those things."

My gut dives, and what she says sinks in. I want to deny it, but I blatantly told her I didn't believe in love, last night.

Do I?

No, I don't.

Maybe it would be different with her?

That's what I thought all the other times.

For the first time in my life, it hits me that I'm looking at a woman who isn't ever going to let me have her.

And it's my own damn fault.

Fifteen

GEORGIA

We return to the house, and Sebastian's quiet most of the night. When it's finally time for everyone to sleep, I go into the bedroom, get ready in the bathroom, and crawl into bed.

He joins me, but unlike the night before, he doesn't try anything. At four in the morning, I hear him get up, and I see the faint outline of him in his exercise clothes as he leaves.

I doze off until I hear the door creak again. I keep my eyes shut, hear him in the shower, and assume that he's going to leave, but he doesn't. He slides back into bed and scoots closer to me until his body is flush with mine. He secures his arm around my waist and takes a deep breath as if he's trying to inhale me.

My heart beats faster, and my pulse races. I don't move, keeping my eyes shut. I should tell him to return to his side of the bed, but I don't. Sebastian's body around mine feels right, yet I know it's wrong.

I'll elbow him if he tries any funny stuff.

Surprisingly, he doesn't try anything. Within a few minutes, his breathing pattern slows, and I realize he's sleeping.

When the clock hits six a.m., I gently pry myself out of his arms and sneak out of bed. I go into the bathroom, shower, and change. Then I prepare myself to tiptoe through the bedroom. I open the door and run right into him. I blurt out, "Oh, sorry."

He drags his eyes over my body, stating, "Morning, Sunshine."

Tingles pop up all over my skin. I reply, "Good morning. Did you sleep okay?"

"Eventually," he answers, drilling his blues into mine.

We stare at each other in awkward silence. Ever since we went to the secret garden, things have been off between us. It's as if he took my statement about how there's no way he could ever give me my dream wedding personally. I didn't mean to hurt his feelings, but he wanted honesty.

Anyway, I'm not sure what Sebastian wants from me. He's the one who wanted the fake bride and to annul the marriage on January 2nd. Yet my statement seemed to upset him.

I can't deny it also upset me. Part of me regrets agreeing to this. I'm trying to keep the end goal in sight, but the more time I spend with Sebastian, the more complicated things seem to become. And I'm starting to think we're both confused, yet he's Sebastian Cartwright. I doubt he's ever not one hundred percent sure about every situation he's in.

He finally orders, "Don't make any plans tonight."

I arch my eyebrows. "Why? What are we doing?"

He hesitates, but then declares, "I'm taking you on a date, Sunshine."

My dimples turn into intense sting. Then I remind myself that it's not a real date. We're fake. So I reply, "That's not necessary."

His face flashes a moment of hurt before he hardens it. He claims, "My family would expect me to take you on a date."

I take a deep breath and square my shoulders, nodding. "All right. What time?"

"Five work for you?"

"Sure."

He doesn't move, and more time passes. He continues staring at me as if he wants to say something.

His intoxicating scent grows stronger, teasing my senses until I shift on my feet. I ask, "Is there something else?"

He opens his mouth, then snaps it shut. He slowly shakes his head, then steps back.

What is that all about?

I step past him, leave the bedroom, and relief floods me. Staying away from Sebastian might be the only way I'll survive this month.

If only I wasn't attracted to him.

I'm not a dumb woman. I realize there's no future with him. Yet I never expected it to be this hard. The more I get to know him, the more I like him. Well, except for when he infuriates me.

I walk down the hall and into the kitchen. Ruby's making breakfast, so I jump in and help. Soon, the entire family is seated in the dining room, eating.

Sebastian sits next to me, and the uncomfortable tension continues. I'm sure no one else notices it, but I can't shake it. In some ways, I feel like he's on his best behavior. Part of me is relieved.

The other part wants to beg him to return to his normal grumpy, arrogant self so I know what to expect. Because this Sebastian Cartwright is throwing me off. I'm unsure what to make of him.

As soon as breakfast is finished, Ruby declares, "We need to leave. The wedding boutique will be opening soon."

Sebastian takes advantage of our PDA clause, kissing me several times until my body is on fire.

"Okay, you're going to have to let her out of your sight for a bit," Ruby teases.

He only uses her statement to study me, making me squirm. He finally squeezes my ass, murmuring, "Have fun."

"Thanks," I manage and struggle not to run from him.

Sebastian's sisters, mom, nieces, and I split up into two SUVs. We drive into town where the shops are.

The entire way, my nerves skyrocket. All the chatter in the car about wedding details means we're closer to making our fake marriage official. It only makes the guilt around what Sebastian and I are doing grow stronger. Plus, I can't get his kisses off my mind.

The more I get to know the Cartwrights, the worse it seems that we're tricking them. But I signed a contract and agreed to this. The last thing I need to be is in breach with Sebastian. I'm pretty sure he'd sue me for everything I have—not that I have anything. Still, I don't need to be in a legal mess.

Evelyn veers into a parking spot in front of a wedding boutique. She claims, "This is the best one in town."

I force a smile, feigning my excitement, wondering again how I got myself into this. I declare, "The dresses in the window look beautiful."

We all get out and go into the store. I glance around and freeze. The most beautiful gown I've ever seen is draped artfully on a mannequin. It's white with an A-line skirt. It's not puffy like a princess dress with tons of tulle, but it still has some flowy girth.

It's sleeveless, has a heart-shaped bodice, and the back dips to the hip level. A satin underlay has an outer layer over it. Delicate lace flowers are scattered across it, and 3D petals give it a textured appearance. I reach out and touch one of them, surprised by the soft material.

The saleslady clears her throat, then I hear, "Well, if it isn't the Cartwrights."

"Sally, great to see you," Ruby states, and all the women exchange greetings.

"I heard Sebastian had a new fiancée in town," she says with a bit of haughtiness in her voice, as if I'm not even there.

Anger flares inside me like gasoline pouring over a match. Sebastian's past relationships sound horrible, and the women he was with clearly hurt him. If this is what he has to deal with when he comes to town, then I can't blame him for bringing me home. I'm about to say something but don't have to.

Ruby's voice turns sharp. She slides her arm around my shoulders and declares, "This is my soon-to-be daughter-in-law, Georgia. We'll be trying on dresses, so let's keep your gossip inside your head and the spoken comments about lace and tulle."

Sally's cheeks heat. She forces a smile and replies, "Yes, of course. I didn't mean to offend anyone."

Ruby lifts her chin higher, tightening her embrace around me.

Sally changes the subject, informing us, "We just got that dress yesterday. Isn't it divine?"

Trying to ignore her previous comment, I nod. This dress is everything I would ever want for my wedding dress.

What's going to happen when I actually get married for real? I can't wear this again.

There won't be a dress better than this.

I should pick something average.

"You have to try it on, Georgia!" Isabella exclaims and points to the child mannequin next to it. "Emma and I can wear those!"

"Isabella! This is Georgia's choice," Evelyn scolds.

"But, Mom! It's so pretty!" she states.

"Yes, but it's not your decision," Evelyn reprimands further.

Unable to disappoint Isabella, I cave. I reply, "Can I try this on?"

"Yes!" Isabella shouts and jumps up and down, tossing her arms around me.

I laugh, hugging her.

Sally replies, "Yes, right this way." She leads me to a rack, pulls three dresses, and shows me to the dressing room. She puts two dresses on a rack outside the dressing room and one inside it. She points to it. "I think that's your size, but just in case you need a different one, and I got it wrong, here's the next size up and down."

"Thank you," I reply.

"Do you need me to help you get it on?"

The last thing I want is Sally telling the entire town what I look like in my undergarments.

She's probably seen all of Sebastian's other fiancées.

I can hear her comparing me now.

I firmly assert, "I can handle it myself."

She gives me a disapproving look, exits, and I sit down on the bench, staring at the dress.

What am I doing?

Evelyn's voice hits my ears. "Who are the bridesmaids? Georgia needs dresses for them too."

I place my hands over my face and cringe. Sebastian and I have done a horrible job discussing the details of this shindig.

I'll just have all of his sisters.

Sebastian said he only wanted his family and a few friends. I can't have the entire family up there if it's only a small wedding, can I?

I continue to fret, then grab my phone out of my purse. I text Sebastian.

Me: *What are we doing about a wedding party? Evelyn's asking questions about the bridesmaids, and I'm in the dressing room. She'll ask me when I get out, and I don't know what to say.*

Sebastian: *Just pick somebody. I'll have my brother Alexander be the best man.*

Me: *Who should I pick? You have four sisters.*

Sebastian: *It doesn't matter. Just pick one.*

Me: *That's going to be hard. I don't want to offend anyone.*

Sebastian: *Why don't you invite one of your friends?*

I think about Melanie. I would love for her to be here, even if this is fake, but that brings up an entirely different issue.

Me: *I can't exactly tell my friend I'm getting married but it's fake.*

Sebastian: *Can she keep her mouth shut?*

Me: *Confidentiality clause.*

Moments pass. He finally replies.

Sebastian: *Just tell her in January that you made a mistake and we got it annulled.*

I don't respond, debating if I really want Melanie to be a part of this. If I don't, she'll never know what I've done.

He sends another text.

Sebastian: *Don't overthink this. It'll be good for you to have a friend here. Just invite her.*

Me: *She has a husband, a four-year-old son, and a two-year-old daughter.*

Sebastian: *So? Invite them. There's plenty of room. Plus, it looks odd you have zero friends in attendance.*

The debate continues in my head until I decide he's right. Plus, I've never wanted to see my friend so badly before. So I text her.

Me: *Hey, girl. I can't talk right now because I'm picking out my wedding dress with Sebastian's family, but we're getting married on Saturday. Can you guys come? I want you to be my maid of honor.*

The phone rings. I send it to voicemail. I text again.

Me: *I can't talk at the moment.*

Melanie: *Are you pulling my chain?*

Me: *No.*

Melanie: *What is going on, Georgia?*

I lie, adding the overwhelming guilt I can't shake.

Me: *I'll tell you all about it later, I promise.*

Melanie: *You don't even know him. How can you be getting married?*

Me: *I know it seems weird, but it's fine. Can you all attend the wedding? You can come sooner rather than later, and we can hang out. There's plenty of room for you and your entire family to stay.*

Melanie: *Of course we'll come.*

I blink back tears, not realizing how much I need my friend.

Me: *Great. Send me your size so I can pick out your bridesmaid gown.*

Melanie: *Georgia, are you being serious right now?*

I toss out more untruths.

Me: *Yes, I promise. Everything's good though. I'm happy.*

Another moment goes by.

Melanie: *You need to call me as soon as you can.*

Me: *I will, but it might not be until tomorrow. There's a whole day of things going on. Picking out your bridesmaid dress now. Talk to you later. Bye.*

I get another message.

Melanie: *Georgia!*

I don't respond and stick the phone back in my purse. I step into the dress, and because of how low the back is, I can zip it myself. I stand in the mirror, assessing myself, blinking back more tears.

My grammy would've loved this dress. She would be crying, and I would be crying.

This dress is made for somebody who actually loves me.

I need to stop thinking like this. I signed a contract.

There's a knock on the door. Sally chirps, "Georgia, do you need help?"

I call out, "No," and then I open the door.

"Oh, sweet Jesus," Ruby chirps, throwing her hand over her mouth.

"Dang, girl," Paisley says.

Ava just nods with a big smile on her face.

Evelyn points at me. "That's definitely your dress."

Emma and Isabella clap.

Willow steps behind me, then holds out the train. "Wow. Georgia, this is amazing. Sebastian's going to go nuts with you in this."

My stomach flutters burst to life again. I curse them, wishing they didn't react so much over him.

"I have some other dresses for you to try on," Sally states.

I lift my chin and pin my gaze on her. "No, I don't need to try anything else on. This is it."

"Are you sure?" she asks.

"Yes."

"Okay. Let's go look at shoes," she directs.

I follow her to another part of the store, where there are shoes worth more than my entire month's paycheck. I've never had any designer shoes, and I blurt out, "These are really expensive!"

Ruby chuckles. "Don't worry about it, dear. Everything's on me."

I gape at her. "No, this is too much."

She gives me her no-nonsense expression. It reminds me of Sebastian's. She declares, "I insist."

Deciding I won't win, I say, "Thank you." The guilt over tricking Sebastian's family increases. I look at all the shoes and point to one that stands out.

It's a beautiful white shoe with a glamorous, tall half-moon heel. There's a single wide strap over the toes and a mix of floral crystals that twinkle and circle around the ankle. It's complete with a tied blue ribbon.

"Perfect. You've got your something blue," Willow proclaims.

I try on the shoes, and I have to admit that they're amazing. I declare, "Okay, I'll take these."

"You're a really easy bride," Sally comments.

I shrug. "I guess when you know, you know."

She lowers her voice and wiggles her eyebrows. "Kind of like when you first laid eyes on Sebastian?"

Her attempt to find out details about Sebastian and me only irritates me. I smile at her and stay quiet.

She takes the hint and adds, "Everything's beautiful. You picked right."

I go into the dressing room, take off the dress, and put my clothes on. I carry it to the checkout counter, and Sally takes it from me.

She notes, "I think you're the first bride to come in here who doesn't need any alterations."

How can everything fall into place so perfectly when it's not real? I ask myself, but there is no answer.

"What about the bridesmaid dresses?" Evelyn questions.

I force another smile. "I need one for my best friend, Melanie. She'll be here later in the week."

"When will she arrive?" Ruby asks.

"She needs to figure it out with her husband. She has two children. Sebastian said it was fine for them to stay at the ranch. Is that okay?"

"Of course. Our home is now yours. Any friend you want can stay with us," Ruby states.

I blink hard. This is all too much. How can the Cartwrights be this nice and welcoming to me when I'm a total stranger?

"What color are you thinking for the bridesmaid dress?" Sally asks.

I try to push my anxiety out of my head and go straight to a chocolate-brown satin dress that catches my eye. I hold it up, looking it over. I decide it's perfect, then find one in Melanie's size. I turn to Isabella. "Did you pick out your flower girl dress?"

Her face lights up, and she runs to the rack with the matching dresses. Evelyn joins her and pulls two off it.

Ruby pays for everything, and we eat lunch in town. When we return to the ranch, it's early afternoon. Sebastian sends me a text almost the moment I get through the door.

Sebastian: *Are you back?*

Me: *Do you have ESP?*

Sebastian: *Maybe where you're concerned.*

My heart skips a beat.

Me: *Did you need something?*

Sebastian: *Don't forget about our date tonight.*

My chest tightens. I struggle to fight the excitement forming in my belly.

Me: *I'm going to take a shower. What should I wear?*

Sebastian: *It's on the bed.*

Me: *What is?*

Sebastian: *I got you a gift.*

I cringe. Knowing Sebastian, he got me something over the top that won't feel like me. I glance at my ring and wish I could appreciate it.

Me: *Thanks.*

Sebastian: *You don't know what it is yet.*

I stroll into the bedroom and freeze. There are several boxes on the bed.

Totally Sebastian-style.

I prepare myself for something super expensive, out of my comfort zone, and flashy.

Slowly, I open the first box, then stare at the contents in awe. Brown suede cowgirl boots with several shades of blue and turquoise running through them, along with little streaks of orange. They're the most beautiful boots I've ever seen. I've only imagined having boots like this. I try them on, and they fit perfectly.

I remove the boots and open another package. A pair of dark designer skinny jeans, a brown leather belt with a hammered gold abstract design on the buckle, and a form-fitting white V-neck shirt are inside. I place them on the bed with the boots over the bottom of the jeans.

What else could he have possibly got me?

I carefully open the last box. It has a fuzzy-textured, trim-knit cardigan shawl. There's a heart pattern and a matching fur collar. It's blue but has a tad of brown running through it.

Still in awe, I stare at everything on the bed.

My phone dings with another text.

Sebastian: *Did I get it right this time?*

My gut continues to flutter. I glance at everything once again, then answer.

Me: *Yes, everything is perfect.*

Sixteen

SEBASTIAN

There were so many people in the house that I worked most of the day in my father's office. Well, that was the plan.

I kept staring out the window into the garden, imagining what Georgia will look like in her dress. Then I became obsessed with finding her an outfit she'd love for tonight. I scoured the online sites of the boutiques in town, debating about what to get her. I finally narrowed it down, called my order in, went and picked everything up, then returned to the office.

I still can't concentrate on the merger I need to close in the next few weeks. Every time I look at something I need to review or figure out, Georgia's smile pops up in my mind.

I glance at my watch. It's four thirty, so I give up. I go to the house and into our bedroom, expecting to find Georgia, but she isn't there. Disappointment fills me, but I jump in the shower to get ready for our date.

When I'm ready, I text her.

Me: *Where are you, Sunshine?*

Georgia: *I'm in the library playing board games with the girls.*

The warm feeling in my stomach grows. It happens whenever I'm around Georgia, and I can't seem to shake it.

I knew she'd fit in well with my family. Everybody adores her differently than I anticipated. It's not that my family didn't get along with my other fiancées, but something is different with Georgia. I can't put my finger on it, but there's no denying it.

Yet it isn't just my family who loves her. She genuinely seems to care about my family too.

My family will kill me once they find out I'm no longer with her.

My stomach flips for the hundredth time today. A voice in my head says I shouldn't be doing what I'm doing, but I don't know how to get out of this.

It's not like Georgia doesn't know what's going on.

She agreed to it.

She negotiated like a rock star.

Pride mixes with distrust whenever I think about how she got me to agree to a million dollars.

She's going to hate me when this is over.

I should stop this before it goes any further.

I stare at myself in the mirror, telling myself to push all these feelings away. I've made my own bed. Now I have to sleep in it.

I make my way through the house and get to the library. My heart stammers when I see Georgia. She's wearing all the new items I got her, and she looks more gorgeous in them than I could have ever imagined. I give myself a high five for finally getting something right. And it's another thing

that my exes wouldn't have gone for—it's just too country
ish.

Except for Molly.

She would've worn some of it if I added something with bling to
it, like a diamond-studded buckle or piece of new jewelry. But I'm
learning that's not Georgia. She doesn't like flashy. But I already
know she'll still be the one everybody stares at in the room. Not
only because she's new in town and with me, but because it's her.
She lights up every room she steps into. No one can outshine her.

"No!" she declares as her smile grows.

"I win!" Emma cries out.

"Ugh!" Isabella groans.

My stomach flips faster and faster, and I question again why I feel
so nervous. It's not like I've not been on dates before.

This isn't a real date.

It's just to fool my family.

Is it?

Yes. Stay the course.

It'll be good for us to get off this ranch for a night.

She really is beautiful.

It doesn't matter. Stop confusing things, I reprimand myself.

I interrupt, "Are you ready to go?"

She glances at me, and my heart misses a beat. Then she holds out
her two fingers. "Two seconds. Let me help the girls clean up."

I blurt out, "Where's your ring?" My pulse creeps higher.

She freezes, then checks out her finger. Her cheeks grow red. She winces. "Sorry. I forgot it. Let me go get it." She rises.

My chest tightens again.

How did I get it so wrong?

She hates the ring. She won't come right out and say it, but I know she does.

Georgia tells the girls, "You gals clean up while I get my ring. Okay?"

"All right," Emma says.

"On it," Isabella exclaims.

Georgia passes by me, and her sugary-rose perfume fills the air. She states, "Be right back."

"No rush," I tell her, then go over and help the girls clean up. I give each of my nieces a kiss on the head, inquiring, "Did you have a good day with Georgia?"

Emma nods. "She's so much fun."

"We love her," Isabella claims.

I love her too.

Shit. What am I thinking?

Georgia bounces back into the room, chirping, "Got it," she holds her hand out.

The diamond glares on her finger. I stare at it, annoyed that it's so blatantly obvious how incorrect it is for her.

"What's wrong?" she questions.

"Nothing. Ready?"

"Yep."

"See you girls, later." I give them a wink, grab Georgia's hand, and lead her out of the house.

We step outside, and she asks, "Where are you taking me tonight?"

I answer, "Simmers."

"What's Simmers?" she inquires.

I boast, "Only the best barbecue in town, but we're going there for something else."

She arches her eyebrows. "What would that be?"

I grin. "They also have award-winning pecan pie."

Her face lights up brighter than I've seen it before. I pat myself on the back for getting one more thing right. She freezes and tilts her head. "Are you teasing me?"

"Nope!"

"Really? Are you going to have some?"

I cave, knowing it'll make her happy. "I'll have a couple of bites of yours."

Satisfaction fills her expression. "Okay. That sounds good."

I open the truck's passenger door, and she gets in. I shut it and slip into the driver's seat. I turn on the engine, then pull down the driveway and through the gate. I glance at her, quizzing, "How was your day with my sisters and mom?"

"It was good," she answers.

"Overwhelming?"

A tiny laugh escapes her. It's another thing I can't get enough of —the sound...the way her face glows...the joy I feel just from experiencing it. She admits, "There were some moments."

"But you got what you wanted?" I prod, wanting her to have everything she wants for this wedding, even though she told me it will never be what she imagined.

I don't know why that stings so badly, but it does. And I wish I could get yesterday's conversation out of my mind, yet it only plays on repeat.

She answers, "I did. But your mom paid for everything, which I feel bad about."

I grunt. "Don't feel bad about it. What did you think? That you'd pay for your own dress? If my mom didn't pay for it, I would have. But my mom loves that kind of stuff, so you made her happy."

Georgia stays quiet a minute, then softly adds, "Well, it was extremely generous of her."

More silence fills the cab. *Why can't I think of anything to say?* I wipe my sweaty hand on my jeans, then finally state, "Thanks for playing with Isabella and Emma."

Georgia beams. "They're adorable. I really love them."

"Yeah. They love you too," I answer, then turn on the street the restaurant's on. I find a parking spot and turn off the engine. "Ready for the world's best barbecue?"

She smiles. "Bring it!"

I exit the truck, go around, and open her door. Then I take her hand and lead her into the restaurant. It's one of those restaurants where you seat yourself, so I grab the booth toward the back in a quieter location.

One of the longtime servers, Nancy, approaches us within a few seconds. She booms, "Well, Sebastian Cartwright, I heard you were in town."

I groan inside. Of course she heard. The whole town's probably talking about the fact I'm here. There's no doubt they know about Georgia as well. I force myself to be nice. "Hey, Nancy, how are you?"

"I'm as perfect as a glass of lemonade on a hot summer day," she replies.

I nod, then point to Georgia, announcing, "This is my soon-to-be wife, Georgia."

Why am I so proud to say that?

I need to get my head straight. This isn't real.

Nancy turns toward Georgia, claiming, "It's so nice to meet you, darling. I heard you were in town from Sally. She said you were different from Sebastian's other girls." Nancy wiggles her eyebrows.

Seriously? Heat creeps into my face.

Georgia gapes at her, speechless.

I snap out of it and firmly state, "Nancy, we'll need some time to look at the menu. Could you give us a few minutes?"

She looks at me, disappointed she's not getting any gossip, replying, "Okay, sure." She walks away.

I shake my head, declaring, "I'm sorry about that."

Georgia shrugs. "It's okay. I guess I understand why you have some issues coming back home."

"You have no idea," I mutter.

She gives me a look of pity, and I hate it.

Get back on track.

"But you had a good time today, right? You had fun with my family?"

She assures me, "Of course I did. Also, Melanie texted me and said that she and her family will arrive Friday morning. That's still okay, right?"

I grab her hand, caressing the top with my thumb. "Of course it is," I say. "Are there any other friends that you want to invite?"

She glances at our hands but doesn't remove hers. Then she locks eyes with me. "No, I don't have any friends left in Texas. They've all gone off to other states where their hometowns are or moved for jobs."

I don't hesitate. "I can fly them in for you if you want."

She bites on her lip a few moments, then shakes her head. "No, that's not necessary."

My gut sinks. It's another reminder she's not marrying me for any other reason besides the fact that I needed a fake wife and she wanted a million dollars.

She slowly pulls her hand away, stabbing me in the gut. She reads the menu and questions, "What are you going to order?"

I don't need to look at the menu. It's my favorite place in town for barbeque, and it's never changed since I was a kid. I answer, "They have a family platter with everything on it. I thought we could split it so you can try everything?"

"Sure. That sounds great."

I motion for Nancy and place the order.

She asks, "What do you two lovebirds want to drink?"

"I'll have a draft beer," I state, then look at Georgia, realizing I don't even know what she likes to drink.

Is it champagne?

Rare wine?

I begin to freak out. This isn't the type of place that offers anything expensive. It's beer and very bad, cheap wine. The food's amazing, and the beer is great, but the wine sucks. It'll give you a headache for days.

Why did I bring her here?

I should have taken her to the country club.

Georgia surprises me and says, "I'll have the same as Sebastian."

"You drink beer?" I blurt out.

She jerks her head back. "Is there something wrong with that?"

"No, not at all," I happily answer. I've never had a girlfriend who drank beer. They all thought it was disgusting and beneath them. In fact, two of them tried to get me to drink scotch, which I'm not a fan of and refused to do.

Nancy furrows her eyebrows, and her voice drops to the one she uses when she's gagging for gossip. "How is it you're getting married and don't know that your fiancée drinks beer?"

I wince inside and retort, "Well, you can't know everything about a person, can you? There's always some mystery left, right?"

Georgia chimes in, "Yes. Sebastian's right. Plus, I usually drink wine, especially at all the restaurants he takes me to."

That's my girl.

"No offense, Nancy, because you know this is my favorite place, but my schedule doesn't allow me to deviate away from the five-star restaurants in Dallas. The wine is the finest in the world and hard to avoid. You know what I'm saying?" I add.

Nancy thinks for a minute, then agrees. "Yeah, I guess you're right."

I continue, "I'm really thirsty, Nancy. Do you mind bringing some water with the beer?"

"Got it," she declares and leaves.

I breathe a sigh of relief. Nancy's one of the biggest town gossips. The less I can speak with her, the better.

Georgia asks, "So what did you work on all day?"

I think about all the times I thought about her, wondering what she was doing or how I spent hours fretting over what to order her.

Don't tell her that.

I tell a half-truth. "I worked on the merger."

"How's it going?"

"It's coming along," I lie. I'm far from close to closing it. But it'll eventually get done.

Georgia stares at me.

"What?" I uncomfortably ask.

"Do you like what you do?" she questions.

I don't have to think about it. "I love it."

"That's good. But don't you miss your family, with you living in Dallas?" she quizzes.

I open my mouth to say no, but then I shut it. Being home these last few days makes me realize how much I miss them. I should come back more to see them, especially my nieces and nephews. They've gotten so big, and I'm missing out on their lives. So I decide to be truthful, replying, "Yeah, I do miss them."

"So why don't you come home more?"

I glance at Nancy, mumbling, "Pretty obvious, isn't it?"

"You shouldn't let what other people say stop you from seeing your family. One day they might not be here. Trust me, I know," she points out.

Guilt and sadness wash over me. I haven't thought too much about what it must be like for Georgia to have zero family left, but her statement hits me like a ton of bricks. Grief fills her face, and I'd do anything at this moment to take it away from her. Plus, I'd be devastated if anything happened to anyone in my family, including Evelyn. I finally agree, "You're right."

"Yes. I am," she firmly asserts.

More shame hits me.

An awkward silence fills the air until she asks, "Sebastian, what do you want out of life?"

It's another question that surprises me and leaves me speechless. How is it that she's so much younger than me but seems to have her life together more than I do?

Before I met Georgia, I thought I was doing everything right. I was continuing to build my family empire, and everyone in Texas knew about me. I was happy.

That's a lie.

I've not been happy in a long time.

She makes me feel happy.

"Sebastian?" she pushes.

I don't know how to answer her question, so I flip it on her and tease, "I don't know. What do you want? A husband, a dozen kids? Your cupcake store, and you'll live happily ever after?"

Disgust mixed with anger fills her expression. She seethes, "What if I do? What's wrong with that?"

My gut dives like I'm at the top of a hill and the ground just broke underneath me. I hold my hands in the air. "I didn't mean to offend you."

"No?"

"No. I swear I didn't," I claim.

She challenges, "So you don't want a wife who loves you? You don't want any kids? You want to be by yourself forever and only make more money?"

My mouth turns dry. *Is that how she sees me?*

It's what I've portrayed.

Is that what I want?

Yes.

No.

I could see that life with Georgia.

Christ. What's happening to me?

She's going to divorce me on January 2nd.

Annulment...not divorce...like it never happened.

This isn't real.

Her blue eyes swirl with something I haven't seen before. My heart thumps hard against my chest as I realize what's growing more intense the longer she drills her gaze into mine.

She thinks I'm pathetic.

Am I?

I finally confess, "I used to, but then I learned it just wasn't in the cards for me."

"Why isn't it in the cards? You can have anything you want. You're Sebastian Cartwright," she claims.

Nancy arrives with the beers and water. For once, I want to hug her for saving me. But my gratitude is short-lived when she lowers her voice and asks, "Did you hear about Matteo?"

My chest tightens. I almost tell her that I don't care and to not talk to me the rest of the time we're here. But curiosity kills the cat, and I'm apparently the cat. I can't resist and fall into her trap, responding, "No."

Nancy glances to both sides of her, then leans down even farther. "They lost the ranch. She couldn't stop racking up debt." She cocks her eyebrows, waiting for my reaction.

A mixture of emotions fills me. On the one hand, I feel bad for Matteo. I warned him. Yet the bad person in me feels some satisfaction knowing that she did to him exactly what I told him she would.

"Nancy, order up," the cook calls out.

"Back soon," she states, pats me on the shoulder, and leaves.

Georgia tilts her head, her eyes turning to slits, questioning, "Who's Matteo?"

I take a big gulp of my beer, swallow, and finally inform her, "My ex-best friend."

Her eyes widen. "Why is he your ex-best friend? Why isn't he still your best friend?"

I shift in my seat, tapping my pint glass.

"Sebastian?" she softly inquires.

"It's hard to stay friends with someone when they marry your ex-fiancée, who was also your high school sweetheart that only wanted you for your money."

Georgia gapes, then recovers, and a look of pity crosses her expression. I hate it. She quietly asks, "He married Molly?"

"Yep." I down half my beer.

Georgia puts her hand on mine. "That must have hurt."

"I don't need your pity," I tell her.

"Sympathy for others isn't the same as pity, Sebastian."

I think about her statement. *Is that true?* I tell myself to google the difference between sympathy and pity because I don't know if it is. So I stare at her hand on mine.

My silence must be a dead giveaway for my thoughts because Georgia adds, "Sympathy implies a deeper, more personal level of concern...because you care about the person. Pity is just an expression of sorrow. So what's wrong with sympathy?"

Once again, my little peach has me stumped. I decide she's way smarter than me and ask, "Can we change the subject?" Then I hold my beer out and say, "Cheers."

She sighs, then clinks my glass and takes a sip. She swallows and informs me, "Hey, Isabella has a surprise for you tonight."

The previous night I had makeup all over my face. By the time Isabella had to go to bed, I looked like a drag queen. I groan. "Do I want to know?"

Georgia cringes, then answers, "You get to be the first guest in her nail salon."

I groan, then chuckle. "I guess it's good I'm keeping you out past her bedtime."

"You are?"

"Yep."

"We're going to be here all night?" she asks, glancing around.

I chuckle again. "Nope."

She tilts her head, and I wish I were sitting beside her instead of across from her. She asks, "Well, where are you taking me?"

"On the best date ever."

She bites her lip.

I take another sip of beer.

She says, "You aren't going to tell me where?"

I lean closer. "If you slide over here and give me a kiss, I'll tell you."

She pretends to pout.

I shrug but wish she'd sit her pert little everything next to me. I offer, "Okay. Have it your way."

"Tell me," she begs.

I shake my head. "You'll see later, Sunshine."

Seventeen

GEORGIA

"That was delicious," I state.

Sebastian grins. "Told you. If there's one thing I know, it's barbecue. I'll leave the pecan pie to you." He glances over at Nancy, who's fixing a slice for us.

"Sebastian Cartwright," a woman in a booth behind me says in a low voice.

His face hardens.

The other woman declares, "I'm sure she won't last long either."

Sebastian's face turns red and heat ignites on my cheeks too.

I love this quaint town, but I don't understand these people's manners. The gossip is out of control. I can't blame Sebastian for staying away, except that his family's amazing.

The women continue talking, and I glance behind me, glaring. A redhead catches my leer, but she doesn't seem to care. She leans closer to the table, refocuses on her friend, and states, "The wedding is Saturday. We'll see if she gets down the aisle."

Appalled at her audacity, I jump up, slide next to Sebastian, and tug his head toward mine.

"What are you doing, Sunshine?" he asks.

"I can't wait to marry you," I declare, then smash my lips to his and slip my tongue in his mouth. It's a bit clumsy, but he quickly slides his hands in my hair, then takes control of our kiss.

He sets the pace, slowing me down. He pulls back from time to time, intensely staring at me, his thumbs tracing my jaw and lips.

Every time he does it, I catch my breath, dying for him to put his mouth back on mine. No one kisses like Sebastian Cartwright. It makes me wonder how any woman could have ever let him go.

He appeases my wishes several times, and I soon forget we're in a restaurant. I barely hear Nancy when she clears her voice and chirps, "Pecan pie, lovebirds."

Flustered and flushed, I retreat, but he keeps his eyes locked on mine. I barely glance at Nancy. "Thanks."

"Do you need anything else?" She smirks.

"No, we're good," Sebastian says, still holding my cheeks and staring at me.

My insides quiver. No man has ever looked at me the way he does. It's like he's seeing me at a depth others can't.

He releases me, and Nancy walks off. He motions to the table. "Eat your pie, Sunshine."

I catch my breath, but my pulse still races. I pick up a fork and take a bite. The gooey mixture melts in my mouth, and I moan. "Mmm."

Sebastian watches me, cocking his eyebrows.

I chew and swallow, then take a sip of water. "Well, you did it."

"What's that?" he questions.

"You found the world's best pecan pie for me."

He tosses his arm in the air. "Yes! Score one for me."

I lean my face toward his. "Are we keeping score?"

His face falls. "No. But I'm tired of getting things wrong."

The hairs on my neck rise. I inquire, "What have you gotten wrong?"

"Pretty much everything," he claims.

A lump forms in my throat. I put my fork down. I cautiously ask, "Do you want to clarify that statement?"

He picks up my hand and holds it in front of me. "I think this says it all, don't you?"

Guilt eats at me. I shake my head, asserting, "It's a beautiful ring."

"But it's not you, is it?" he insists.

"I wouldn't say—"

"Don't lie to me, Georgia."

"I wonder how old she is. She looks pretty young compared to him," the brunette in the booth says in a loud voice.

I tear my eyes off Sebastian, wondering how people can be so rude.

Sebastian states, "Ignore those hags. Answer my question. Honestly."

I turn back, and it pains me to look at him. I can tell he's upset, but I also can see he doesn't want me to lie. So I choose my words carefully and reply, "I'm not a flashy kind of gal."

His lips curl up. He takes my hand and kisses it. "Yeah, I love that about you."

I freeze, as does he. Heated tension grows between us.

Did Sebastian Cartwright just say he loved something about me?

It's just a statement. Don't confuse it with actual love.

He's not in love with me.

"What do you think the prenup says?" the redhead questions.

I glare at her again, shaking my head. Then I lean into Sebastian, inquiring, "Do you know those women?"

"Unfortunately so," he mutters.

"Well, tell me their dirt," I order and shove another bite of pecan pie in my mouth.

He pretends that he's in shock.

I chew, swallow, and ask, "What?" I take another sip of water.

He taunts in my ear, "Little Miss Sunshine wants to gossip?"

Zings fly to my core. I reply, "Sure. Why not? If you can't beat 'em, join 'em," I declare, then hold up a fork of pecan pie under his nose. He opens his mouth, but I shove it in mine.

He chuckles. "You're evil."

I shrug, finish my bite, and command, "Spill it, Cartwright."

Amused, he glances at the table. He sits back, slings his arm around my shoulder, and tugs me into his chest. He quietly informs me, "The red-haired lady is Holly. She got so drunk one year at a holiday party that she screwed the other town drunk, who dresses up as Santa every year. So now everyone calls her Ho-Ho-Holly."

"No!" I laugh so hard, tears fill my eyes.

"I'm not joking."

"That's horrible," I say and continue to laugh.

"Wait until you hear the brunette's story."

"Do tell."

His lips brush my ear, and I shiver as he states, "Casey's husband left her for another man."

"Oh, that's sad," I say, feeling sorry for her.

"Yeah, but..." Sebastian trails off.

I turn and lock eyes with him, asking, "But what?"

He clenches his jaw and stares at me for a moment, then answers, "He came back home and begged for forgiveness. So she pretended it didn't happen for a few months. Then she brought home her new friend." "Another man?" I question.

Sebastian shakes his head. "Nope. She brought home another woman."

I gape at him.

"You want to know the final kicker?"

"There's more?" I ask, wondering what else could top that situation.

He adds, "She moved her new friend in, but her hubby moved his friend in as well."

I throw my hand over my mouth.

"True story," he states, then sits back.

"Their story's way more interesting than yours," I proclaim.

"Sorry to disappoint you, Sunshine." He winks, and my heart melts more. I take a fork full of pecan pie and hold it to his mouth. This time I let him take it.

He groans, chews, swallows, and admits, "This is good."

"One thing I know is my pecan pie, and I agree."

He wipes his mouth with his napkin, then questions, "What would you be doing over Christmas if you weren't with me?"

My chest tightens. I admit, "I'm not sure."

"What do you mean?"

"I don't know. This is the first year my grammy's not alive. Melanie's my only friend in town, so maybe I would have spent it with her. Or maybe I'd be alone." Grief lodges in my throat.

Sebastian takes my hand.

I force a smile and add, "I thought about going to Iceland for the holiday."

He wrinkles his forehead. "Are you looking to freeze your ass off?"

I laugh and shrug. "It's supposed to be really cool at Christmas. It was that or the North Pole, but Iceland seemed not as scary."

Amused, he asks, "The North Pole is scary?"

I put my hand over my face and groan. "I don't know. I didn't research it yet, but I figured the population has to be bigger in Iceland?"

He leans closer. "And that would be important because?"

I shake my head. "No clue. It just seemed safer? I don't know! It was just a silly idea."

"Oh, I don't know. I can see where you were going with it," he states then asks, "What did you do for Thanksgiving?"

I take a deep breath and relay, "Melanie and her family were supposed to come over, but they got sick. I had already started cooking everything, so I finished making it and dropped it off at her front door. Then I spent the rest of the day baking the Black Friday Cupcakes."

His expression turns guilty. "I'm an asshole. I'm sorry, Georgia."

"For what?"

He glances at the ceiling, shakes his head, and then states, "For giving you so much shit about your cupcakes all the time."

"It's fine," I offer.

"No, it's not," he says.

I stay quiet, feeling nervous again. I'm not used to this side of Sebastian. The rare moments when he gets vulnerable and doesn't hide behind his grumpy, arrogant persona make me want to know everything about him.

And that scares me. All this is ending soon. I don't need more heartache.

I finish my pie, trying to ignore the little pieces of grief popping up, thinking about my grammy and all the confusion around Sebastian. When I get done, I turn to him. "You have to tell me where we're going now."

"Why is that?"

I huff. "Because I kissed you."

His lips twitch. "That was more of a pity kiss, not a real kiss."

I scoff. "Is that right?"

He stares me down and challenges, "Definitely. You need to give me a real kiss if you want to know."

The voice in my head tells me to scoot out of the booth and run, in order to save the future of my heart. I ignore it and reach for his face. I tug him toward me, then kiss him as if my life depended on it.

He kisses me back and slides his hand under my shirt, palming my bare skin. Tingles race down my spine. We kiss until I force myself to pull an inch away from his mouth and murmur, "Where are we going?"

He looks nervous, and it strikes me as odd. Sebastian Cartwright is not an unconfident man, at least not that I've seen. But he definitely looks anxious. He answers, "I assume you're into holiday stuff?"

"Duh!"

His nerves disappear, and the arrogant confidence that makes my knees weaken appears. "Perfect!"

"So, where are we going?" I repeat.

"The entire month of December, there's a Christmas Wonderland on the river."

"That sounds fun," I chirp.

He nods. "They have games to play, vendors for shopping, and the river is full of lights. Is that something you'd want to go to?"

"Do snowmen need snow?" I question.

He bites on his smile. "Did you just make that up?"

"Yep."

"That was pretty good, Sunshine," he praises.

I confess, "You know I'm a Christmas junkie, right?"

He chuckles. "I had a feeling you were." He gives me a chaste kiss. He tosses money on the table and orders, "Let's get going."

I slide out of the booth, and he follows, grabbing my hand. He leads me out of the restaurant. I hold my head higher and squeeze his hand tighter as we pass the women.

We get outside, and instead of leading me to the truck, he guides me the opposite way, stating, "It's only about three blocks. Are you good to walk?"

"A walk sounds good after all that food," I admit.

We stroll through the town in silence, and excitement builds inside me when the lights start to come into view.

We spend hours playing games and looking at items the vendors are selling. We get to the last one, and I ask, "What time of day do the vendors get here?"

"I think around noon," he answers.

"I want to come back and do my Christmas shopping here," I declare.

"I can make that happen," he states.

I smile, unable to stop the giddy feeling growing inside me. I like the Sebastian in front of me more than I ever thought I would.

We get to another booth, and he booms, "Ah, here we go."

I glance at it. It says "Mistletoe Booth."

"It's for charity," he claims as he slaps money on the table. His eyes twinkle, and he bends me slightly backward.

I laugh, but he silences it, sliding his tongue against mine with so much enthusiasm, he steals my breath. A bell rings, and the vendor says, "That's it. Kiss over, unless you pay more."

Sebastian pulls more money out of his wallet, tosses it at him, then returns to pressing his lips against mine. When the bell rings again, my knees are weak.

He chuckles, holding me tight to him, and states, "Come on, Sunshine. We're going for a ride."

"A ride?" I question, trying to return to reality.

"Yep."

I glance at the Ferris wheel. I fret, "You know I'm afraid of heights, right?"

He answers, "Not that type of ride." He moves me farther down the walkway. We approach a gondola with lights strung around it. He points. "You're not scared of boats, are you?"

I clap my hands. I've always wanted to go on a gondola. "Nope! This looks fun!"

Sebastian helps me onto the boat and pays the driver, who turns the Christmas music up. We make our way down the river, and Sebastian slides his arm around my shoulders.

I rest easily into his body, taking in everything.

Lights wrap around the trees and decorate the buildings, and there are special displays. I've never felt so in the holiday spirit. I say to Sebastian, "Tell me you feel it."

"Feel it?" he asks, flames growing in his eyes.

"The holiday spirit," I say, but my voice cracks. I squeeze my thighs together, wishing the pulse between them would calm down.

He rolls his face in front of mine. "Is that what you want to call it?"

Heat rushes to my face. I open my mouth, but nothing comes out.

He kisses my forehead, then leans back.

I stare at the lights for a bit, then question, "What would you be doing in Dallas if you weren't here? And you can't say working."

"I don't know. Probably exercising."

I laugh. "Come on, Sebastian. You have to do more than work and exercise."

Another moment goes by. He adds, "I guess dining with clients."

"That's working," I claim.

He stays quiet, then admits, "Nothing exciting, Georgia. What would you be doing? And you can't say baking."

His statement saddens me and also surprises me. Does he just work?

I answer, "Okay, but I might be baking," and then I put my hand over my face, peeking at him through my fingers.

"You really love it, don't you?" he asks.

"Yeah, I do. I always have. My grammy and I used to do it together. She started teaching me when I was three."

"Wow."

Nostalgia hits me, thinking about my grammy teaching me her recipes when I was little.

He asks again, "All right, so if you weren't baking, what would you be doing?"

"I might be volunteering at the children's hospital."

"You do that?" he questions.

"Yeah. I started doing it when I was in college. I felt like I was making a difference, so I continued with it," I reveal.

He softly says, "That's amazing. What else would you be doing?"

I ponder the question, then answer, "Maybe hanging out with Melanie and her family."

"What about dating?" he asks.

My butterflies mix with dread. I toss it back to him, quizzing, "What about you and your dating life?"

He squeezes his eyes shut, groaning, "You don't want to know."

I chirp, "Oh, but I do. Let me guess. You have a new girl in your bed every night."

He scoffs. "I'm not that bad."

"Right," I snicker.

"Do you think I'm that bad?" he questions.

I consider if I do, then decide I'm not sure. So I respond, "Am I close?" My chest tightens. The thought of Sebastian with any other woman makes me feel ill. It shouldn't. I know this isn't real between us.

He admits, "No. I usually stick with the same woman for a few months."

Something about his statement irritates me. I add, "Then you get bored?"

"Ugh," he moans. "You make me sound horrible."

"Sorry," I offer, but hurt annihilates me.

I'm not even lasting a few months, and I'm marrying him.

A moment of uncomfortable silence fills the air. Then he pushes, "Okay. I spilled the beans. What about you? Longtime boyfriend who you put on pause to make your million with me?"

More pain ignites within me. It's not because I'm no longer with my ex; it's sadness over how things ended and why. I admit, "My boyfriend and I broke up shortly after Valentine's Day."

Sebastian furrows his brows. Confusion fills his face. "You haven't dated anyone since?"

"No," I answer.

"Why not?"

I shrug. "No one seemed interesting to me."

Something passes on his face and I'm unsure how to interpret it. He asks, "Well, why did you break up?"

I blurt out, "He dumped me."

Shock overtakes Sebastian's face. "Why would he do that?"

I shift in my seat and reveal, "He said my head was in the clouds."

"Meaning?"

"He had a lucrative job offer in Alaska. I had mentioned it to my professor, who recommended me to his contacts. They said that they would hire me once I graduated in May, so he wanted me to move to Alaska with him."

Sebastian waits a moment, then asks, "Why didn't you go with him?"

The grief I wish I knew how to stop rises in my chest. My mouth turns dry, and I swallow a lump in my throat. I somehow manage to get out, "My grammy was ill. I moved her from Savannah to Texas. She lost her house because of medical bills, so I moved her into my apartment. Plus, she was sick, and I wanted to take care of her."

Sebastian stays quiet but tightens his hand around mine. "You said she passed about six months ago?"

"Yes." I blink hard, but a tear falls down my cheek. I swipe at it and continue, "James wanted me to put her into a home and go with him. I told him I wouldn't ever do that, and that was the end of us."

"What a dick," he states.

I force a smile. "It is what it is."

The gondola ride comes to an end. Sebastian hesitates, opens his mouth, but then snaps it shut. We get off the boat, and he takes my hand again. He asks, "Is there anything else you want to do here?"

"No, I'm tired," I say, suddenly drained from the day I've had.

"Let's go home," he says, leading me back to the truck.

Home. If only it were my home.

We walk in silence, and when we get to his truck, he doesn't open my door. He puts his hand on my cheek and proclaims, "You deserve a lot better than the hand you've been dealt, Sunshine."

Another tear falls down my cheek. I swipe at it and turn away from him.

He steps in front of me, stating, "Your ex is a fool for letting you go."

All I can think is, *Why is James a fool when Sebastian has me but already has my expiration date picked out?*

The questions create more emotions within me that I'm not prepared to deal with, nor do I want to in front of Sebastian. I clear my throat, spin, and yank open the truck door. I claim, "It's fine. Let's go home." I jump in the truck with my pulse skyrocketing, wondering how I can protect my heart when I already know he's going to break it.

Eighteen

SEBASTIAN

Three Days Later

Things only feel more confusing between Georgia and me. In front of my family, she's relaxed. There's no boundary between us. Yet when we're alone, things become strained.

I've asked her if I've done something wrong, but she keeps saying no. I even stopped trying anything in the bedroom with her. Yet every morning, we wake up with one of our bodies draped over the other. And it's getting harder to resist my urge to do anything with her.

No woman's ever given me blue balls for so long.

Still, she's made it clear where she draws the line, and something is cautioning me not to try to move her over it.

The last few days have been a whirlwind of wedding planning. I've done way more than I ever anticipated, but like everything I do with Georgia, she makes it fun.

My work is piling up. I keep delegating more things to my staff that I normally would handle. Yet I'm so distracted by wanting to spend more time with her that it's not even on my mind most of the time.

Plus, there's the issue that I got things wrong. I can't escape the nagging voice in my head. Now, I'm hoping I can correct it.

I step inside the jewelry store my family always uses. I came here the day after our date. I spent a few hours looking at different rings, feeling so out of my comfort zone that our family jeweler, Bobby, told me to sit down. He asked me a ton of things about Georgia. Then he pulled a dozen different diamonds from his safe. None of them were anything like what I gave her. They were smaller. Simpler. Each diamond was nothing to sneeze at and flawless, yet more of what I guessed is her style.

After I chose the diamond, he drew a design. It was so perfect, my heart almost stopped.

He called me this morning to tell me it was finished. I raced over here, unable to wait any longer to see it.

Bobby booms, "Sebastian." He pulls a box out of the drawer and removes the lid.

My pulse quickens. I stare at the triangle rose-cut diamond set on a 24-carat gold band. It's something else I noticed about Georgia. She always wears yellow gold. It was another thing I got wrong. The platinum band on her seemed dull next to her cheerful attitude.

The ring isn't flashy, but it's elegant. The triangle is set sideways, so the one side of the band has one prong, and the other side has two. I can envision it on her finger, plus it's flatter, so it won't interfere with her baking as much as the current one.

"It's perfect," I state, hoping she loves it as much as I think she will. I can't get this wrong a second time. I curse myself again for not even taking a moment to think about what might be good for Georgia. But then again, I didn't really know her.

I still won't claim to know her. There's so much more I want to know about her. She's only let me into a tidbit of her life, but everything about her fascinates me.

I pay Bobby and leave. When I return to the ranch, I grab the shopping bag I tossed into the truck.

When I was strolling down Main Street, there was a boutique with a mannequin wearing a jacket. I instantly thought of Georgia and had to buy it for her.

The moment I step into the house, I pull the coat out of the bag. I hang it up in the closet. I go into the kitchen, where I know she'll be.

Georgia insisted on baking the wedding cake, and Isabella and Emma wanted to help. She said it would be fun, so they woke up at the crack of dawn to start. Nobody was allowed in the kitchen. Breakfast was already in the dining room on covered plates when I returned from my workout. I could hear Georgia, Isabella, and Emma giggling when I left.

The feeling I can't seem to escape, and I don't remember ever having before this week, reappears when I lay eyes on Georgia. The three of them are all standing over the wedding cake. Four tiers are stacked one on top of the other in an off-white color.

The kitchen's a mess. Winter-white pansies, blue forget-me-nots, and pale-pink cyclamen flowers from the secret garden are every-where. Twigs, pine cones, and little wooden hearts that she had the girls help her design last night litter the counter. They took a burning tool and engraved them. One has S and G on it. Another displays "Just Married."

A while passes, but I can't tear my eyes off her. Her apron has flour on it, and there's a little mark of frosting on her cheek. My nieces have a lot more on them.

She takes a forget-me-not and breaks the stem. She places it on the top tier, then says, "This is a trial run. On Saturday, we'll need to add fresh flowers and replace these."

"Can I put one on?" Isabella asks.

"Sure. You can too, Emma," Georgia states, handing both of them a flower.

She'll be an amazing mom.

I can see her with a dozen kids.

Georgia observes them, then glances up. She beams at me, and my pulse races quicker. "Hey!"

"So, that's what you needed the tree for," I assert, pointing at the wooden base of the cake.

Georgia asked Alexander to cut her an eighteen-inch diameter circle from one of the logs she chose last night. She wouldn't tell us what it was for, claiming it was a secret between her and the girls. They helped her put clear lacquer on it before they went to bed, and all three of them were tight-lipped.

She chirps, "It looks cool, right?"

I answer honestly, "I love it. It's going to fit perfectly with the rest of the decor."

Relief floods her face, which I find odd. Everything she does is perfect, so it's surprising to me she would question anything, especially when it involves baking. She asks, "What have you been doing all day?"

Nervous flutters kick off in my gut. I admit, "I had to go to town for some stuff. I'm going to go work for a few hours, but are you up for a walk later in the afternoon? We can go check out what the workers have been doing in the garden."

Her face lights up. "Sure, I'd love to go see it."

"Great." I stare at her another moment, then tear my eyes off her and leave the room.

When I get to my father's office, I shut the blinds so I can't see everything the workers are doing to get the garden ready for the wedding. I have to work. I somehow force myself to concentrate on what I need to do and get way more done than I anticipated.

At four o'clock, my mind begins wandering again with visions of Georgia's smiling face. I decide I've done enough and leave to find her. She's near the front hall when I walk in, wearing the cowboy boots I got her. She never seems to take them off, which makes me happy. It's always a reminder that I got one thing right.

She announces, "There you are. I was going to find you."

My heart pounds faster. It's innocent, but I like that she was thinking about me. I open the closet and remove the new coat I bought for her. It's a slim-cut, button-up, light denim blue jacket. It has a cream Sherpa lining and an oversized collar that lays flat on the shoulders. "I got this for you when I was in town."

She gazes at it, then puts her hand over the material. "It's really soft."

"So you like it?" I ask, wanting more than ever for her to say yes, and to know that I got one more thing right about her.

She smiles. "Of course! I love it."

I give myself an internal high five, then hold the jacket out for her to slip into. She does, and I lead her outside.

We don't talk on the way to the secret garden. My stomach continues to flip, and I motion for her to go through the door first.

She steps in and freezes. "Wow!"

I glance around and admit, "It looks amazing."

The last of the workers have left. She studies everything, and as much as I'm impressed by the landscape, she's the only thing I can look at.

"They got it done so quickly," she mutters.

"I'm having the glass ceiling washed a few hours before the ceremony to remove any new residue," I inform her. It had a thorough cleaning, and the inserts were placed on the sides so that it's not as cold, but I'm going to make sure everything's sparkling clean.

"This is insane," she says, peering around again.

Dark wooden chairs have been placed in two sections on a wooden floor with a cream satin runner between them. After the ceremony, the chairs will be removed and the space will turn into a dance floor. The whole setup is situated in front of the ivy wall.

The oversized hanging beds in the back corners have clear lights strung around the chains. They're always there. My mom had them installed when we were little. The cream-colored mattresses are spotless, and new pillows add an extra pop of color.

There are more lights on the tree trunks, and lanterns hang across the yard. Heat lamps are strategically placed around the garden. Bars and food tables line both sides of the hedge walls. Circular dinner tables are set from the middle of the room to the back. The right front corner has an area for a band, and the left front corner has one for a DJ.

"I can't get over this," Georgia states.

"It does look great," I agree.

"It's perfect," she claims.

Yes! I got it right.

It's not perfect though. She made it clear it'll never be the perfect day for her because she's marrying me.

I shrug off the comments in my head that have plagued me since she told me why this could never be the perfect wedding for her.

The lights and the heaters flip on. Soft music begins to play through the surround sound.

She laughs, asking, "Is this garden haunted?"

I chuckle. "No, everything's on timers. I scheduled the music to give you the overall vibe."

She bites her lip, continuing to be fascinated by it all. Then she arches her eyebrow and focuses on me.

My anxiety takes off again. I order, "Follow me." I lead her to one of the oversized beds and suggest, "Let's sit here and take it all in."

"You don't have to ask me twice!"

I chuckle and point to the heater. "It's going to get hot. Let me help you out of your coat."

She allows me, and I set it on the end of the bed, along with my coat.

She climbs onto the mattress and then I grab her calf, hold it in the air, and start to unzip her boot.

She pulls her leg toward her, questioning, "What are you doing?"

"Just chill. It's comfier this way. Trust me," I assert.

She relaxes, and I take off her boots and then my own. I lie back against the pillows and slide my arm around her.

Thankfully, she doesn't resist.

We sit in silence for a few moments. Her sugary-rose perfume teases me until I feel like I'll break out in a sweat.

She adds, "I can't get over how incredible this is."

"I think you're incredible," I blurt out, and my stomach flips faster.

She slowly meets my eye.

My pulse beats so hard against my ears that I wonder if she can hear it. To buy some time, I ask, "Is there anything you don't like?"

She doesn't tear her gaze from mine as she shakes her head. "No, this is more than I could have ever imagined."

Relief fills me, then dies as my nerves overpower it. I grab her hand and claim, "I know something that's wrong."

She furrows her eyebrows, reassesses the garden, and asks, "What? Everything is perfect."

"No, it's not," I insist.

She scrunches her face, trying to figure out what isn't perfect.

I summon my courage and assert, "I can't marry you if it's not right."

Her face scrunches in confusion. She admits, "I can't figure it out."

I slide the oversized diamond so wrong for her off her finger.

"What are you doing?"

"Do what you want with this." I slip it into her coat pocket, then turn back toward her. I reach into my jeans, pull the new ring out, and curl my fist around it. It takes me several breaths to gather my thoughts. The speech I thought about all week becomes a mish-mash of words. I scold myself for not being more prepared, even though I thought I was, and then I open my fist.

Her eyes dart between the ring and me until she's gaping.

I state, "I was an idiot getting you that other ring. It's not you. I should've known it wouldn't be you. All I saw were the women in my past, but you aren't like them, are you?"

She swallows hard, remaining quiet, and I think my heart will pound out of my chest.

I push a lock of her blonde hair behind her ear and continue, "I chose to marry you because I knew everyone here would fall for you. I knew you'd fit in, and deep down, I knew you weren't like anyone I'd ever met. So, I don't know why I didn't put any effort into something so important."

"Sebastian, it's okay," she claims.

I firmly state, "No, it's not. You deserve a ring that represents you, not something that screams for attention. You don't need to scream, do you? You walk into a room and everyone naturally sees you. They're drawn to you. Yet you aren't vain or selfish or have any hidden agendas. You're genuine, and that's really hard to find."

Her eyes tear up, and her lip slightly trembles. She glances away, blinks hard, then relocks her gaze with mine, questioning, "Why are you telling me this?"

I don't know how to answer her. There are too many emotions running through me. It's been like this ever since I met her, if I'm being honest, but especially the last few days.

However, one of them is fear. I'm unsure what I'm trying to tell her, and I wish I could just man up and figure it out. But my inse-curities get the best of me.

So I hold up the ring and say, "Because I want to, and I hope I didn't get this one wrong, because if I did, just tell me. I'll go back and—"

"I love it," she interjects.

"You do?" I question, just to make sure.

"Yes, it's perfect," she declares.

Happiness fills me. It's not arrogance like I often feel when I do something correctly. It's a genuine joy that I actually got something right that makes her happy.

I slide it on her finger, and her eyes dart between me and the ring. I want to kiss her. I move closer to her, but then I freeze an inch from her lips.

I don't need to push myself on her. I do it as often as I can in front of my family, and I don't know if she likes it or not. I think she likes kissing me, but I never know if it's just an act for my family or not. She's not let me kiss her when we've been alone since our date night.

I chicken out and retreat. I focus on the sky, wishing I knew the right way to act around her. It hits me how much I want her to like me. But not just like me as a person.

I want her to like me as a man.

Yet everything I've done is so backward. And I'm so far in, I don't know how to fix it or what I want from her going forward once this is over.

Can there even be anything once January 2nd hits?

She bites her lip, staring at me. I can feel it. Awkward silence mingles with tension and hangs in the air.

I release a stress-filled breath and then decide to put my cards on the table however they might fall. I turn toward her and say, "Georgia, I—"

She surprises me when she puts her fingers over my lips, then straddles my body. She cups my cheeks, gazing at me with her glistening eyes as if she's looking for my soul. She's never looked at me so intensely before, and it chokes me up. She leans closer and whispers, "Thank you."

I don't think I've ever felt so nervous in my life. I can barely reply, "You're welcome."

More silence grows between us, with our breath merging and our hearts pumping harder. I stay frozen, unable to make a move, scared that if I do that, this moment will end, and whatever's going on between us will be ruined.

Then she breaks the tension, softly pressing her lips to mine in the sweetest of kisses.

There's no more holding back. I'm a man, and she's the woman I need to have.

Nineteen

GEORGIA

Sebastian doesn't move when I first kiss him, making me think I shouldn't have been so forward. So I begin to retreat, but his hand slides into my hair and his other arm circles around me.

His tongue plays with mine, gradually taking over our kiss, setting the pace. It's different from our other kisses. It's a slow burn, igniting in my toes and dancing up my legs, growing hotter and hotter until my core pulsates in anticipation.

He flips me onto my back, his mouth still latched to mine, caging his hard frame over me. I gasp as he pulls back an inch. His hitched breath merges with mine. He locks his blues on mine and swallows hard.

I reach for his head to tug him back to me, but he resists.

I ask, "What's—"

"I don't want you to regret me, Sunshine," he declares, his intoxicating scent mixing with the garden's flowers.

My butterflies flutter so fast, I shift my hips upward. It's only a slight movement, but the friction of his hard shaft against me sends a shudder down my spine.

He clenches his jaw, breathing harder.

"Sebastian..." I mumble, not sure what I'm trying to say.

The blue flames in his eyes roar hotter, drilling into me. He deeply inhales and demands, "Tell me you won't regret me."

"I won't," I say with no hesitation.

He stays locked in place, as if questioning my answer.

I reiterate, "I won't," and lean up and press my lips back on his.

It's all it takes for his worries to dissolve. His warm palm slides up my shirt, then under my body. He unclasps my bra. Then his large hand moves over my breast. His fingers graze my nipple, teasing it until it can't harden anymore and I'm whimpering into his mouth.

His face drops to my neck. Tingles dance along my skin, and he murmurs in my ear, "What do you taste like, Sunshine?"

Zings pummel me, and his hand moves to my jeans, releasing the button and zipper with ease. His long fingers slip under my panties and glide through my slit.

I moan, arching into him, squeezing my arms tighter around him.

He taunts me, flicking me, sliding into me, then removing his fingers and flicking some more until I'm a quivering mess. In an arrogant voice, he challenges, "Tell me to lick your pussy."

I've never said that word. The first time I heard Sebastian say it, something sparked inside me. Now is no different. And since he mentioned it the first night we arrived at the ranch, I've imagined his tongue down there every night when he held me in bed. So I don't hesitate, ordering, "Lick my pussy, Sebastian."

His lips twitch. He shoves his tongue back in my mouth as if he owns it, and I grind my lower body against his erection.

He groans, then undresses me. I'm soon naked, underneath him, and throbbing. I reach for his belt, but he grabs my hands and pins them to a pillow. His eyes twinkle, and the faint hint of stars appear in the night sky.

He removes his shirt, and it's like his cut torso's glowing.

I lean up and kiss him, but he cuts it short. He slides his mouth down my body, leaving a trail of endorphins under his hot lips.

When he gets to my hips, he glances at me with his cocky expression.

I take a deep breath, not believing this is happening, unable to stop it if I tried.

But I'm not trying. I want Sebastian more than I've ever wanted anyone. There's too much between us not to give in. And I have to have every part of him, no matter the consequences.

He pushes my thighs out and slithers his tongue over my pussy. I arch up and cry out. He takes his palm, pushes my chest down on the bed, and then slides it up. His fingers circle my neck, grasping me in a stranglehold, right to the point he's not cutting off my air but any tighter he would be.

My insides quiver harder. He pins his blues on me and challenges me for a moment, until my body relaxes and fully submits.

"Good girl," he murmurs, then buries his face between my thighs, whirling his tongue on my clit until I'm thrusting my hips faster and faster.

Incoherent sounds fly out of me. Adrenaline pools in my cells. Then it explodes like a shaken soda can when it opens.

The yellow stars in the sky turn white, then blurry, and his hand clasps my neck even tighter. I draw shorter breaths, and somehow, my high skyrockets to another level.

The music continues to play, but my cries drown it out. His digits slide inside me, moving deeper and deeper until there's nowhere left to go.

He curls his fingers, creating new quivers within me, and my body turns into a volcano, erupting from everywhere.

The garden disappears. His scent permeates me, and he sucks me so hard, I get dizzier. Sweat coats my skin, and the cool night air does nothing to ease it.

He slides up my body, his warm torso making me hotter, his pants somehow lost among our other clothes. The scent of my orgasms mixes with him, and he mutters, "Taste yourself," before sliding his tongue into my mouth.

He releases his hand from my neck, re-pinning my wrists to the pillow. He takes his other hand and drags his knuckles from my thighs, over the curve of my waist, and up my arms until they meet his grasp.

Determination lights up his expression. He studies me, and with a slow thrust, he slides his cock over my clit.

"Sebastian," I whimper, but he doesn't let up, continuing to own every part of my body like it's second nature to him.

"Beautiful woman," he mumbles against my lips.

Tremors continue to roll within me. I curl my fingers between his, squeezing the back of his hand like a vise.

"Ready, Sunshine?" he questions, but my eyes are rolling toward the back of my head from his cock that isn't showing my clit any mercy.

"Oh...oh..." I moan.

His small chuckle hits my ear, and he sucks on my lobe, then adjusts his hips, thrusting into me in one motion.

My eyelids fly open. I arch into him, and he puts his face in front of mine, studying me with his arrogant expression as he shimmies his body slowly in and out of mine.

I don't know how much more adrenaline I can take. My senses are on overload. I've never felt anything so intense. And he's filling me more and more. Every time he pushes back in, I think that's it.

But it's not. Somehow my body accepts every inch of his.

A bead of sweat drops down his cheek, and he pauses, his hips flush with my pelvis, his breath merging with mine.

My voice cracks when I say, "Sebastian."

He strokes my cheek, saying, "Shhh, I've got you."

My eyes water from the onslaught of never-ending zings. I blink hard, then refocus on him.

His palm holds the side of my head. He releases my wrists, and I cling to him, pressing my fingertips into his shoulder blades.

"Hold on, Sunshine," he orders, then returns to thrusting, moving faster and even deeper than before.

"Oh...oh...oh..." I whimper, rocking my hips with his, destroyed by so many sensations, I close my eyes and just feel.

He buries his head into the curve of my neck, declaring in a low voice, "You're mine, Georgia."

"Yes," I agree, wanting nothing more than to be his, not wondering if it means only tonight or tomorrow or however long.

The pressure in my body grows until he growls into my neck, "Christ."

His frame convulses against mine in a violent wave of tremors.

And I cling to him. Through all the earth-shattering sensations of his body and mine, I hold on to him because I realize there's nothing I want more than him.

Our climaxes disintegrate, and the garden comes back into view. I don't move, nor does Sebastian. Our bodies remain joined, and the beating of our hearts slowly dwindles to a normal rate.

He slowly turns his face and kisses my chin, then cheek. His eyes meet mine as if he's searching for something, but I don't know what.

"Hi," I say, suddenly feeling shy.

His lips twitch. "Hi."

We stay frozen for a moment longer. Then he rolls off me.

My body instantly misses his. I feel empty where he was inside me. I attempt to get up, but he tugs me into his arms.

"Where are you going?"

"Nowhere," I say, unsure what I would have done if he hadn't pulled me into him.

He kisses my head, takes several deep breaths, then points to the sky. "When I was a kid, I used to pretend I was in space and living inside the Big Dipper. Do you see it?"

I glance up. "Yes. Why did you want to live there?"

He absentmindedly says, "My teacher told me it wasn't possible. I guess I always wanted what people told me I couldn't have or do."

My heart almost stops. I lift my chin and furrow my eyebrows.

"What's wrong?" he asks.

Fear fills me. I swallow hard and question, "Is that why you wanted me? Because I told you that you couldn't?"

His face falls. He shakes his head and runs his thumb across my lips. "No, Sunshine. I wanted you because I've never met anyone like you. You're special."

I take a deep breath.

He tilts his head and moves his thumb across my jaw. "You don't believe me?"

"I'd like to," I confess.

Hurt washes over his features. His eyes turn to slits. He accuses, "You're regretting me, aren't you?"

"No," I adamantly say.

"Then why don't you believe me?"

I choose my words carefully, answering, "You're Sebastian Cartwright. You can have anyone you want."

Something passes in his expression, but I'm unsure how to take it. He waits several moments, then says, "I'm pretty sure, out of the two of us, you're the one who can get anyone you want. While I'd like to believe I'm holding the cards between us, I'm not. And I think we both know it's the truth."

His statement shocks me. I stay quiet, pondering it.

He kisses the top of my head and states, "We should get back. My mom will have everyone looking for us for dinner."

"Guess it would be bad if they caught us here naked, huh?" I tease.

He grins. "Might not be our best public moment." He hands me my clothes, and we both get dressed quickly.

On the way back, he never lets my hand go. From time to time, he kisses it.

There are no more borders between us. Everything is blurry. And when I look at him, I see the future, yet I'm also fully aware he's going to crush my heart.

There's no avoiding it.

We're a disaster in the making.

Nothing I can do will stop it. No matter what Sebastian says, he's the one holding the cards. All of them. The full deck and even the box. I'm just a card he'll shuffle into his life, yet I can't stop myself from volunteering.

Twenty

SEBASTIAN

When I wake up, I go into the kitchen. Georgia's there making breakfast with Isabella and Emma, which shouldn't surprise me. She does it every morning.

Today, she's wearing her new ring. It's the first morning she's cooked wearing it, and everything about seeing it on her finger gives me satisfaction.

I'm starting to get used to seeing her. And I wonder what it would be like to live the remainder of my days with Georgia in my kitchen.

Naked under her apron.

Wearing my ring on her hand.

I sneak behind her and circle my arms around her waist.

She tilts her head up, smiling.

My heart stammers, and it hits me for the millionth time how she's a rare beauty. I kiss her on the cheek. The light in her eyes flickers brighter, and joy shoots through me. I ask, "What are you making?"

She chirps, "Mini Belgian protein waffles and a vegetable egg casserole. It's in the oven staying warm."

"Smells good," I admit.

"Everyone's in the dining room. Go sit down. You're just in time to eat," she says.

I give her another kiss, pat her on the ass, and obey. She enters the room carrying two casserole dishes. Emma and Isabella follow with the platters of waffles. They set everything down, and I pull out Georgia's chair for her when the doorbell rings.

"They're here," Isabella shouts, jumping up and down.

Georgia beams.

"Who's here?" I ask.

"Melanie and her family," she states.

"Oh yeah. I forgot they were coming this morning." I rise and go to the door with her. A short redhead, a man about six inches taller than her, and two kids that look just like the woman step inside.

Georgia makes introductions, and Melanie glances over me for so long, it makes me slightly uncomfortable. She finally states, "It's nice to meet you, Sebastian. I want to say I've heard a lot about you, but I haven't really heard that much to get to this stage."

My stomach flips.

Georgia groans. "Melanie, don't start."

"Melanie," her husband Greg warns.

I tug Georgia closer to me, stating, "No, it's okay. I know things happened quickly between us."

Melanie's eyes dart between Georgia and me, then she starts the interrogation. "So tell me, what do you love about Georgia the most?"

My stomach dives, but my heart seems to expand. I blurt out, "Everything. She's amazing."

"Yes, I agree. But what specifically about her do you love?" she repeats.

"Melanie," Georgia reprimands.

I lock eyes with Melanie, asserting, "I love how she finds the good in everything and how the room lights up the moment she steps into it."

"That's a good start. And?" Melanie pushes.

"Ugh," Georgia mutters.

I don't hesitate. "She's the nicest person I know, but she's genuinely happy. It's not fake. As I said, I love everything about her," I state and glance at Georgia.

Her face flushes slightly.

I suddenly wonder if I'm still pretending. I meant what I said, with the exception of love. I'm not capable of love.

Or am I?

We've not known each other that long. So love can't be true.

But this feels true.

"What do you think about her career goals? Are you going to support them?" Melanie questions.

Georgia's body stiffens.

I cock an eyebrow. "Of course I will. She's going to open her bakery come the New Year," I proudly state.

"You are?" Melanie asks.

"Yes," Georgia replies.

"So you're getting your franchise off the ground?" she excitedly quizzes.

Confused, I blurt out, "Franchise?"

Melanie's eyes turn to suspicious slits. "Yes. So you aren't in support?"

Georgia interjects, "I've not discussed that with Sebastian yet. I want to get my feet wet first and then decide if I'm going through with it."

Melanie tilts her head. "What are you talking about? It's your dream. You've done all the work for it. You got your MBA so you could be successful when you did it."

The puzzle pieces start coming together. I don't know all the details, but I recover from my initial shock and tighten my grip on Georgia's waist. "I can assure you if Georgia wants a franchise, she'll have it. But it seems like we have some more things to talk about," I say lightheartedly, then gaze at her.

She gives a tight smile, then adds, "Yes. We do. We just haven't gotten that far."

Melanie continues, "You're marrying him, and you haven't told him? How do you know he'll support you and won't try to stop you from achieving what you want?"

I adamantly state, "I would never stop Georgia from achieving what she wants."

259

"Let's go eat. I just put breakfast on the table. Plus, you need to meet Sebastian's family. You'll love them," Georgia quickly interjects.

"And give poor Sebastian a break!" Greg declares.

I give him a grateful look. I can appreciate Melanie trying to protect her friend, but it makes me nervous. I reply, "I can't blame her for wanting to protect Georgia. But I can assure you I only have good intentions."

Melanie gives me another suspicious glare.

"Let's go," Georgia says, grabs her hand, and tugs her toward the dining room.

We eat breakfast, and Melanie drops her interrogation. When we finish eating, the kids run off to play.

Georgia asks, "Do you want to see where we're going to get married? It's a secret garden and one of the most beautiful places I've ever stepped foot inside."

"Sure. We'd love to," Melanie claims.

"A walk would be good," Greg adds and rises.

My mom says, "You go ahead. I'll watch the kids."

We get bundled up and go outside. I take Georgia's hand, and we start down the road. We approach the area with the horses, and my brothers are about to train a new one that got delivered yesterday.

Greg whistles. "That's a beautiful racehorse you've got there."

"Are you into racing?" I ask.

Melanie laughs. "He's obsessed with it."

"Why don't you guys stay here, and Melanie and I can go to the garden?" Georgia suggests.

"That sounds good," Greg states.

"All right," I agree, then kiss Georgia on the forehead.

The entire time that we're with the horses, I try to pay attention, but I can't get the fact out of my mind that Georgia has business plans and didn't tell me.

Why would she tell me?

She should have. We're getting married.

But I've already told her we're getting an annulment.

There's no dream of only one silly cupcake bakery?

It's not silly. She's super talented and smart.

How would a franchise even work for what she wants to do?

Curiosity starts to morph into an obsession I can't shake. I don't doubt she can pull off whatever she dreams of, but I can't stand not knowing her plans.

I could help her.

Maybe she doesn't need my help.

Of course she does. I have money to help her make it happen.

Is that why she needed the million dollars?

Did Georgia out-negotiate me because her entrepreneurial goals are bigger than I ever gave her credit for?

A wave of guilt hits me. My ego was so big, I underestimated her. And as the day goes on, I only reprimand myself more.

Everything is so busy that I don't see Georgia until we're in the bedroom before the rehearsal dinner.

I step inside and freeze. A tingly, tight feeling ignites in my chest. My eyes dart from her face, down her form-fitting, icy-blue dress, to her matching stilettos. I drill my gaze into hers, claiming, "You look amazing."

She shyly replies, "Thanks."

My curiosity reappears. I demand, "Want to tell me about this cupcake franchise?"

She shrugs. "It's not a big deal. Don't worry about it."

"It is a big deal if it's something you want to do."

She walks to the dresser and reaches for her earrings, repeating, "I said not to worry about it."

"Georgia, why won't you tell me?" I ask, hurt lacing my tone.

She sighs, pushes her gold earring through her lobe, and utters, "Melanie shouldn't have opened her big mouth." She spins toward me. "You need to get ready, or we'll be late."

I shake my head. "I don't care. I want to know about this franchise you got an MBA for."

"Just drop it, Sebastian," she orders, then walks out of the room.

Disappointment wells within me. I get ready and try to push it away, but it's bugging me that she's keeping it from me. We go to the rehearsal dinner. Georgia remains mostly by my side, but everything now feels off between us.

My father moves me into a conversation with a group of his friends. When I turn to find Georgia, the hairs on my neck rise.

Andrew Duncan, another oil tycoon whose family is close with mine, has her cornered. I've never been a fan of his, but I put up with him because of our business dealings. He's leaning into her ear and saying something. She pushes on his chest, but he's a lot bigger than her and doesn't budge.

I fly across the room just in time to hear him slur, "We all know you're not going to make it down the aisle. My door's always open. And I can assure you I'll show you a better time than Sebastian Cartwright."

I grab the back of his suit jacket and slam him against the wall so fast, he cries out. I grasp his shirt, seething, "Don't you dare ever talk to her again."

He recovers from his shock and challenges, "I'll speak to whomever I wish."

I pull my arm back, and Alexander grabs it. "Whoa."

I spin, warning, "Get him out of here, or I'm going to."

My other brothers circle us, and Alexander nods at them.

"Sebastian," Georgia says.

I glance at her. She's slightly shaking, and her expression is filled with fear. I grab her and guide her down the hall while my brothers are dragging Andrew the other way.

"Sebastian, I didn't do anything," she claims.

"I know you didn't," I reply as I push her into the bathroom and lock the door.

Her lips quiver. "Then why do you look so mad at me right now?"

I ignore her question and press my mouth to hers, parting her lips with my tongue. I slide it farther into her mouth until her body submits to mine.

She mumbles, "Sebast—"

I spin her quickly, move her two steps forward, and push her down so her forearms are on the counter.

Her blues burst with flames. She drills them into the mirror, locking them to mine.

I press my erection against her ass, lean into her ear, and question, "How much does your tight pussy miss me?"

Her breath hitches. She swallows hard and then presses her ass into me.

I slide my hand on her thigh, crumpling her dress higher, then tear her delicate thong off.

"Oh!" she gasps. Her mouth hangs open.

I release my pants, then take my foot and move her leg to the side while sliding my finger inside her, never removing my challenging stare from her.

Her face flushes. She closes her eyes and then opens them.

"I think you're trying to drive me nuts," I state, removing my hand and pressing it over the back of her neck. A curled lock of her blonde hair falls over one eye. I graze my cock over her wet heat, and she shudders. I add, "Do you know what it's like for me having to watch other men flirt with you?"

"I didn't do anything," she claims.

"Ah, but you did, sweet Sunshine," I assert.

"No. I didn't—" She gasps again as I thrust, going as deep as I can into her until my pelvis is flush to her round ass cheeks. She whimpers.

I kiss the back of her neck and continue, "You were yourself. Maybe I'll have to lock you up once you say 'I do.' Keep you away from all the temptation." I begin to slowly inch in and out of her in long strokes.

"I don't...oh..." Her eyes flutter. "I don't want any of them."

My ego grows, and arrogance washes over my expression. I demand, "Who do you want?"

She takes a few breaths, pushing her hips into me as I enter her again.

"Tell me," I order.

She answers, "You. Only you, and you know it."

Do I?

Is she telling the truth?

Why am I even questioning this?

I move my hand to the front of her body and circle her clit at a faster speed than my thrusts. My cock swells, but I refrain from releasing inside her.

Her moans grow louder.

The handle jiggles, and then there's a knock.

"Go away," I bark, then move my hand off Georgia's neck and clasp it over her mouth.

Her eyes widen with worry, but then they roll in pleasure. Her body trembles against mine, and her muffled cry fills the air.

"Tomorrow night, when you're my wife, I'm going to make you come so hard, you won't be able to walk the next day without thinking about what I can do to you," I warn.

She shakes harder. Her walls spasm around my shaft, forcing me to use all the restraint I have not to be selfish and bury my seed deep within her.

The knock turns more urgent. "I have to go!"

I shout, "Find another bathroom." Then I thrust faster, continuing to manipulate Georgia's clit and keeping my body caged over her and the counter.

Her deep moan fills my ears as her knees buckle.

"Tell me you can't wait to marry me," I demand.

She squeezes her eyes shut.

I slow everything down.

"Sebastian...don't...I...please don't stop!" she says between choppy breaths.

"Admit it, Sunshine. Say the words." I thrust fast three times, then slow it down again.

"I can't wait to marry you," she blurts out in a desperate voice.

I pound into her like there's no tomorrow.

Her pussy clenches me like a vise and there's no more restraint left in me. I detonate inside her, my vision flashes to white, and I groan louder than I should.

The room slowly returns into focus. Georgia's still trembling underneath me. And I love everything about it.

There's another knock. I turn toward the door and order, "Find another bathroom!" I glance back at my juicy little peach. I kiss her on the cheek and pull her dress over her ass. I rise but don't step away from her. Then I pick her ripped panties off the floor and toss them in the trash.

She slowly rises but still grips the counter.

I wait a moment to ensure she's steady on her feet, then take a step back.

I ask, "Are you okay standing on your own?"

She nods, nervously looking at me.

I state, "Don't worry about whoever's outside."

She opens her mouth, then shuts it.

"What?" I question.

She spins and says, "I need a minute to freshen up."

I almost quiz her further but decide against it. I slide my hands over her flushed cheeks, staring at her.

"What?" she nervously asks.

"You're really beautiful," I state.

"Thank you," she replies.

There's another knock.

She rolls her eyes. "We should get out of here."

I peck her on the lips. "I'll wait outside." I slip out the door and then shut it.

"I need the bathroom," one of my mother's friends says, trying to push me aside.

I point down the hall. "There are more bathrooms."

"They aren't as nice as this one. It's a bunch of stalls," she says.

"So? Go use them. This one is still being used," I assert.

Confusion fills her expression. Then it turns to shock. "Sebastian Cartwright! If you think it's appropriate—"

"Save it," I bark.

She jumps and glares at me.

I point down the hall again. "I suggest you go use those."

She finally takes my advice, and I lean against the wall. The high of my orgasm wears off, and my previous frustration over Georgia not telling me her franchise plans reappears.

She told me she can't wait to marry me.

She did it so she could come.

When she opens the door, I slide my arm around her waist and lead her toward the back exit.

"Where are we going?" she asks.

"Why are you hiding things from me?" I blurt out, opening the exit door.

Confused, she replies, "Who said I was hiding things from you?"

"I want to know about this franchise," I state, steering her toward my truck.

"It's none of your business, Sebastian."

"So you're not going to tell me anything," I state and open the passenger door.

She glares. "Why are you pushing this?"

I motion for her to get into the truck.

She refuses for a moment, but I don't back down. She caves, sighing and then sliding inside.

I shut the door, get in the driver's side, and admit, "I couldn't understand why you would go through the hassle of getting your MBA only to have a silly little cupcake bakery. Now, I find out you want a franchise, which makes the MBA make sense, but why didn't you talk to me about this?" As soon as I say the words, I regret them.

Anger flares on her face. "And what if all I wanted was one bakery? Sorry, a *silly* little bakery."

My gut dives. I claim, "I didn't mean it like that."

"Yeah, you did," she says.

I take a deep breath, scolding myself for my choice of words. "I'm a dick. Sorry for saying silly. I didn't mean it," I restate.

"Yes, you did. But why would that be so bad if that's what I wanted?" she scolds.

I sigh. "I'm not saying it would be bad. I'm just saying that a woman as smart as you, who's worked as hard as you have, you know, there's something more for you."

"More for me? Why? Because everything's about money with you?" she accuses.

I've never felt bad about having or making money in my life until this moment. I'm unsure why, but Georgia sounds so disgusted right now that I cringe inside. I try again. "I'm not trying to be an asshole. I just want to know what it is that you want."

"What I want?" she asks, then blinks hard and looks away.

My insides flip. I lower my tone. "Yeah, Sunshine. I want to know what you want."

"What are you really asking me about, Sebastian?" she challenges.

My mouth turns dry. I stare at her, and tense silence builds between us.

She huffs. "Fine, I'll tell you about my career goals. I want to open a cupcake franchise, okay? I've done all the pre-work and got my MBA so I would have a higher chance of not failing. I know what it will cost down to the penny. Are you happy now?"

I try to process her statement.

She snaps, "Oh, sorry. Is that silly too?"

I groan. "Georgia, don't hold that word over my head for the rest of my life."

She scoffs, shaking her head.

"What did I say now?" I question.

She drills her blues into mine. "Don't worry, Sebastian. I won't hold anything over your head for the rest of your life." She jumps out of the truck before I can stop her, rushing back into the restaurant.

I follow her, and the DJ announces, "All right, it's time for dinner. Have a seat, lovebirds."

We sit down and get through the meal and the rest of the evening. She focuses most of her time on others. When the night is over, she gets into the back of the truck with Melanie and makes Greg sit in the front.

We arrive at the house, and Evelyn chirps, "Time for you guys to separate. It's bad luck for you to see the bride tomorrow morning when you wake up."

I groan inside. The last thing I want to do is sleep without Georgia next to me.

Evelyn orders, "You're in the other wing, Sebastian."

Once again, I'm annoyed with my sister, but I'm unsure how to get out of this situation.

"Goodnight," Georgia says and starts to leave.

I grab her wrist and pull her back to me. "Hey."

Sadness laces through her hardened expression. I don't understand what I've done, but everyone is looking at us. She quietly asks, "What?"

"You weren't going to kiss me goodnight?" I challenge.

"Sorry. I'm tired," she claims.

I try to give her a kiss, but she's not having it. My stomach just flips faster and faster.

She says, "Goodnight," spins, and I watch her leave me, feeling horrible. When I get to the guest room, I text her.

Me: *Are you going to show up tomorrow?*

A few minutes pass. The sick feeling in my stomach grows.

Georgia: Yes. I signed a contract.

It feels like a knife stabs through my chest at her words.

Me: *So is that all this is between us?*

I pace the room, grinding my molars, staring at my screen.

Georgia: *That was the agreement, Sebastian. It's what you wanted, right?*

My heart pounds harder. I start to text, erase it, and retype it several times. So much time passes that I get another text from her.

Georgia: *That's what I thought. I'll see you tomorrow. Let's not complicate things more than they are.*

I start to text her again, then stop.

What am I trying to say?

Why can't I just admit how I feel about her?

I finally get some balls and reply.

Me: *I really like you, Sunshine.*

Georgia: *It's not about like, Sebastian. Go to sleep. We have a big day tomorrow. I'm turning my phone off.*

And just like that, I've been silenced, except for a final text.

Georgia: *And stop worrying. I always hold up my end of deals.*

I should feel relieved I have her reassurance, but nothing feels good about it. All I can think is that she's only marrying me because she signed a contract.

I'm getting exactly what I wanted.

Yet nothing feels further from what I want.

Only, I still can't pinpoint what I want to happen between us.

Twenty-One

GEORGIA

"Time to get up," Melanie chirps.

I roll over in bed. I've been awake for hours, pretending to be asleep. My stomach won't stop flipping in a nervous heap of butterflies. I open my eyes, claiming, "Still too early."

"It's almost nine o'clock, girl. Everyone's going to be in the room soon," she scolds.

I groan, then roll over, opening my eyes.

She sits on the edge of the bed. "That's my girl."

"You look like you've been busy."

She points to a small cart in the room. "There's your breakfast."

"Wow. How'd you do that?" I ask.

How did I not hear her?

Because I'm so lost in my thoughts.

273

"Thanks," I offer.

She stares at me for a minute, and I cringe inside. It's the look she's been giving me since she arrived yesterday.

I ask, "What is it now?"

"Are you sure you want to do this?" she questions.

My chest tightens.

Am I sure I want to marry Sebastian Cartwright, god of sex and the hottest man on the planet?

It's not real.

"Melanie, can you stop, please?" I beg.

She turns toward me more. "Okay, but, Georgia, I don't understand the rush. Like, how do you know that Sebastian is the one? A week ago, all you could talk about is what a jerk he was."

"Things have changed. He's not a jerk," I announce.

She tilts her head. "Is something else going on?"

My pulse quickens. I ask, "Such as?"

She peers at me closer. "Sebastian Cartwright is known for being sneaky and callous."

Offended, I declare a little too loudly, "He's not sneaky and callous!"

She huffs. "Please. He's known all over Dallas as ruthless."

My head spins. I wish I could think of Sebastian as ruthless, but I can't. I've gotten to know him, and he's generous, kind, and even funny at times. "He's only ruthless in business. And never with me."

She gives me a challenging look, stating, "He was at the start."

"Drop it! And you should get to know him. It's not right for you to think about him that way. I'm marrying him!" I cry out, my insides quivering.

I'm marrying Sebastian Cartwright for less than thirty days.

She holds her hands in the air, surrendering. "Okay." Then she adds, "But you're positive?"

"Melanie. Stop," I firmly assert.

My door opens, and Emma and Isabella come running into the room. Relief hits me with their entrance.

"Georgia! It's the wedding day!" Isabella shrieks.

Emma jumps up on the bed and hugs me, along with Isabella. I hold them tight. I'm going to miss them so much. They've won my heart over, and the thought of them not being in my life hurts. Tears well in my eyes, but I blink them away.

All of Sebastian's sisters and his mom come in, beaming. Ruby chirps, "Time for the bride to get up."

"I know, I know. Okay, girls, you got to get off me, or I'll get in trouble." I give them a wink.

They jump off the bed, and I rise. A makeup artist and hair stylist enter the room. Within minutes, I'm behind the vanity. Excited chatter fills the air, but it only makes my nervousness intensify.

Melanie tries to get me to eat breakfast, but I can barely stomach more than a few bites of toast.

"How do you want to wear your hair?" the stylist asks.

"I was thinking down with curls, with a small section pulled back," I state.

She glances at my hair and picks up a handful of my locks. She nods. "Perfect choice."

The room becomes full of chatter while my hair and makeup get done. Melanie takes me aside and hands me a box when I'm finished.

"What is this?" I ask.

"Just a little gift," she chirps.

Suspicion fills me. "Why do I feel like I shouldn't open this?"

She smirks. "You totally should."

I remove the lid and pull out a white lace thong. It's delicate and probably costs way more than she should have spent.

My flutters dance in my belly. I glance at her. "Thanks."

She winks. "If you're going to do this, you might as well have a good time tonight."

My face heats. Sex with Sebastian is unlike anything I've experienced. My normal rule about only sleeping with a man who loves me and who I love no longer exists. Now that I gave in, I'm like an addict jonesing for another hit of him.

"Time for your dress. We have to get moving here," Ruby announces.

The nervousness flares all over. I stare at my wedding gown hanging against the door. It's beautiful. It's everything I could have ever wanted.

Too bad it's for the wrong guy.

Is it?

Of course it is. He's going to get our marriage annulled come January 2nd.

Ruby helps me get in my dress, and I stand in front of the full-length mirror. Too many emotions race through me as everybody fawns over me.

Evelyn claims it's time to leave.

We go outside, and a limo's waiting to transport Melanie, Emma, Isabella, and me to the secret garden.

The drive is short—too short. I've never felt so nervous. Emma and Isabella get out, then Melanie. I tell her, "I need a moment alone."

She scrunches her face, then sticks her head back inside. "Are you sure you're okay? We can still run."

Maybe I should.

No, I signed a contract.

He's already breaking my heart.

I fight more tears and somehow answer, "No, I'm fine. I just want a minute."

She reluctantly agrees and shuts the door.

For several moments, I breathe slowly, trying to calm my racing heart and flipping stomach.

Am I really going to do this?

Yes.

Besides, I can't leave Sebastian in there all alone. That would be worse than what anybody else has done to him.

I muster my courage and exit the limo. Melanie hands me a huge, beautiful bouquet. Dried chocolate-brown and cream flowers and the same color feathers create an exquisite work of art.

It's perfect. Everything about this entire situation is, except for the fact that it's fake. And it hits me harder than I ever anticipated.

The music plays. Emma and Isabella step through the door, tossing soft pink petals on the runner.

Then Melanie leans into me, whispering, "Last chance."

I glare at her.

She holds up her hands. "Kidding."

"No, you aren't."

She kisses my cheek. "You look incredible. I'll never say another word."

I exhale. "Good."

She steps through the door, and the wedding planner shuts it.

It takes less than a minute before the music changes to the traditional wedding march.

Too many thoughts hit me at once.

No one's walking me down the aisle. I didn't feel right asking anyone. I don't know the Cartwrights well enough to do that. And something about asking Sebastian's dad felt wrong when this isn't real. Now, I wish I would have because I've never felt so alone.

I miss my grammy. Even though this isn't real, her absence is felt.

The never-ending question about what I'm doing persists.

The door opens, and the wedding coordinator motions for me to come through. My knees wobble, but I step through the door.

Sebastian appears from behind a row of people, and I almost freeze. My blood pumps so hot, I feel slightly dizzy.

He's picture perfect in a chocolate-brown tux. Never in my wildest dreams did I imagine a man as stunning as him, standing at the end of the aisle, waiting for me. And not once did I anticipate my future husband giving me a look like the one he's giving me. It's as if he could have his way with me at any moment, and no matter where we were or what he wanted to do, I'd let him.

Somehow, I manage to make my way down the aisle. Sebastian steps forward, away from the crowd. His blues never leave mine, nor does that dirty expression on his face. It's the look that always makes me squeeze my thighs, and I reprimand myself.

This isn't the time to think about sex.

He takes my hands, leans down, and says, "Wow, you're more beautiful than I imagined you'd be, Sunshine."

My heart soars. I take another breath and smile, telling myself to pretend this is real. Then I'll be able to get through it.

The officiant says, "Should we start?"

Sebastian takes another moment, keeping me entranced in his gaze, then leads me closer to the officiant. I barely hear what he says, grateful Sebastian has his arm around my waist, helping me stay on my feet.

All I can smell is his praline, citrus, and sandalwood scent. And his palm grasping the curve of my waist has a constant supply of tingles racing several inches below it.

When it's time for the vows, Sebastian turns and grabs my hands.

I realize I'm shaking.

"Give me a minute," he quietly says to the officiant, squeezes my hands, then leans into me, whispering, "You okay, Sunshine?" He puts his face in front of mine and arches his eyebrows.

I nod and force a smile.

He studies me closer, and I nod again.

He murmurs in my ear, "Do you wish I invited Ho-Ho-Holly?"

I burst out in a laugh.

He grins and caresses the back of my hand with his thumb.

It helps calm me, and he mumbles, "That's my girl."

The officiant turns to Sebastian. "Ready?"

I nod at Sebastian again.

"Yes," he states.

The officiant says, "Repeat after me. I take you, Georgia Peach, to be my lawful wife."

Sebastian looks at me. "I take you, Georgia Peach, to be my lawful wife. I vow to love, protect, and cherish you beyond what you or anyone else would expect me to. I promise to put your needs first, mine second, and not take you for granted. I pledge this in sickness and health, for richer or poorer, for better or worse, until the day I die."

I gape at him. This isn't what we discussed. We agreed on normal, boring vows.

His statement affects me. I try to hold back tears, but one escapes.

What is he doing?

Why did he say that?

His words are everything I would ever want to hear from my husband-to-be. I don't understand why he's doing this to me.

Maybe I was wrong and Sebastian is cruel.

Is it part of his ruthlessness?

No, he's not anything but good to me.

The officiant glances at me. "Would you like to make your vows, Georgia?"

Panic fills me. My insides turn into a quivering, chaotic mess. Flustered, trying not to cry more, and wondering what I'm going to say, I close my eyes briefly.

Sebastian cuts in, ordering, "State the regular vows for Georgia, please." He squeezes my hands again and refocuses on me.

I open my eyes, grateful he stepped in. He gives me his award-winning smile, and a part of me calms.

The officiant comments, "I take you, Sebastian Allen Cartwright, to be my lawful husband."

My voice shakes and then it grows stronger. "I take you, Sebastian Allen Cartwright, to be my lawful husband."

Sebastian clenches his jaw, his eyes twinkling.

"To have and to hold from this day forward," the officiant adds.

My lips tremble and my knees wobble more. I repeat, "To have and to hold from this day forward."

Sebastian steps closer, caressing my hands again, and somehow it magically reduces my anxiety.

The officiant states, "For better or for worse, for richer or for poorer, in sickness and in health."

I repeat, "For better or for worse, for richer or for poorer, in sickness and in health."

The officiant continues, "To love and to cherish until death do us part."

I swallow hard, then raise my chin and square my shoulders, locking eyes with Sebastian. "To love and to cherish until death do us part." My insides roll so fast that I feel like I might get sick.

Sebastian gives me a small smile.

The officiant beams at us. "By the power vested in me by the glorious state of Texas, I now pronounce you husband and wife. Let me introduce you to Mr. and Mrs. Sebastian Cartwright."

The entire room breaks out in applause and shouts.

Mrs. Sebastian Cartwright.

The officiant looks at Sebastian. "Well, you may kiss your bride."

Sebastian tugs me into him and slides his hand under my hair, grasping the back of my neck. He briefly studies my face, then brings his lips to mine.

The room disappears. My body submits against his, molding into his hard frame, and he owns me once more. Only this time, I'm legally his wife.

He pulls back and murmurs against my lips, "You did good, Sunshine."

I stare at him, still processing everything.

"Or should I say Mrs. Cartwright?" He winks, then takes my hand and leads me past the chairs.

Everyone begins to congratulate us. By the time we've been hugged and kissed by all the guests, the chairs have been moved out of the way. That space is now a dance floor. Servers in tuxes and short black dresses roam the garden with trays full of appetizers. Champagne toasts are being made all around, yet I barely hear anything the entire time.

All I want to do is leave and be alone with Sebastian.

He never leaves my side the entire night. His hand's always on my bare back. I scold myself a million times for getting a dress that didn't have a back. I should have known he'd have his hand on my bare skin all night, putting my spine in an overload of tingles.

After dinner and a few dances, it's time for the bouquet toss. I go to the dance floor and throw it in the air. Paisley catches it and shrieks with excitement.

Alexander moves a chair to the dance floor and orders me to sit. Sebastian gives me his dirty, sexy look, and my butterflies reignite.

The song starts. Sebastian slides his hand up my leg slowly, his lips twitching. I try not to squirm, but I can't help it and shift in my seat.

He puts his lips on my ankle, moving up my calf, over my knee, and past my garter to the highest part of my inner thigh as possible.

And I swear that I feel him inhale deeply. That only creates more heat searing through my veins.

He finally removes the garter, and I'm positive my face is as red as a tomato. It's so hot, I'm going to break out into a sweat.

Sebastian's arrogant expression doesn't help cool me off. He tosses it, and I don't know who catches it.

Paisley and the man who caught the garter dance to a song. Halfway through it, Sebastian tugs me into him, and we dance.

There's no room between us. He can't get any closer. He leans into my ear and murmurs, "Glad your pussy's on fire for me, Mrs. Cartwright. I'm over this party. How about you?" He gives me a challenging, dirty stare.

There's no other answer I can give him. "Yes," I say breathily, wanting more than ever to be alone with him.

Satisfaction erupts on his chiseled features. He guides me away from everyone, and we don't even say goodbye.

There's a limo waiting for us. We get in, and he pulls me onto his lap, kissing me with a newfound fire.

I barely realize we've passed the house, but when I do, I question, "Where are we going?"

His eyes twinkle. "I'm taking you on a honeymoon, Mrs. Cartwright."

Twenty-Two

SEBASTIAN

Georgia freezes. She hesitates, then says, "A honeymoon?"

The hairs on my neck rise. I question, "That's what married people do, right?"

She swallows hard and turns toward the window.

I pull her chin back in front of me. "What's wrong? You don't want to go away?"

She opens her mouth, then shuts it. She takes a few deep breaths, then swallows hard.

The bad feeling in the pit of my stomach grows. I quietly ask, "Are you going to tell me what's wrong?"

She furrows her eyebrows, cautiously inquiring, "I thought you had to stay at your parents' until the New Year?"

"My parents were fine letting me leave for a week. It's a special occasion," I say.

She leers at me.

Dread fills me as I inquire, "Why do I get the feeling that isn't your concern?"

She stays quiet, but it's written all over her face that I'm right. The longer the silence continues, the more disturbed she looks.

"Why don't you tell me what this is really about?" I suggest.

She finally quizzes, "Why did you change your vows?"

My heart pounds harder. I debate about how to answer her, then finally choose the truth. "I don't know. It just came out when I opened my mouth."

She tilts her head. Her eyes turn to blue slits.

"Are you mad at me?" I ask.

"You just opened your mouth, and it came out?"

"Yes."

"You expect me to believe that you, Sebastian Cartwright, Mr. Prepared For Everything, didn't rehearse that?" she accuses.

"I didn't," I claim.

"So it wasn't part of the show?"

Confused, I question, "The show?"

She huffs. "Yeah, Sebastian. The show. You know, the one that you wanted? The big event to fool your family and the entire town?"

All the guilt and frustration I've felt over the last few days slaps me in the face. The closer we got to today, the more I regretted having Georgia sign the prenup. I wish I could have a redo, but there are no do-overs in life. I'm fully aware of that reality. And now we're in this situation. I don't even know where I'm at with her or how to morph this from something contractual to what I want.

Hell, I'm not even sure what it is I want.

"At least answer me," she demands, her cheeks heating with anger.

I quietly confess, "It wasn't for show."

Her bottom lip trembles. "Then tell me what it was about. I deserve an answer."

Tension grows between us. The limo rolls to a stop, and I glance out the window at my private jet. I mutter, "We're here."

The driver gets out of the car and shuts his door.

Georgia states, "I want an answer, Sebastian. If you didn't change your vows for a show, then why did you say those things to me?"

All my feelings for Georgia that I'm still trying to decipher jumble in my mind. I reach for her cheek, but she jerks her head backward.

The door opens, and our driver says, "Time to get in the air."

Georgia slides over me and steps out of the limo. She hightails it to the stairs.

"Georgia," I call after her, close on her heels and trying not to step on her train.

She holds her dress and marches up the staircase.

"Georgia," I repeat, reaching for her arm.

"Don't touch me!" she seethes, spinning on the top step. Her blue eyes glisten.

My heart feels like it's being squeezed by a pair of pliers. I've never seen her so angry, except after what I did to her by the pool the first night we got to the ranch. I'm unsure what's happening or causing her to be so upset, but I hold my hands in the air, yielding. "Okay."

She drills her glare into me further, then shakes her head. She turns back and nods to the flight attendant, Carmine. She goes directly to the bedroom and shuts the door.

I step past Carmine and open the door, trying again, "Georgia—"

"Get out, Sebastian," she cries out.

"I don't understand what's going on right now," I admit.

She laughs, and a tear falls down her cheek. "How convenient for you."

"Sunshine—"

"I said to get out, unless you can be honest with me," she demands.

I stare at her for a moment, feeling hollow. She's the most beautiful bride I've ever seen, and I don't know why I'm tongue-tied.

She's my bride.

I've hurt her.

I need to tell her how I feel about her.

I open my mouth, but the coward in me wins. I snap my mouth shut.

She looks at me as if I'm pathetic.

I wish I could say I wasn't, but it's an appropriate word to describe how I feel. I decide to give her space and offer, "When you're ready to talk about whatever this is, I'll be here."

She laughs, wiping at more tears. "You can talk to me when you're ready to be honest."

"How have I not been honest?" I question, but as I say the words, I know I'm lying to her and myself.

She scoffs. "Figure it out. Now, get out." She squeezes her eyes shut and turns away.

Defeated, I shut the door and plop down on a seat.

"Mr. Cartwright, would you or Mrs. Cartwright like a drink?" Carmine asks.

Mrs. Cartwright.

Hearing Georgia called that fills me with pleasure and sadness.

How is it my wife is so pissed at me on our wedding night?

Because I'm a heartless asshole.

"No, thank you," I answer.

Carmine smiles. "Jeffry said we're ready to take off."

"Very well," I reply.

Carmine nods and then goes to the front of the plane.

Within minutes, we're in the air. I glance out the window, staring at the fading lights until there's nothing but blackness. And that's how I feel right now—dark, void of any light.

Georgia's light.

Why can't I tell her how I feel?

What exactly do I feel?

Hours pass. The longer I go without telling her I have feelings for her the worse it gets. I'm unsure how to undo the damage I've done by making her agree to this arrangement, and it only makes me feel sicker.

I go to the bedroom door several times but chicken out before I can knock or open it. When we're six hours into the fourteen-hour flight, I finally get sick of my inability to be a man.

I've never felt so nervous. I rise, go to the bedroom door, then knock softly.

She doesn't answer.

I knock again, this time louder, but no sound comes from inside. I slowly open the door, slip into the room, and lock the latch.

It's dark, but Georgia's white dress glows from the little light streaming in from the blinds. She's curled on the bed, hugging a pillow.

She's so quiet, I barely hear her raspy whisper, "Why are you here, Sebastian?"

I lie on the bed, slide my arm under her, and wrap my other around her. I inhale her sugary-rose scent, then kiss her on the head.

"Why?" she repeats.

I realize this is my moment of truth. I either lay my cards on the table, or I'm never getting things back to where they were between us. So I flip onto my back and tug her toward me.

She takes a shaky breath. Her lashes are wet, and her mascara is smudged under her eyes.

I scoot down, so my face is in front of hers, and reach for her cheek.

She closes her eyes and sighs. She states, "I can't do this, Sebastian. I thought I could, but I can't. Not like this."

My stomach dives. I blurt out, "I like you, Georgia. A lot. More than anyone I've ever dated or was engaged to."

She holds her breath.

I continue, "I wish you never signed the contract. More than anything, I wish we could start all over."

She blinks hard, then says, "We can't, can we?"

"No. I messed that up for us," I admit, tracing her lip with my thumb.

She presses her palm on my chest and traces the outline of my shirt. Zings erupt under her finger, and my heart races faster. She states, "You didn't do this alone, Sebastian. I agreed to it."

The hum of the engine is the only sound filling the air. A million thoughts spin in my mind, but no solutions to our problem appear. I finally say, "You're the most beautiful bride I've ever seen. And I mean that. You stole my breath when I saw you."

Her eyes glisten more. A tiny smile erupts on her lips, giving me a twinge of joy. She continues moving her finger over my skin and states, "You clean up well too."

More time passes, and neither of us tear our gaze off the other.

"I hate how I couldn't give you the wedding you deserved."

Her face falls. She replies, "It's tough not being able to love anyone, isn't it?"

Without hesitation, I say, "What if I regret saying that?"

She freezes, holding her breath.

I ramble, "What if maybe there was a woman I think I could fall in love with?" My pulse pounds between my ears.

She opens her mouth and then shuts it.

The roller coaster in my gut reappears. At record speed, I fall down the first hill and assert, "I lost my chance with you, didn't I?"

The silence is excruciating. I decide I've lost her, and there's no recovering from it, when she asks, "Is that what you want, Sebastian? A chance with me?"

"Yes. I want a real chance. No lies. No deceit. Just you and me," I claim.

"What about your family?" she asks.

My chest tightens. I shake my head. "I don't know what to do about that. If I tell them before Christmas—"

"Alexander will become CEO," she finishes.

I move over and put my hands over my face. "I'm done. My father will never forgive me."

A moment passes, and Georgia slides on top of me. She locks eyes with me and quietly says, "Or we can wait to fess up to them until after you're named CEO."

"But I don't want to pretend with you anymore," I admit.

She smiles. "Okay, then don't."

"I'm... Now I'm confused," I admit.

She tilts her head. "You've worked too hard, Sebastian. No one deserves to run Cartwright Enterprises more than you. And Alexander told me he doesn't want to take over, so what's the point of your father making that decision?"

"To teach me a lesson that I deserve," I offer.

She scoffs. "Maybe you do, but that's pretty harsh."

I caress her back, which is another thing that's been driving me crazy all night. No woman's back has ever turned me on so much. I ask, "What are you saying?"

"I'm suggesting... Well, I'm suggesting we finish out what we started, let you take over as CEO, then we can figure out what to do about this situation."

I don't speak for a while.

"Do you now want to be CEO?" she asks.

"Of course I do."

"Good. You're meant to be it," she claims.

"Thanks for your confidence," I tease.

"You're welcome. But I only say it because it's true. And I don't want to screw that up for you, Sebastian."

"You wouldn't be. It would be my fault," I assert.

She bites her lip.

"What?" I ask.

"Maybe so, but you couldn't have done this without my assistance," she declares.

I tighten my arms around her. "You are a pretty good assistant."

A tiny laugh escapes her.

"I love hearing you laugh," I confess.

"I love hearing you laugh," she states.

I admit, "I do it more when you're around."

Her face lights up. "Then maybe you should keep me around."

I flip her onto her back, and she screeches. I cage my body over hers and insist, "Oh, I'm keeping you around, Mrs. Cartwright."

She reaches for my cheeks, then stares at me.

I lean down and kiss her, and every fear I have seems to melt away.

But then she yawns.

"Did you just yawn in my mouth?" I ask, feigning shock.

She giggles and puts her hand over her face. "Yeah. Sorry!"

I roll to my side, move her to hers, then curl into her. "You can make it up to me when we're in our hotel room."

She turns her head. "Where are we going?"

My nervousness makes another appearance. I thought long and hard about where to take Georgia. I don't want to disappoint her again. I announce, "Iceland."

She spins into me. "Iceland!"

I chuckle. "Yes. Iceland. I assume you're okay with that?"

"Iceland during Christmas? Are you kidding me?" she cries out.

I wiggle my eyebrows. "So, does this mean I'm the best husband ever?"

She laughs. "Why yes. Yes, you are, Mr. Cartwright."

"Maybe we can enjoy the week and deal with the other stuff when we get home?" I suggest hopefully.

She takes a deep breath and nods. "Yeah, let's do that."

"Thank you." I kiss her, but she yawns again. I groan. "You're killing me, Sunshine. Roll over."

"Sorry." She cringes, then obeys.

I wrap my body around her again and order, "Go to sleep." I kiss her cheek, and she closes her eyes.

For once, everything seems right in my life. I'm unsure how we'll figure everything out, but right now, I don't care. I have my Sunshine in my arms and nothing has ever felt better.

Twenty-Three

GEORGIA

"Time to get up, Sunshine," Sebastian softly says, stroking my cheek.

I open my eyes, taking in my surroundings. I'm still in my wedding dress, and Sebastian's in his tux, minus the coat and bowtie.

Where am I?

Oh, the plane.

I sit up. "Are we here?"

His eyes light with mischief. He replies, "We are, but I think it's time I take you out of this wedding dress."

My butterflies take off. I tease, "Now we're going to have sex? I could have joined the mile-high club."

Heat travels to his eyes. "Don't worry, Sunshine. We'll make sure we do that on the way back."

I squeeze my thighs together. *Maybe we should stay here a bit longer...*

He interrupts my naughty thoughts, ordering, "Come on, time's ticking."

I rise, and he steps behind me. He drags his knuckles down my spine until he gets to my zipper. I shiver. "Don't tease me."

He brings his lips to my ear. "I told you how amazing you look, right?"

I glance behind me, my lips an inch from his. I state, "I'm sure I look fabulous right now."

"You always look good," he declares.

My heart flutters again.

He unzips my dress and it falls to the floor. His warm hands palm my ass cheeks. His lips tease the curve of my neck and he murmurs, "Too bad we need clothes."

Zings explode in all my cells and I lean against him. I ask, "Since I didn't pack any clothes, I'm assuming you did?"

He chuckles. "Don't worry. I've got this handled. Do you want to go to the bathroom and wash your face? You've got some makeup running down it."

"Oh geez." I cringe.

He shrugs. "I assume you don't want to go out like that. But I'm okay with it if you are."

I shake my head. "Absolutely not. Is there anything to wash it off with?"

"There's stuff inside." He points to the bathroom door.

"Of course there is," I chirp, loving that Sebastian is always prepared. I step into the bathroom, and horror fills me.

Mascara streaks down my face in thick, black blurry lines. My lip stain faintly outlines my mouth but isn't on the rest of it. The white in my eyes is red.

"Let's see what's in here," I mutter, then open the medicine cabinet. My heart swells. Sebastian's stocked it with all of my skincare products, makeup, and other toiletries. There's also a bottle of eye drops.

I wash my face and add the drops. Then I put on a small amount of makeup and deodorant. I spritz three sprays of perfume and step back outside.

Sebastian wears a pair of designer jeans and a beige sweater. His eyes drift down my body. I realize all I'm wearing is the little thong Melanie gave me. He pins his blues on my lower body and smirks, "Nice touch."

I try to avoid his heated gaze and blurt out, "Oh gosh, please tell me you have clean underwear for me too."

He points to the pile of clothes on the bed. "That I do."

"Thank goodness!" I exclaim, wishing I could take a shower.

We quickly get dressed. I slide into a pair of skinny jeans, a nude tank top, and a pale-pink cable-knit sweater. I beam. "This is really nice. And thanks for stocking the plane with all my bathroom things."

Pride fills his expression. He tosses his arm in the air in victory, proclaiming, "Yes! I got another thing right."

"You get a lot right," I blurt out.

His face falls. He lowers his voice, questioning, "I do?"

I nod. "Yeah, you do."

A humble grin graces his lips. It's rare I see it; he normally wears his cocky one, but I like it just as much. He gives me a peck on the lips and says, "I'm glad you think so."

"I do," I reiterate.

He retreats, stating, "Let's get out of here. Coats, hats, scarves, and gloves are at the front of the cabin."

I give him a little salute. Excitement fills me. I still can't believe I'm in Iceland for Christmas! "Okay then, let's do this."

We enter the front of the cabin and put on our outdoor gear.

The flight attendant smiles. "Good morning, Mrs. Cartwright. Did you sleep well?"

Mrs. Cartwright. My heart swoons again.

It's not real.

Or is it?

Since Sebastian admitted he had feelings for me, I don't know what to think. But before I fell asleep, I decided to enjoy Iceland and figure out the rest later.

Slightly embarrassed that I rushed past her and didn't really introduce myself when I stepped on the plane, I reply, "I did. I'm Georgia. I'm sorry I was rude earlier." I hold out my hand.

She shakes it, beams, and says, "I'm Carmine. Nice to meet you, and you weren't. Congratulations on your big day."

Relief fills me that she seems genuine and isn't going to hold my bad manners against me. I reply, "Thank you!"

Sebastian puts his arm around me, then addresses Carmine, "Have a good time in Iceland, Carmine. We'll see you in a week."

"You too," she responds and opens the door.

Sebastian motions for me to go first, and I step out on the landing. I freeze, muttering, "Holy moly!"

The morning sun is trying to rise, and the sky is a mix of green and blue hues with just a hint of purple. The buildings glow gold from the Christmas lights. Ice and snow are everywhere. I declare, "I've never seen anything so majestic."

"Incredible, isn't it?" Sebastian agrees.

I glance up at him. "This is so sweet that you brought me here."

The arrogant expression I love about him takes over his face. He proclaims, "I thought you'd enjoy it."

"I do," I restate.

Amused, he asserts, "We haven't done anything yet."

"Yeah, but this is going to be insanely cool," I insist.

He chuckles.

A driver standing near an SUV waves his hands and shouts, "Welcome to Iceland."

My excitement level increases. We make our way down the tarmac, and Sebastian shakes his hand, announcing, "This is my beautiful wife, Georgia Cartwright. And I'm Sebastian."

Georgia Cartwright.

His wife.

My stomach flutters again. I push the mystery of what's going on between Sebastian and me and where this is going to the back of my mind. This is too awesome of a trip to worry about that. Plus, he admitted he likes me and wanted to do something nice, so at least I'm not just here because he wanted to trick his family further.

The driver says, "My name is Helgi."

"It's great you speak English, because I don't know a word of Icelandic," I fret.

He gives us an amused smile as he says, "You don't need to worry about knowing Icelandic. Almost ninety-eight percent of the population speaks English. It's taught as a second language in school, so you'll be fine."

"Really? I had no clue," I confess.

"Yes." He opens the back of the vehicle.

I slide in, and Sebastian follows. As soon as the door shuts, my stomach growls.

Sebastian admits, "I'm starving too. What do you say we figure out breakfast?"

I nod. "Sounds good to me."

Helgi puts the luggage in the car and then gets in the driver's seat.

Sebastian inquires, "Helgi, where can we go eat? We're starving."

"I know the perfect place. It's not too far from here. It's a popular bakery and eatery, and you have to go there when you're in our town."

"Sounds great. Let's go," Sebastian commands.

It doesn't take long, and we're soon dropped off in front of a bakery. The moment we step inside, the smell of pastries hits me. My stomach rumbles again. I declare, "This place smells amazing."

Sebastian nods.

I glance at him. "You're not going to stick to your crazy diet, are you?"

He grins. "Nope."

I tilt my head, not sure if I believe him. Then I question, "Are you telling the truth?"

He makes a cross over his heart, stating, "Cross my heart and hope to die. I promise I'll indulge in everything with you."

I toss my arms around his neck and rise on my tiptoes. I give him a kiss on the lips. "That's good. We'll get back on track when we get home."

He nods. "Deal."

I spin, take his hand, and lead him toward the front of the counter. When the line thins out, a woman says something to us in Icelandic.

Sebastian states, "We just got off a plane from the U.S."

Her face lights up. "Welcome to Iceland! I'll switch to English."

"Thank you," I say.

"We've not been here before, so I'm assuming Georgia's okay with this." He eyes me and then asks her, "What's the most Icelandic breakfast you have?"

I clap my hands. "Yes, that's what we want."

She beams. "You're going to want skyr, which is a thick, creamy sour cheese. It's eaten like yogurt, and we'll add some berries and seeds to it. And then you need some rye bread with meat and cheese."

"Sounds delicious," I proclaim.

She adds, "I also recommend the hafragrautur."

"What's that?" Sebastian questions.

"It's an oatmeal porridge with milk and brown sugar. Also, do yourself a favor and get one of these." She points to a big pastry behind her.

I inquire, "What is that called?"

She answers, "Snúður. It's a cinnamon bread roll filled with chocolate or caramel."

I ask Sebastian, "Can we have both?"

Sebastian chuckles, then tells the woman, "My wife has a sweet tooth."

Her eyes get brighter. "You'll love them. Both of you!"

"We'll take one of each, please," Sebastian declares.

"Great. Can we get some coffee too?" I ask.

"Sure." She hands us two mugs and motions to the counter with several urns, sweeteners, and creamers. "Anything else?"

"I think that's it," Sebastian answers.

She punches in the order, hands us a number, and instructs, "Just take a seat. We'll bring it all out."

Sebastian pays and we fill our coffee.

I choose a table by the window. People rush past it, and I chirp, "This is so cool."

"You already said that," he says, a new look of amusement on his face.

"Yeah, but it really is. What made you pick this place?"

He takes a sip of coffee and admits, "You said you thought about going to Iceland for Christmas. It was that or the North Pole. Unlike you, I did some research. The North Pole was pretty inaccessible this time of year, so I didn't want to take any risks."

"You chose well," I praise, then lean over and kiss him on the lips.

He tugs me in for a longer one, and someone clears their throat.

I retreat, sit back in my seat, and blurt out, "Oops!"

A young man grins at us. He sets food on the table until it's full, I stare at our breakfast, not sure what to try first. Overwhelmed, I state, "This is a lot of food. Do you think we went a bit overboard?"

"Nope!" Sebastian answers, then takes a spoonful of what I assume is the skyr and holds it to my mouth. "You're the guinea pig."

I laugh. "Is that so?"

He wiggles his eyebrows. "Yep. Try it."

I take a bite, chew, then swallow.

"Well?" he asks.

"It's good!" I claim.

He tries a spoonful and declares, "Way better than yogurt."

I dip my spoon in it, replying, "Agreed."

We spend the next hour eating, tasting each item, unsure what we like the best. When we're done, we're full.

I'm happy Sebastian tried everything and didn't worry about any of the ingredients. It's the first time I've seen him relaxed around food that isn't part of his normal routine. And he shows no sign of stress. While he's been calmer at the ranch than what I saw in Dallas, he seems worry free, engaged in the present, and that makes me happy. I love this side of him.

He leads me out of the cafe and Helgi's waiting for us. He states, "I called the hotel. There's a plumbing issue in your suite. It won't be ready until six. The hotel said they'd discuss how to compensate you when you arrive. I asked if there was another room you could utilize, but with the holiday season, the hotel is full."

Sebastian groans. "I'm dying for a shower."

"Me too," I confess.

Helgi suggests, "Let me take you to the Blue Lagoon. It's under forty kilometers, and there are geothermal swimming baths."

"That sounds incredible," I declare, a rush of excitement bubbling up again.

Sebastian agrees, "You heard the boss. Let's go."

I gasp. "I'm the boss?"

"Happy wife, happy life," Sebastian teases.

Wife.

Not real.

Shush it.

I bat my eyelids. "Smart man." I kiss him and sink into his body.

The trip takes about an hour. I keep staring out the window in amazement, unable to believe I'm actually in Iceland. Everything about it is beautiful and unlike anything I've seen before.

We arrive at the Blue Lagoon. As we exit the SUV, I see the steam rising off the water. I can only mutter, "Wow."

"Have you ever been to one of these?" Sebastian asks.

Unable to take my eyes off it, I reply, "No. Have you?"

"Yeah. Years ago, I went to New Zealand," he replies.

I glance at him. "Did you like it?"

"Loved it. I'll take you there next if you want," he says, his eyes filling with hope, which takes me by surprise.

My heart swells again. I reveal, "I'd love to go with you."

He kisses the back of my hand. "Great. I'll plan it."

I turn back to the steaming water. "I guess you get to pop my cherry."

His eyes widen. "Did you just say pop your cherry?"

I laugh. "Yep. My geothermal cherry."

He chuckles, then adds, "You're always full of surprises, Sunshine."

"I like to keep you on your toes," I claim.

"That you do. Let's go change," he directs and leads me to the changing area.

We change and he hands me a claw clip. "I thought you might want this so your hair doesn't turn to ice after we get out of the water."

My heart skips a beat. I tease, "Well, Sebastian Cartwright. Are you a secret claw clip lover?"

He chuckles, then slides his arm around my waist. He leads me to the water and I secure my hair on top of my head. We dip in the hot springs. The warm water heats up my cold skin. I moan. "I'm in heaven."

Sebastian pulls me into him, wrapping his arms around me, giving me his intense expression. He replies, "Good way to describe it."

My stomach flutters some more. I blurt out, "Are you trying to permanently win me over?"

"What if I am?" he questions, his blues looking semi-arrogant and semi-nervous.

My butterflies flutter faster. I confess, "Then I'd say you're off to a good start."

Satisfaction and relief flit across his features. He kisses me, and for several minutes, we stay lip-locked.

For hours,, we swim, talk, and laugh. After we dry off, we change and return to the car.

Sebastian inquires, "Where to now, Helgi? It looks like we've got more time to kill."

He turns around in his seat. "The village of Hafnarfjörður. It's thirty-two kilometers from here, but it's on the way back to Reykjavik. It's known as the Christmas town. There's a ton of shopping, restaurants, and you'll see a bunch of elves."

"Elves?" I chirp.

"Yes. There are also art galleries, craft beer tastings, and free live entertainment in the marketplace."

"Sounds good. Let's roll," Sebastian orders, leans back, and slings his arm around me.

I relax into him, which is starting to feel normal. I'm still in awe, and so happy, I wonder if I've ever felt this way. When we get to Hafnarfjörður, we walk around the marketplace. We visit lots of different shops, buying Christmas gifts for Melanie's family and Sebastian's.

For his sisters, mom, and Melanie, we decide to get skincare products and wool blankets. For the kids, we buy Icelandic candy, including licorice shoelaces, praline-peppermint chocolate, chocolate raisins, and chocolate Draumur, which in English means dream.

I hold the praline-peppermint chocolate in front of Sebastian, admitting, "You smell like praline."

He cocks his eyebrows. "I do?"

I inhale the scent of the candy. "You sure do."

"And this is a good thing?" he questions.

I admit. "It's a sexy, good thing."

His grin grows. "Well, I guess I won't change my cologne, then."

I warn, "Don't you dare!"

"Noted," he states with a chuckle.

We continue finding gifts, buying the little boys Viking books and toys. For the girls, we buy jewelry made from lava rock and some Icelandic dolls.

"Here we go," he booms, picking up a bottle of Icelandic alcohol.

"Are you into schnapps?" I ask.

He shrugs. "Not really, but when in Iceland..."

A sales clerk states, "Brennivín, or sometimes called Svarti dauði, is a distilled brand of schnapps. It's considered Iceland's signature liquor. It means black death."

"This will be perfect for my dad, brothers, and Greg," Sebastian claims.

I interject, "It sounds like a really bad hangover."

The sales clerk answers, "Sometimes."

Sebastian's face fills with mischief. He adds, "We'll have to see, won't we?"

"You're evil," I state, laughing. I turn to the cashier. "How do they make this?"

He replies, "It's from fermented potato mash, and we use caraway seeds to flavor it."

"Interesting," I say.

Sebastian leans close to my ear, questioning, "Are you also an alcohol connoisseur?"

I shake my head. "No, but ingredients interest me."

"Ah. I should have known."

I hold my hands in the air. "I'm an ingredient whore. What can I say?"

"Did you just call yourself a whore?"

"An ingredient one."

"Sunshine, you kill me." He chuckles. He turns to the clerk and points to several bottles. "We'll take four of each." Then he spins back toward me, announcing, "I'm getting hungry again. It's way past lunch. Want to go eat?"

The cashier points across the street. "They do craft beer tasting there, and the food is top notch."

"Great. Sounds perfect," I reply.

We check out, and Sebastian texts Helgi to pull up to the store. The clerk helps Helgi load the alcohol into the car, and Sebastian leads me across the street. We're seated in a booth and Sebastian slides next to me.

The server sets down a loaf of homemade bread and recommends a fish sampler. It includes cod, salmon, and haddock paired with dipping sauces.

Sebastian orders that and adds lobster, a side of roasted root vegetables, and a beer tasting for each of us.

Everything is just as delicious as breakfast. We finish all the food, and I put my hand on my stomach. "I'm officially full."

"It was good, wasn't it?" Sebastian asks.

"Delicious," I declare.

He glances at his watch. "It's after six. Do you want to go to the hotel and check in? I could do with a little nap before we go out tonight. Unless you decide you want to stay in?" he adds and gives me his lewd, challenging stare.

My face heats and I answer, "We have been out all day."

He murmurs, "Maybe we should shower and double-check they fixed the plumbing."

I lean into his ear, drag my fingers over his inner thigh, then suggest, "I am feeling a bit dirty. Maybe you can help make sure I get clean?" I retreat and give him an innocent stare.

"Time to go," he states, rising and holding his hand out.

I laugh, take it, and we walk to the SUV. Before we get inside, he gives me a kiss on the lips and studies me for a moment.

My nerves ignite. I question, "What?"

He hesitates and says, "I think this is the happiest I've ever seen you."

I confess, "It is."

"Really?"

"Yeah, this was the best day of my life so far," I tell him honestly.

A huge grin forms on his face. He takes my hand and kisses the back of it. "That's good, Sunshine. It's mine too."

"It is?"

He nods. "Without a doubt."

We get into the car. He tugs me into him, and I stare out the window, happy, content, and with a stomach full of food. I'm so full of joy I think I might explode, but I realize it's not just Iceland. It's spending time with Sebastian that I love so much. Within minutes, I drift off to sleep, curled into his warm chest, dreaming about us.

Twenty-Four

SEBASTIAN

A Few Days Later

"After you," I say, opening the door to our hotel. Georgia and I were downstairs eating breakfast. She finally agreed to show me her franchise concept. I've been bugging her all week to show me, and I could tell she was closer to caving. Now that she's agreed, I'm chomping at the bit to see it.

"Aren't you the eager beaver?" she teases and steps inside.

"Yep. And proud of it," I declare. I grab my laptop off the desk. "Sit."

She obeys, and I take the seat next to her. I turn on the laptop, punch in my security code, and place it on her lap. "Go ahead and log in."

She bites her lip and winces.

My gut sinks. "What's wrong? You're not backing out, are you?"

She hesitates, stating, "No. It's just... Well, I've not shown anyone this."

"Melanie has seen it," I point out.

"Melanie doesn't count," she claims.

I dramatically gape, then lean closer and lower my voice. "Does Melanie know this?"

Georgia puts her hand over her face and groans. "No. That sounded bad, didn't it?"

"Yep. So why doesn't she count?" I question.

Georgia turns more toward me. "She's my friend. She'll tell me she likes it, no matter what."

I arch my eyebrows at her. "I doubt that. Melanie seems like she'll always tell you what she thinks. But do you think if I see something wrong with it, I'm not going to point it out?"

She cringes. "Yeah. That's what I'm kind of scared of."

I chuckle. "Come on, Sunshine. I'm sure it's fabulous. Let me see what you've planned. Plus, you know I'd only point something out if I thought there was a major mistake that could hurt you."

She takes a deep breath and logs in to the cloud. She inquires, "What do you want to see first?"

"Whatever you want to show me."

She scans the different folders, then pulls up one labeled *graphics*. She clicks several times, and a logo pops up on the screen. It's a huge gourmet chocolate cupcake with pink frosting, and the word "Grammy's" is written in a scripted font, and "Cupcakes" is in a bold block script.

I blurt out, "That's badass."

"You like it?"

I scoot closer. "Yes, I do. Your fonts are great. They pop. And so do the colors. I can see that on a wall."

She beams proudly. "It will be. Right behind the counter!" She clicks on another folder, and a layout appears. Excitement grows in her voice as she informs me, "I hired a designer to create this. I know it would have to be scaled to each building, but this is the basic design I want."

I study it for a moment, looking at all the details, impressed with how thorough the specs are.

Before I can say anything, Georgia points to the kitchen. "The appliances have to be here. The ovens I want to buy can make over a hundred cupcakes an hour. The number per building will depend on the location and kitchen size. And I wanted to make sure that things run efficiently. So this is why the sink needs to go here, the ovens here, and the mixers here. The dishwashing station is there."

"That makes sense. I wouldn't have thought about that stuff. You put a lot of time into this," I state.

She nods, then moves her hand out to the front of the store. "The display case with the cupcakes has to be first. I can't stand it when you go into a bakery, and you're supposed to order, but the display case is after the cashier. It doesn't make sense."

I've never really thought about it, but she's right. I proudly declare, "Once again, genius idea."

She tilts her head. "Are you being condescending?"

I furrow my eyebrows. "No, not at all. Why would you think that?"

She exhales but avoids answering my question. "Okay. So the hot drink station for the fancy coffees and teas will be here. The cold case for the sodas and water will be here." She points to the area before the customer would order.

"Makes perfect sense. What's this?" I ask, pointing to an area that looks like couches.

She motions to the front of the building. "These are normal tables, but I thought this could be an area where people can meet and stay awhile. Kind of a lounging area, so I thought couches and overstuffed armchairs would be comfier." She motions to the corner. "This is going to be a quiet area. There'll be a glass wall so people can go inside and work."

Impressed, I study it, commenting, "You really have thought of everything."

"I want Grammy's Cupcakes to be a place where people come in and stay. Somewhere they feel welcome...kind of like home," she admits.

I slide my arm around her shoulder and kiss her cheek. "You have good ideas. I love everything about it. Thank you for showing me."

Her cheeks slightly flush. She smiles and inquires, "Do you want to look at my spreadsheets?"

I rub my hands together. "Of course I want to look at your spreadsheets."

She laughs and rolls her eyes. "That was a dumb question, wasn't it?"

"You know it," I reply.

She opens another folder and pulls up a spreadsheet with a dozen different tabs. She clicks on one and states, "This is the one for the build-out."

I know a lot about build-outs, so I study it. I whistle, "You're pretty bang on with your numbers."

She beams, then opens another tab. "This is what the franchise costs will be based on from when I last researched it. I updated it about a month ago. Not much changed."

I review her costs. Her attorney fees are sky-high. I move the mouse over them. "Where did you get the numbers for this category?"

"I got several quotes," she answers.

"I have the firm you should use. It'll cost a third," I claim.

Her eyes widen. "Seriously?"

"Yes."

"That's a ton of money to save!"

I do everything I can to not smile. I don't want her to think I'm being condescending again—I'm not. I'm so impressed by what she's already planned, I can't even describe it. I hold my serious face and assert, "I'll introduce you when we return to Dallas."

"Thanks."

"Of course. What's this tab?" I question.

She opens it. "This is the monthly fixed costs and then I have the variables on this side. Because of my ingredients, I can't be certain what they'll be. And the more I buy, the cheaper the costs will be, so it'll change. I did run this spreadsheet." She clicks on another tab. "And these are the base prices for ingredients for bulk for the last five years."

Every single day for the last five years has a date and price. Shocked, I ask, "How did you get this?"

She shrugs. "I researched it."

"This is ridiculously detailed," I claim.

"Too much?" she asks, wincing again.

"No, not at all. This is impressive, Sunshine."

"It is?" she questions again.

"Of course it is. Why are you second-guessing yourself because I'm looking at it?" I inquire.

Her face turns red. "I am, aren't I?"

"Yes. And you shouldn't," I declare.

She releases a stress-filled breath. "You're right."

"You know this inside and out. Don't ever doubt yourself," I tell her.

She smiles, and my heart swells. She quietly replies, "Thanks."

I know the perfect spot for her first bakery in Dallas.

I rise, announcing, "I have to go to the restroom. I'll be right back."

"Okay."

I lean down and put my face in front of hers. "This is a killer plan. You're going to be super successful with it."

She beams. "Thanks. I appreciate your confidence."

"There's no reason for you not to do this," I add, then peck her on the lips. "I'll be right back." I go into the restroom and grab the phone receiver off the wall, then hit the extension for the spa. A woman chirps, "Good morning, Mr. Cartwright. This is Anna. How can I assist you?"

"I need to schedule my wife for a manicure and pedicure today."

She answers, "I'm sorry, but we're fully booked today."

"I figured, but I'll give your entire staff a generous bonus, and I need the appointment to be within the next half hour," I state.

"Oh...umm..."

I continue, "I don't care what else I need to add to this, but I need my wife to get a manicure and pedicure."

Anna asserts, "Mr. Cartwright, just a moment, please."

"Sure." I stare at myself in the mirror, tapping my hand against my thigh.

Anna returns to the line. "Okay. We can make that happen. Please send your wife over."

"Thank you," I state and hang up. I pretend to flush the toilet and wash my hands. I leave the bathroom and announce, "I have a surprise for you."

Georgia turns her head. "Another one? You're spoiling me."

I pull her off her feet. "You have an appointment at the spa."

"What?"

"Pedicure and manicure. You need to go now, or you'll be late," I declare.

"I thought we were going to go downtown?" she asks.

"We will, but you have an appointment first."

She glances at her nails. "Are they that bad?"

I chuckle. "No, but when we were at our massages, the lady kept claiming how amazing the manicures and pedicures were here. So I booked you one."

She grins, rises on her toes, then tosses her arms around me. "Thank you. You're the best."

"Can you say that again?" I ask.

She softly laughs. "Nope. You'll have to do something else for me to say that again."

I challenge, "Something like what I did to you last night?"

Her face turns beet red. She admits, "Yeah, something like that."

I pat her on the ass and move her toward the door. "Good. Challenge accepted."

"What are you going to do while I'm there?"

"I have to take care of a few things for the merger. Let me get that out of the way. You get your pedicure and manicure and then we can spend the rest of the day together. Okay?"

She smiles. "All right."

I walk her to the spa, kiss her, then tell her I'll pick her up when it's over. I hurry back to the room and turn on my laptop. I make copies of all of her plans, and then I call Victoria.

She answers, "Sebastian, I thought you were on your honeymoon."

"I am, but I have something I need you to do," I reply.

"Getting right down to business. Normal Mr. Cartwright that I know well," she teases.

"Sorry. Victoria, how are you doing?" I ask.

She chirps, "Well, I'm great, Sebastian. Thank you for asking. Now, what can I do for you today?"

I drop the bomb. "I need you to make sure that the new lease in the Main Street district doesn't go through."

Silence fills the line.

"Are you still there?" I ask.

She clears her throat. "Why would we not close that deal? It's high rent and a huge profit."

"I'm fully aware," I assert.

"Would you like to tell me why we're not doing it?" she asks.

"No, not really. I'll let you know soon though."

She groans. "Are you serious right now? You're not going to tell me why?"

I debate, then give in. "This is between us, but I'm giving it to Georgia for her bakery."

More silence fills the line.

"Hello?" I say.

"That's... That's incredible, Sebastian."

"Make sure it doesn't close, Victoria," I direct.

She answers, "I'm on it."

I get off the phone with her and call my builder, Liam.

He booms, "Sebastian, what do I owe the pleasure?" Hammers and saws hum in the background.

"I have something I need you to do, and it needs to get done today," I assert.

He groans. "Why do I have a feeling you're about to make my day a pain in the ass?"

I chuckle. "Because I am."

He sighs. "What do you need done?"

"The building down in the Main Street district—I need you to pull permits for it. I want them issued today."

He whistles. "That will cost you at least six figures. We're going to have to grease Eduardo."

"Yeah, I know," I say, hating that I have to give Eduardo money. I can't stand the pig, and he can't stand me, so it'll cost me a pretty penny. However, whatever it takes, I'm going to get it done.

"Why don't you tell him you need it in a few days? It'll cost you a fifth of the price," Liam suggests.

I stare out the window at the icy snow and the buildings gleaming with lights. "Liam, I don't care what it costs. I want permits, and I want them today. Go grease the fat bastard, and let me know when it's done."

"All right, boss," he concedes and hangs up.

I text him.

Me: *I'm sending you plans. I need them fitted to the current space.*

Liam: *On it.*

I email him the plans that Georgia's designer made.

I call the company I use for our logos. Normally my assistant does this, but I'm not leaving this to anyone.

The receptionist answers, "Dallas Logos. This is Sabrina. How may I help you?"

"Hi, Sabrina. This is Sebastian Cartwright. I need to talk to your boss."

She clears her throat. "Yes, Mr. Cartwright, just a moment. Can you hold, please?"

"Yep," I reply.

Not long passes before her boss, Mark, answers. "Sebastian, what's going on?"

"I just emailed you a logo with the materials I want it made with. How long will it take? And don't tell me a few months," I demand.

"Well, everything can be done for a price," he dangles in front of me.

"I don't care what it costs, Mark. I need it, and it's got to happen soon," I state.

"Worst-case scenario is probably a week. For a price, of course."

"Of course," I sneer, then pull up the calendar on my phone. A week gives me enough time. Still, I tell him, "A week's pushing it, Mark. I want it before then."

He concedes, "Maybe five days, Sebastian, but you have to understand. Some things need to sit and cool off before we can attach other materials to them. Five days is the soonest possible if you don't want it falling apart."

"Fine. Get it done," I instruct.

"Done. Since I have you on the phone—"

"Call my office. Bye," I interject and hang up.

I send an email to my legal team to start the process of franchising Georgia's concept. I attach the documents they'll need and tell them to put it in her name. I start to write Peach, then pause.

I don't debate long. Her name's not legally changed yet, but I still put Georgia Peach Cartwright on it.

I spend the next hour making plans for the rest of the day. There's a Santa Claus hunt in the downtown area. It has thirteen hidden hologram Santa Clauses around the city, and you walk around trying to find them. When Georgia and I read about it, she stated it would be fun.

Then I buy tickets for a Christmas concert scheduled before the Reykjavik Food Walk. We'll visit five to six unique Icelandic restaurants and get to eat a different cuisine at each of the venues. It's supposed to be super authentic, and I don't doubt Georgia will be pumped about it.

Finally, I buy tickets for ice skating. I know I'll spend most of the time on my ass since I'm not a skater, but Georgia's eyes lit up when she saw the rink. If it costs me bruised ass cheeks to see her glow like that, I'll do it all night long.

By the time I'm done planning, Liam sends me a text.

Liam: *Permit's done, but it's 120k. Enjoy writing the check.*

Me: *Thanks. Now get your night crews on this. Whatever it takes, you need to be done by Christmas Eve.*

Liam: *That's pushing it.*

Me: *I don't care. Get it done.*

Liam: *Someone have you by the balls or something?*

Yep. And happily so.

Me: *It's for my wife. Now, get it done.*

Twenty-Five

GEORGIA

A Few Days Later

The plane shakes with turbulence and more sweat coats my skin. Adrenaline sears through my cells. I cry out, "Sebastian!"

He removes his tongue from my clit and meets my eye. He challenges, "Do you want me to stop?"

"Sebastian Allen Cartwright! Don't you dare!" I shriek, trembling, and push his face back down on my body.

A spark ignites in his blues. He chuckles and latches on to my pussy like a vacuum cleaner.

"Oh...my..."

He stops and demands for the fifth time, "Say it if you want it, Mrs. Cartwright."

Caving, I blurt out, "You're the best husband ever!"

"That's my girl," he praises, then turns my pussy into his dinner.

Endorphins unfurl through me right as the turbulence turns rougher. The high is so intense, the dark bedroom turns white. My incoherent cries get drowned out by the overhead bins rattling so loudly, it sounds like they're going to fall on us.

Before I know it, Sebastian flips me over. He pushes my face to the pillow, and his warm torso hits my spine. He moves my hands to the bars and orders, "Hold on, Sunshine, it's rough."

I grip the headboard, and his girth fills my pulsating body. I arch my back into him, but he leans closer, pinning me to the mattress.

The pilot comes on over the speaker, saying, "It's going to be bumpy, but we're landing. Please remain buckled up."

Like the previous warnings, Sebastian ignores it and thrusts faster inside me.

I moan, closing my eyes. Every time we have sex, it's like a new cupcake flavor I've perfected. I would have thought I'd be used to him after all our encounters in Iceland, but I'm not. And every time, we seem to get better.

"Christ, you're always so tight," he mumbles in my ear.

"You love it," I blurt out.

"Damn right," he agrees, then claims, "My wife's got the tightest pussy in all of Dallas. And it's mine." He moves his hand to the front of my body and manipulates my overly stimulated clit.

"Oh...I...oh...yes! Don't stop," I demand, returning to the bliss train.

The sound of the wheels lowering fills the cabin.

"Tonight, you're sucking me off in the pantry while everyone's at the dinner table," he states.

My adrenaline mixes with excitement. I'm convinced that no man on Earth has a better cock than Sebastian. And one of my new favorite tasks is giving him blowjobs and making him beg me to finish him off. I had a bit too much to drink last night. He told me I had to choose something naughty to do when we returned. So I admitted the fantasy I had one morning when I was in the pantry looking for ingredients to make him his pancakes.

"You'll wear the apron only and a bun," he asserts, pounding into me harder, hitting my G-spot.

"Y-y...oh!" I cry out as the wheels hit the ground and the brakes screech.

"And a pair of stilettos. The red ones I just got you," he demands, then buries his head into my neck and groans. His body convulses over mine, long after the plane's come to a full stop.

The pilot comes over the speaker again. "Welcome back to the great state of Texas."

"Hallelujah," I utter.

Sebastian chuckles and rolls off me. He grins and pulls me into him. Both of us try to catch our breath, not saying a word.

I turn to him. He reaches for my cheek, and I admit, "I had the best time. Thank you."

"In here or Iceland?" he teases.

My smile grows. "Both."

He leans forward and kisses me, then states, "Me too, Sunshine. You ready to go home?"

I nod. We get dressed, I freshen up in the bathroom, then we make our way out of the plane. A driver is waiting for us on the tarmac. We get into the car, and Sebastian puts his arm around me. I lean into his chest, feeling the happiest I've ever felt.

Neither of us talk. When we get to the ranch, the house is bustling with excitement.

"Georgia!" Isabella squeals the moment I walk through the door.

"Hey!" I crouch down, and she runs and jumps into my arms, followed by Emma. "I missed you two."

"We missed you!" Isabella declares, and my heart soars.

"Where's my hug?" Sebastian asks.

They redirect their energy to him, and he picks both of them up.

It takes a while to hug everyone, but I don't mind. I love everyone in his family. And they've been nothing but kind and loving toward me.

We're led into the family room and answer questions about Iceland for a few minutes. Sebastian kisses the top of my head, declaring, "I need a shower."

"Me too, but you go first," I state.

"I'm not arguing with you," he declares, kisses my head again, then winks. He leaves.

I continue telling his family about Iceland and all the things we did. After a while, I wonder why Sebastian isn't back. I excuse myself and go to our room. I step inside, then freeze outside the bathroom door.

Sebastian scoffs. "Huck, that's not exactly a loophole."

The hairs on my neck rise. *A loophole?*

Sebastian continues, "Georgia's too smart for that. Remember when she signed the prenup? She's not a moron."

My gut dives so fast that I reach for the wall to steady myself. Silence fills the air as I realize he's looking for a loophole in our prenup.

After everything we've been through, he's trying to get out of our deal?

Not just get out. Screw me out of it.

I haven't thought about the prenup since the day of our wedding when I had to convince myself to make it down the aisle. Sebastian claimed he had feelings for me, and we agreed to figure out this mess together. But he's been lying to me the entire time.

I believed he was telling the truth.

I trusted his words.

I fully gave myself to him the entire trip, believing we had something real between us.

How could I be such a fool?

Sebastian firmly asserts, "Listen to what I'm saying. That's not a loophole."

Bile climbs up my throat. In my entire life, I've never felt so betrayed. Sebastian's been using me this entire time, and I'm the idiot who fell for it.

Before I can think, I take off my wedding rings and toss them on the bed. I grab my purse, then glance around the room.

His truck keys are on the desk. I snatch them, then sneak through the house, trying to avoid everyone. It's not easy since there are so many people, but I finally get outside.

My pulse races faster. I run to Sebastian's truck, jump in the driver's seat, then start the engine. I step on the accelerator and barrel down the driveway, screeching to a halt for the gate to open.

"Georgia!" Sebastian yells from out of nowhere.

I glance in the rearview mirror. He's running toward me, barefoot. My heart pounds against my chest cavity. I mutter at the gate, "Come on. Come on. Come on."

Sebastian gets ten feet from the truck and the gate finally opens.

I peel through it, then increase my speed until Sebastian is no longer in sight.

Two streets away, my phone rings. Sebastian's name pops up on the screen.

I send it to voicemail.

He calls again.

I turn my phone off and blink through my tears, but nothing will stop them. I can't see, so I pull over on a dirt side road and into a wooded driveway so the truck's hidden. I turn off the engine and sob.

How could I have been so stupid?

I don't know if I would claim he loved me, but it felt like it. At the very least, I believe he cared deeply for me.

This entire time, he was playing me.

I can't sit here. He'll try to come after me.

Somehow, I manage to pull it together. A numb feeling sets in. The two-hour drive to Dallas is a blur. It's after ten when I arrive. I pull up to the office building, park in the garage, then go up to Sebastian's office.

I toss his keys on his desk, along with my security key card. I turn on my phone and ignore his text messages and voicemails. Then I go back downstairs and order an Uber.

It pulls up to the curb within minutes. I finally get into my apartment and crawl into my bed. The tears fall freely until my chest heaves with so much emotion that bile climbs up my throat. I run to the bathroom and get sick, hugging the toilet and wondering how I could have allowed myself to get into this situation.

I sit against the wall for hours, replaying my time with Sebastian and all the things he said to me over the last few weeks. It's well after midnight when I convince myself to take a shower.

I'm about to step under the hot water when I freeze.

I still smell like him. He's all over me, and once I wash him away, it's over.

It's already over, I reprimand myself.

Another river of tears falls. I force myself to shower but don't use the soap until the water begins to turn cold. I rinse off, shaking from the freezing temperature. Then I quickly shampoo and condition my hair.

After I'm dry, I get back under the covers, but the shaking doesn't stop. I'm colder than I was in Iceland. But I had Sebastian's body around mine, keeping me warm. Now, I'll never have it again.

The waves of grief never stop. To torture myself further, I pull up his text messages.

Sebastian: *Georgia, answer your phone.*

Sebastian: *I don't understand what's going on, Sunshine.*

Sebastian: *Answer your door. Whatever's going on here, we can work through it.*

Answer my door?

He's here in Dallas?

I glance at the timestamp, then cringe. I must have been in the shower.

It's good I didn't answer.

Maybe I got something wrong.

No. I didn't. I need to stop being naive. He's Sebastian Cartwright. Ruthless and cruel.

He's not ruthless or cruel.

He is. He just proved it.

There's a loud pounding on my door. Sebastian's voice booms, "Georgia!"

Goose bumps break out on my skin. I sit up in bed.

Another pound fills the air. He shouts, "Let me in, Georgia."

I creep out to the main living area and stand on the other side of the door. A bang thuds from the thin wood, and I jump.

"She obviously doesn't want to talk to you. Do I need to call the cops?" my neighbor, Tina, threatens.

"Mind your own business," Sebastian warns.

"When you're waking me up, it is my business," she claims.

Another knock makes me almost jump out of my skin. I hold my hand over my mouth and squeeze my eyes shut as he declares, "Georgia, I love you. Open the door."

My knees give out. I crouch down on the floor, shaking.

He loves me?

No. It's another trick. He wants me to finish the contract so he can become CEO and screw me out of the money.

"In three seconds, I'm calling the police," Tina announces.

Desperation fills Sebastian's voice. He knocks again, only not as rough. His voice is lower, and he asserts, "Whatever I've done, I'll make right. Please, let me in."

More than I've ever wanted anything, I want to open the door and believe him. But I can't. I stay frozen, except for my quivering body, staring at the door, with a puddle of tears forming on the wood floor.

A while passes before I check the peephole. He's finally gone, which only hurts my heart more.

I crawl back into my bed, and my phone lights up.

Sebastian: *I love you. Please, talk to me.*

More pain rips through me. I wonder how he can be so cruel. And then all my demons come rushing to the surface.

What was it that made me so eager to be his victim?

Is my self-esteem so low that I was okay subjecting myself to him?

Did my loneliness cause me to agree to his contract so I could be around people over the holidays?

The hard questions continue to pop up all night long. I beat myself up until the sun comes up, but there still aren't any answers. And there's only one question I'd do anything to know the answer to but never will.

Did Sebastian have any feelings for me, or was it all one big lie?

I don't get out of bed the entire day. He pounds on my door several times, sends more messages, and attempts to call. I ignore all of it. It's after midnight when I fall asleep.

The next day, I force myself to get out of bed. I turn on the shower and step under the hot water, vowing to never again trust Sebastian Cartwright.

I was wrong about him.

And I'll never make that mistake again.

Twenty-Six

SEBASTIAN

Nothing I do gets Georgia off my mind. Working out doesn't work. Pacing my penthouse doesn't work. I can't eat or sleep, and it doesn't matter how many times I've gone to her house or texted or called her. She won't give me the time of day. She wants nothing to do with me, and it's starting to sink in, making me crazier.

I finally go to work, hoping she'll be there. I know it's a long shot, but I have to try. So I get to my office early in the morning.

My gut drops when I turn the corner and see her empty desk. I step into my private office, and it dives even further.

The keys to my truck and the security card to get into the building sit on my desk. It's like a final rip to my heart. Victoria walks in, inquiring, "Sebastian, what are you doing here?"

I spin, admitting, "I don't know."

She studies me, then states, "You look like shit."

"Yeah, I'm aware."

She arches her eyebrows. "Mind telling me what's going on?"

I sigh. I don't even know what to say anymore. I finally confess, "I screwed everything up."

"Regarding...?" she asks.

Numbness sets in. I offer, "With Georgia."

Shock fills her face. "What did you do?"

I hold my hands in the air and, in a defeated tone, answer, "I honestly don't know. Everything was amazing, and now she won't talk to me. She fled my parents' house the night we got back. And I just don't know what to do."

Victoria tilts her head, thinking, then asks, "Have you gone to her house?"

"Victoria, I've done everything. I've texted her. I've called her. I've gone to her house. I've banged on the door. Her neighbor has threatened me too many times to count that she will call the police and have me arrested. That's how many times I've shown up," I confess.

Victoria's lips twitch.

"This isn't funny," I blurt out.

"Well, I never thought I'd see it," she mutters.

"What?"

"You finally met your girl," she claims.

I groan. "I need to get out of here."

She jerks her head backward. "You're not staying to work since you're in town?"

"No," I state.

"Are you going back to your parents'?"

Dread fills me. I don't even want to think about how upset my parents will be. I followed Georgia, and I've been ignoring all of their phone calls and text messages, as well as my siblings', for the last two days. I grumble, "Don't ask me about them." I brush past her, step into the elevator, and leave.

Obsessed, I swing by Georgia's and knock on the door again. Nobody answers. I finally give up and return to my penthouse, feeling like I'm going crazy.

When I walk in, my chest tightens. My father and mother are there, along with Alexander. He gives me a sympathetic look and the hairs on my neck rise.

This isn't going to be good.

What do I even tell them?

My mother doesn't waste any time. "Sebastian, what's going on between you and Georgia?"

I stay quiet, debating how to fess up. Then again, I don't know what's wrong between Georgia and me.

"We deserve answers," my father declares.

Alexander shifts uncomfortably on his feet.

Why did they bring my brother?

Because my father's going to take away my CEO position.

No, he won't. He knows I'm the only one capable and willing.

Does it even matter anymore?

"Sebastian, where's Georgia?" Mom repeats.

I shake my head, confessing, "I don't know."

"What do you mean you don't know? She's your wife," my father states.

"I don't know," I repeat and scrub my hands over my face, feeling like I'm on the brink of a nervous breakdown. Yet I shouldn't feel sorry for myself because obviously, I've done something wrong that Georgia's this upset with me.

My father booms, "Stop stalling and start talking, Sebastian! We aren't getting any younger!"

I finally give in. And once I start talking, I can't stop. I admit, "I convinced Georgia to become my fake wife."

The blood drains from my mother's face. "What?"

Alexander's eyes widen, and my father's glare deepens.

"Why on Earth would you do something like that?" Mom questions.

I answer, "I didn't want to deal with you pushing all of the Dallas socialite wannabes on me. Plus, I didn't want the whole town talking about my failed relationships."

Hurt and dismay fill Mom's expression. "So, you lied to us?"

My insides quiver. "Yeah, I did. I'm sorry."

"No, you're not," my father asserts.

"Yes, I am," I declare.

My father scowls. "What are you sorry about? Are you sorry you convinced a nice woman to do something for your selfish benefit?"

Bile crawls up my throat. I swallow it down and claim, "Yes. All I have is regret, and I wish I wouldn't have done it."

"Why would Georgia agree to something like that?" Alexander asks.

My gut dives again. "Because I offered her money."

"But Georgia doesn't care about money," my mom states.

"Yes, I know. But she wanted money for her cupcake bakery. I offered her a hundred grand, and she negotiated a million. I thought she was another greedy woman trying to use me for my money. I didn't know what she wanted it for," I admit.

"She's nothing of the sort," Mom professes.

A wave of shame overtakes me. "I know that now. She's not anything like it. I didn't know she had plans to franchise her cupcake business, which made sense why she got me up to a million. But I know that doesn't even matter."

The room turns silent, filling with more tension.

I add, "I don't understand why she left the ranch and won't talk to me. Everything was perfect between us in Iceland."

Mom drills her blue eyes into mine, making me cringe inside. She finally shakes her head, steps as close to me as possible, and jabs me in the chest. "I never thought the day would come where I would say you disappointed me, but you have. I've always been proud of you, Sebastian, but I have to say, this is beneath you."

I swallow hard, wishing there was some moisture in my mouth because it's so dry. All I can utter is, "I agree."

She sizes me up again, tsks, and turns to my father, announcing, "I'll be in the truck when you're ready to leave." She throws darts at me with her glare, then leaves.

The tension only grows after she departs. My father continues scowling like he wants to kill me. Alexander's sympathy has turned to disgust.

My father finally states, "I'm naming Alexander CEO."

Alexander asserts, "No, you're not."

Shocked, my father spins to him. "Excuse me?"

Alexander lifts his chin higher. "I am not moving my children to Dallas."

"You don't have to. You can come into the office a few days a week," my father claims.

I snort, interjecting, "Do you have any idea what goes on here, Dad? It's not the same company as when you stopped coming into the city ten years ago."

He snaps his head toward me. "I suggest you be quiet before I throw you out on your ass and cut off your trust fund."

I shut my mouth, my insides continuing to quiver, and I try to regulate my breathing. I don't put it past him to do that. And I wonder how I screwed up so badly, when a few weeks ago I almost had everything I ever wanted.

It's not worth it without Georgia next to me.

He turns back to Alexander. "I can't trust him. I need you to step up."

Alexander shakes his head. "No, Dad. My kids have lost enough. I'm not moving them to Dallas, and I won't travel here a few days a week, coming back and forth, so I barely see them. They don't have a mother; all they have is me."

"That's not true. They have the rest of us," my father states.

"It's not the same. I'm their only parent, and I am not stepping into the CEO's shoes. I never wanted that position anyway. This is what Sebastian wants. He's the one who's capable of fulfilling the role. He's the one who should have it, no matter how stupid he is."

"Thanks," I mutter.

"Yeah, no problem. But you know you're a jackass for doing what you did to Georgia," my brother hurls.

"Noted."

My dad stands there, not used to being told what's going to happen from one of us. We normally just do what he says. He finally spins and assesses me. I think he's going to cave, but then he throws another wrench into the situation. He informs me, "I will not have somebody running our legacy who can't be trusted. I'm not stepping down as CEO."

My entire life feels like it's going away very quickly. I've now lost everything. I've lost the position I've worked so hard for and the only woman I've ever actually loved.

Dad studies me closer.

I finally ask, "Is there anything else?"

He gives me another disgusted look. "No." He leaves the room.

My brother steps closer. "I'll talk to him. You should be CEO."

"I fucked up," I admit.

"Yeah, you hit a new level. I suggest you go get your wife back. You're a better man with her."

I nod. "Yeah, I am. But I don't know what to do."

He crosses his arms. "Begging is a start, but I don't know how to get you out of this, bro. You really did pull a dumb-ass move."

"You can stop telling me that now. I'm clear on how big I messed up," I assert.

He shakes his head, then pats me on the back and leaves.

If I had learned a few weeks ago that I wasn't going to be CEO, it would have driven me nuts. It would have derailed me. But I can't even think about that right now. All I can focus on is that I need to get Georgia back.

An hour passes with me pacing. I decide to return to her apartment. I get in my truck and easily reenter her building, reminding myself again that if she doesn't forgive me, then I need to give her one of my condos. She cannot stay in this run-down place. I climb the stairs to avoid the rickety elevator and knock on her door.

The same nosy neighbor steps out, claiming, "She's not home, but it's clear she doesn't want to talk to you, so go away for good. You really are becoming a stalker."

I grumble, "Mind your own business."

She snaps, "Like I've told you 18,000 times, I live in this building. You don't. Now, I suggest you leave, or I'm calling the police. This time, it's not a threat."

Something tells me not to mess with this woman. I don't need the police here. So, I give up and leave.

I sit in my truck and wait on the side of the road, hoping that Georgia will arrive. I'm there for several hours, replaying our time at the ranch, our wedding, the trip to Iceland, and when we returned home. It's starting to turn dark when I finally see her.

A car pulls up. Georgia steps out of it. My heart thumps harder looking at her. Then my gut also dives.

Melanie opens the driver's door and gets out.

Still, I rush toward them on the sidewalk, calling, "Georgia!"

She spins. Her bottom lip trembles. Her eyes are bloodshot and she orders, "Go away, Sebastian. I have nothing to say to you."

My heart sinks. I reach for her, begging, "Please. We need to talk."

Melanie steps between us, directing, "Go inside, Georgia."

"Georgia, don't. We need to talk."

Melanie spins so her back's to me. She repeats in a stern voice, "Go inside, Georgia."

"Melanie, this isn't your business. This is between my wife and me. Stay out of it," I warn.

Melanie huffs. "Wanna bet?"

Georgia's eyes dart between Melanie and me.

"Georgia, please," I beg.

"Go home, Sebastian. I have nothing to say to you," she claims and disappears inside.

As soon as the door shuts, Melanie spins on me. "Do not ever step foot near her again. You picked the wrong woman to use for your fake wife."

The hairs on my neck rise. "She told you?"

"Yeah, she told me everything. Are you going to sue her for the little possessions she has? Maybe steal the few items she inherited from her grandma?" Melanie seethes.

Shocked, I declare, "I would never do such a thing. I'm not that low of a person."

"Aren't you?" Melanie hurls.

"No, Melanie. I'm not."

She snarls, "You know what, Sebastian? Take your loophole and shove it up your ass."

I freeze. *Loophole?*

She shoots daggers at me with her eyes and continues. "Don't try to deny how you planned to screw Georgia over all along."

Guilt reignites in my belly.

How does she know about a loophole?

Melanie continues, "And then you're so twisted that you made her believe that you actually cared about her. What kind of sick bastard are you?"

"I do care about her. I love her! But why would she think—" I freeze, and goose bumps pop out on my skin.

She overheard the conversation with Huck.

Melanie's face turns into a smirk. "Yeah. You know what you did."

"Listen, you have this wrong. *Georgia* has this wrong. Huck, my attorney, called me. He told me if I signed the annulment but Georgia didn't show up on January 2nd, she'd be in contempt of our contract. I didn't want to explain to him over the phone that I no longer cared about the loophole," I admit.

My confession only makes Melanie angrier. She accuses, "You can't help yourself in your web of lies, can you?"

"I'm not lying."

"Sure you aren't. And pigs fly too, don't they, Sebastian!" she shouts.

I try again. "I swear, Huck didn't know he wasn't looking for a loophole anymore. And I hadn't thought about it since before the wedding. I was trying to get him off the phone instead of going into a long conversation about my change of mind."

Melanie scoffs. "But when you signed the agreement, you did want a loophole, didn't you?"

The truth hangs in the air. I don't think I've ever felt so sick.

She snarls, "Admit it, Sebastian."

"Yes. Originally, I did. But I would never do that to her. All I want is my wife back," I admit.

"You wanted a loophole. You would have screwed her over without even thinking twice. This entire time, you were in cahoots with your attorney to avoid paying Georgia the money that she earned...the money you *agreed* to. So don't tell me you would never do that to her!" she hurls.

I shake my head, so ashamed, but I still add, "I don't feel the same way anymore. I haven't since before I married her. Yes, those were my intentions, but they aren't anymore, I promise you. When I talked to Huck the other day, he didn't know how I feel."

She snarls, "God, Sebastian, you make me sick."

"I'm telling the truth," I claim.

Melanie's brown eyes turn wilder. "Do you ever listen to yourself? You just admitted that you had a woman sign a contract to marry you and go into a fake marriage. She was supposed to spend a month with you, with your family, and get to know everybody. And everything she did, she did for you. She negotiated a fair and square settlement amount. And then you, from day one, were trying to screw her out of it. All the while claiming to have feelings for her. Do you see how sick that is?"

"I'm a horrible person. I know it was wrong, but it doesn't change the facts. I don't just have feelings for Georgia. I *love* Georgia," I declare.

"Rot in hell, Sebastian. And whatever you do, you stay away from her, or you're going to have me to deal with," she threatens.

"She's my wife. You can't keep her from me," I claim.

Melanie's face turns almost purple. She lowers her voice and steps forward. "She may be your wife, but in a few weeks, she won't be. Don't make me tell you again, Sebastian." Melanie spins and goes inside, slamming the door.

I want to crawl into a hole and never come out. My entire life is in a collapsing brick building. There are only a few floors between us, yet I've never been farther from getting what I want.

For the first time in my life, I don't care about my career, or success, or anything else. All I want is my wife back.

And I'm Sebastian Cartwright, a man who always gets what he wants. But I don't know how to fix this or save the one thing that makes me happy. And that's my marriage.

Georgia's the only person who never wanted anything from me. All she asked for was there to be no lies between us and for me to be honest about how I felt about her. Now, she thinks my feelings were false. She believes our marriage was fake.

Nothing is less true. Not a moment since marrying her did I feel like anything between us was a sham. There wasn't a second where I wanted January 2nd to come so I could alleviate her of her duties.

I'll do anything to fix this misunderstanding between us. Yet I've never been so unsure about how to make something happen.

I stare at the building for a long time, willing her to come to the window. She never does. And the more time that passes, the deeper the truth sinks in.

I've lost her forever.

Twenty–Seven

GEORGIA

A Week Before Christmas

Sebastian never stops contacting me. He texts, calls, and sends gifts with notes. I should block his number, send his email directly to spam, and refuse the gifts.

But every time I try, I stop myself. I just can't. I don't know why. I know it's the best thing for me. If I'm ever going to get over him, I need to stop thinking about him. Yet I can't seem to push the buttons.

The gifts started arriving earlier in the week. He's sent an array of things, all of which surprised me.

He sent me a bag of sugar and roses on the first day, along with a note.

Georgia,

. . .

I miss everything about you.

Your scent is fading off your wedding dress. I keep trying to recreate it, but I can't seem to.

I miss you so much and wish we could talk, Sunshine.

I love you,

Sebastian

I read it so many times that my tears smeared the ink. And it doesn't matter that I can no longer read it. The words are imprinted on my mind.

The thought of my wedding dress, and Sebastian smelling it, got to me. I had a hard time not calling him. Somehow, I found the strength not to.

The next day, silicone cupcake molds arrived. They were in several different sizes. There was another handwritten card.

Georgia,

I saw these online. Then I went to the store to make sure they weren't crap. They seem to be good, but I'll let you be the judge of that.

I miss you more than you'll ever know, Sunshine.

I love you so much,

Sebastian

. . .

Like the first note, that one too became unreadable and etched into my mind.

Then business cards with the Grammy's Cupcake logo were left in front of my door...all six sets.

Each box has a different name for me.

The first says, *Georgia Cartwright, CEO.*

The second reads, *Georgia Peach, CEO.*

The final box has cards with *Georgia Peach Cartwright, CEO.*

Each card had *georgia@grammyscupcakes.com* on them.

Boxes four, five, and six have the exact same writing as boxes one, two, and three, except for one thing.

They include a business phone number.

Sebastian hand wrote a quick note.

Georgia,

I'm hoping you pick one of the cards with Cartwright on them.

I love and miss you,

Sebastian

All that did was compound my confusion. On January 2nd, we're annulling our marriage. What is the point? He can't possibly mean he wants to stay married.

It's all a trick to make me help him secure his CEO role.

He can stop worrying. I'm not telling his family.

The next day, another six sets of cards were delivered. These cards had a black background instead of white. There was a new note.

Georgia,

I'm not sure what version you like better.

I wish we could talk. I could ask you these things.

I'm so proud of you, and I know you'll crush everything you set out to accomplish.

It hurts how much I miss you.

I love you.

Your husband,

Sebastian

Of course the waterworks started again.

But today is a new day, and I'm determined to not cry. I force myself to not stay in bed until ten a.m. by setting my alarm for five o'clock.

When I wake, my eyes are swollen from crying myself to sleep. I give myself a pep talk and make myself get up. I shower, put on fresh clothes, and don't look at my phone. If I do, I'll see Sebastian's messages.

It's getting harder and harder not to text him back or pick up the phone when he calls. Several times, I almost went to his office.

Each day I wake up and haven't, I pat myself on the back. Then the pain comes back, and the vicious cycle starts again.

I brew coffee and fill my mug. I add sugar and cream. It's the only thing I can seem to stomach these days. I know I need to eat, but I just can't seem to force myself to. Every now and then, my stomach growls, but when I try to eat food, it just makes me feel ill.

I'm about to take a sip of my coffee when the doorbell rings. My stomach flips. I quietly go to the door, expecting to see Sebastian.

I glance out the peephole, and my breath catches. My pulse increases, but it's not Sebastian.

Ruby and Evelyn stand on the other side. I freak out, and I take so long that there's a knock.

Ruby calls out, "Georgia, sweetheart. Can we barge in? We really want to see you. Please?"

Guilt fills me. I can't turn them away. After all, it's not their fault that Sebastian did what he did.

What do they know?

"Auntie Georgia!" Isabella calls out.

"Doesn't she want to see us?" Emma asks.

My heart pounds harder. *Why are the girls here?*

I fight the emotions lodging in my chest and reach for the lock. I unlatch the chain and open the door.

Isabella and Emma shriek, "Auntie Georgia!" They fly past the doorframe and jump up on me.

I crouch down and hug them, laughing but also crying. They hug me tighter, and I'm suddenly sobbing.

Isabella retreats, puts her hands on my cheeks, and asks, "Auntie Georgia, are you okay?"

I swipe at my tears. "Yes. I'm just so happy to see you. I missed you."

"We missed you too," she says.

"What are you doing here?" I inquire.

Emma says, "We get to go to the zoo. We're going to see lions and monkeys and bears."

Isabella claims, "And parrots! They talk!"

I laugh again and wipe my eyes. "Well, that sounds really exciting." I glance up at Evelyn and Ruby.

Evelyn states, "They have a class field trip. Their friends' mom is chaperoning and downstairs. She's going to take them over to the zoo. My mom and I thought that we could take you to breakfast?" A hopeful look fills her expression.

I almost say no, but Ruby steps forward and hugs me. I start to cry again. She tightens her arms around me and softly asserts, "Let's go to breakfast. We can catch up, okay?"

I sniffle. "Okay, let me get my coat." I grab it and my purse, and we all go downstairs.

The girls give me another hug, get into a minivan, and I watch it pull away. I take a deep breath, then turn and get into Ruby's truck.

She asks, "Where's a good place to eat?"

"There's a diner right down the street."

"Sounds perfect," she answers and turns on the engine.

Silence fills the cab.

Evelyn turns in her seat. "So, how have you been, Georgia?"

"Okay," I lie.

She gives me a look like she knows I'm not telling the truth. She adds, "My brother's an asshole."

"Evelyn," Ruby reprimands.

"Sorry, but he is."

"Yes, he is, but let's cool it a bit," Ruby orders, which I'm grateful for. I don't want to sit and bash Sebastian in front of his family or at all, really. I just want to figure out how to get over the pain he caused me.

We pull up to the diner and go inside. Since it's so early, it's not very busy. Ruby points to a booth in the back and announces, "We're going to sit back there."

The hostess nods, grabs menus, and says, "Follow me, ladies." She leads us to the back booth.

We slide in, and she sets the menus down. She states, "Your server will be with you shortly." She leaves.

We study the menu. I'm suddenly starving but can't seem to make up my mind about what to order. Maybe it's the nerves about Sebastian's family being here and not knowing what he's told them about our situation.

Ruby puts her hand on mine, "Georgia. Have you been eating? You look really thin, dear."

I open my mouth but close it. There's no point in lying to Ruby.

She adds, "Let's get some food in you. Okay?"

I nod and then look closer at the menu. All I can see are pancakes, which remind me of Sebastian. I'm not a super big pancake fan. I prefer French toast or waffles, but all I suddenly seem to want are pancakes.

The server comes, and Ruby orders eggs and bacon. Evelyn chooses a Denver omelet, and I order the pancakes. They bring us our coffee, and we settle into the booth.

Evelyn leans forward. "My dad's really angry with Sebastian."

I freeze, wondering again what they know. I choose my words carefully, before I say, "It's not all his fault."

"Yes, it is. He told my parents what he did," she claims.

My insides quiver. I gape at her, then clear my throat. "What do you mean?"

Ruby interjects, "He admitted that he created a deal with you for you to become his wife...his fake bride," she says in disgust, but sympathy fills her face.

Embarrassment floods me. My cheeks heat. "It was stupid of me to agree to it. I'm sorry we lied to you."

Ruby puts her hand over mine again. "This is Sebastian's fault, not yours, honey."

"I did agree to it," I state.

"It's not your fault," she reiterates.

I glance away, trying to gather my thoughts. It doesn't seem right for Sebastian to take all the heat for this. He couldn't have done it without my involvement.

Ruby continues, "Jacob is very angry, but he's angry with Alexander and Sebastian."

Surprised, I question, "Why would he be mad at Alexander?"

She glances at Evelyn, then answers, "Alexander's refusing to become CEO. He doesn't want to move to Dallas with the kids.

And to be honest, I'm glad he doesn't want to. I don't think it'd be good for them, but he also doesn't want to commute and be away from them all the time."

My heart pounds in my chest. "What about Sebastian? He's supposed to be the CEO."

Evelyn shakes her head. "Dad will not name him CEO after what he did to you."

"But that's not fair," I claim.

Ruby admits, "Well, Jacob sees it as a character flaw."

My chest tightens.

She adds, "It's fine. Alexander will figure out how to do this without having to move."

I blurt out, "Sebastian deserves the position. He's brilliant at what he does. And Alexander told me he doesn't want to be CEO. This isn't right."

Compassion fills Ruby's face. She leans closer. "You know how Jacob is when he gets an idea in his head."

I disagree, declaring, "But Sebastian's worked his whole life for this."

"Well, sometimes there are consequences to our actions," Ruby asserts.

"This seems extreme," I say.

"He hit a new low. There's no reason he had to lie to all of us. And gosh, to put you through what he did. I mean, he's a monster," Evelyn proclaims, then takes a sip of her coffee.

I don't know why I stick up for Sebastian, but I don't like hearing Evelyn talk bad about him. And nothing will convince me he's not meant to be CEO. "Sebastian only created a fake marriage because everybody in town talks about him."

"So? He should deal with it like a real man," she asserts.

Her answer only upsets me further. I spout, "He is a real man. And have you ever heard the gossips talk about him? Even in front of his face? Because I have."

Evelyn tilts her head, questioning, "What do you mean?"

"We couldn't even go to a restaurant without women talking about him, knowing we were right there. They said horrible things and not just about him, but me too. That has to get old after a while. I mean, Sebastian has feelings too," I declare.

Evelyn scoffs. "Does he?"

"Yeah, he does," I reply, glaring at her.

"Of course he has feelings. Don't talk about your brother like that," Ruby reprimands. She takes a deep breath and refocuses on me. "Georgia, it's not up to me who becomes CEO. That's Jacob's business."

"But this isn't right," I add.

She slowly shrugs. "It is what it is, dear. No one's going to change Jacob's mind."

Silence fills the air.

The server places our food on the table. I stare at it, thinking about how I made Sebastian pancakes and figured out a recipe he actually enjoyed. It makes tears well in my eyes.

Ruby taps her fork on my plate. "You need to eat, Georgia. Go on, take a bite."

I glance at her, then back at the pancakes. To appease her, I cut a piece off and shove it in my mouth, but I can barely taste it.

Several minutes pass while everyone eats in silence.

Ruby clears her throat and drills her eyes into mine. "We'd love to have you for Christmas. And I don't think Sebastian will be there, but I can also tell him not to come if he plans on it."

Shock fills me. I tear up again but say, "Sebastian's your son. If anyone deserves to be at your house at Christmas, it's him."

She smiles. "You deserve to be there too."

I look away. This is all too much. I love the Cartwrights, but I'm not with Sebastian. I'm never going to be with Sebastian again. The longer I'm with them, the more this will continue to hurt. I reply, "Thank you for the offer. But I have other plans."

"Oh?" she asks.

"Melanie invited me over to her house," I admit.

Ruby pats my hand. "I'm sure that will be nice. We'll miss you though."

My heart hurts more. I confess, "I'll miss all of you."

We finish our breakfast, keeping the conversation to things that don't have to do with Sebastian or me. They drop me off at my apartment, making me promise to let them know if I need anything or change my mind about Christmas. I go inside, relieved to be alone again.

All day, I can't stop thinking about how Sebastian lost his CEO role. It's not fair. By nighttime, I can't handle it anymore.

Part of this is my fault. I didn't hold up my end of the bargain. I ran out on Sebastian, and no matter what he was going to do or not, I was the one who left. I'm part of the reason he lost his dream. And I know how much I want my dream to happen with my cupcake franchise. So Sebastian's no different.

Plus, Melanie told me he wasn't thinking about a loophole anymore. Part of me wants to believe it because I thought I could see how much he had changed during our time together. But he's already made a fool out of me. I'm not looking to do it twice, so I need to stay away from him.

Regardless, I pick up the phone and dial his dad.

He answers in his gruff voice, "Jacob Cartwright."

I take a deep breath. "Jacob, this is Georgia."

Silence fills the air.

"Hello?" I ask.

He recovers, softening his tone. "Georgia. How are you doing, sweetheart?"

I smile, blinking hard again, trying to hold down the emotions. "I'm good. How are you?"

"Id be better if my son wasn't such a moron," he declares.

I softly laugh. "Yeah. I guess we're all morons sometimes. Right?"

Jacob doesn't answer me. He finally asks, "To what do I owe the pleasure of this call, Georgia?"

I muster all my courage and assert, "No one's more capable of running your corporation than Sebastian."

"Did he put you up to this?" Jacob questions.

I talk fast, informing him, "No, I haven't talked to him. I had breakfast with Ruby and Evelyn, and they told me that you were trying to make Alexander the CEO. And I know Alexander doesn't want the role. Plus, I've seen Sebastian in action. He's brilliant. He knows everything about your company. And he has all the relationships. Everybody respects him. He can negotiate better than anyone I've ever met."

Jacob grunts. "I don't know. I heard you're a pretty amazing negotiator."

Embarrassment floods me, but I also know he means it as a compliment. "Maybe so, but I know Sebastian deserves to be your CEO."

More silence fills the air.

My stomach twists. I add, "Please don't hold what happened between Sebastian and me against him."

Jacob finally answers, "Georgia, I'll take your words under advisement, but I can't give you an answer right now. I'm not happy with how my son has acted. And character is a big thing in our family, as you know."

I lift my chin. "Yes, I know, sir. However, I was part of this too."

"I can assure you, Georgia, that not one part of this is your fault."

I don't like how everyone keeps claiming I'm not at fault, because I am. It's not fair to only blame Sebastian.

When I don't say anything, Jacob inquires, "Will we see you on Christmas?"

I tear up again and manage to get out, "No, I have other plans, but thank you for the offer."

He hesitates, then adds, "You'll always be Ruby's and my daughter-in-law, no matter what happens between you and my son, understand?"

My tears fall. My voice breaks as I say, "Thank you." I hang up because I can't get anything else out, and I'm about to lose it.

I wish I could have Sebastian. I know that I can't. So I wish we could have peace between us in this situation, yet I'm unsure how we'll ever find it.

Twenty-Eight

SEBASTIAN

It's Christmas Eve. I still haven't given Georgia her present. I've held off going to her place all week, but I get into my truck and drive over to her apartment.

As I pull onto her street, she gets into her car. My pulse increases and my heart skips a beat. I've not seen her since the day Melanie and I got into it on the street, but she's more beautiful than I remember.

Like a psycho, I follow her, staying a few car lengths behind her. She pulls up to a house, goes up to the porch, and rings the doorbell.

Melanie opens the door, and they hug.

Great. She's probably going to be here all night.

But I'm only half right. It's worse than I anticipated. She not only stays for hours but sleeps over.

Early the next morning, I watch through the window as kids jump around opening presents. She's in her pajamas with her coffee. Her beautiful face shines, but there's also a hint of sadness. And I wish there wasn't. Because I know I put it there.

They're halfway through opening gifts when my phone rings. I glance at the screen and groan, answering, "Merry Christmas, Dad."

"Get your ass to the ranch," he orders.

"I'm not coming to town."

"I'm only going to tell you one more time, son. Get your ass over here," he demands.

I sigh. I don't even go home and change. What's the point? I make the two-hour drive and pull up to my parents' house. I walk in the door, and all my siblings are there, along with my nieces and nephews.

My father motions for me to follow him to his den.

Annoyed he took me away from spying on Georgia, I ask, "What's this about?"

He crosses his arms. "Your wife called me."

My heart beats faster. "Georgia called? What did she say?"

He stares me down for a minute.

"Dad, tell me what she said," I demand.

He makes me wait another moment, then announces, "Seems like your wife pleaded your case for you to become the CEO."

I jerk my head backward, blurting out, "Why would she do that? I don't understand."

My father snorts. "I don't know, but that woman's too good for you."

"Tell me about it," I mutter.

He glares at me, then questions, "So you didn't put her up to it?"

"Put her up to it? She won't even talk to me. I've tried everything, and she refuses."

He shakes his head. "You brought that on yourself, son."

"Is there anything else you want to tell me?" I snap. I don't need his guilt trip. I have to live with myself and my decisions every day.

His nostrils flare. He inquires, "Do you still want to be CEO?"

I freeze. I never would've thought about whether I wanted to be CEO or not a few weeks ago. Now, I feel like my life's upside down and everything's changed.

"What else did Georgia say?" I inquire.

He grinds his molars, then replies, "She said that you're the most capable CEO I could have and that I'd be a fool to name anyone else but you to the position."

"She did?"

"Not in those words but close enough," he claims.

I stare at him.

He huffs. "So I asked you, do you still want to be CEO?"

"Yeah, of course I do," I admit.

"Good. Don't screw it up," he adds.

I arch my eyebrows, then double-check I'm not hearing things. "Are you naming me CEO? You're actually going to step down?"

"Don't make me say it twice," he threatens.

"Is it the same deal as before? January 2nd, I'll be named CEO?" I quiz.

He nods. "Yeah. But you better not screw it up this time."

"I won't," I assure him.

"Good."

Why would Georgia call my dad and go to bat for me?

Does she still care about me?

Is not all lost?

He warns, "You better make it right with Georgia. A woman like that doesn't come around twice."

Mom steps into the room, informing me, "Yeah, she was a mess. She looks like she's lost a lot of weight."

I spin toward her. "You've seen Georgia?"

"Well, of course. Evelyn and I dropped the girls off for their field trip to the zoo in Dallas. Isabella and Emma needed to see her first. Then we took her to breakfast. She barely ate... I don't think she's eating," Mom frets.

My stomach turns. "I have to go."

"Where are you going now? You just got here," Mom accuses.

"I haven't given Georgia her Christmas gift, and I need to."

My mom doesn't hesitate. She points to the door. "Then get your booty moving."

I leave, ignoring everyone, and get into my truck. I barrel out of the ranch and return to Dallas. I shower, then go back to Melanie's and see that Georgia's car is still outside. I wait and wait. Finally, around eight o'clock, long after dark, she steps out of the house.

My heart squeezes as Greg helps her carry gifts to her car. He hugs her, and she drives off.

I follow her to her apartment. The moment she parks and gets out of the car, I rush up to her, grab her arm, and spin her. "Georgia."

The color drains from her face. "Sebastian, what are you doing here?"

"Please just give me a minute."

She takes a deep breath and clenches her jaw. She lifts her chin higher, stating, "Sebastian, you need to stop sending me gifts, texting, and calling me."

I hurriedly state, "I made a request for Huck to give me a prenup with loopholes. I'll forever be sorry. But I have your Christmas gift if you just give me a few minutes."

She scrunches her face, admitting, "I don't have a Christmas gift for you."

"I don't need a Christmas gift. I only want you," I blurt out. My pulse beats hard between my ears.

She looks away. Her voice shakes as she says, "I can't give that to you, Sebastian."

My heart drops. It was a long shot anyway. I quickly add, "I understand, but I still need to give you your gift. I don't want you side-swiped with it when you receive it. So if you can give me an hour, I promise I'll leave you alone after I give it to you. If that's what you want," I add.

She glances at the truck and asks, "What is it?"

"I can't tell you that. You have to see it."

"If this is a trick, Sebastian, I swear—"

"No, I promise you it's not a trick."

She stares at me.

I lower my voice and grab her hand. "Please just come with me. It's only for an hour. I promise I'll drop you back off after you see it."

She finally takes a deep breath, nods, and says, "I have to get my packages inside first."

"I'll help you," I state.

We carry her Christmas gifts into her apartment and then come back outside. I open the door to the truck and she gets in.

My stomach's flipping hard, but I have hope again. At least she's finally talking to me. I run around the truck, get in, start the engine, and veer onto the road. Her sugar-and-rose scent flares in the cab, and everything about it reminds me how much I've missed her and how much it's hurt.

She asks, "Did you have a good day with your family?"

I glance at her, admitting, "I was only there for about ten minutes."

Horror fills her face. "Why? It's Christmas day."

"I followed you to Melanie's last night and was waiting for you to come outside. Then my dad called," I confess.

She looks at me like I'm crazy, ordering, "You have to stop this, Sebastian."

"I know. But listen, I needed you to talk to me, and my dad called and ordered me to the ranch. I didn't know what was going on. I didn't want to go, but you know how my dad is. So I went, and he told me that you called him." I glance at her.

Her face turns red. She claims, "I just did what was right. Is he naming you CEO?"

Everything about being CEO feels off. I should be elated. I should be jumping up and down and thanking my lucky stars. I'm finally getting what I've always wanted, but now it just doesn't seem right without her. I reply, "He is, but it doesn't feel that good."

She furrows her eyebrows. "Why not? It's the only thing you've ever wanted."

I admit, "Maybe in the past. But it doesn't feel right without you by my side."

She inhales sharply and turns, staring out the window.

"Georgia—"

"You were fine before me, Sebastian. You'll be fine again," she claims.

"That's not true," I declare.

We travel the rest of the way in silence. When we get on the street her bakery is on, I park a block away and turn off the truck.

"What are we doing here?" she questions.

I pull a blindfold out of the glove compartment, answering, "I need you to put this on."

She gives me a funny look, warning, "Sebastian, if this is one of your tricks—"

"I told you, I'm not trying to trick you. But I need you to trust me right now."

She snaps, "That's a little easier to say and harder to do."

It stabs me in the heart a bit, but I can't blame her. "I understand. I promise you, I'm not tricking you, but I need you to put this on." I hold it out to her again.

She sighs, then takes the blindfold and slips it over her eyes.

"Okay, stay there. I'm coming around to get you." I jump out of the truck, help her out, and guide her down the street.

It feels so good to have her in my arms again, right next to me.

This is how it should be.

We get in front of the bakery, and I unlock the door, turn on the lights, and move her inside.

"Are you ready?" I ask.

"Sure," she answers.

My stomach fills with flutters as I untie her blindfold and study her.

She blinks a few times, and all the color drains from her face. She opens her mouth to speak, but nothing comes out. She finally swallows hard and stares at me.

"Merry Christmas," I offer.

She questions, "How...?" She continues to gape.

I've never felt so nervous in my life. I admit, "When we were in Iceland, and you showed me your plans, I called the spa to book you for the manicure and pedicure. Once you left, I arranged for it all."

Her mouth drops closer to the floor. Then she glances outside at the boutique across the street. She declares, "Sebastian, this is prime real estate."

"Yes, I know. It's perfect for foot traffic," I add.

She frets, "I can't afford rent on a place like this."

My face falls. I go to the counter and pick up a thick envelope. I hand it to her and state, "There is no rent. The title was trans-ferred to your name yesterday. My attorneys filed for your fran-chise. They want to meet with you. Whenever you're ready though. It can be soon or down the road. It's a standing meeting. The paperwork is all in here."

She puts one hand over her mouth and her other on her stomach.

I chuckle. "You really should see your face right now."

"Sebastian, are you serious?"

"Yes. Here, let me show you around your kitchen." I guide her through the swinging door and ask, "Is everything how it's supposed to be?"

She studies the room, goes to the ovens and opens them, then slides her hand over the mixers. "This is amazing," she says reverently.

Happy that I got it right, I guide her out of the kitchen to where the customers will sit. I show her the lounge area and then I open the glass door for the quiet room. I inform her, "I had them noise proof it. And you didn't have this on your plans, but I had them add the electrical outlets so people can charge their phones or laptops. I hope that's okay?"

She nods. "That's a great idea."

I ask again, "Is this what you imagined? I tried to get it as close to scale as possible to your design, but if anything's off—"

"It's perfect," she claims. Her eyes glisten, and she locks them with mine. She adds, "It's exactly as I imagined."

I step forward and place my hands on her cheeks.

She squeezes her eyes shut and whispers, "Sebastian, I can't do this with you again."

I feel ill, so ill. I've felt like this since she left me, but this is the worst I think it's been. I declare, "Georgia, all couples have issues they have to deal with. We can get past this."

She opens her eyes, asserting, "We were never meant to be. We just got wrapped up in things because of the situation."

"I don't believe that. Tell me you don't believe that," I plead.

She tilts her head, questioning, "Would you have ever asked me out if you didn't need a fake wife?"

"That was stupid of me to ever ask you to do. I'm sorry."

"Sebastian, answer my question. Would you have asked me out?"

My mouth turns dry.

"You thought I was an annoying woman with a silly cupcake bakery dream, didn't you?"

I hate that I called her bakery silly a few weeks ago and how ignorant I was. I confess, "Georgia, I was an unhappy, arrogant idiot."

She squeezes her eyes shut again and takes a deep breath. She opens her lids, raises her chin, and firmly states, "You never would've asked me out. I wasn't the type of woman you were attracted to."

"I've always been attracted to you. And the fact you aren't like anyone else is exactly why I fell in love with you," I declare.

She freezes.

I lower my voice. "I do love you. And once I got to know you better, I would've asked you out."

She drills her gaze into mine, "Sebastian—"

"I'm in love with you, Georgia. I was stupid and wrong. I should have told Huck on the phone I didn't care about the loophole anymore. I just wanted to get off the phone that night. He's my attorney. He would have tried to talk me out of it. I didn't want to deal with it and that's the truth. I'm sorry you heard that. I'm sorry that I hurt you."

She cries out, "You didn't just hurt me. You broke my heart."

Silence fills the air.

She jerks her head toward the door.

I've never felt so bad in my life. Hurting her is the worst thing I've ever done. I take a deep breath and add, "I'm sorry I broke your heart. I didn't mean to. My heart's broken too, and if you forgive me—"

"I have forgiven you," she claims quietly.

Hope fills me. "Then let's move forward."

She glances at the ceiling, then pins her gaze on me, declaring, "I'm sorry, Sebastian. I can't. Forgiveness doesn't mean you repeat the same mistakes." Tears flow down her cheeks.

My heart sinks. I beg, "We aren't a mistake. We—"

"Please don't keep trying to win me over. It's just hurting me more," she interjects.

Once again, my life's crashing around me.

Is there really nothing I can do?

The look on her face tells me nothing will make her change her mind. I've never felt so defeated.

She pleads, "Please. I'm tired of hurting."

I don't want to hurt her anymore, so I agree. "Okay, I'll stop." The moment the words come out of my mouth, I regret them. But now that I've promised her, I need to uphold my word.

"Thank you," she says, then steps away from me. She gazes around the bakery, adding, "This is too much though, Sebastian."

"No, it's not. You deserve it. And I know this is just the start of whatever you want to accomplish," I insist.

She stares at me for a while, then adds, "I don't know what to say besides thank you. It feels like it's not enough though."

"It is," I confirm.

Another moment of silence passes and she suggests, "We should get going."

More disappointment fills me. I walk her back to the truck, and we don't say anything on the way home. All my words are jumbled in my head and seem like the wrong thing to say.

I get out of the car, and she stops me when we get to the front of her building.

She repeats, "Thank you so much for the bakery. It's incredible."

I smile sadly. "You're welcome." I hand her the key. "You're going to have an amazing company."

She hesitates and then hugs me. Nothing's ever felt so good. I want to kiss her, but I stop myself.

She retreats, offering, "Merry Christmas, Sebastian."

I force another smile. "Merry Christmas, Sunshine."

She spins out of my embrace, and once again I'm empty.

Twenty-Nine

GEORGIA

Melanie whines, "It's New Year's Eve. You can't spend it by yourself. Come over."

I sigh. "Melanie, I'm just not up for it, okay? You and Greg have a great time with the kids."

"Come on, Georgia. Just come on over," she pushes for the hundredth time.

"Okay, I'm hanging up now," I chirp.

She groans. "You're annoying."

I laugh. "You love me."

She grumbles, "Yes, I do. Tomorrow we're definitely getting together."

"All right, sounds good. I'll talk to you later. Have a great New Year," I offer.

"Happy New Year, Georgia," she softly replies.

I hang up the phone, sit back on the couch, and glance at my watch. It's only five in the evening. I've been in the house all day, not feeling in the festive spirit. Now, the walls are starting to cave in on me.

I need to get out of here.

I bundle up and decide to go for a walk. There's barely any daylight left. The streetlights blink on, and I walk for over an hour, aimlessly strolling through Dallas, trying not to think about Sebastian.

Suddenly, I'm in front of the bakery. I've not gone inside since I was here with him last. I don't know why. I've walked by it several times this past week. I've read and reread the paperwork he gave me so many times that I've lost count. Yet I've not stepped foot inside of it.

I'm still blown away by what he's done. It makes me want to tell him everything is fine between us, but I know it's not. I miss him so much that I wish I could get over it. But I don't know how to trust him again. And I'd do anything to get past this pain.

I reach into my pocket and pull out my key ring. The key that Sebastian gave me is on it, so I unlock the door and walk in. I stare around the space, feeling a swell of excitement and pride. Then I notice a light shining through the crack of the kitchen door.

We must have forgotten to turn it off.

I go over to the kitchen door, push it open, and freeze. The hairs on my neck rise.

Sebastian's standing against the counter, his hands covering his face.

"Sebastian?" I softly say.

He slowly looks up. His blue eyes are glassy.

I immediately rush to him. "What's wrong?"

He clenches his jaw, admitting, "Everything."

I take a deep breath, then reply, "It shouldn't be. You're the CEO now. You have it all." I offer a smile.

"No, I don't," he states, drilling his bloodshot eyes into mine.

"When did you sleep last?" I ask.

He shrugs.

"When?" I push.

"I don't sleep well without you," he confesses.

My butterflies kick off, a mix of flutters and nerves.

He tilts his head, studies me, then murmurs, "I miss you. Nothing's ever hurt this badly."

I start to object, then stop. He's right. What's the point of denying it? I slowly nod. "I miss you too. And you're right. It does hurt badly."

"Then why are we doing this?" he questions.

I glance at the ceiling, trying to stop my eyes from watering. I wish I had answers for us. All I know is I don't know how to trust him again.

"I'm sorry. I shouldn't have asked you that," he adds.

I refocus on him. "Are you going to be okay?"

He just stares at me. Uncomfortable silence fills the room. I shift on my feet, and he inquires, "Have you had any dinner?"

I shake my head. "No."

He hesitates, then asks, "Do you have New Year's plans?"

For some reason, a laugh comes out of me. "No. Melanie keeps asking me, but I'm just not feeling it."

His lips form a tiny smile. "I understand. Me too." He pauses, then continues, "Do you want to have dinner with me?"

Yes.

I blurt out, "I don't know if that's a good idea."

"Georgia, it's just food."

More tense silence fills the air.

"Let's have dinner," he quietly repeats.

I blow out a big breath and ask, "What are you making?"

He grins, and my heart skips a beat. He answers, "I ordered a tray of enchiladas and chips from my favorite Tex-Mex place. Plus, one of our clients sent a homemade pecan pie to the office. I snagged it and took it home last night." He wiggles his eyebrows. "But I haven't cut into it yet."

"Stop teasing me!" I exclaim, then add, "Are you going off your diet?"

He shrugs. "Someone amazing told me I needed to live a little."

I softly reply, "That's good, Sebastian."

He steps closer. "What would you say if I told you I had ice cream and whipped cream for the pie?"

"Now you're really tempting me," I state.

His eyes twinkle, then his face falls. In a serious tone, he pleads, "Please come have dinner with me."

I think about it for a minute, then cave. "Okay."

"Yeah?" he asks with hope in his voice.

"Sure. It would be horrible for your wife to let you eat dinner alone on New Year's Eve, wouldn't it?" I say, then instantly regret bringing it up when a sad smile fills his face. I reprimand myself and add, "Sorry. I shouldn't have said that."

"No worries." He swiftly places his arm around my waist and guides me out of the bakery.

An ache in my heart appears. It feels so normal, like I'm meant to have his arm around me.

He says, "I only live a few blocks from here."

We make our way through the crowds and get to his building. I feel at ease with Sebastian, like before when I thought we fit together. But I can't escape the awkwardness that's also present...and I see it in his expression too.

We go inside and take the elevator to the penthouse. I gravitate toward the window and stare at the beautiful night view of Dallas, commenting, "This is really nice."

"It's what sold me on the place," he admits.

I glance around. "I can understand why. It's beautiful."

Sebastian goes into the kitchen and I follow. He opens a bottle of champagne and fills two flutes. He hands me one, holds his glass out, and says, "Happy New Year."

I clink his glass and offer a smile, replying, "Happy New Year."

We each take a sip, and things become awkward again. "Georgia —" He snaps his mouth shut.

"What do you want to say?" I ask.

He hesitates, then shakes his head. "Nothing. Let's get dinner in the oven." He spins and turns on the oven.

I open his refrigerator and laugh.

"What's so funny?" he questions.

I point to the contents. "You have the most organized fridge I've ever seen." Several days' worth of precooked meals are stacked on shelves, with labels describing each dish and the macro count.

"It would probably drive you nuts, huh?" he questions.

I lock eyes with him. "No. Not at all. You should see my pantry."

He grins. "Don't tell me your baking ingredients are alphabetized."

I put my hand over my face, admitting, "Guilty."

He chuckles.

I spin back toward the fridge. There's a large throw-away casserole dish with a matching silver lid. I pull it out and ask, "I assume these are the enchiladas?"

"Yep."

I set it on the counter and remove the lid. "These look really good."

"They're the best," he claims as he picks up the tray and puts it in the oven. He sets the timer and adds, "But wait until you try the salsa."

"Oh! Salsa. Now you're spoiling me," I tease.

He wiggles his eyebrows and removes a container from the fridge. He opens it and a brown, grease-stained paper bag. Then he takes a chip out, dips it in the salsa, and holds it in front of my mouth. "Try—"

I bite it before he can finish.

His eyes widen, and he laughs. "Hungry?"

"Starving," I confess with a mouth full of chips and salsa. I suddenly feel like my appetite is back. "This is so good," I say on a moan.

"Told you!" he exclaims, then stuffs one in his mouth.

We finish off half the container of salsa, then the oven beeps. Sebastian removes the enchiladas and orders, "Come here."

I step next to him.

He leans down and wafts the steam toward his face. "You have to smell it."

"I already can. It's making me hungry," I declare.

"Nope! You have to inhale it, Sunshine," he asserts.

I humor him, take a deep breath, and then look up. "You're right. It smells even more amazing!"

"Right?"

"Totally!"

He kisses me on the top of my head and murmurs, "Wait until this hits your tongue." He fills a plate, hands it to me, then makes one for himself.

We sit at the table, and he opens two bottles of Mexican beer.

I hold mine out. "Cheers."

He clinks my bottle, repeats, "Cheers," and we both take a sip.

I take a bite of the enchilada and say, "You were right. This has to be the best in Texas."

His eyes sparkle brighter. He watches me eat a few bites, then takes one himself. He groans.

I laugh. "You look like you're in heaven right now."

He locks his blues to mine. "I am."

"All it takes is some enchiladas and a good beer, huh?" I tease.

His face turns serious. "And you."

My heart swoons, and my chest tightens. I scold myself for my mixed emotions. Being here with Sebastian is dangerous. It feels like nothing bad happened between us, but it did.

I still love him.

I can't let him hurt me again.

He takes a chip, adds enchilada to it, then holds it in front of my mouth, ordering, "Try it this way."

I bite it and nod. I chew, then swallow. "Yum."

For the rest of the meal, we keep our conversation light. Then he fixes a piece of pecan pie for me exactly how I like it.

After we clean the kitchen and do the dishes, the awkwardness reappears. I don't want to leave but convince myself it's best. I force a smile and say, "I should get going."

He clenches his jaw and stares at me.

"Thanks for dinner. It was nice seeing you," I add.

"You can't go yet."

I turn, speechless, unable to move or figure out what to say. I know I should go. But the part of me that doesn't want to be without Sebastian won't let me budge an inch.

He takes my hand and tugs me to the couch. "There's a marathon on."

"Oh?" I question. My flutters do the happy dance at the possibility of staying.

He points, challenging, "Sit, and you'll see."

I don't argue and obey.

He plops down next to me, pulls the ottoman closer, so there is no room between it and the sofa, and tosses a blanket over us. His praline, citrus, and sandalwood scent makes me edge closer to him. He slides his arm around my shoulders, tugging me so I'm resting on his chest. He moves his face in front of mine. A smile plays on his lips as he announces, "*Cupcake Wars* is on all night."

A nervous laugh escapes me. I inquire, "You watch *Cupcake Wars?*"

He gives me his look—the one that always makes me think he's undressing me without even taking his eyes off my face.

I squeeze my thighs together, trying not to squirm or think about what I'd love for him to do to me.

He answers, "Yeah. It intrigues me."

To create some space between us, I turn toward him. I immediately regret the loss of his warm, hard body against mine. I quiz, "It intrigues you?"

He shrugs. "It does. But I'm sure you can run circles around them. And I bet your cupcakes would kick theirs to the curb."

"I'm not sure about that," I reply.

He grunts. "Sure they would." He grabs the remote, turns on the TV, and the show appears.

"How often do you watch this?" I question, surprised he didn't even have to change the channel.

Nerves fill his expression. I wait him out until he confesses, "I started watching it when we returned to Dallas. It reminds me of you. Plus, I wanted to learn more about the business."

My heart skips a beat. I decide it's safer to lean back against him, so I do.

He comments, "I took some notes."

I return to my previous position. "Notes on what?"

His expression turns to that of a kid caught with their hand in a cookie jar. He answers, "I have a few different sections."

"On?" I push.

"Ideas you might want to implement, lessons you can take from the show to avoid problems, things I didn't understand."

I gape at him, then finally ask, "Can I see it?"

"It's probably stupid—"

"No, it's not. I want to see it," I declare.

He pauses, then reaches over into the side table drawer. He hands me a black leather notebook.

"I would have thought this had women's contact info in it," I tease.

He smirks. "Ha ha. Funny."

I open the book, and I'm struck with awe. I blurt out, "This is really detailed."

"Like I said, probably stupid," he mumbles.

I firmly attest, "No. It's not. Grab a pen."

He arches his eyebrows.

I point to the drawer. "Go on. Let's add to it."

"Really?"

"Yes! This is awesome information! I watch this show all the time, but I've never thought of doing this. It's a great idea," I praise.

His cocky expression that I love so much appears. He grabs the pen out of the drawer and slides down on the couch, tugging me with him.

We watch episode after episode, laughing, screaming at the screen at times, and having a great discussion about different business aspects.

The last episode finishes, and the screen switches to the ball dropping in Times Square. There are five minutes until midnight.

Sebastian jumps off the couch. He refills our champagne flutes, then sets them on the side table. He reaches for me, and I allow him to help me off the couch.

He palms my cheek and drags his thumb over my lips.

I close my eyes, forgetting about all our issues and enjoying being under his spell again.

He kisses my eyes and murmurs, "This has been the best New Year's Eve ever."

I open my eyes and smile. "I agree."

He clinks my glass, we take a sip, and a new song blares from the speakers. He takes my flute out of my hand, sets them down, and circles his arm around my waist.

Our bodies collide together and effortlessly sway to the music. We dance the remaining minutes until the countdown, then shout, "Happy New Year!" when the clock strikes midnight.

Sebastian's hand slides through my hair. He gently tugs on it and leans over my mouth. Zings fly all over my body, mimicking the fireworks going off across the Dallas skyline. Our breaths merge, and he closes the gap between us.

His lips and tongue slowly caress mine until we're a fire out of control, burning everything in its path, only to gain more intensity.

Before I know it, I'm in his room. Our clothes come off as the sky bursts with colors, lighting up his chiseled features and intense gaze.

Then I'm on top of him, straddling his hips, taking all of him in me as fast as I can.

He groans as I shudder. He tightens his grasp around me, kissing me with a renewed passion, letting me ride him until I'm a quivering mess.

Then he flips me to the mattress, cages his body over mine, and murmurs against my lips, "You're still mine."

I nod, tearing up, not thinking about any consequences and wanting it to be true. I palm his ass, pulling him to me as soon as he thrusts backward. Within minutes, we're coming, violently trembling against the other. It's faster than normal, but it's as if our bodies can't hold back, unable to stop the reaction the other creates.

In the aftermath, he rolls onto his back, bringing me into his arms. We say nothing, and I'm almost asleep when I hear him murmur, "I love you, Sunshine."

It's so faint, I question if he really said it. I keep my eyes shut, bury my face into his neck, and reply, "I love you too."

He tightens his arms around me, and states, "You've never said that to me before."

I stay quiet, trying to shut up the voices in my head that are arguing about what all this means. One is telling me to get up and leave. The other to curl up into him and never go home. That's the voice that wins, so I sink farther into him, closing my eyes.

We both fall asleep, and I don't know which of us crashes first. I wake up the next morning, and Sebastian's body is strewn across mine. My heart starts beating faster as my fears turn to fresh panic.

What did we do?

I slowly move out from underneath him, then stare at him for a few more minutes. He's peacefully sleeping, and I want to stroke his cheek but don't. I almost slide back against his warm body. Then my conscience doesn't allow me to. I toss on my clothes and sneak out of his penthouse.

It takes a while for me to walk home, but when I finally get there, I go into the bathroom and stare at my reflection in the mirror.

I'm never going to be free of him.

I'm in over my head.

My phone dings. I glance at the screen, and my stomach drops.

Huck Peterson, Esq.: This is an appointment reminder from Huck's office for your 10:00 AM annulment appointment on January 2nd. Please let us know if you cannot attend.

My stomach dives.

He didn't cancel the meeting.

I pace my apartment. This has always been the plan, no matter what happened between Sebastian and me.

Does he want this?

I didn't hold up my end of the bargain.

He probably wants to sign and get off the hook for the million dollars.

He already gave me more than a million. The building alone is worth at least three, and that's without the build-out he orchestrated.

I open my laptop and sign in to my email account. Then I start typing.

Huck,

Please make sure the paperwork states that I'm not to receive anything. I will not sign anything unless it states this. I waive my right to claim Sebastian is in breach of the contract since I won't have a week to review the paperwork.

Thank you,

Georgia Peach

Several minutes pass as I stare at the email. Sadness washes over me. I'll no longer be Sebastian's wife, but the desire to use his name at least once before he lets me go wins. I erase the Peach and type Cartwright. Then I hit send.

Thirty

SEBASTIAN

All day, I've been going crazy. I woke up expecting to see Georgia in my arms, but she was gone. I looked all over the penthouse. I texted and called her, but she's not responding again.

It's dinnertime when I drive to her apartment, feeling crazy again. She doesn't answer. I pound on her door, calling out, "Georgia!"

"You can't take a hint, can you?" her neighbor sneers.

I groan and spin. "You can't keep your nose in your own business, can you?"

She smirks. "I'm not the one chasing a woman who wants nothing to do with me."

I scowl. "Mind your own business, bat."

"In ten seconds, I'm calling the police," she threatens. This time, she holds out her phone, punching her finger on the screen, stating, "Nine. One. One." She shoots me a challenging glare. "Should I push the green button?"

"You're a horrible person," I mutter and leave the building.

I get into my truck, and my phone vibrates in the cup holder. I pick it up and glance at the screen, hopeful it's Georgia, but it's a work contact. I pull up my inbox to see if she messaged me, and my stomach churns.

There's a missed appointment reminder from Huck's office.

Bile rises in my throat. I text him.

Me: *Cancel the annulment meeting. We can't attend.*

Huck: *Your wife's already confirmed.*

Georgia confirmed?

No. No. No.

"Damnit!" I shout, hitting the steering wheel so hard, my hand stings.

Huck: *This isn't the time for second-guessing yourself, Sebastian.*

Me: *Stay out of it.*

Huck: *I'm your attorney. This is why you pay me the big bucks—to get you out of your messes.*

Defeated, I turn on the engine and drive home. I don't sleep at all. The next day, the closer it gets to that ten o'clock appointment, the more I know there's no way I'm signing those papers.

I debate about going to Huck's office to convince Georgia not to sign, but something holds me back.

A little after ten a.m., Huck calls me. He asks, "Sebastian, are you on your way?"

"I'm not coming."

"What do you mean you're not coming? This is a done deal," he booms.

My heart sinks. I close my eyes and utter, "Did she sign?"

"On the dotted line," he confirms.

I feel sick. I take several deep breaths, trying to control the bile rising in my throat.

He adds, "You made out well. She didn't want her million."

My heart feels like it might explode out of my chest. I demand, "What are you talking about?"

"She would only sign annulment forms that stated you didn't owe her anything," he informs me.

Once again, Georgia surprises me. I stare at the Dallas skyline, repeating, "She didn't want anything?"

"That's correct."

More confusion fills me. Georgia earned every penny of what she negotiated. Why didn't she want it?

Huck continues, "She said she got enough. She didn't need anything else from you."

She doesn't need anything from me.

Something about that makes me feel sicker. I order him, "Put the million dollars in her account anyway. I'm sending you an address to one of my condos. Retitle it in her name."

He blurts out, "Are you crazy?"

"I don't want to talk about it, Huck. Put the money in her account as soon as we get off the phone. And I want the condo retitled in her name within the next hour. Send a courier with the finished documents to her apartment," I instruct.

He whistles. "You're a sucker for punishment, aren't you?"

"Just do it," I direct and hang up.

I text him the address, pace some more, then go into my gym. I work out for a few hours, trying to figure out how I'll get her back.

It's over. She signed.

I'm not signing.

Everything was perfect last night. It hurts she signed the annulment paperwork, but I won't give her up without a fight.

I step off the treadmill, soaked with sweat. I get in the shower, quickly scrub down, then step out. I'm about to shave when my buzzer goes off. I go to the front door and hit the button. "Yeah?"

"There's a Georgia Peach here to see you," my security guard states.

Goose bumps break out on my skin. I reply, "Give her full access and send her up."

It takes a few moments, and I open the door, too antsy to wait any longer. As soon as the elevator opens, she takes a step out and then freezes. She drags her eyes down my body, back up, and her cheeks turn red.

I realize I'm still in my towel. "I just got out of the shower. Come in."

She hesitates.

I open the door wider and motion for her to enter. "Georgia, I'm not going to bite you."

She nervously laughs, lifts her chin, then brushes past me.

The electricity I always feel whenever she's around hits me like a fresh bolt of energy.

Goddamn it, I've got to figure this out.

We get inside and an awkward silence hangs between us. I'm trying to figure out what to say when she holds an envelope out toward me. She takes a deep breath and asserts, "This is yours."

I glance at it. "What is it?"

She squares her shoulders. "It's the title you just sent to my house. And I need to transfer that money back to you. Did Huck not tell you I don't want anything? Besides, it was only supposed to be a million dollars. Why did you want to give me this condo too?"

"You know why," I answer.

She slowly shakes her head. Her voice shakes as she says, "No, I don't."

I step closer, deciding to lay it all on the line, even though I feel like I've already done that. But if she needs to hear it again, I'll say it. "I love you. I've told you so many times that I love you. What part of that do you not understand?"

She swallows hard. "Sebastian, we were supposed to sign annulment paperwork today. That was always the deal."

"I don't care about the deal. When I took my vows, I meant every word."

The color drains from her face. She gapes, slowly shaking her head.

I continue, "You wanted to know why I changed them? I'll tell you what I should have told you when you asked on our wedding night. I knew you were the one. I was stupid not to admit it. And I'll be damned if I break my vows."

She stands perfectly still, as if frozen, minus her chest rising and falling faster.

I keep talking, stating, "I'm not going to sign anything saying that our marriage didn't happen, because it did. Maybe it wasn't real for you, Georgia, but for me, it was nothing but real."

Her eyes fill with tears. She blinks hard and whispers, "Why are you doing this to me?"

I close the gap between us. "I love you. Nothing you say is going to change my mind. I'm not annulling this marriage."

"Sebastian..." Her head moves side to side.

"Tell me that you don't love me," I challenge.

It takes her a minute, but she claims, "I don't. You don't love me either. It was just—"

"I heard you tell me last night. Was that a lie?" I interject.

She opens her mouth and then shuts it. She looks away. I turn her chin back.

"You aren't a liar. So don't start now," I declare.

She scrunches her face.

"Admit you don't love me, Sunshine. Tell me you don't love me, and I'll let you go."

Nothing comes out of her mouth.

I back her up to the glass and cage myself around her.

She glances up. "Sebastian, we can't do this again. It hurts too much."

"We can't what? You're my wife, Georgia. Whatever I have to do to make you happy and keep you happy forever, I'm going to do. If I have to spend the rest of my days making up for what an asshole I was, I will. And it hurts because we both know we belong together," I profess.

Her lips tremble.

"Tell me you want to be with me," I demand.

She stays quiet. Anguish paints her beautiful features.

"Tell me you want me as your husband," I plead.

Teardrops roll down her cheek.

I squeeze my eyes shut, feeling more desperate than ever to earn her love again. I beg, "Please tell me you want me." My heart's breaking in two. It feels like it's never going to be back to normal.

Then she quietly admits, "I do want you."

I open my eyes. "As your husband?"

She nods, confessing, "Yes."

"Forever?"

She sniffles. "Yes."

I swallow the lump in my throat. It's everything I've wanted her to admit.

She reaches up and pulls my face toward her. Her lips move an inch from mine. I lean closer to kiss her, but she retreats, then warns, "Don't hurt me again, Sebastian. Make a new vow to me."

I hold her cheeks with both of my hands. I declare, "I won't. I promise you. I'll never do anything to break your heart again."

She stares at me some more.

"I mean it, Sunshine. I'll spend the rest of my life proving it to you," I adamantly assert.

She finally kisses me, and I'm back in heaven. When she retreats, she's smiling.

I murmur, "You're missing something."

She cocks her eyebrows. "What?"

I lead her into the bedroom and open my drawer. I pick up her wedding rings and slide them on her finger. "These."

She studies them, and her smile grows. The blues in her eyes twinkle, and she says, "I think it's time you called the movers."

GEORGIA

Almost One Year Later

"Thank you all for coming. This past year has been a whirlwind of dreams coming to fruition, including this store. And congratulations to our franchisees, Donna and Zach Martin. Austin will be a great market for you and Grammy's Cupcakes," I declare, glancing over at them.

Zach tugs Donna closer to him. Their excitement is palpable, and it increases the joy I feel.

I turn to my right, and my heart swells so big, it might burst. I add, "It wouldn't be right for me not to express my gratitude for my husband, Sebastian Cartwright."

Sebastian's blues twinkle with pride and his arrogant gaze is nowhere to be found. It's always absent whenever it comes to my business. He's always humble, which is the only time in business I typically see him that way.

I continue, "You've helped me in ways I can't even describe. I'm forever thankful for your knowledge, support, and curiosity about cupcakes."

The crowd laughs.

He winks at me, and my stomach flutters.

"You're my biggest cheerleader, an amazing mentor in business, and the best husband a gal could ever have. I love you."

He grins and mouths, *"I love you too, Sunshine."*

I gaze around the room. Everyone I care about is here, even though it's a three-to five-hour round trip, depending on where they came from. Melanie and Greg beam at me and so does Sebastian's entire family. And I might as well be blood because they've never once treated me as anything else.

Since Sebastian and I committed to each other, we've both changed. He's more relaxed. He still keeps up on his crazy workout schedule, but he's learned to have some balance in his meals. And the late nights at his office are rare. We're both busy with our careers, but we try to be home by six every night. Not because we feel pressured, but because we can't wait to see each other.

Most of my growth has been with my naivety. I've learned to speak up where Sebastian is concerned. He's not perfect, and neither am I. What goes on in his head isn't always clear to me, so when I need to, I ask him what his intentions are about whatever is confusing me. He's aware if I do ask him that, he needs to stop doing whatever it is and think before he speaks. Sometimes his ghosts reappear. It's typically during a vulnerable conversation, so I try to stay patient and gently ask him point-blank if what he's saying is how I'm interpreting it.

Normally, he's trying to tell me something completely different than what I'm hearing. So we've both learned the more we can talk about an issue, the stronger our marriage grows.

When I think about my life before him, it seems so dull. He's opened a new world for me, not only due to his lifestyle but because of the love he shows me daily.

I tear my gaze off him and motion to the Martins. They step forward next to me, and the mayor hands them a huge pair of scissors. I grab Sebastian's hand, and he kisses it then releases it. He slides his arm around my waist, tugging me against him, right where I belong.

The Martins cut the red ribbon, and everyone cheers louder than before.

Sebastian spins me into his arms and gives me a chaste kiss. Then he leans into my ear. "Well done, Mrs. Cartwright."

I beam at him. "We did it!"

He shakes his head. "No. You did it."

I open my mouth to protest, but he puts his finger over my lips. He leans into my ear and states, "Sunshine, I think it's time I showed you how proud of you I am." He gives me a challenging stare.

My favorite scent of praline, citrus, and sandalwood teases my nostrils. I squeeze my thighs together, arch my eyebrows, and reply, "Oh? What's involved?"

His lips twitch. "Now, what fun would it be if I told you?"

I put my fingers together, bat my eyelids, and whine, "Just a little hint?"

He chuckles, undresses me with his eyes, and my cheeks flush with heat. His hot breath hits my lobe, and he teases, "What would you say if it involves sugar, roses, my tongue, and your naked body?"

I inhale deeply, shift on my feet, and lift my chin. "I think that would be perfect, Mr. Cartwright."

The Auction

CLUB INDULGENCE DUET: BOOK ONE

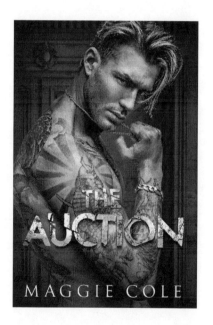

DESTROYING my partner became sweeter when his daughter stepped on stage at a charity auction.

But I don't want her for a month.

I'm upping my bid to make her sign for a year.

Her strong will, independence, and defiant attitude toward her family indulges my carnal desires and need for revenge.

I'll break her, train her, and turn her into the compliant woman she didn't know existed within her.

Every second, she'll be my pawn in the secret game of retaliation I'm going to win.

Then I'll present her as my pet to all of L.A., including her father.

After our year is up, the damage will be done.

She'll be free to go, and I'll move forward with my life without her father, or anyone associated with him in it— including her.

Schemes Unleashed is the first book of the Club Indulgence Duet. It's a forbidden love, age-gap, dark billionaire romance with forced proximity.

Click to get your copy of The Auction, Club Indulgence Duet's Book One!

The Auction Prologue

Riggs Madden

Seven Years Ago

"Riggs?" Hugh Gallow nudges me, pulling me out of my trance. I've barely heard a word of my business partner's stifling conversation for the last few minutes.

It's his daughter Blakely's fault. She stepped into the garden wearing a nude slip dress and matching four-inch designer stilettos. Her blonde hair cascades along her shoulders in long curls, and when her blue eyes met mine, she quickly broke our stare as if she were caught with her hand in the cookie jar. Since then, I've been too captivated to tear my eyes off her, pleased every time I catch her gazing my way and trying to pretend she's not looking at me.

The attraction between us started three years ago. She turned eighteen and was no longer Hugh's little girl. It didn't take long for me to notice the little flush in her cheeks when she glanced at me or her nervous finger tapping on whatever she could find to torment. Her usual victims consist of a table on her thighs, the latter of which I'm dying to get between. Right now, her champagne flute is taking a beating.

Hugh demands, "Riggs, confirm my numbers."

I clear my throat, recover from my absence, and answer, "That's right. We're up over thirty percent." I down the rest of my scotch and add, "Excuse me. The men's room is calling." I escape Hugh and the circle of his stuck-up friends he's always trying to impress, hightailing it to the restroom, glad to exit their presence.

Blakely's father and I have been partners for over a decade, and while his mentorship influenced many things in my life, there's one thing he couldn't change about me—I just don't care about impressing people like Hugh does. I couldn't give a shit about what anyone thinks unless I need to impress them to sell one of our companies for a huge profit.

After growing up on food stamps in Compton, where most adults didn't have a job and addiction was rampant, you'd think anyone with business acumen would have impressed me. I'd escaped the gangs and pitfalls of poverty in the absence of anyone molding me into a successful young man. Yet most of the entrepreneurs I came across didn't strike me as anything special.

Then I met Hugh. I was in my late twenties and he was in his forties. Our first discussion led to a six-hour meeting. I impressed him for my age, and I was craving a business mentor even though I didn't realize it at the time.

Hugh was different. He would speak of things I hadn't heard of or show me new ways to manipulate others to get deals done. When I told him the story of how I got scholarships and put myself through school to get my MBA in finance, he instructed me to never speak of it again. He claimed successful people—rich people—wanted to know you were born with money. So I listened to him, and he created a backstory about me growing up in Northern California, which was just far enough away that no one ever questioned it.

Within a few months, we created an investment capital firm. Hugh had money and I had grit, along with an unquenchable work ethic. Slowly, I've earned my shares and we're now fifty-fifty partners. And even though I've always done more work than Hugh, including finding and closing almost all the deals over the last five years, I wouldn't be here without him. You have to have money to make more, and Hugh had plenty at a time when I had none. The combination of his start-up resources and my overzealous determination to be the best allowed us to create a dynamic partnership. Our start-up firm is now the largest in the country and a global name.

It's the exact reason why nothing can happen between Blakely and me. I'll forever be loyal to Hugh for giving me the chance and knowledge to create my life. So she's off-limits. And the last thing I need is to have daddy's little girl run to him, crying about how I broke her into submission and didn't marry her afterward.

Plus, she's sixteen years younger than me. I don't normally even think about women who aren't at least thirty years old. The things that quench my appetite are considered a bit taboo. Full consent is required, and I don't need a woman claiming she didn't know what she was getting into. You go below thirty, and you're asking for a wishy-washy woman who's still trying to find herself and can't be relied on to understand what she's dipping her toes into.

But my rules aren't helping my predicament every time I see Blakely. The desire to have her at my fingertips only gets harder to ignore. Hell, I knew before I arrived at the party and laid eyes on her that I would be in agony the entire time. And every time she sneaks a glance at me only reiterates that I should have given Hugh an excuse about why I couldn't attend tonight. So my time here is up and I need to go before my partner realizes his daughter is giving me a hard-on.

I do my business in the bathroom and make my way through the mansion, determined to return to the backyard and say my good-byes. Halfway there, I turn the corner and run into Blakely.

Her champagne splashes on my shirt, and she frets, "Oh my gosh! Riggs, I'm so sorry!" A pink flush crawls up her cheeks, her doe-eyes widen, and she swipes at my shirt.

I grab her hand, and she freezes, her palm an inch from my pecs. My heart pounds harder in my chest and I curse myself for reacting like a teenager. It's another thing that's been happening when I'm with her, and it makes me feel exposed, instead of my normal controlled self. I state, "It's okay. It's only champagne. It'll dry."

She stays silent, her cheeks growing hotter, and I can only wonder if her ass would turn the same color after a good slapping.

I have to stop these thoughts.

Blakely lifts her chin, and the remaining room in my pants disappears. My cock painfully strains against my zipper. I scold myself again, but it's pointless. Her expression is another reminder how different she is, yet exactly what I look for in my conquests.

She doesn't have the snotty Beverly Hills air about her that most women at this party have. Her little gesture is a confident stance. It indulges my cravings further. I love nothing better than dominating a woman with a backbone, and Blakely's always had one. It drives Hugh and his wife Madelyn nuts. I'm one of the few they don't put on a show for when it comes to their daughter. Over the years, I've heard them complain too many times to count about their daughter's stubbornness, or how she forged ahead with something they forbade her to do.

Attempting to regain some control of this situation, I nod to her half-empty glass, questioning, "So you're legal now?"

She glances at it, then locks eyes with me again. Her lips curve into a small smile. She answers in a low voice, "Yes. Totally legal as of today." She inhales deeply then licks her lips, and her cheeks turn redder.

I clench my jaw, keeping my breathing controlled, trying to convince myself she doesn't mean anything by that admission, but I can't. There's a tornado of lust and hope swirling in her blues, and no matter what lie I tell myself, it's impossible to ignore.

Christ, she's young.

I bet she's tighter than any woman I've been with in years.

She'd look good on her knees, with her hands bound and those plump lips around my cock.

She opens her mouth, then snaps it shut. She glances behind her, then refocuses on me.

More visions of her in positions I can never have her in assault my brain. Several moments pass before I state, "Happy birthday."

Her face lights up even more as her lips curve into a bigger smile. She shifts on her feet. "Thanks."

"Twenty-one is a big occasion. I assume you're going out and getting crazy with your boyfriend later?" I question, prying for information.

It doesn't matter. She's Hugh's daughter.

She shakes her head, and a blonde curly tendril falls over her eyes. She replies, "I don't have a boyfriend."

Thank God for that.

Not that he'd have anything over me.

Mesmerized, not thinking clearly, and unable to stop myself, I reach for the lock. She holds her breath as I slowly drag my fingers over her forehead, then even slower onto the side of her head, pushing her strands behind her ear. Just as I suspected, her hair's soft, unlike the typical overprocessed blondes roaming all of L.A. I've always known she's a natural blonde, but finally feeling it only adds fuel to my thoughts. I have to stop myself from wrapping all of it around my fist.

She arches her eyebrows, waiting for me to answer, the heat from her cheeks radiating past the inch of air between her skin and my hand.

We've never been this close, nor have I touched her before. Now that I breached my self-control, I step closer, studying the flecks of blues in her eyes. I admit, "Your eyes remind me of the favorite part of my morning surf."

Her voice falters as she inquires, "How so?" She swallows hard but doesn't flinch or retreat.

Her ability to stand in front of me and not break our heated gaze challenges me. It stokes a deep-seated craving I can't seem to shake. I contemplate taking her to my house—not the club—which is another surprise. I don't bring my play things home. They stay at the club and out of my private life. Yet the thought of breaking her into submission in my personal environment, somewhere she can't come and go from, with no one else around, takes root.

I trace the edge of her ear, and she shakily inhales, her lips parting enough I could slip my tongue between them if I attempted. My blood heats to the point I might sweat, and I curse myself for putting myself in this position. Yet I can't stop. Now that I have her attention, I need to keep going. I answer, "When the sun rises over the water, and the light hits it just right, there's calm chaos."

She furrows her brows. "Calm chaos? That's an oxymoron. It doesn't make sense."

I clench my jaw, trying to contain my pleasure that she's not just a pretty face. She has a brain and uses it, which is another thing I don't often see with many beautiful women in L.A. I flip my hand and lightly graze my fingertip over her chin, enjoying how her eyes quickly shut then reopen. I answer, "When the tide's rolling away, barely giving way to any waves, and the water looks like it's full of sparkles trying to jump into the air, that's calm chaos."

She ponders my statement for a moment, her expression morphing into a soft smile I assume she'd make after I wore her out with my demands. She asserts in approval, "I suppose your oxymoron works."

It's all too much. I might as well be a reckless teenager unable to control his urges instead of a sexually experienced, normally always in control thirty-seven-year-old man. I reach behind her, grab a fistful of her hair, and firmly tug her head backward. It's nothing like what I've done to women in the past, but it's enough to make her gasp and get an idea of what I'd do to her if I had the chance.

Whatever her perfume is flares in my nostrils. It reminds me of the surf, along with something else I can't put my finger on besides the combination of sea salt and driftwood. I lick my lips, studying hers, then pin my gaze to her widened one, murmuring, "There are many things I do that perception would claim don't work but do."

Her bottom lip quivers, but she catches it and takes a deep breath. Her chest rises higher, and I give it a lewd glance, then pin my most challenging stare on her. She opens her mouth, tries to speak, but nothing comes out.

I tug her head farther back, leaning so dangerously close to her mouth her breath hits mine.

She whispers, "What kinds of things?"

I don't hesitate, running, "Things that would make your father despise me."

Her plump lips part again, but her mother's voice calls out, "Blakely!"

Goddamn it!

I release her and step back just as Madelyn turns the corner.

She beams. "There you are! We're about to cut the cake." Then she turns to me, bats her eyes, and puts her hand on my bicep. Vodka overpowers Blakely's sea salt and driftwood scent, and Madelyn coos, "Riggs. I didn't know you'd arrived."

I groan inside. Madelyn and Hugh are no saints. They both fuck whatever walks, and for years, she's made it clear she's into me. But I'd never do her for two reasons.

One, she's my partner's wife. I don't need that kind of drama in my life.

Two, I'm not interested. She's another product of Beverly Hills, overindulging in alcohol and prescription pills, and void of anything interesting. The only difference between her and the people I grew up with is she has money. She's as predictable as they come and might as well be a junkie on the corner.

All of it bores me.

I step out of her grasp and nod. "Madelyn. Good seeing you. Please give my regards to Hugh. Something's come up." I hightail it down the hallway, ignoring her questioning calls after me. I move to the front door, step outside, and get into my Porsche, racing out of the subdivision and driving directly to Club Indulgence in L.A.

Something has definitely come up.

Yet it's not anything the Gallows would expect.

As I pull into the club's secret parking garage, I already know I'll be here well into the night, trying to get Blakely out of my head. It won't be the first time I've dealt with my frustration here, but this time, I curse myself for stepping over the line that I know I can never cross.

Click to get your copy of The Auction, Club Indulgence Duet's Book One!

Mafia Wars Ireland
Spinoff Series

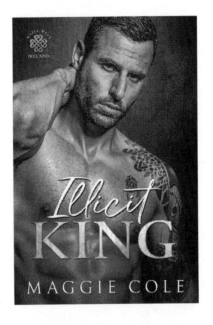

Are you ready for the O'Connors in Mafia Wars Ireland? Cover Reveals and Titles Coming Soon!

Book One (Brody)- May 1, 2023

Book Two (Aidan) - June 1, 2023
Book Three (Devin) - July 15, 2023
Book Four (Tynan) - Sept 1, 2023

BUT BEFORE MW IRELAND….I'VE got some other goodies for you...

Holiday Hoax (A Fake Marriage Billionaire Romance - Stand Alone and all new characters) - Nov. 15

Club Indulgence Duet - A Dark Billionaire Romance

The Auction (Book One) - Feb. 1

The Vow (Book Two) - March 1

Keep flipping for sneak peeks!

Illicit King – Brody & Alaina

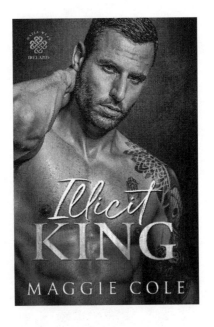

He's not my King.

TALL, rugged, and focused on destroying my family, Brody O'Connor's the one person I need to avoid.

He seduced me on purpose and now I'm paying the consequences.

Every step I take, he's there, lurking in the shadows, studying me, waiting for any chance to undermine my efforts to become my father's successor.

He's succeeding.

No matter how much I try to shake him, or our heated encounters, I can't.

He insists I'm naive, in the dark about what my family is really about, and what he tells me I can't fathom.

He's lying.

Screwing with my head.

It can't be true. My father is cruel, but he wouldn't do this.

Or would he?

If Brody's right, then where does that leave me?

Where does it leave us?

Illicit King is book one of Mafia Wars Ireland. It's a forbidden love, enemies to lovers, age gap, dark mafia romance.

Ready to read Brody and Alaina's story? Download now!

Binge Now!

Ready to Binge the Original 10 Book Mafia Wars Series? Get to know the Ivanovs and O'Malleys!

He's a Ruthless Stranger. One I can't see, only feel, thanks to my friends who make a deal with him on my behalf.

No names. No personal details. No face to etch into my mind.

Just him, me, and an expensive silk tie.

What happens in Vegas is supposed to stay in Vegas.

He warns me he's full of danger.

I never see that side of him. All I experience is his Russian accent, delicious scent, and touch that lights me on fire.

One incredible night turns into two. Then we go our separate ways.

But fate doesn't keep us apart. When I run into my stranger back in Chicago, I know it's him, even if I've never seen his icy blue eyes before.

Our craving is hotter than Vegas. But he never lied.

He's a ruthless man...

"Ruthless Stranger" is the jaw-dropping first installment of the "Mafia Wars" series. It's an interconnecting, stand-alone Dark Mafia Romance, guaranteed to have an HEA.

Ready for Maksim's story? Click here for Ruthless Stranger, book one of the jaw dropping spinoff series, Mafia Wars!

A Favor

CAN I ASK YOU A HUGE FAVOR?

Would you be willing to leave me a review?

I would be forever grateful as one positive review on Amazon is like buying the book a hundred times! Reader support is the lifeblood for Indie authors and provides us the feedback we need to give readers what they want in future stories!

Your positive review means the world to me! So thank you from the bottom of my heart!

CLICK TO REVIEW

More by Maggie Cole

Club Indulgence Duet (A Dark Billionaire Romance)

The Auction (Book One)

The Vow (Book Two)

Mafia Wars Ireland

Illicit King (Brody)- May 1, 2023

Illicit Captor (Aidan) - June 15, 2023

Illicit Heir (Devin) - Sept 1, 2023

Illicit Monster (Tynan) - Oct 15, 2023

Standalone Holiday Novel

Holiday Hoax - A Fake Marriage Billionaire Romance (Standalone)

Mafia Wars New York - A Dark Mafia Series (Series Six)

Toxic (Dante's Story) - Book One

Immoral (Gianni's Story) - Book Two

Crazed (Massimo's Story) - Book Three

Carnal (Tristano's Story) - Book Four

Flawed (Luca's Story) - Book Five

Mafia Wars - A Dark Mafia Series (Series Five)

Ruthless Stranger (Maksim's Story) - Book One

Broken Fighter (Boris's Story) - Book Two

Cruel Enforcer (Sergey's Story) - Book Three

Vicious Protector (Adrian's Story) - Book Four

Savage Tracker (Tibrocht's Story) - Book Five

Unchosen Ruler (Liam's Story) - Book Six

Perfect Sinner (Nolan's Story) - Book Seven

Brutal Defender (Killian's Story) - Book Eight

Deviant Hacker (Declan's Story) - Book Nine

Relentless Hunter (Finn's Story) - Book Ten

Behind Closed Doors (Series Four - Former Military Now International Rescue Alpha Studs)

Depths of Destruction - Book One

Marks of Rebellion - Book Two

Haze of Obedience - Book Three

Cavern of Silence - Book Four

Stains of Desire - Book Five

Risks of Temptation - Book Six

Together We Stand Series (Series Three - Family Saga)

Kiss of Redemption- Book One

Sins of Justice - Book Two

Acts of Manipulation - Book Three

Web of Betrayal - Book Four

Masks of Devotion - Book Five

Roots of Vengeance - Book Six

It's Complicated Series (Series Two - Chicago Billionaires)

My Boss the Billionaire- Book One

Forgotten by the Billionaire - Book Two

My Friend the Billionaire - Book Three

Forbidden Billionaire - Book Four

The Groomsman Billionaire - Book Five

Secret Mafia Billionaire - Book Six

All In Series (Series One - New York Billionaires)

The Rule - Book One

The Secret - Book Two

The Crime - Book Three

The Lie - Book Four

The Trap - Book Five

The Gamble - Book Six

STAND ALONE NOVELLA

JUDGE ME NOT - A Billionaire Single Mom Christmas Novella

About the Author

Amazon Bestselling Author

Maggie Cole is committed to bringing her readers alphalicious book boyfriends. She's an international bestselling author and has been called the "literary master of steamy romance." Her books are full of raw emotion, suspense, and will always keep you wanting more. She is a masterful storyteller of contemporary romance and loves writing about broken people who rise above the ashes.

Maggie lives in Florida with her son. She loves sunshine, anything to do with water, and everything naughty.

Her current series were written in the order below:

- All In (Stand alones with entwined characters)

- It's Complicated (Stand alone with entwined characters)
- Together We Stand (Brooks Family Saga - read in order)
- Behind Closed Doors (Read in order)
- Mafia Wars
- Mafia Wars New York
- Club Indulgence Duet
- Mafia Wars Ireland

Maggie Cole's Newsletter

Sign up here!

Hang Out with Maggie in Her Reader Group
Maggie Cole's Romance Addicts

Follow for Giveaways
Facebook Maggie Cole

Instagram
@maggiecoleauthor

Tik Tok
https://www.tiktok.com/@maggiecole.author?

Complete Works on Amazon
Follow Maggie's Amazon Author Page

Book Trailers
Follow Maggie on YouTube

Are you a Blogger and want to join my ARC team?
Signup now!

Feedback or suggestions?

Email: authormaggiecole@gmail.com

twitter.com/MaggieColeAuth

instagram.com/maggiecoleauthor

bookbub.com/profile/maggie-cole

amazon.com/Maggie-Cole/e/B07Z2CB4HG

Made in the USA
Columbia, SC
11 December 2023

28282721R00252